BREAD AND MURDER IN ARAMEZZO

MURDER IN AN ITALIAN VILLAGE · BOOK 2

MICHELLE DAMIANI

RIALTO
PRESS

BREAD AND MURDER IN ARAMEZZO

MURDER IN AN ITALIAN VILLAGE · BOOK 2

RIALTO PRESS
P.O. Box 1472
Charlottesville, VA 22902
michelledamiani.com

CAST OF CHARACTERS

CASALE MAZZOLI

Stella   *arrives to Aramezzo to take over her family's bed-and-breakfast*

Mimmo   *the former caretaker of Stella's bed-and-breakfast*

JOBS IN ARAMEZZO

Domenica   *owns the local bookshop*

Matteo   *the streetsweeper*

Cosimo   *the antiquarian and expert on local lore*

Romina   *owns Bar Cappellina, married to Roberto*

Roberto   *owns Bar Cappellina, married to Romina*

Don Arrigo   *the village priest*

Marcello   *the mayor*

Marta   *raises sheep, mother of Ascanio*

Leonardo   *an ex-racecar driver who now operates the family porchetta van*

Antonio   *the red-bearded baker*

Dario   *apprentice baker*

Jacopo   *apprentice baker*

Christiana   *owns the alimentari with her father*

Orietta   *the pharmacist*

Bruno   *the butcher*

Flavia   *the florist*

VILLAGERS

Victoria   *the mayor's wife*

Benedetta   *the butcher's wife*

Celeste   *the baker's wife*

Luisella   *lingers at Bar Cappellina*

THE POLICE

Luca   *police officer*

Salvo   *Luca's partner*

Palmiro   *the local police captain*

SATURDAY

*T*he baker did not look well.

In the few months Stella had lived in Aramezzo, she'd come to think of the baker as the real-life equivalent of a Muppet character. How could she not, with his ruddy cheeks and lustrous red mustache that glimmered in the barest thread of light? Now though, the baker's wan face echoed the pale dough appearing and disappearing beneath his hands. That vibrant mustache sagged, parentheses around his frown.

Stella shifted her weight as she waited in the line snaking out of the tiny shop, past the bakery's double doors thrown open to the street. She narrowed her eyes, her gaze following Antonio, now stalking to the oven to fling wood into the already roaring fire.

Gazing down the line of villagers waiting to enter the diminutive bakery, Stella wondered if any of them noticed the baker slapping the dough against the counter with a thwack that carried in early spring's brittle air. Everyone's conversations must be far too engrossing. Not one face peered curiously into the *forno*, as Antonio's hands—famed for coaxing flour and water into loaves beloved throughout Umbria—now punched the dough as if holding it accountable for its sins. She amended her earlier thought. He didn't simply look unwell... he looked enraged.

As she took in the preoccupied townspeople, Stella had to acknowledge herself to be the only person in line not gathered with a neighbor or two, debating the chance of rain or the merits of the Italian National Soccer team, affectionately known as Azzurri, or the Blues. She'd grown used to being the odd woman on the block and usually felt lucky that, as an outsider, she'd been able to form her few friendships. Except at times like this when she wished for eye contact with someone, to lift a quizzical brow at the smudge obscuring the baker's usual sun.

Antonio turned, and Stella couldn't help but notice the dullness in his eyes. She watched as he sniped at a junior baker, barking at him to clean up his station while he himself ran a handheld razor—called a bread lame—over the top of six loaves to score the dough, giving the rising bread room to expand in the oven, creating an airy, tender crumb.

At the sight of the junior baker now wordlessly scrubbing his station, Stella realized that though the villagers queued up for bread hadn't picked up on Antonio's seething, his apprentices couldn't miss it. All the young men had their eyes fixed on their tasks, with none of their usual banter and teasing. The stiff hush suggested their determination to avoid Antonio's notice at all costs. Quite a change from the usual boisterous clanging and calling out, laughter echoing joyfully down the street.

After all these months, Stella considered that joyfulness as much a part of the *forno* as the bakers' uniforms. Though, Stella remembered, those uniforms had initially thrown her. Manhattan bakers certainly didn't work in white tank tops and boxer shorts. The first time she'd caught sight of Antonio standing on the cobblestone street in what she thought was his underwear, she'd thought he looked as out of place as she felt. It had taken her at least a month to not startle at the bakers' matching white garb, topped with a blue apron for the apprentices and white for Antonio.

She used to think she'd never grow used to the sight of barely clad men, pulling at each other, bursting into song, teasing and chiding and arguing good-naturedly even as they worked the dough and piled it into the blazing ovens, heat glinting off the sweat on their foreheads. But now she realized she had stopped remarking internally on the outfit altogether. Though back in December, she remembered Antonio joking about getting her into the *forno* to help with all the orders and maybe feed the bakers the sweet treats his operation didn't have the time or capacity to manage. She'd responded that she didn't think she'd look good in the uniform, and he'd looked down at his white boxer shorts, undershirt, and sneakers and roared with laughter.

Funny how time softened edges. If Antonio made the same joke today, Stella likely wouldn't have the presence of mind to quip back about the outfits. There were many ways that Stella still felt like an outsider, but she supposed that acclimating to bakers in their underwear was a sign of her immersion into her ancestral village. In fact, in retrospect, she thought the get-up lent a familiar, almost intimate, tenor to the bakery. Except in moments like this, when the stiff silence bumped up against the delicate apparel in a way most unseemly.

A roar from the bakery cut off Stella's thoughts. The villagers standing in the street fell silent. Stella couldn't make out the words, only the volume of the tirade. Faces craned, staring into the *forno*, but Antonio was nowhere to be seen. On the bakery floor, the apprentices glanced at each other and then through the doorway that connected the floor with the shop.

Antonio couldn't be yelling at the woman who sold the bread, could he? Stella tried to remember the woman's name, but she found it hard for names to stick and constantly defaulted to calling the villagers the baker, the butcher, the greengrocer, the florist—the legacy of a childhood spent devouring Richard Scarry books from the library (her mother refused to buy them for her daughters, considering Lowly Worm's fixation on occupations entirely too American, even while she tossed the Italian books sent by family directly into the trash). In any case, what infraction could that mild-mannered bread seller possibly have committed that was worthy of Antonio's snarl of rage?

Just then, a stocky stranger, thin hair combed greasily across his scalp, emerged from the bakery. He walked stiffly, refusing to acknowledge Antonio, now looming at the threshold of the shop, arms folded across his chest.

Could Antonio have raised his voice like that to a *customer*? Stella knew Italian notions of customer service were different from the States, where she had to sound remorseful when a diner sent back a properly cooked, medium-rare, steak. But still.

Stella felt a tap on her shoulder and turned to find the owner of Aramezzo's *alimentari*. She hadn't gotten to know Cristiana well, but she always enjoyed their casual exchange of pleasantries. "Who is that?" Cristiana asked, gesturing at the stranger ambling by, rolling his shoulders as if to shed Antonio's thundering look of death.

Stella almost turned to check if Cristiana had meant to ask someone else. But Cristiana's eyes stayed fixed on her and Stella remembered that, of course, with her bed-and-breakfast, she would be likely to know a stranger in Aramezzo.

She shook her head. "No idea."

Cristiana clarified, "He's not staying at Casale Mazzoli? I thought you had guests this week."

Stella nodded. "I do. An American couple. Young. Not this guy."

Cristiana watched the stranger's back recede down the street. "*Allora*, whoever that man is, he did something to get on Antonio's bad side."

"And I would have thought that impossible."

Chuckling warmly, Cristiana said, "I know, he even smiles when Bruno makes snide remarks about his 'stupid mustache.' "

Stella nodded, remembering all the times she'd heard the butcher mutter unintelligible insults at the passing baker. "I figured Antonio chalked all that up to Bruno's sour disposition."

Cristiana grinned. "Your Italian is coming along."

Laughing, Stella said, "I know, right? I'm finally expanding past my elementary school whining and restaurant bawdy talk."

Shaking her head, Cristiana said, "I meant your accent. You said that like an Umbrian. Not the usual medley of dialect."

Stella wanted to volunteer that her Italian was a potpourri of Tuscan slang from working in Florence and Lombardian vowels from her time in Milan, blurred with her mother's barbed commentary, but she couldn't think of the Italian word for potpourri. So maybe her language wasn't as advanced as Cristiana thought.

Cristiana went on, "Anyway, Bruno and Antonio used to get along. Before the whole television show debacle."

Stella stared at Cristiana. "What?"

"The national news spot. The one that might have made them famous. Surely you know about this." Cristiana gestured at the moving line. "Oh, you're almost up. You getting bread or *torta al testo*?"

Stella stepped forward without wondering why Cristiana only figured on two options—that's all the bakery sold, mostly to area restaurants but also to the village's residents and those who ventured within Aramezzo's walls for a bite of the slow-fermented, naturally risen bread. Usually, these visitors were treated to better manners than a cursing out by Aramezzo's perennially sunny baker.

Stella realized she had yet to answer Cristiana. "A loaf. My guests are leaving today to drive to the Amalfi coast and asked me to pack them a lunch they can eat on the road."

Cristiana frowned. "Eat on the road? You mean . . . in the *car*? While they *drive*? Why wouldn't they stop at an Autogrill or something to have a proper meal?"

Shrugging, Stella answered as she stepped forward again. The line seemed to be moving swiftly now. "They said they tried the Autogrill on their way here from Rome, but found the system confusing—where they order, where they pay. I tried to explain it, but I could tell the idea made them too nervous." It had been one of those complicated interactions she often had with guests—she liked this couple from Maryland (not only because they requested she make their dinners, a financial boon, but also because she never failed to warm to people who grew quiet with appreciation as they tucked into her food) and wanted them to have a memorable first trip to Italy. Which, by rights, should include a stop at Italy's illustrious answer to fast food, a staple of road trips up and down the Boot. But Stella didn't feel she could challenge them to push past their comfort zone. So to-go sandwiches it was. She finished the thought aloud: "They seem determined to travel only uncomplicated roads."

Nodding slowly, Cristiana said, "How in the world did they wind up in Aramezzo?"

"A fair question," Stella laughed. Aramezzo lay so far off the tourist trail, tucked in the hills behind Assisi, most travelers didn't know of its existence. "The family I had at Christmas—you remember, they bought out all your decorative jars of Nutella. They're part of the same supper club as this couple." At Cristiana's furrowed eyebrow, Stella went on, "It's a thing in America. People schedule a night every month or so where they gather at a member's house, and they all bring a dish on a theme, or from the same cookbook."

Cristiana shook her head slowly, "I will never understand you Americans. If you want to have a meal with friends, have a meal with friends. Why must you turn it into a chore?"

Stella tamped down the pinch at Cristiana's easy lumping of Stella in with a continent of people who didn't know how to live. She pretended an ease she didn't feel as she said, "Anyway, the family at Christmas told everyone about all their great Umbrian meals and inspired this couple to come. Originally, they had only planned on Rome and Amalfi."

Laughing, Cristiana said, "You are underselling yourself, Stella. I suspect they praised *your* Umbrian meals."

The comment eased some of the sting from Cristiana's earlier words. Since she'd arrived, Stella had been working to weave in an understanding of the food of her ancestors with her education from stints at restaurants throughout Italy. She'd tired the butcher to impatience asking questions (which, granted, did not seem hard to do—any sentence beyond, "I'd like those pork chops cut on the thick side" seemed to annoy him) and spent several long afternoons with Adele, the woman who cooked at Trattoria Cavour, Aramezzo's only restaurant. Stella had even considered asking Antonio for a bread-baking lesson, but hadn't yet worked up the courage. For all his open cheer, she'd noticed a thread of steel around his methods. Mostly in the form of changing the topic whenever she got close to shop talk.

Along with her ad-hoc training, Stella had cleaned Domenica out of all the Umbrian cookbooks in her used bookstore. Luckily, Domenica gave Stella the friends-and-family discount, even steeper when Stella remembered to bring something tasty to sweeten Domenica's generosity. "Ah, well, they may have mentioned something about that." Stella shifted uncomfortably, never gifted at accepting compliments, before realizing she was next in line.

Cristiana said, "Sounds like another five-star review coming your way. I bet you're glad of that."

Stella nodded, fairly certain this couple would be writing that glowing review on the drive to Amalfi. They seemed the type, and anyway, Stella had learned to hint for reviews in the footers of emails and in conversational asides. She had to. Flipping this bed-and-breakfast so she could return to the States and start over with a restaurant of her own, well, it was all part of the plan. The only question was where she'd land. Certainly not New York, after the debacle that led to her flight to Aramezzo.

Yes, that was the plan. Though lately, sometimes, she lost the shape of that particular plot, as she poured a swirl of olive oil from her own trees onto greens sautéed with plenty of garlic, or added bay leaves from the bush outside her back door to a bubbling ragu. In those moments, she only noticed the satisfaction derived from cooking for people she had some sort of relationship with—new friends, neighbors, or guests at Casale Mazzoli—rather than a roomful of strangers.

With a laugh of remembrance, Cristiana said, "Then again, you probably love any guest that doesn't die on your watch."

Trying in vain to smile, Stella could only say, "Ah, I'm still trying to forget about that." She'd stopped jumping at sudden shadows, but only because the cat that came with the property, that she'd named Barbanera for his pirate-like black chin and missing ear, seemed to delight in taking her by surprise.

Cristiana patted Stella's arm. "Aren't we all? Better to enjoy making road panini for your living American guests than remembering . . . all of *that*."

A white-haired woman in a navy blue dress and matching crepe heels stepped out of the shop, and Stella started to walk in before Cristiana pulled her back. "*Torta al testo*! Why aren't you packing that for your guests? It's so much better than a loaf of bread for a . . . picnic on wheels? It's portable and far, far better."

Stella made a noncommittal noise. Cristiana glared at her. "You still haven't had a *torta al testo* sandwich, have you?"

Edging into the bakery, Stella stammered, "Well, I already told them what I'd be packing them. I'd hate to change the menu this late in the game." At Cristiana's stare, Stella added, "But later today I'll drop by your *alimentari* and get one for myself. So I'm ready next time."

"Promise?"

Stella grinned. "Promise."

Cristiana half patted Stella's arm and half nudged her into the shop as she said, "You'd better. You can't call yourself an Umbrian without being well versed in our staples."

Stella returned the smile before ducking into the shop to order her customary *filetta*, the local term for a simple loaf of country bread. Her eyes passed over the wheels of Umbrian flatbread. She had, it was true, thus far avoided *torta al testo*, what Umbrians called both the bread and the lunch it made when sandwiching any kind of cured meat. It wasn't that she didn't enjoy sandwiches—there were times she'd offer up her whisking arm for a *bahn mi* from her favorite Vietnamese dive on the Lower East side, or even a basic corned beef on rye. But she figured dry bread filled with nothing but cured meat had to be boring. Shouldn't flatbread be slathered with hummus or lentils or something?

Perhaps, but as she handed over the euro for her bread, Stella decided Cristiana had a point. If she wanted to be part of Aramezzo, she had to at least sample their ways. Then again, she wondered, as she passed Cristiana with a farewell wave, how much did she want to be part of a town her own mother found so objectionable she never spoke of it without sneering?

Stella could now admit to herself she'd arrived in Aramezzo ready to hate it. But the labyrinth of cobblestone alleys had grooved its way into her heart. Moreover, she'd warmed to the villagers, grounded as they were in the countryside, with a dedication and curiosity about food that she found endearing. She could feel how much her heartbeat had slowed as she adapted to Umbria's quieter rhythms.

Slowed, that is, as long as she didn't stumble across any more dead bodies. She'd had enough of that for two lifetimes.

Stella caught sight of a man walking toward her in a blue sanitation worker's uniform, his curly hair mostly clasped back in a ponytail, except for the premature silver tendrils that sprang up around his temples. Her thoughts drifted away like fog disappearing in warm sunshine as she raised her hand, calling, "Matteo!"

Her friend grinned. "Well, look what the cat dragged in."

She made a show of looking behind her and he laughed, his eyebrows jumping like cricket legs. He said, "I figured you'd be seeing off your guests or already curled up by the fire with a mystery."

Stella laughed. How did Matteo know this had been her first order of business once her guests checked out? One of her neighbors had given her a whole stack of *gialli*, Italian mysteries termed "yellow" for their trademark goldenrod spines. She'd thought it too generous of a trade— she'd only brought over a jar of pasta sauce made from pancetta and early spring greens after hearing his wife had sprained her ankle getting off her Vespa—but he'd insisted, saying the books belonged to their son, a hot shot lawyer in Rome who came regularly for Sunday dinner but no longer had time to read. "Isn't it too warm for a fire? I wasn't sure."

"Ah, I don't abide by these rules," Matteo declared airily.

Stella stared at him, unsure if he was being sardonically self-critical or practicing willful self-delusion. He cut his eyes away from her and said, "Your guests seemed easygoing. Domenica said you even had time to go with her to Perugia for that installation on Raphael's journey through Umbria."

Stella nodded. "Super easygoing. They only asked for lots of dinners in so they could avoid having to translate menus in restaurants, but I'm okay with that."

Chuckling, Matteo said, "I bet you are."

"You should have seen them with the gnocchi and goose ragu."

His eyes widened. "They allowed you to make them goose? I thought they weren't adventurous."

"Well, I didn't tell them it was goose until after."

Matteo laughed and then grew serious, his eyes fixed on Stella.

"What?" she asked. Matteo didn't answer, and Stella realized. "Oh! Yes, I saved some for you. It's in a container. You can pick it up anytime you're passing."

Matteo patted Stella's shoulder. "That's what I like to hear."

As he continued walking, Stella turned to fall into step with him.

"You don't have your broom. Or your truck."

"Not on duty yet. I told Domenica I'd stop by. She got a new stack of spy thrillers in, and I'm seeing if I want any before she shelves them. You have time for a coffee before you head back?"

She nodded, thinking aloud. "Yes, but a quick one. I have to go to Cristiana's, and I want to catch an episode of *Don Matteo* before my guests come back from their hike. Have you watched it? It could take place here in Aramezzo!"

"Mysteries aren't my thing," he said, as he retied his silver-threaded ponytail, spinning the rubber band around it in a practiced motion.

Stella considered teasing him about what kind of worry it took to cause a guy in his thirties to gray, but she wasn't sure that their friendship had advanced to that level of joking. Instead, she mused, "They filmed Don Matteo in Spoleto. I need to get there. It looks beautiful, and I hear there's a shop with fabulous pistachio gelato. I guess when I have a car." She sighed. "Well, a problem for a different day. A day with more money in it."

He grinned and then said, "Speaking of watching television—"

"Were we?"

"I heard Luca has been watching a lot of American television shows lately. In *English*." He smiled widely, cuing Stella that there was more meaning to his words than he let on.

"Luca . . . the police officer?"

"Who else?" Matteo shrugged.

"Well," Stella ventured. "That's good, right? It's more broad-minded than I would expect of him, but Domenica keeps telling me I sell Luca short. That he may act condescending sometimes, but it's part of the uniform. She keeps reminding me how, when she told him I was in danger last fall, he listened to her and raced to help. Then again, Domenica would pin a gold medal on any person under the age of fifty who reads books. The way she gushes about their conversations about historical romance..."

"*Madonna mia*," Matteo muttered.

"What?" she asked.

Matteo shook his head with a sigh. "Not a thing. So what's the bread for, anyway? The sheep shearing?"

Stella wondered if she'd had enough coffee today, she seemed to have a hard time keeping up. "Sheep shearing?"

Matteo smacked his long forehead with the heel of his hand, releasing a fall of curls from his ponytail. "Oh, man. I can't believe I forgot."

Stella shifted the bread to her other arm.

"Marta is shearing her sheep tomorrow. She asked me to bring you, but I forgot to let you know, didn't I?" At Stella's non-response, Matteo went on, "It's fun. Well, aside from getting a year's worth of Mimmo in one day. Please come?"

At Matteo's eyebrows creeping up to his hairline as he exaggerated a pleading expression, Stella laughed. "I don't know how much good I'd be. I'm too citified to be comfortable with sheep."

"Pssh. No problem. Bring something to eat and nobody will care if you volunteer to be the one hauling the baskets of wool rather than throwing the sheep."

Stella gulped. "Throwing sheep? That's a thing?"

Matteo laughed. "It's not as dramatic as it sounds, trust me. Domenica will be there, some other people you'll like. Don Arrigo, for sure."

"I haven't seen Don Arrigo for a while," Stella realized aloud. She missed her conversations with the village priest. Every time they spoke she realized anew that perhaps Catholicism had more merit than her mother led her to believe.

"It's almost Easter." At Stella's blank look, Matteo went on. "Confirmations, plus all those preparations, you know. So you'll come?"

Stella hedged, "Is there something I would need to bring?"

"Something for dinner. Marta won't care what... anything really..."

He let his voice trail off.

Grinning, Stella said, "But Matteo cares... okay, what's your request?"

Matteo's face lit up as though a sudden sunbeam had unfurled through the clouds at this precise moment. "I've been dreaming about your focaccia since you made it when Domenica and I came over for dinner last time."

Her mind raced... she'd need to pick up supplies from Cristiana's, but she was headed there anyway. Plus, her favorite focaccia method demanded a long rise, perfect for cozy hours getting lost in *gialli*. But did she want to juggle sheep or whatever? Stomp through fields with their messes? What a weenie, she chastised herself. Here Marta wanted to include her and Stella worried about soiling her shoes? Before she could talk herself out of it, she said, "Focaccia, no problem. What time tomorrow?"

"Anytime after lunch. She starts earlier, but needs the big push in the afternoon."

They passed the spot where Stella had been waiting in line just a bit ago. Stella's eyes flicked into the bakery, but she didn't see Antonio. She wondered if he'd gone home. "Do you know if everything is okay with Antonio? He seemed... off this morning."

Matteo ran his hand over his long face in thought. "He seemed good yesterday when I went in. Normal, which would be anyone else's ebullient. Asked after my sisters. Said he wants to set one of them up with his son if things don't work out with the current girlfriend. He keeps forgetting one of my sisters is married and the other one went to school with his son and didn't like him much then. You know how hard it is to get over those early opinions."

"Not me, I never have opinions," Stella mugged.

Matteo laughed, then his steps slowed as they approached Domenica's bookstore. "The *forno*..." he muttered. "Now that I think of it, I remember my boss mentioning something. About Antonio requesting a change of service."

"Trash service?" Stella asked, her head cocked to the side.

Matteo nodded. "I can't remember exactly. Either they were sus-pending trash pick up or adding in debris pick up. All I know is I remember picturing some work happening at the bakery that could have them closed for some time."

Stella pushed the door of Domenica's open as she said, "Would that be enough to rattle Antonio, do you think?"

Domenica looked up from her desk, pushing up her glasses as she smiled. "Something is rattling Antonio?"

Stella took a moment to breathe in the familiar scent of Domenica's bookshop—old books, hot coffee, and a scent she could only articulate as sun-warmed dust motes. Light slanted in through the front windows, illu-minating the maze of bookshelves that wound into the back of the shop. Stella dragged a folding chair out from behind the desk and sank into it, leaving the cozy armchair for Matteo. She cut off his protests by saying, "You're going to be on your feet all day, might as well be comfortable now. Besides, this way you're closer to the thrillers." Stella gestured to the stack of books with dark covers piled next to the overstuffed armchair.

As Matteo leaned over to grab one, a long-haired white cat leapt nimbly into his lap, blocking his reach. He grumbled, "If Attila lets me, that is."

Stella grinned at Domenica. "What is it we were saying about Matteo's priorities last week?"

Domenica adjusted her myriad scarves to better cover her throat and grinned back. "Plum out of whack."

"Just so," Stella said with a laugh. She looked from Domenica, her iron-gray hair held back with a burgundy velvet headband, to Matteo, begrudgingly stroking Attila. Stella never would have predicted, in a zil-lion years, that her exodus from Manhattan would culminate in having a should-be-retired bookstore owner and a gangly sanitation worker as her closest friends. *Amici di cuori*, as Matteo toasted her and Domenica at their dinner at Trattoria Cavour last month. Friends of the heart.

Stella's reflections faded as Matteo muttered, "Cat hair all over my uniform."

"You know where the roller is," Stella and Domenica said at the same time before breaking into peals of laughter.

"Jinx," said Stella, in English.

"What?" asked Matteo.

"Never mind. Just a thing kids say back home."

Domenica pushed her glasses higher on her nose. "So what were you saying about Antonio?"

"*Buongiorno*, Ravioli," Stella said as she picked up a passing cat, this one a patchwork of orange, white, and charcoal. "It's probably nothing. But Antonio wasn't himself this morning. Yelled at a customer, and I wondered if—"

"He *what*?" yelped Matteo. Attila ricocheted off his lap. Despite his earlier complaining, Matteo stared longingly after the cat before saying, "You didn't tell me that part."

Domenica asked, "Who did he yell at?"

Shrugging, Stella said, "I don't know. Some guy not from Aramezzo. The whole thing was kind of surreal. If someone yelled at me in public, I'd be humiliated. Or maybe angry. But this guy... he looked pleased."

"Pleased?" Domenica asked, leaning forward.

"Smug, even," Stella said. "Anyway, Matteo was telling me that there might be something happening at the bakery, some change. Maybe it's overwhelming for Antonio?" She wondered if she should bring him dinner. But under what pretense? *You were kind of a jerk, so I figure you have a lot on your mind and could use a hot meal?* No, certainly not.

Matteo said, "But what kind of change would make him tense enough to yell at a customer?"

Domenica mused, "Maybe he's selling the *forno* and that guy was the new owner. A new owner who has requested permits from the city to remodel the space, and that's what you heard?" Domenica directed the end of her thought to Matteo.

"He's gotten enough offers over the years," Matteo said. "But if he sold the bakery to that guy, why would he be so angry at him?"

Domenica leaned back and stared at the cracked plaster ceiling. "Hmmm. Maybe if financial trouble forced him to sell. I could picture his being resentful of a new owner stalking what he still thinks of as his territory."

Matteo gave up cajoling Attila and settled for plucking a gray tabby off the printer and trying to hold him in his lap. Stella and Domenica rolled their eyes at each other. For a guy who carped about Domenica having more cats than books, he sure spent a lot of energy cajoling them. Matteo caught the look and said, "What? I can't look at the books with you two chatting. I need something to do with my hands."

Stella lifted Ravioli off her lap and stood up, cradling the calico against her chest for a moment before saying, "I'll let you get to it. I have to head to Cristiana's, anyway. She should be open by now."

"Her father opened the shop about a half hour ago. I saw on my way here." Matteo suddenly straightened. "What are you getting from Cristiana's? Something you'll need help tasting?"

"You are nothing if not consistent," Stella laughed. "I promised Cristiana I'd finally try *torta al testo*. And I need tomatoes for tomorrow's focaccia."

Matteo yelped, "You haven't had *torta al testo*?"

Stella glanced at Domenica to see if she shared Matteo's horror, but the older woman straightened her headband, saying, "You know how Umbrians are about their food, *cara*. This shouldn't be a surprise."

Stella's eyes widened. Domenica herself was born in Trevi, not that far south, and definitely in Umbria. Then again, the woman had traveled so much before settling in Aramezzo, she seemed more global than of any particular place.

Shaking his head, Matteo said, "But this isn't just any Umbrian food. It's *torta al testo*. What farmers eat when they break from picking olives and what we bring on picnics and what we stuff with grilled sausages at festivals. It's *famous*."

Stella's slide into guilt for neglecting an Umbrian standard was forestalled by the familiarity of the word. She sat back down. "Famous?"

Ravioli sat down with her back to Stella and only a flick of her ear suggested she noticed Stella trying to draw her back to her lap. One thing about cats, Stella noticed, they knew how to hold a grudge. But not for long. She knew Ravioli would soon forget being summarily discharged from her lap and only remember Stella's knack of scratching her in just the right place under her white chin.

"Famous," Matteo nodded. He turned to Domenica. "You've heard this story?"

Domenica blinked from behind her overlarge glasses. "Of course."

Stella said, "Well, I haven't. Will somebody fill me in?"

Domenica gestured for Matteo to take the proverbial floor. "You tell it, I wasn't here when it happened."

"Well, I was little, so I don't remember it, but I've heard the story more times than I can count." He turned to Stella, leaning forward a touch. She could read his pleasure in being the one to spin a local yarn for her. "Okay, so, about twenty years ago, maybe more, a news team from Rome stopped in Aramezzo on their way to cover Assisi's Easter celebration. They wanted to grab a quick bite and decided not to battle with the tourists in Assisi. Probably hard for you to imagine since you came off season, but Assisi at Easter is packed. A total *casino*."

Stella nodded, wondering where this was going.

"Anyway, the news team stopped into Bruno's butcher shop for *torta al testo* sandwiches."

Stella frowned. "Bruno sells *torta al testo*? I've never seen any prepared food in his shop. Not even *porchetta*."

"This was before his wife got sick. Now, he sticks to meats. Are you going to let me finish the story?"

"Okay, okay," Stella mimed zipping her lip to show she wouldn't be interrupting again.

"Anyway, *torta al testo* is super regional, so the news team hadn't tasted it before. They loved it! How could they not? I mean, Antonio's perfectly tender bread and Bruno's prosciutto that he cures himself from local pigs. They decided it would be an excellent candidate for the regional food segment they aired once a week. So they invited Bruno and Antonio to come on the air and talk about why *torta al testo* is such a signature of Umbrian cuisine, how it's so simple and so delicious at the same time."

"I can't picture Antonio and Bruno being in the same room, let alone doing a news segment together."

Matteo laughed. "I know, right? But the way Mamma tells it, they were once great friends. Vacationed together in Sardinia with their wives and everything. But as it turned out, they didn't make it on the news."

"Why?"

Matteo sat back, pleased to arrive at the punchline of his story. "A series of disasters! First, Bruno got food poisoning, of all things. So mortifying, you can imagine the rumors, how he got sick off his own meat. They were going to cancel, but then Bruno's wife offered to stand in for him. He tried to refuse—she's always been shy, can't imagine her in front of cameras—but Benedetta insisted all she had to do was slice the prosciutto, she'd done it a zillion times, and Antonio could do the talking. They took the train to Rome the morning of the shoot, but they didn't plan on," Matteo paused for effect, "the *Mafia*."

"The Mafia!"

Domenica batted her hand into the air like she didn't brook with such nonsense as organized crime. The woman's unflappability was a wonder.

Stella's knowledge of the Mafia was limited to installments of the

Godfather playing in the background at parties. She'd sort of imagined the Mafia's escapades as largely overdramatized or fictional. Perhaps a mistake.

Matteo retied his ponytail as he went on, "The Mafia. The morning of the shoot, the Mafia called the news station and warned they would detonate a bomb in the studio unless the station changed its coverage of some government thing or another. Antonio and Benedetta didn't even make it onto the stage! The producers put them up in two rooms at the hotel across the street, saying maybe they could do it the next day. But of course, the next day, the news had to cover the bomb threat, so Antonio and Benedetta came home and that was that."

"Oh, how tragic. They missed their chance."

Domenica and Matteo exchanged glances. Domenica shook her head with a small smile as Matteo asked, "What do you mean?"

"What do you mean, what do I mean?" Stella said. "Their chance! They had this shot at glory and it disappeared!"

Domenica chuckled warmly to herself. Matteo shrugged and said, "That's life, Stella. The world doesn't owe us anything."

Stella frowned in thought. Before coming to Aramezzo, she would have assumed the villagers to have a provincial, limited view of life. Like in the memes—grannies leaning out of windows, bragging about their handsome children, or arguing about whose side of the property line an apricot tree grew. Instead she discovered, time and again, the villagers' rounded understanding of life. Like now, for instance. Stella practically heard a gear clicking into place as she realized how little the people of Aramezzo believed they were entitled to riches, literal or metaphorical. This one simple deviation from the American perspective allowed these small-town residents to be grateful in gentle moments and prosaic in challenging ones.

Every day, Stella's interactions with her neighbors gave her fuel to rethink her assumptions. She wondered . . . was that unique to Aramezzo?

Or was it simply living somewhere new that forced you to bend what you thought was straight, and flesh out unexplored parts of your understanding? Could this be why she liked her new friends? Domenica, whose travels had created a ground fertile for all manner of novel perceptions; and Matteo, so totally of Aramezzo he challenged her American opinions, but at the same time, so open, he left space for accepting her for who she was.

Yes, she'd worked in restaurant kitchens and so came into contact with people from around the world. But the focus had been solely on food. So she'd felt her knowledge and intuition about ingredients and processes growing, but hadn't thought to wonder about herself.

She shook her head. She needed coffee if she was going to wrestle with deep thoughts before noon.

Stella rose again, ignoring the baleful glance Ravioli tossed over her shoulder. "Sounds like it's time I further my culinary education."

She said goodbye to Domenica, who wished her a happy day of reading, and Matteo, who added that he'd let her know if he heard more about the change of service to the bakery.

Stella nodded, distracted by her revelations, and stepped into the lightening morning air.

As Stella walked Aramezzo's ring road to the *alimentari*, she remembered her last trip to the little grocery store. She'd stopped in to pick up olive oil and a packet of fresh mozzarella and ran into Antonio, buying prosciutto. It must have been Sunday, the bakery's closed day. She remembered noticing how the red in Antonio's hair and extravagant mustache gleamed, even in the low light of the shop.

Stella had been trying to decide if she should buy a bottle or a tin of oil when Antonio asked how she could have already run out of the supply she'd pressed from her trees. She told him she was trying to stretch her private supply—for sentimental reasons, since even with her refined palate she couldn't detect a difference between the oil from her grove and what the *frantoio* took as payment from growers and combined to sell in local shops—and reminded him of how few olives she'd been able to harvest from her beleaguered trees.

He had laughed then, a booming laugh that filled the space, before saying, "That's right. The bucket." Stella had nodded. The bucket. Antonio had been behind her in the queue to have her olives pressed, and therefore been witness to her embarrassment as she stood in line with her single bucket of olives, while those around her pulled their three-wheeled trucks in, the beds groaning with teetering towers of crates. She'd tried not to notice more olives bouncing out of those trucks than she had filling her bucket. When she'd made a self-deprecating crack to Antonio about the American with the paltry haul, he'd launched into what a good year it was for olives and how next year was sure to be the same, and by then she'd have pruned the abandoned grove that came with her ancestral home and olives would be so plentiful they'd pull down the boughs like Christmas trees laden with ornaments.

The image had stalled her.

As Stella walked down the now familiar road that made up the lowest level of Aramezzo, which was constructed like a birthday cake with tunnels connecting the tiers, she remembered standing in the *alimentari* with Antonio that last time and thinking that she'd been wrong to think of him like a Muppet character. The man had depth.

Just as she'd stood, silent, her hand wrapped around a tin of olive oil, Antonio had asked her how to cook *topinambur*, what Italians called Jerusalem artichokes. His wife, he had added in an aside, had a cold and he wanted to make dinner for her. Stella had offered to cook for the both of them, but he'd shaken his head with a smile. "Baker's hours mean I'm not home much," he said. "Early to bed and early to rise. I like to dote on her when I can."

Stella had smiled as the flavor profile of Jerusalem artichokes, the root of a kind of sunflower, flashed through her. Nutty, sweet . . . it would be lovely in risotto, especially with a few threads of saffron. Stella used to assume saffron came from some dusty country in Central Asia or the Middle East, but the villagers had been quick to educate her—saffron grew right here in Umbria, and even Marta with her sheep farm grew enough to sell a bit at local markets.

Stella had walked Antonio through how to make a simple risotto with Jerusalem artichokes, not mentioning that part of the reason for her suggestion was her long-seated, probably very American, belief in the power of chicken broth. Risotto, with its long cooking in ladle after ladle of hot broth, would both soothe his wife's symptoms and make her feel warm and cared for.

Antonio had taken a little pad of paper out of his pocket and borrowed a pen from Cristiana to write down the instructions in careful script while Cristiana's father sliced the prosciutto. It had been one of those little Aramezzo moments that plucked a chord of tenderness Stella had never known to seek.

Almost at the *alimentari* now, Stella remembered the end of that conversation with Antonio, the last she'd had before seeing him so altered today. Cristiana had been ringing up his basket of prosciutto and Jerusalem artichokes and arborio rice for the risotto when he tossed in a roll of black licorice candies.

Smiling, Stella had said she didn't peg him for a lover of black licorice and Cristiana had answered before he could, "They're for Celeste. He always brings her a roll when he does the shopping."

Antonio had shrugged. "They're her favorite."

Stella had offered, "It's funny, I love anise flavors in drinks and desserts, but can't stand the candies."

He'd chuckled and patted her arm before stepping outside, whistling as he walked away.

Stella remembered that she'd almost stopped him to ask about getting a bread lesson right then. She baked a great sourdough loaf, even a worthy country loaf, but there was something about Antonio's Umbrian bread that made her want to understand it better. She suspected it had something to do with his yeast, which she knew came from wild strains. When toasted in her fireplace and drizzled with olive oil then sprinkled with sea salt, the bread developed a crisp exterior yielding to a succulent interior that reminded her of a sourdough donut she'd had once at a bakery around NYU. She wasn't a huge fan of Umbrian bread for ordinary uses, but for bruschetta, she'd never had better.

But he'd walked away before she could work up the courage, and anyway, she needed to get back with the olive oil if she was going to have dinner prepared in time for her guests. In the moment, she'd consoled herself with remembering how often she met Antonio walking to work, his daily fresh white apron tucked under his arm. There'd be plenty of chances to catch him.

Little had she known that what seemed like Antonio's boundless cheer did, in fact, know bounds.

Stella pushed open the door of the *alimentari*, the bell over her head ringing merrily to announce her presence. Cristiana called out from behind the counter as she restocked the display case with tubs of marinated anchovies and red peppers *sott'olio*, soaking in olive oil, "Stella!"

Stella smiled as she took a red plastic basket from the stack by the door. "*Ciao*, Cristiana. Long time no see."

"I was just telling Orietta about the scene at the *forno* this morning," Cristiana said, gesturing to the pharmacist who had no groceries. She'd probably popped in for chat rather than food.

Orietta said, "I'd assume Cristiana was pulling my leg, no way Antonio would yell at anyone, but I'd already heard about it from Flavia."

Softly, Cristiana said, "He was so mad. I've never . . . I never would have thought it of him."

Orietta checked her phone. "*Madonna mia*, where is the morning going? I have to open up the pharmacy. I'll see you later."

Stella and Cristiana waved goodbye, and then Cristiana turned to Stella with a grin. "*Torta al testo* time?"

Stella nodded, "*Torta al testo* time."

Cristiana's face wreathed in smiles. "Finally! Mortadella or prosciutto?"

Stella cocked her head. Which went better with dry bread? "What do you suggest?"

Cristiana frowned in thought. "Mortadella. But only by a hair."

"Mortadella for the win!"

As Cristiana laughed and opened the case to remove a log-size roll of mortadella onto the gleaming meat slicer, Stella reflected on the absurdities of language across time and space. Mortadella came from Bologna, and so when it arrived in America (losing the pistachios and spices that made it such a treat in Italy), it became known as bologna.

Stella watched as Cristiana cut a triangle from a round of flatbread and then sliced it open before heating it momentarily on a hot grate while she simultaneously sliced the mortadella. When the bread had toasted to her liking, Cristiana carefully piled on layers of the mortadella and topped the sandwich with the remaining triangle of bread. Wrapping the sandwich in a waxy napkin, Cristiana handed it to Stella, who put on her game face. "Looks great!" She hoped she sounded more convinced than she felt.

She bit into the sandwich, and the look of determination left her eyes. She chewed, stunned. The bread, it practically melted away on wings of mortadella. Unlike Umbrian bread, which lacked salt, the flatbread had enough salinity to bring out the yeasty tones of the dough, and the fat of the meat melded into the crumb of the bread for one resonant, triumphant chorus. "Wow."

"Right?"

"No, I'm serious. This is spectacular."

"I *have* been trying to tell you."

"I know, I know."

Cristiana grinned as she went back to refilling the display case. "Orietta told me about a *forno* in Montefalco. No, *aspetta*, I think Bevagna. Right, she mentioned it was on the other side of the canal from the historic center."

Stella tried to concentrate but found it difficult to focus.

Cristiana didn't seem to notice. "That *forno* had to close because state inspectors came in and said the pipes—or was it the equipment? Something like that. Anyway, the bakery hadn't been updated in fifty years. The inspector said they had to bring the *forno* up to code or close."

Stella took another bite and concentrated on not letting her eyes roll back in her head before gesturing for Cristiana to continue.

Cristiana tucked a stray lock of caramel-highlighted hair back behind her ears. "So we think that's what's happening at Forno Antico. That guy Antonio yelled at, he must have been the inspector."

Stella chewed slowly, processing this new information with what Matteo had mentioned about the change of service to the bakery. Finally, she said, "That does fit."

Nodding, Cristiana said, "For sure we'll know soon enough. But my money is on that guy being an inspector. I just hope Antonio can afford the renovations."

Stella finished her sandwich and stacked ingredients for focaccia in the red plastic basket. If Antonio couldn't afford to update the bakery, would he shut his doors? What would that mean for Antonio? For the bakers? Stella paused in thought.

What would it mean for Aramezzo?

Stella couldn't imagine this little village without the *forno* anymore than she could imagine a cake without sugar.

As Stella stepped outside with her groceries and her bag of bread, she considered. Did she have time for a coffee before heading home to make sandwiches? Her guests were probably just starting the descent down the hill from Subbiano. She'd missed her window to catch an episode of Don Matteo, but soon enough she'd be in front of her fireplace, book in hand, putting it down from time to time to jot down notes about a baking project to tackle or a new combination of meat and vegetables that might please Barbanera.

Yes, later she'd savor her alone time. For now . . . coffee. After all, she'd neglected to get herself a cup at Domenica's.

Stella walked down the cobblestone street, enjoying the sunshine on her face, even as she realized it was indeed too warm for a fire. She turned into the tunnel that led to the middle of Aramezzo's ring roads. Climbing the steps, Stella reminded herself she should never leave the house without her reusable bag. It tucked neatly into her pocket, ready for spontaneous shopping, and the handle fit much more comfortably over her shoulder than the *alimentari*'s plastic bags.

Stella arrived in front of Bar Cappellina. The bar had once been a chapel, hence its name (*cappella* meaning chapel in Italian) and the open area spreading out before the entrance. Italian churches often boasted a mini-*piazza* for people to congregate before or after Mass. Though those spaces rarely included the kind of sweeping vista of hills rolling out to sharp mountains, like this one. Even after months of living in Aramezzo, Stella hadn't stopped losing her breath at the view.

After drinking in the greenness of the hills, Stella pushed open the door to Bar Cappellina, breathing in the scent of grinding coffee—chocolatey and rich. As she unwound her scarf, she waved at Romina, who waved back from her helm at the espresso machine before brushing her white hair away from her forehead.

Romina gestured to Stella, above the heads of the chattering villagers, if Stella wanted her usual espresso and Stella nodded. At the pitch and volume in the room, Stella momentarily assumed the villagers were discussing Antonio's outburst. But she quickly realized that they were talking about Leonardo, the *porchetta* guy. Apparently, Leo had taken Marta out for a drive in his red sports car, of some make or model that made the men in the bar grow wide-eyed, but Stella couldn't commit to memory.

Roberto, Romina's husband—similarly white-haired, but as lanky as his wife was stout—moved toward Stella and ducked his head to ask if she wanted anything to eat. She smiled, "Just the coffee, *grazie.*"

He nodded and moved to the other end of the bar, leaving Stella adrift in what seemed a sea of chatter. Leonardo? And *Marta*?

Stella could hardly envision a less likely pairing. She couldn't deny that Leo's swagger had a bit of dashingness to it, but surely that kind of display could hardly sway pure, sweet Marta.

Thanking Romina for the coffee, she reached for a pack of sugar and decided that Marta had probably been polite in accepting a ride. Or maybe her feet had grown tired, chasing after her sheep. This idle speculation about Leonardo and Marta must be just that—idle speculation.

Even so, the crowd refused to be deterred from the bit in their teeth. Some pointed out Leonardo's charisma, and she did have to admit to herself he did have his own kind of charm. Others commented on Marta's romantic beauty, which could be particularly attractive to a gristle and grease guy like Leonardo.

Stella noticed Cosimo standing at the other end of the bar. She realized that he knew everybody in town; in fact, sometimes it seemed he knew everyone in Umbria, what with all his gallivanting from place to place to restock his antiques shop. He may well be able to shed light on the mysterious bakery customer. Was he really an inspector or somehow mixed up in the fate of the *forno*?

She moved to stand next to him, figuring Cosimo couldn't possibly be interested in the dating life of young people, especially since she happened to know he didn't think much of Leonardo, finding him entirely too interested in faddish technology and not at all interested in the lore of Aramezzo. Inexcusable, in Cosimo's book, and yet Cosimo leaned across the bar, swapping rumors with Romina about how long Leonardo and Marta were gone for, and who saw them when they returned.

Stella tugged Cosimo's elbow and when he turned to her, she asked if he'd heard anything about the bakery lately. Cosimo merely blinked his mismatched eyes, one green and one blue, and turned away, muttering that whatever the baker was up to was hardly any of his business. Odd, given that Leo and Marta's romantic entanglement wasn't any more related to him, but Cosimo didn't seem to notice as he turned to wonder aloud to Romina if Ascanio had been with Marta when she accepted Leonardo's offer of a ride in the countryside.

Romina shook her head and said that Ascanio had been with his grandparents.

This brought Stella up short. "I didn't know Marta had family here."

Romina nodded. "The paternal grandparents, dear."

Stella opened her mouth to say she had heard nothing about Marta's husband or boyfriend, or former husband, or partner. She clearly managed the sheep farm on her own. But the conversation rushed on without her as Flavia, the florist, said, "It's strange, though, right? I mean, nobody has ever seen the two of them together and suddenly they're driving around where nobody can see them? And don't we always see Leo riding around in his fancy car with women that look like models? I mean, that's not Marta at all, is it?"

Cosimo furrowed his brows, deep in thought. "Perhaps the boy has finally elected to settle down. About time, I'd say."

This prompted Stella to wonder if Cosimo himself had ever "settled down." He didn't seem to have a partner of either gender nor children. Then again, even without these trappings of domesticated life, they didn't come much more settled down than Cosimo, the antiques dealer. Unless there was romance in the air, apparently. When he fairly shivered in schoolgirl delight.

Stella dropped a euro at the register to pay for her coffee, which practically went unnoticed as all the villagers continued their tidal wave of gossip. All the villagers, that is, except the trim woman with the dress which could have been from the 1960s, though its timeless quality made it hard to tell. Luisella sat as erect as ever, at the edge of the action, letting her eyes drift along the tops of the villagers' heads, removed from it all.

As Stella passed Forno Antico, she peered inside and caught sight of Antonio, the skin around his eyes pulled taut, his shoulders hunched and folded like a baby bird, despite his tall frame.

One of the young apprentices stepped out of the bakery to lean against the wall and take out a pack of cigarettes. He caught her eye and smiled. "Stella, right?"

She nodded, hoping she wasn't supposed to know his name.

"I'm Dario."

"*Piacere.*"

"*Piacere.*" He paused for a moment as if in internal debate and then added, "Listen, I've been meaning to tell you, but you're in and out of here so fast . . . "

"Guilty," she held her hand up. "I'm always on the move."

He lit his cigarette. "Anyway, what you did for Aramezzo back in the fall . . . I'm sure you're sick of everyone thanking you, but I wanted to add mine to the mix. Catching the murderer, that was heroic."

She blushed. "Oh. It was nothing."

He shook his head, his dark hair falling over his eyes as he smiled a lopsided grin. "Not true. The police would never have figured it out if it wasn't for you."

Stella wondered if she'd earned enough cachet to ask her question, but the words escaped her mouth before she had decided either way. "I was here this morning and Antonio . . . Is he okay?"

Dario's face darkened. "He is." Stella felt relief flood her body. He cocked his chin to the side, thinking before adding. "Look, I don't want to contribute to village gossip, but you're obviously going to find out one way or another. Jacopo is taking a job at another bakery. In Assisi."

Jacopo? Who was Jacopo? Was this related to the inspector? Finally, Stella asked, "Jacopo?"

Dario gestured with his cigarette toward the men kneading bread. "One of the apprentice bakers." He looked up, curious. "You must have met him, he has quite the fan following."

Was it Stella's imagination, or were Dario's words laced with ice? Perhaps he had adopted some of Antonio's irritation. Which made sense if Jacopo's leaving made Antonio harder on all the apprentice bakers.

She shook her head. "I don't get out much."

Dario grinned and exhaled a plume of smoke over his shoulder.

She frowned for a moment. "Wait, so Antonio is worried about being short-staffed?" Why would this make him yell at a customer? Unless the customer was somehow related to Jacopo?

Dario laughed before his face grew serious. "He's worried about another baker getting his secrets. It probably sounds paranoid to someone working in New York City restaurants, but it's been known to happen. This bakery gets by because it's the one *forno* in Umbria where bread and *torta al testo* are made the old way. You can't blame him for not wanting to put those secrets in a rival baker's hands."

She smiled. "Okay, confession time. I planned to ask Antonio for a baking lesson."

Dario grinned and thought for a moment. "You know, I think for you, he'd probably spill it. Not all of it, but, you know, some of it."

Her mouth dropped open, and he laughed.

"Seriously, you bring in some of your pine nut cakes he's still raving about, talk like equals, promise you won't sell his secrets . . . I betcha he'll be putty."

She considered this as Dario took one last drag of his cigarette before dropping it to the cobblestones and grinding it out with the toe of his shoe.

"Anyway, he'll be okay. I keep telling him he's still got a crew of us, and we'll work extra hard. He won't lose his reputation. We wouldn't let him down."

Stella wanted to ask about the renovations at the bakery, but it wasn't her business, and anyway, Matteo might have misheard, or it might have just been normal service disruptions. She waved goodbye as Dario slipped back into the *forno*, now humming with a tense energy. She heard Antonio mutter, "Next time you're taking a break, let me know, would you?"

Dario laughed, though the tone sounded more defensive than cheerful. "Relax. It's all good."

Antonio's bitten-off reply did not sound in the least relaxed. Stella, as averse to Italian cursing as she was to the English variety, covered her ears and hurried home. The Americans would be arriving soon, she needed to hustle.

That hustle was impeded as she opened her front door and tripped over a silver-spotted tabby who appeared at her knees as if summoned from the shadows.

"Barbanera!" she breathed. "You've got to stop getting underfoot!" The cat narrowed his eyes, as if doubting the sincerity of her aggravation. She grinned and scratched him under his chin. He paused for only a moment before leaning into the scratch, sticking his head forward, and closing his eyes. She tentatively stroked the fur growing over the scab where his ear used to be before it fell victim to her tussle with a murderer.

He widened his eyes briefly before pulling away to sit, staring through the still-open door.

Forgetting her haste for a moment, Stella watched the cat's eyes, fixed on a bird that had landed in the street. Stella whispered, "Is today the day you finally venture out into the great outdoors?"

Barbanera spun around to retreat into the house, no doubt to perch on the back of the armchair she'd moved to the kitchen all those months ago and left for him to watch over her kitchen shenanigans. She sighed. How could this cat have gone from feral beast to homebody in the space of a few months? Then again, what a few months. Domenica kept telling her to give it time. Barbanera's ear would recover much more quickly than his spirit.

Stella hoped so. She couldn't bear to think of his wild heart so bruised.
 lights.

SUNDAY

*S*tella stirred the oregano she'd dried from the riot of herbs in her garden into the tomatoes simmering in her battered aluminum pot. She reached for her bottle of olive oil and poured a generous spoonful into the tomatoes. As the oil hit the warmth of the sauce, the smell wafted up to her, green and spicy, like raw artichokes. She inhaled, savoring the scent. Lifting the bottle, she realized she'd inadvertently slipped beyond the halfway point. Should she ration the small amount of oil she'd been able to press from her trees?

Stella shrugged and poured in another circle of the oil, admiring its glossy spiral pattern on the tomato sauce. She'd never been good at waiting.

After all, when she finished her oil, she could easily go back to buying oil from the town cooperative. Her lanky, fruitless trees aside, this slope of Monte Subasio had experienced a banner year, not only more yielding olives, but those olives produced more oil than anyone could ever remember. Next year, she told herself, she'd show up at the cooperative with at least two crates of olives. No buckets.

Cosimo's friend Basilio, who had shown her how to harvest her "crop", had assured her he'd seen olive orchards in worse shape than hers rebound quickly with proper care. He'd returned soon after to teach her how to rehabilitate her orchard; and after weeks of pruning, Stella decided she'd never look at a bottle of olive oil the same way again. How her arms had ached with the removal of diseased and dead branches, as well as thinning out boughs to create more airflow and cutting down the ungainly upright branches to lower the profile of each tree.

The bow-legged Basilio had guffawed when Stella grumbled that olive oil bottles should come with photos of the backbreaking work involved in the care and keeping of olive trees. And the cost should be twice as high. "You're past the hardest part," he'd said. "Now we fertilize this summer and keep an eye out for fungus and mold."

"Fungus?" Stella's voice had scaled up. "And mold?"

Chuckling again, Basilio had reassured her, "Don't worry. Trees are mostly sound, this side of the mountain. Clouds split along that ridge," he'd pointed a gnarled finger at a distant peak, "so we get more sun. And less rain, when it comes to that." He'd squinted at the sky as if looking for confirming information. Finally, his gaze had returned to Stella. "Even if you get mold, checking the trees often means we know early. You ring me up, we can sort it no problem."

Stella had nodded and held out her hands, covered with blisters. "And the pruning? Please tell me this gets easier."

In answer, Basilio had held out his own hands, covered with callouses. "Your hands get used to it like anything else. And next year the pruning won't take more than a week of light work. But you need to keep the undergrowth clear, all year long."

She had nodded, remembering the harvest. "For the nets? So they don't snag on weeds?"

He'd nodded slowly, waiting for her to catch on, and when she didn't, he prompted, "Those weeds...you remember..."

"Right!" Stella had practically yelled. She'd never been a star pupil in school. Her mind struggled to stay focused on boring marches of facts unless those facts included the meals served at historic events. She was unused to having an answer. "The weeds! They soak up the rain! And probably nourishment in the soil!"

"*Brava*," Basilio had nodded, a small smile twitching across his weathered cheeks. In that one word, Stella had felt a surge of triumph.

She remembered that moment, the moment when the life of an olive tree made sense to her, whenever she visited her grove. Which was almost every day. She'd linger, stroking each side of a leaf, delighting in the shiny blue-green topside and the silvery-gray underside that sparkled like tossed tinsel when the wind rustled the trees. Even when ice made her stomp her feet to keep her circulation going, she weeded at least once a week. The lines of trees looked nicer, she had to admit, without the undergrowth. All that lovely light swirling under the gleaming boughs, trimmed and tidy.

Even though Basilio laughed whenever he caught her staring at the space between the olive leaves and the stems, reminding her the trees wouldn't bud until the weather warmed, she couldn't help her obsessive checking. Buds meant flowers, and those flowers meant olives, and she wanted some sort of tea leaf reading to estimate the success of her next harvest.

Then again, would she even be here for the next harvest? Her stay in Aramezzo had not gone according to plan. Finding that dead body back in the fall had slowed down the work of transforming her ancestral property into a thriving bed-and-breakfast so she could sell it. But since then, she reminded herself, business had definitely improved, one five-star review pulling in more inquiries. It could only be a matter of time now.

Stella pulled out the baking sheet heavy with focaccia dough, rising in the warmest corner of her kitchen. Admiring the dough's loft, Stella spread her fingers and used them to poke divots all over the surface. What in the world was cheerier than focaccia dough, freshly dimpled?

Smiling, she poured more olive oil over the stretchy dough. Self-regulation was for other people.

As if in dissent, Barbanera leapt nimbly onto the counter to stare at the pooling olive oil. He cocked his one-eared head, and Stella could have sworn she felt his judgment. Shouldn't you save that for my dinner?

She laughed as she washed her hands. "Oh, Barbanera. Don't worry, I made your meal. It's waiting in the fridge."

After a brief sniff of the dough, Barbanera sat down and lifted his black chin, slowly blinking at Stella. She scratched him on his cheek, on the spot he liked best, behind his missing ear. He closed his eyes, his purr rumbling out of him.

"Let me get this into the oven, and I'll feed you, I promise." She spread the tomato sauce carefully over the surface, drizzled a touch more oil (ignoring Barbanera's stare), sprinkled it with flaky sea salt, and then stepped outside.

Like many houses in Aramezzo, Stella's had a wood-burning oven built into the outer wall. Since her kitchen oven barely got hot enough to brown the top of a lasagna or a pan of roasting fennel, she'd taken to using the outdoor oven for baking that required a blast of heat. Luckily, all that painful pruning meant a seemingly never-ending supply of olive branches. Even luckier, she loved how olive wood added a slightly smoky perfume to her baked goods.

The oven door's hinges squealed as she pulled it open, extending her hand into the cavern to assess the heat. Perfect. She slipped the focaccia into the oven and stepped back, her arms crossed with satisfaction.

"Smells like we're in for a treat."

Stella turned and smiled at Don Arrigo, the village priest, carrying a bag with the necks of three wine bottles poking from the top. "On your way to Marta's?" she asked.

"She called and asked if I could bring wine. Mimmo was supposed to, but—"

She raised her hand. "No explanation necessary."

"To be fair, he did bring it. Only he drank most of it at lunch."

Stella shook her head. "Sounds on-brand. I bet it's not slowing him down."

"Nope," Don Arrigo said. "Marta said the sheep's coats are particularly thick this year, but he's already done the lion's share of the work."

Not for the first time, Stella wondered about Mimmo and his brand of country ethics. He had no problem swindling her out of renter's money when she was a faceless name on the other side of the ocean, but he showed up early for a neighbor's sheep shearing. Three sheets to the wind, obviously, but he showed up. So he wasn't entirely a bad sort. At least, she didn't think so. Nobody could make wild boar salami like his and be thoroughly objectionable. Right? Even with his stained shirts and mismatched buttons, and his bumpy nose always sniffing for something to complain about.

Don Arrigo breathed in with a flourish, as the scent of crackling crust and caramelizing tomatoes tripped out of the oven. "I swear, you could give Antonio a run for his money."

"I wouldn't dare. We have a gentlemen's agreement," Stella smiled, wondering what the parallel for this term was when one of the gentlemen was a woman.

Don Arrigo's finely arched eyebrows went up, and Stella realized that the term probably didn't translate. Nevertheless, understanding flashed across his face. Until he frowned and said, "Speaking of Antonio. You've heard about Jacopo leaving?"

Word did indeed travel fast. Especially in a country village. "I did, yes."

He shook his head. "Quite a blow, the boy is a gifted baker." Don Arrigo sighed and then asked, "Shall I wait for you?"

She shook her head, a curl escaping the bandana. She wiped it off her forehead with the back of her hand and said, "You go on, I'll catch up."

Don Arrigo nodded and stepped away, using his free hand to pop Bluetooth earbuds in and cue up the hip-hop music his younger parishioners got him hooked on. Stella watched him stride away, head bobbing. She chuckled to herself.

Opening the oven door, she gave the bubbles forming on the top an approving nod. Almost done. She closed the iron door and as the squeaking faded, Stella heard the familiar undulating of a distant flute. Or pipe. Even after hearing the haunting music at least once a week for months, she still couldn't be sure. She thought about asking someone, but the tune was so wistful, so ethereal, she half considered it a figment of her imagination and didn't want anyone to know of her brain's intricate loops.

Stella listened as the melody rose and then faded into a steady quiet, only a flutter of leaves rustling in the distance. Picking up the peel, she stopped at a sudden realization. She had only ever heard the music at night. Sometimes when she stepped outside to clip rosemary to add to a pot of creamy white beans, sometimes as she leaned out of the window to admire the sea of olive trees tossing a blur of light into the midnight sky. She remembered once she heard it as she fell asleep after a trying day of refinishing floorboards, and she half convinced herself that the moon's rays made the music as they tumbled to Aramezzo. But now . . . she frowned. Why would the mysterious musician choose today to break the nighttime ritual?

She shook her head. That mystery would no doubt remain unsolved. Music and moonlight left no footfalls to trace, no matter how attuned she became to hidden clues and red herrings with all her *gialli* reading.

In short order, she removed the focaccia and brought it back into the house, slipping it onto a wooden board to take to Marta's. As she walked to the door, Barbanera let out a rusty meow.

"Right," she said. "Sorry, old boy." She removed an antique china saucer from the refrigerator, this one rimmed with faded silver and wild strawberries. "Your favorite. Lamb liver and cooked carrots. *Buon appetito*."

The cat seemed to nod before burying his black chin and feasting, his eyes practically rolling back with pleasure. Stella chuckled and called goodbye once more as she headed out the door, but Barbanera ignored her.

As Stella walked the ring road, she wondered if Leonardo would be at the sheep shearing. She had a hard time picturing this always fastidious, former race car driver mincing his way through a field of sheep droppings. But maybe there was more to this guy than met the eye.

Marta welcomed her at the door, the braids wound around her head adorned with bits of wool fluff. Stella smiled and followed Marta to the field behind her house, where she greeted Mimmo, Don Arrigo, Flavia, and some other people Stella recognized, but didn't know. Domenica, Marta told her, was walking Marta's dog Orlando with Ascanio, who hated watching the sheep lose their "fluffy, fluffy, skin." Marta shook her head fondly, adding that she had been unable to convince Ascanio that the sheep's wool was more akin to a jacket than skin.

A young man introduced himself as Jacopo, and Stella paused for a moment, realizing this must be the baker's apprentice leaving the *forno* to work in Assisi. In the brief time she'd known of his existence, she'd internally written him off as a trifling young man, someone who only cared about the almighty euro.

But Jacopo didn't look the part of a frivolous money-grubber. Throughout the day, he sheared more sheep than anyone there (save Mimmo), singing old country songs he seemed far too young to know. Jacopo chuckled at Stella's discomfort with handling the sheep, which seemed too big and too dumb at the same time. He wrestled one into his arms and flipped it onto its rear. It stopped moving all together. Jacopo motioned for Stella to stand behind the sheep, propping it up. Stella, grateful to be relegated to the task of not doing much more than standing, held the animal against her legs while Jacopo ran the electric razor down the wooly coat. He explained, "The thump on the rear puts them in a kind of trance."

He gestured for her to back up, releasing the sheep. The shaved animal toddled around a little drunk before it ran off, kicking its back legs in glee. He grabbed another sheep and flipped it, and Stella hurried to stand so the sheep's back rested on her legs. "How long have you been doing this?"

"Throwing sheep?" Jacopo looked up in thought for a moment before returning his attention to sliding the shears along the sheep's body, thick curls of fluff piling around him. "Middle school, I guess? I used to help my uncle in Bettona and once Marta got her flock, I've been coming here. It's weirdly satisfying, you know?"

She frowned. It wasn't as bad as she expected, but she couldn't admire it.

He grinned at her expression and then rolled the sheep forward until it bucked away in freedom. "You cook, right?"

"I do, yes."

"You know that feeling when you deseed a cucumber? You take a spoon and run it down and all the seeds fall away and you're left with this perfectly crisp valley..."

Now he was speaking her language. She smiled.

He laughed as he caught another sheep. "See?"

"I guess I get it."

"So, Signorina—"

"Stella, please. We've thrown sheep together. I think we can be on a first-name basis."

"Stella, then." He looked up at her, the sky reflected in his clear brown eyes, crinkling at the corners. "Why did you move to Aramezzo?"

She accepted the sheep against her legs and considered how to answer. "Is it possible you don't know the story?"

He winked, all innocence. "You tell me."

She chuckled. "New York... there's so much pressure to be something. I kept messing it all up, shooting myself in the foot. I could see it, but I couldn't change it. I felt—"

"Trapped," he finished the sentence, the sun glinting copper off his dark hair. His animated face grew still. "I get that. As much as I love baking, when I'm at the *forno*, I can feel that way. It's intense. And it makes me want to run. Fast. Anywhere."

Stella wondered what Jacopo could be referring to. But given Antonio's recent moodiness, she suspected it had something to do with his putting pressure on Jacopo not to quit.

Jacopo blinked, as if surprised by his admission. His face regained its motion, and he tilted his head to the sky, belting out some folk song about a pious woman who drew water from a well for a pilgrim and found it to be wine. Only there were clearly some bawdy parts in dialect that she didn't get, given how much everyone guffawed.

She pulled on Matteo's elbow for him to translate Umbrian Italian to the general Italian she'd picked up over the years of staging in restaurants from Rome to Milan, but he was slapping his knee so didn't give her more than a pat of sympathy.

When they finally broke for dinner, Don Arrigo asked Jacopo where he learned the songs, adding, "It's been my understanding that the old music is dying, so few younger people take an interest."

Jacopo nodded. "Even before I could help with the shearing, I visited my uncle annually on shearing day. His friends descended from the hills and sang the songs as they worked. Papà loves music and pushed me to take lessons. These were the songs I loved to irritate my teacher by playing."

Marta smiled affectionately at Jacopo. "Did you bring your accordion?"

"Ah, Marta," he whined, unable to suppress his smile.

"*Ma dai*, Jacopo, come on," Matteo added. "A shearing isn't a shearing without a little music."

Jacopo's flush was hardly noticeable in the gathering darkness. He nodded and sprinted into the house. In the quiet left by his departure, everyone praised the meal, with a smattering of applause for Stella's focaccia.

Mimmo grumbled, "Red focaccia isn't as good as plain. Were you out of rosemary or something?"

Stella stared at Mimmo as he took the last piece, angling it into his mouth and chewing as he looked around the table. "What?" he grumbled. "Someone had to eat it. You can't leave it for the werewolves."

Stella opened her mouth to ask what he was talking about but at a stare and slow head shake from Matteo, she changed her mind.

Jacopo returned, accompanied by Domenica and Ascanio. Ascanio, dressed in his pajamas, clamored onto Marta's lap, indifferent to the wool now dusting her clothes as if she'd turned into a cotton blossom. He curled up and popped his thumb in his mouth as Domenica took a seat on the bench. Stella leaned toward her friend. "How did you get the cushy job of hanging with Ascanio while the rest of us wrangled sheep?"

Domenica grinned. "Privileges of being old, my dear." Stella decided not to point out Mimmo's age. He could hardly be called anyone's role model, as he sat shirtless, bunches of wool erupting from his shoulder blades like a parody of an angel.

Jacopo unsnapped the case and shrugged the accordion over his shoulders, the mother-of-pearl instrument gleaming in the fading light. It might have once been ivory, but over the years had taken on the patina of a spring onion. After a swift run up and down the keys and buttons to warm up, Jacopo broke into a melody. Mimmo sang along, swinging his wine glass until it sloshed purple across the beige wool sticking to his chest.

Stella's knee bobbed. It was impossible not to sway to this music that brought to mind birthday candles or sunsets or the fall of confetti over an exuberant parade. Stella couldn't decide and realized it didn't matter what the music reminded her of. What mattered was how she felt—liberated, easy, joyous.

Matteo pulled Stella up and twirled her around the yard as stars dropped into place above. Don Arrigo tugged Domenica up and Marta wrapped her arms around Ascanio, rocking him back and forth with the music. Mimmo plucked a drowsy Ascanio out of her arms and spun him wildly around the yard while Marta clapped and laughed. Stella danced with the florist and then with Don Arrigo. She even danced with Mimmo, surprised by his unstudied grace as he spun Stella into Domenica's arms.

As Stella danced, she looked into each partner's eyes and felt a wash of thrumming connection. They might not share a backstory, they might not share a future, but they shared this moment. This one spell in time where their bonds felt deeper than family.

The pace increased into a flurry of notes, and Stella, not particularly graceful in the best of times, stumbled over her feet. She laughed until her side ached, begging to sit back down, but Matteo refused, twirling her anew.

When the song ended, Jacopo sat down, breathless, as the assembled guests applauded wildly. Domenica twirled one more time, her skirts flowing around her legs as she beamed up at the inky sky. "Oh, this puts me in the Carnevale spirit! All I need are some *strufoli*."

Stella kept forgetting about Carnevale—though she had enjoyed the schoolchildren walking to school last week in an array of costumes. In bigger towns, she knew from her stages at restaurants around Italy, the bakeries would be full of seasonal treats, mostly fried and drizzled with honey or alchermes, the sweet, bright red liqueur with a spicy edge from the cinnamon, anise, cloves, nutmeg, orange peel, and rose water.

But something niggled at her. "I thought *strufoli* were a Christmas thing?"

Flavia laughed. "No, no, that's *struffoli*. Two *f*s, right?"

Stella frowned. "Is that different?"

Everyone exchanged glances. But in dancing's afterglow, Stella didn't feel stupid but rather cherished like a fluffy pet or an innocent child. Marta explained, "They are both made from fried dough, but in Naples, the balls are small and then bound together in a ring or a mound with honey syrup. Ours are bigger and... I guess you'd say puffier. Like doughnuts."

Domenica sat with her chin in her hand. "I like them with powdered sugar."

Jacopo looked up as he packed his accordion. "Powdered sugar!"

Domenica waved off his objection. "Oh, I know honey and alchermes are more common. But that dusting of powdered sugar...." She didn't seem to notice she'd left the sentence unfinished.

Lifting the accordion, Jacopo said, "Great sheep shearing, as usual, Marta. Thanks for the invite."

Marta rose, hitching Ascanio higher on her hip. "You're leaving already?"

He nodded, his lips a sharp line. "I'm late for my next round of harassment at the bakery." Jacopo seemed to register the bristle in his voice because he added with a grin, "Besides, I need a cigarette, and Marta, I know how you feel about that around the little one."

Everyone laughed and waved goodbye as Don Arrigo poured the rest of the wine. Mimmo left, too, citing a need to feed his dogs. He turned away from Marta's thanks with a gruff noise of dismissal, but Stella noticed how his hand lingered on Ascanio's head when he said goodnight to the child.

The rest of them lingered in the twilight, taking turns guessing how much wool they got, where it would end up. Would a child in Sweden be wearing a sweater made from this wool? They laughed at things Stella wouldn't ordinarily have found funny, and when she pointed that out, they laughed some more. She wished all Umbrian spring evenings could be like this—full of warmth and promise.

Stella rolled her shoulders. Even though Jacopo had done the bulk of the lifting, she could tell she'd be sore tomorrow. She stood with the others to say goodbye. Domenica pointed out her short sleeves and begged Stella to accept a scarf from her own neck. Stella refused the scarf, as well as Marta's offer of a sweater. It was a short walk home. She'd hustle.

As she leaned in to kiss Marta's cheeks goodbye, Marta breathed,

"Thanks for coming, Stella. New York's loss is our gain."

The easy affection of her words nestled into Stella's heart.

Stella rubbed her arms as she walked. Maybe she should have taken Marta up on her offer of a sweater. She smiled, thinking of everyone's concern at her bare throat, Matteo foretelling her certain pneumonia. Her mother was the same. Stella remembered her mother's insistence on jackets and scarves over her Halloween costume, even when the New Jersey fall was warm enough for boys in togas and girls in hula skirts to crisscross the streets. She and her sister had never talked their mother out of her clenched-jaw determination that they'd wind up in the hospital if they didn't bundle. The girls eventually found it more expedient to shove their outerwear behind the bushes before gallivanting around the neighborhood, hand in hand.

Stella stopped in the street, the familiar tightness building around her heart at the memory of Grazie. As if she were there, standing on Aramezzo's cobblestones, Stella could imagine her sister's eyes alight as she wondered if they could stash Halloween candy behind the bush so their mother wouldn't toss out all their favorites—the ones with the lurid colors and cartoon flavors like blue raspberry.

Closing her eyes, Stella waited, wondering how tightly her chest could clench before cracking. The memories always lingered longer in the darkness. Which is why she sometimes still slept with the light on, to the mixed amusement and then annoyance of her roommates and boyfriends.

The grief pressed once more and then began to flicker before finally fading. Stella breathed and took a step. Then stopped at a sound.

Was that a TV?

Irate tones drifting down the street, perhaps from an open window? No. It sounded closer, and anyway, the residents of Aramezzo were no more likely to leave a window open to cool March breezes than they were to venture out without a carefully curated armor of scarves and jackets.

Stella crept forward, leaning around the bend of the road. Of course, the road was entirely a bend, given Aramezzo's odd layout of ring roads decreasing in girth as they rose to the Chiesa di Santa Chiara di Aramezzo at the top of the town. In any case, she peered around and noticed light shining from the bakery onto the cobblestones. Shadows moved jerkily, like marionettes manipulated by a twitching child. The voices rose, and Stella inched forward, her ears practically stretching to catch the words.

"I can't be hearing you right." Ah, the voice belonged to Antonio, the baker. No wonder she'd had a hard time identifying the speaker. Antonio's speaking voice usually matched his personality, full of sparkling sunshine. This voice bulged with rawness. "You said you'd stay until summer!"

"Why won't you listen to me?" Could that be Jacopo? His voice, too, sounded tight and strained. Nothing like the one belting out country folk songs an hour ago.

"Listen while you make a huge mistake? You don't understand what this means!"

"How could I not understand? Everybody, *everybody*, tells me all the ways I don't understand! I'm—" A clatter cut off Jacopo's words, the sound of pans falling to the ground.

Antonio's voice rose, pleading. "What can I do? To get you to stay? I can't tell you how important it is that you stay. Remember, I promised you . . ."

Jacopo's hard voice cut him off. "I told you, nothing. Not everyone is glad of my being here. I can't stay here any longer." Stella stilled at the edge in Jacopo's tone.

"There has to be something. You can't go!" The baker's voice broke. At the sound, Stella realized she was eavesdropping not on a TV spectacle, but on a situation of emotional import to someone she cared about. Two people, actually. Nothing like a sheep shearing to bring people together.

She retreated into the shadows and went around the ring road in the other direction until she arrived home.

When she opened the door, she found Barbanera waiting in the entryway, sitting still like a statue frozen in time. She picked up the big cat and pulled him against her heart, letting the rough purr settle her jangling nerves.

Settling the cat on the comforter, Stella got ready for bed. Freshly clean, she picked up a book from her nightstand. She flipped it over to examine the back cover, her eyes skimming words like "dark secrets" and "tragedy" and "severed head." She put down the book and turned off the lights.

MICHELLE DAMIANI

MONDAY

The next morning, Stella awoke with sore limbs and a heavy heart. She resolved to get a loaf of bread. Maybe she'd catch Antonio on a break and off-handedly mention all the times she had a chef walk off the line during service. Big egos filled kitchens, a truth as sure as the smell of burnt artichokes never washed out of linens. Each time a chef abandoned her felt like the end of the world, but she always made it work and Antonio would too. After all, he'd been running this bakery forever. Then again, she realized with a start, forever was a different animal in a medieval Italian village than it was in the land of tweets that went from enraging to stale in a matter of hours. Perhaps, for Antonio, his business felt fledgling, vulnerable.

When she arrived in front of Forno Antico, she peered through the doorway to the bakery floor but saw only Antonio's broad back. Ah, well. She got in line behind a stranger. A stranger who nevertheless seemed a little familiar. With a start, she recognized the stocky frame and thinning hairline—the guy. The guy Antonio yelled at on Saturday. In all the commotion of discovering Jacopo's plans to leave the *forno*, she'd forgotten what set it all off. This stranger in front of her.

Who *was* this guy? This guy who smelled like bread. And something else, a floral scent. It kept shifting right as she approached the cusp of recognition. Not a scent she often smelled—not orange blossom, not rose. Rather, something that evoked an image of a fairy meadow, blanketed in purple. Lavender? No, definitely not.

Maybe the previous customer was wearing a floral perfume? Stella breathed in again, pulling in a lungful of air. There it was again. Some flower, and with the deeper inhale, Stella realized though the stranger smelled like flour and yeast, his scent didn't match Antonio's bread. No, the scent was sharper than the usual smells of Aramezzo's bakery.

The man took his bread from the woman behind the counter and turned, catching Stella's pensive stare. A smile stretched across his face, and Stella realized she'd inadvertently moved too close. She stepped back, as the stranger ran his tongue over his bottom lip and said in a high voice, "Come here often?"

Stella groaned inwardly before stepping to the counter to order.

The man put his hand on her arm, stopping her. She stared at his hand until he let it drop, though the leer remained, pushing into her space. "Come on, you know this place serves restaurants, hotels, bars. What's a pretty little lady like you doing here?"

Stella fought down impatience. What did this guy expect, her to blush and liquify at the compliment? She was forcibly reminded of construction workers in Manhattan who catcalled as she passed, as if she'd whip off her shirt and whimper, "Oh, big boy, how you turn me on." In fact, one time, after a particularly hard day on the line when too many male chefs commented on how fast her hands moved the whisk, she'd whirled around and laid into a construction worker who made lewd gestures as she passed. She'd never forget how he paled, his jaw working, while his friends laughed.

She considered giving into her temper again now, but creating a scene in Forno Antico would make her the star of too many thousand stories. Instead, she ignored the guy and turned back to the cashier. As she opened her mouth, the man said, "I'm a baker too, you know. If you're ever in Assisi, you should drop in. I'll give you a free loaf if you give me a smile. Can't get a better deal than that."

She concentrated on not rolling her eyes and then realized what he'd said. "Did you say Assisi? What bakery?"

"Forno Fontana. You've heard of it?" His face lit up like she'd given him a cookie.

She shook her head, not bothering to sugar-coat the implied insult by adding that she couldn't name one Umbrian bakery outside of this one and had only been to Assisi twice, once to get her mobile phone set up and the second time to get cat food with Domenica. She didn't even know why she'd asked, it wasn't like she knew which bakery hired Jacopo.

As quickly as his face had illuminated, it fell, crestfallen. He dropped his head to stare at his feet, grousing, "Should have known. Antonio gets all the business."

Stella cocked her head to the side and deadpanned, "What a shame."

He looked up and said, the whininess gone from his voice, "Don't you worry. Things are about to get interesting. You'll see."

Stella had half a mind to tell him that if the scent lingering on his coat was any indication, she could tell him right now why he didn't fetch as much business as Antonio. The yeast, it smelled . . . tame. Stella knew little about Antonio's methods, but it was common knowledge that he bred his starter, believing in the power of naturally occurring yeasts that flourished on the mountain. She suspected this baker must know that as well—it was hardly a secret—but he likely wrote off this bit of insight as too old-school and therefore unimportant. Stella had no doubt that swapping his dried, jarred yeast out for a wild variety would improve the quality of the Assisi baker's bread.

Antonio must have overheard their voices because he crossed the threshold into the shop, and, drawing up to his full height, crossed his arms over his chest. Stella couldn't help but notice he hadn't gotten much sleep. His brown eyes seemed dull, his face pale. Stella had never seen Antonio with a day's growth of stubble. He acknowledged Stella with a nod before saying, his voice like steel, "Aldo. What are you doing here?"

Aldo stuttered, "I . . . I have a right to be here like everyone . . . anyone else." Antonio's lack of response clearly emboldened Aldo because he added, "More even. I need to see all that will be mine."

Antonio lunged at Aldo, who yelped and leapt backward, dropping his bread, as both Stella and the cashier gasped and jumped involuntarily. Two apprentice bakers in blue aprons—Jacopo and Dario, Stella realized—grabbed Antonio's arms, but he had already stopped short of Aldo. His smile appeared to pain him as he said, "Oh, Aldo. You are so easy."

Dario tugged Antonio back, but he pulled away, raising his hands to show he'd cooled and didn't need a chaperone. He spun on his heel and stormed away.

"You . . . you wish!" Aldo sputtered at Antonio's retreating back. Stella exchanged glances with the cashier, who looked equally mystified at Aldo's words.

Jacopo glanced once more at Antonio before stepping toward Aldo, muttering, "You shouldn't have come. You're making it worse."

"But you said you'd start last week and you won't return my calls!" Aldo said, his voice scaling up.

Jacopo shook his head. "I need a little more time. I told you. I'll be there."

"But I already—" Aldo noticed Stella watching him. He cleared his throat before picking up his bread from the floor. As if nothing had happened, he grinned at Stella. "So, I'll see you in Assisi sometime, yeah? Come by and see what I can do with Antonio's secrets."

Stella turned to order *torta al testo*, which the cashier handed her with a relieved smile, glad to have the drama over.

Aldo waited a moment and then strolled out into the March sunshine, whistling.

Stella turned back to find Antonio back in the doorway.

"What did he say?" he asked.

She pressed her lips together before answering, "Some nonsense about becoming king of the bread castle." She attempted a laugh, but stopped when she noticed him pale. "He won't be able to, Antonio. Don't worry. He's not the sharpest knife in the drawer. And anyway, why would any of your customers do business with *that* guy?"

Antonio shook his head. She wasn't sure at her words or at some internal narrative.

To make him smile, she lifted her bread, "Look! *Torta al testo*! I finally tried it."

Antonio's eyes lit and his face regained a shadow of its usual mirth. "You like it?"

"Incredible. The yeast you cultivate, wow . . . there's a depth of flavor I didn't expect from flatbread." She wanted to ask if he used a warm or cool rise, but seeing how threatened he seemed at a rival baker in his shop, she reconsidered. Maybe she'd follow Dario's suggestion and ask when he was replete with her sweets and trust flowed easily. "I heard you were asked to be on the news to talk about it!"

His face stilled. "It didn't happen, though. Instead, I was stuck in my own hotel room all day and night."

Stella, noting the darkening of his face, wondered if perhaps Matteo had been mistaken. It sure seemed to her that Antonio had some feelings about that news segment never airing. Dario appeared again at Antonio's side. "Papà's *torta al testo* is legendary. Nobody needs the news to tell them so."

She looked from Dario to Antonio, who had turned to walk away, and said, "I didn't know you were related!" Though of course, it made sense. Italian shops were often like that, children working for a parent until the parent retired and the children took over. Like Cristiana and her father at the *alimentari*.

Stella's gaze darted to Antonio now pushing the dough with his muscular forearms, sniping at Jacopo, "Any chance you'll be adding wood to the fire anytime soon? Or do you have more admirers you need to receive?" Jacopo turned red and started to respond, but then stalked to the woodpile.

To Dario, Stella said, "I love that you work with your father. I always wanted to cook with my mother, but she wouldn't let me in the kitchen."

Dario nodded as he straightened his blue apron already streaked with dough despite the early hour. "Not the same in Italy, I suppose. Papà had been trying to lure me to the bakery for years. I resisted for a while, but..." He shrugged with a smile.

Stella's eyes scanned the bakery floor, with its hum and the fire flickering in the corner, warming the *forno* until Antonio's cheeks flushed with the heat. "You enjoy the work?"

"Sure, why wouldn't I? It's not too difficult. I only wish Papà would trust that everything will be okay." Dario dropped his voice. "I probably shouldn't be telling you, but Papà has been complaining about Aldo trying to poach his bakers for years. So *this*—Jacopo actually leaving. I've never seen Papà so angry. Even though he must know that Jacopo had to go. Given the hostility between our fathers."

Stella's brows furrowed—was this the stress Jacopo had alluded to? She tried to remember Jacopo's words, but all she could summon was the haunted look in his still face. "Wait, who is Jacopo's father?"

Dario looked up. "Bruno. The butcher. You didn't know?"

Stella shook her head.

Dario paused before saying, "I guess you wouldn't, since Jacopo works here."

"But... why? Why does Jacopo work here and not with his father?"

Squinting into the middle distance, Dario said, "I don't know for sure. I was too busy starting fires to pay attention when Jacopo started working here—"

"Starting fires?"

Dario shrugged uneasily. "You know how kids are. Getting into trouble, I mean. I'm lucky I was never caught during my whole

I-won't-be-what-my-parents-want phase that kids go through around here."

"Or anywhere." Stella smiled.

"Or anywhere," Dario echoed, his face regaining its cheer. "Anyway . . . my guess? The butcher shop didn't get the same bump we did from the near brush with fame. Bruno doesn't make enough to hire his son."

"Which is strange," Stella mused. "Bruno's *macelleria* and this bakery, they are both excellent. Better than I would have expected in a small village—"

"Stop, I'm blushing," Dario grinned.

"Why wouldn't Bruno's shop get famous, too?"

Dario shrugged. "I've never thought about it. I guess with Bruno's wife getting sick, he didn't have time to capitalize on the wave, like Papà did. Anyway, there's plenty of work around here, so Papà took Jacopo on."

Stella considered. "That was kind of your father. Especially given how Bruno . . . well . . ."

"Ah, Bruno hates everyone," Dario said. "Though Mamma says he didn't used to be like that. She says his wife's illness made him sour at the world. Then again, she also thinks Papà hired Jacopo to get back on Bruno's good side. Like that's possible. So who really knows?"

From the corner of the bakery floor, Antonio snapped at Dario. "Dario, if you're done flirting, maybe you want to bake some bread?"

Dario chuckled to himself. "Don't mind him. Oh, and I haven't forgotten that you wanted to talk to him about his methods. He's been . . . in a mood. But I've been calling our customers and none of them plan on leaving, even if Aldo offers better prices. Once I tell Papà our profits and our reputation are secure, he'll accept Jacopo leaving." Dario's face tightened. Stella wondered about his confidence in the future of Forno Antico.

Stella thought about it on her walk home. Jacopo working for his father's nemesis couldn't be easy, but leaving angered his mentor. She now saw what Jacopo meant yesterday at the shearing. He was well and truly trapped.

Stella walked home from the *forno*, her mind abuzz. Plopping on the armchair next to Barbanera, she cajoled him to climb onto her lap. He squinted at her as if she were bananas. Barbanera was no Ravioli. He did, however, concede to curl into a ball, pressed comfortingly against her leg. Stella tried to slow her breathing, to sync it with Barbanera's light purr, but she couldn't contain her darting brain.

Her mind ran over the events of the last few days, catching and whirring. What was it Domenica said about a Carnevale pastry? It had sounded like a Neapolitan Christmas dessert… *strufoli*! That was it. Well, she needed a cooking project to settle her nerves and sharpen her brain. Maybe *strufoli* would fit the bill.

She pulled out the Umbrian cookbook Domenica had given her for Christmas and flipped through it. Ah, yes, *strufoli*. She read cookbooks like novels, but her eyes must have skimmed over the recipe, confusing it with *struffoli*, which she'd always found too sweet.

Flour, eggs, sugar, milk, olive oil, baking powder, lemon peel. She had all that and decided a bit of orange peel would add a layering to the citrus notes. Wait, the recipe called for mistrà. The word sounded familiar. With a snap, Stella remembered working in a kitchen in Florence. At the end of a grueling night, the head chef poured each of them a jot of star anise-flavored liquor over ice. Mistrà.

That she didn't have. But… hold up. Stella bolted to the cabinet in the living room, suddenly remembering dusty bottles she had debated tossing. She rooted through them but found no mistrà. She did find sambuca, which would add that same hint of licorice. As she walked back to the kitchen, she popped the top of the sambuca. Liquors like sambuca could last for an indefinite period of time, but an off odor would indicate some stray bacteria had spoiled the bottle. Closing her eyes, she inhaled the clean scent of a freshly snapped fennel frond. She instantly remembered that conversation with Antonio last week, about her enjoying black licorice in pastries, but not in candies.

Stella began pulling out her ceramic mixing bowls. She'd make the *strufoli* and deliver them to Domenica. Stella would get her friend's take on the drama playing out at the bakery and then maybe she'd take a box to Antonio. Or Bruno. She couldn't decide who needed the comfort of sweets more. And comforted people tended to open up. At the thought, Stella berated herself—there should be no ulterior motives when it came to feeding people. Then again, most chefs got paid for their endeavors, and she just wanted clarity. Nobody ever seemed to think they got the shorter end of that breadstick.

She took a strip of lemon peel, being careful to avoid the bitter, white pith, and then another of orange and set to work slicing the ribbons into tiny slivers. As she whisked the sugar with the eggs, she thought about Jacopo, how three days ago, she'd known nothing about him. There was a story behind every face, every villager.

Into the eggs, Stella poured milk, oil, and sambuca, then added the citrus peel. She whisked the mixture fiercely as she considered Domenica. Her friend seemed an open book, but Stella constantly discovered new chapters. Like last week, when Stella told Domenica about a trip to Washington DC she'd taken with her high school government class, Domenica mentioned in passing that she'd spent a summer tonging for oysters in the Chesapeake with a fisherman named Louis. Not too surprising, given that the woman seemed to have landed everywhere. But then Domenica grumbled about the sunburn she'd gotten on that trip because she preferred tonging while topless. Stella had seen photos of a young Domenica and felt sure her friend had stopped more than one speedboat cold.

Chuckling now, Stella felt her breathing slow as the mixture thickened. The rising scent reminded her of morning rambles in her grove. Probably because of the wild fennel she couldn't bear to tame. She sprinkled in baking powder, a bit of salt, and enough flour to make the dough stiff enough to cling to the spoon.

As she stirred the batter, she considered Matteo. He hadn't shared much of his backstory, despite the number of meals they'd eaten together and walks they'd taken. From his asides, as well as chatter at Bar Cappellina, she'd gleaned he had two older sisters. Plus the brother he'd once mentioned who, with Don Arrigo's help, had turned his life around.

Then there was Luisella, the strangely silent woman at Bar Cappellina. Who was she, really? What was her history? *That* woman was a total mystery.

And how about Cosimo? The man was steeped in town lore, yet she didn't know much about him. She touched the pendant he'd insisted she wear back in the fall. She didn't believe it warded off the evil eye, but she hadn't found even one dead body since he'd handed it to her, so who was she to say?

Marta and her possible preference for ex-race car drivers . . . Cristiana who ran the alimentari with her father . . . Flavia who ran the flower shop . . . for that matter, Antonio and Bruno.

Every single person . . . a mystery. How astounding. All these people walking around, a whole story behind every face.

Maybe she was high on sambuca fumes.

The dough thoroughly mixed, she covered it with a clean cloth to let it rest. Her heartbeat had slowed. In the quiet, she realized there were places all these villagers' mysteries overlapped, she just didn't know what they were yet. But given time, truths would unfold and reveal themselves. Honestly, they'd probably reveal themselves to be none of her business.

She chuckled to herself and went out to weed in her little grove, checking in vain for flower buds along the olive boughs.

After an hour, she washed up and put on a pot of oil. As it heated, she scooped the dough, passing the batter repeatedly between two spoons, smoothing and scraping until they resembled neat eggs. She dropped the ovals into the oil, turning them to keep the color even. As they crisped, she removed each one to a paper towel-lined tray. Popping one into her mouth, she closed her eyes, savoring the way the crispy exterior gave way to a meltingly soft interior, and the slightly green anise scent, rounded out by the citrus. No wonder these were Domenica's favorite in an imposing line-up of Carnevale pastries.

The recipe said to drizzle the *strufoli* with warmed honey, but she didn't have enough, and anyway, Domenica liked them with powdered sugar and that was good enough for her. She slipped the finished *strufoli* into a few boxes, picked up two of the boxes, and patted Barbanera on the head before stepping out.

Domenica squealed like a toddler at Christmas when Stella whipped off the box lid. "*Strufoli*! My favorite!"

Stella grinned. "I hope so. You dropped enough hints."

Settling into her chair, Domenica shook her finger. "Now, now, missy. I'm far too refined for hints. Those were demands, elegantly given."

Stella settled into her armchair. "Well, I'm lucky I picked up on those elegant demands."

Removing a pastry from the box, Domenica said, "Aren't we both? I didn't much relish bopping you over the head with it."

Chuckling, Stella gestured for Domenica to tuck in.

Domenica did, and with powdered sugar dusting her chin, she moaned aloud. "Oh, my. *Cara*, you've outdone yourself."

As Stella looked around for Ravioli, she said, "They aren't the right shape. I was in the mood to play fine dining, circa 1980. In retrospect, I think the crispy bits of an irregular form would be better."

Domenica didn't answer. Her eyes closed as she chewed.

Stella smiled and settled for Attila, who only sometimes consented to play the role of a lap cat. It must be her lucky day, he stretched across her lap with his front legs crossed and fell asleep. Stroking Attila's long white fur, Stella said, "I'm guessing you know about Jacopo leaving Forno Antico?"

Domenica regarded Stella through powdered sugar-dusted glasses. "I heard today at Bar Cappellina, but sounds like it's been brewing for some time."

Stella nodded. "Jacopo seems like a nice young man. I hope he finds his happy."

Domenica pulled the box of *strufoli* closer, nosing about for one with a thicker dusting of powdered sugar. "That's an unusual way to say it, but I get what you mean. And I agree . . . it can't be easy being Bruno's son when Bruno despises Antonio so much."

Stella nodded, deep in thought as she stroked Attila, his rumbling purr filling the bookstore.

Domenica's face lit up. "Say! Did you hear why Leonardo didn't come to the shearing?"

"I assume because he didn't relish getting covered with sheep's wool. And turds. My Doc Martens will never be the same."

"That's what I thought too, but no. Marta didn't invite him!"

Stella cocked her head to the side. "Maybe she's not as smitten as everyone assumes?"

Domenica adjusted her glasses. "Or maybe she's smarter than everyone assumes."

"I always thought there was a well of iron behind Marta's earth mother exterior." Stella grinned. Seeing the sun slanting in the street, she lifted Attila and said, "I gotta run. I want to get a box to Bruno before he closes." Until she said it, she hadn't known she'd decided who to deliver the batch of *strufoli* to.

Domenica waved her hand, eyes fixed on her *strufoli*. "Go, go. See if I care."

"*Ciao*, now," Stella called as she walked out. She paused for a moment, her hand on the doorjamb, watching Domenica. Stella had no idea how this woman she once confused for a pile of scarves had wormed her way into her life and heart, but she was glad she did. Stella couldn't picture life without Domenica.

As she walked to Bruno's, she realized that eventually leaving Aramezzo meant eventually leaving her friends. Her throat constricted, and she ordered her brain to behave. She had plenty of time before that happened. And once safely ensconced back in her home country, it's not like she couldn't visit. She stopped, thinking. How strange that she now considered this tiny, off-the-beaten-path town that her mother could never speak about without her lip curling in distaste, as a possible vacation destination. Huh. She shrugged, life was certainly, and beautifully, weird.

Stella amended that revelation on entering Bruno's *macelleria*. At the sight of Veronica, the mayor's wife, Stella wished life could be decidedly less weird.

Sure, there were plenty of people in Aramezzo who barely acknowledged Stella's existence. But at least their lack of engagement, when she bought a light bulb or passed them on the street, seemed a reasonable suspicion of outsiders. Whereas every interaction with Veronica led to Stella feeling smaller than her five feet and two inches.

Well, nothing for it now. Bruno offered a grunt of greeting as Stella walked in, but did a double-take at the box in her hands. His lip twitched up in an approximation of a smile. It didn't last long.

"Two of those sausages, Bruno, if you would," said Veronica. "Though I do wish you wouldn't make them so fatty. Marcello and I have our figures to maintain, you know." Her laugh tinkled through the store like rusty nails in an unused box.

Stella flinched. Sausage without fat? An abomination.

Veronica added, "Actually, throw in one more for my babies."

Stella had enough experience with Veronica to know that the babies in question were the copper-colored, long-haired dachshunds currently wagging their tails in anticipation. Veronica didn't seem to notice that she'd categorized Bruno's meats as dog food. Given how long Bruno toiled over those sausages, perfecting the balance of heat and salt, it had to sting.

Veronica turned and gave Stella a once over but didn't find her worthy of more greeting than "Oh. It's you," with an eye roll. Eye roll? Seriously? Veronica rapped the counter and said, "Bruno! Not that sausage! The other one."

To Stella's culinarily trained eye, the sausages looked identical. She figured Veronica needed something to be bossy about. Bruno, exhibiting the patience of a monk, put back one sausage and picked up its twin, pausing to check for Veronica's opinion, but the woman didn't notice. "Like I was saying, before we were interrupted," Stella had to imagine her presence was the interruption, though Veronica barreled forward like a steam train, "what's this I hear about Jacopo leaving Aramezzo?"

In Bruno's pause, Stella imagined he was waiting to see if she planned to answer her own question, or assumed it to be rhetorical. When Veronica made a noise of impatience, Bruno finally said, "Only to work. He'll still live at home."

Veronica clicked on the counter with one perfectly manicured finger. "He can't go and that's all there is to it. Aramezzo's one claim to fame is that bakery. We can't have him in Assisi, cheapening Antonio's work."

Stella winced. Was it her imagination, or did she see Bruno's shoulders tense as he wrapped the sausages in paper? He must have felt the insinuation that his shop didn't matter. He grumbled, which Veronica took as agreement because she said, "Don't fret, Bruno. My husband has a plan." She stood, if possible, even taller at the words. "Well, we came up with it together, obviously. As we do all things. It's amazing how in sync we are! Like two sides of the same heart."

Stella held back her instinctive gag reflex.

Veronica kept talking, her mouth stretched across her teeth. "Jacopo is young and oblivious to what's important in life. Of course, he needs a firm hand. I'm sure you'll thank Marcello for stepping in and giving Jacopo the guidance he needs."

Bruno slammed the parcel onto the counter, startling Veronica's dachshunds, though Veronica herself was too lost in what Stella could only assume was some fantasy where Aramezzo was merely a backdrop and she and her husband pulled the strings of villager-shaped puppets.

Slipping the sausages into the only designer reusable tote Stella had ever seen, Veronica crooned, "It's no problem at all, Bruno. Simply part of being mayor. I'll pass along your thanks."

Stella watched Veronica swan out of the *macelleria* on a cloud of what must be expensive perfume, if the nuanced layers of jasmine and sandalwood were any indication. She stared at Bruno with wide eyes. "What was *that* all about?"

He shrugged. "Everyone has an opinion."

"Apparently." Stella nodded and then set the box on the counter. "*Strufoli*. And I'll take two of those sausages. Which, for the record, have the exact right amount of fat."

A glimmer of a smile flickered across Bruno's face.

Hoping to coax an actual smile from the butcher, she added, "I meant to tell you, I used a few of Thursday's sausages, the ones with garlic and rosemary, in a pasta sauce for Romina and Roberto. You heard about how their grandson was in that motorcycle accident? He's going to be all right, thank heavens, but anyway, they said the *sugo* was the only thing they could stomach while he was in the hospital. It was so delicious I froze some for when I have guests next week."

His gray eyes glazed over as he handed her the package of sausage.

Ah well, too much to hope for chattiness from Bruno. Stella paid for the sausage and told him she hoped he and his wife enjoyed the *strufoli*. Bruno picked up the box with a kind of reverence and headed to the door that Stella knew led upstairs to where the family lived. Softly he said something about bringing the *strufoli* to his wife now. Then he offered his first real smile of the evening.

It was enough.

Stella strolled out into the street with a satisfied heart.

The evening seemed to match her mood... a warm breeze tickled her hair against her cheek, soft as powder. She decided on a *passeggiata*, a little walk through town, before heading home. Might as well enjoy the tender weather while she had it. Umbrian springs could be as wily and unpredictable as soufflés.

She wandered to the second ring road, past Cosimo's shop, but no lights glowed against the gathering darkness. She did, however, hear the eerie music begin to unspool as she stood in front of Cosimo's door. It sounded stronger in this part of the village. She listened for a minute or two before strolling back to the lowest ring road, noticing the pop of color from newly planted blossoms in one neighbor's window box after another. The music faded away; all Stella heard was the stillness of approaching night.

The quiet, interspersed with the drone of white-haired women gossiping in the street as they sorted greens, washed over her with a sense of constancy, like wind through the trees. Her feet wanted to keep walking, but her rumbling stomach reminded her to head home.

Lights illuminated the police station ahead of her and, to her surprise, the mayor's office in the building next door. She saw a figure walk out of the door and close it gently, his hands running down the wood as if being careful to avoid making a sound. It didn't look like Marcello, even in the half-light. One more glance and Stella recognized the figure as Jacopo; he must have been meeting with the mayor. From the way Veronica spoke about it, Stella had assumed it to be upcoming, not in process. Then again, maybe Veronica didn't know as much as she pretended.

Stella lifted her hand to greet Jacopo but stopped when she caught sight of his face, pinched in worry. He lit a cigarette, his hand cupped around the lighter, and then hurried down the street, away from Stella, until the darkness enveloped him. She heard him talking into his mobile phone, his voice tense. What could the mayor have told him? Stella certainly hoped young Jacopo hadn't been fooled by Marcello's bluster into assuming the man wielded more power than he did. He couldn't keep Jacopo in Aramezzo if the boy wanted to leave.

She paused to watch the men sitting outside Trattoria Cavour playing *scopa*, the card game that seemed to Stella like a cross between UNO and Calvinball, the game from the old Calvin and Hobbes comics, where players made up rules on the fly.

As she rounded the corner to her house, she noticed someone sitting on her stoop. Her pace slowed. "Dario? Is everything okay?"

He rose with a smile, waving his piece of paper. "Great, I won't have to leave you a note."

"Isn't that a scratch-off lottery card?"

He chuckled. "It's the only paper I had on me."

"So, what's up?"

"Good news! Papà's in good spirits. He agreed to meet you to talk bread anytime he opens the bakery."

Stella hoped this meant Antonio had accepted losing his apprentice. "Which upcoming days does he open?"

Dario narrowed his eyes in thought. "That's a good question. He's supposed to open tomorrow, but the schedule keeps changing."

Stella nodded and said, "There's no hurry."

Dario's eyes flicked to the side, and he moved closer to lower his voice. "Honestly, Stella? The way he lit up when I said you wanted his expertise? I think he could use the lift. He thinks so much of you...we all do...so to have someone of your reputation interested in his process...well, it seemed a welcome distraction."

She didn't entirely know what reputation he could be referring to—as far as she knew, nobody in Aramezzo knew about her Michelin star—but she had learned that sometimes simply having a job in the United States conferred a kind of cachet, deserved or not.

Grinning, Dario added, "Now, that doesn't mean that you should come empty-handed. Don't forget his sweet tooth."

She smiled. "I made *strufoli* today."

He brought a fist to his chest and said, "Bless you, Stella. You're the best."

"Well, I don't know about that." She had a thought. "What time should I be there?"

"Five."

Her voice scaled up. "In the morning?"

"I'm afraid so," Dario nodded, looking up as a light rain began falling. "The rest of the day, he's too busy. But in the morning it's all about prep and he'll have time, as long as you're okay with him bustling around."

"Are you kidding? I'm pretty sure the secret sauce is in that bustling. Anyway, food is one of the few things in life I can get up early for. I'll be there."

TUESDAY

*T*he warm light from the bakery spilled onto the black cobblestones, shiny with the rain that had fallen on and off throughout the night. Without quite realizing it, Stella's ears reached for the sound of mixing, or the little tinny transistor radio Antonio sometimes had playing.

Nothing.

Stella held the box of *strufoli* against her chest and called out, "Antonio?"

She winced at the sound of her voice ringing in the quiet space. Why was it so quiet? Bakery sounds routinely overflowed into the streets. There were times she heard the flow of banter and teasing rising above the sound of banging pans from as far away as the upper ring road.

Now? All she heard was a hush, like an intake of breath.

For an instant, she thought maybe he was late or not coming, except . . . the lights. The open door. Plus, somebody had to make the bread.

"Antonio?"

No response.

The quiet, the darkness, crept closer.

Stella stepped onto the threshold and leaned in, scanning her eyes across the bakery floor. Empty. Was there a bathroom off a corridor she couldn't see? Or an office? She hesitated, wondering what to do. Part of her wanted to hightail it home and make excuses later. After all, the plans were vague.

There was no reason for silence. Something was wrong.

She sniffed. A smell in the air. Many smells, actually. The smell of a silky, butter-rich dough. Something floral. Cigarette smoke, easy to explain since all the younger bakers smoked. But . . . she inhaled again. What was that? The musky tang of adrenaline. And something else. She closed her eyes to help her nose find the thread . . . .there it was—a smell that reminded her of the swing set at her elementary school. A kind of tinny sweetness. Her eyes scanned the bakery, clocking a pile of fallen pans on the floor.

The scents drew her forward, her eyes now scanning the surfaces. Stella spotted a flour canister knocked over . . . and beside it, the source of the buttery scent—a square of sleek, laminated dough, the kind used in making *cornetti*. But Antonio didn't sell *cornetti*. Did he start the project hoping to get her advice? A kind of tit-for-tat? If so, she'd be happy to swap methods . . . maybe if he diversified he'd worry less about losing his market share.

But then . . . why the quiet? Not an ordinary quiet, a quiet like somebody hid in the shadows, ready to pop out.

Her eyes darted over her shoulder into the blackness of the street.

Nobody there.

Why would there be?

"Hello?" Stella felt pulled forward, almost without her consent, further into the bakery.

Her gaze snagged on something at the other end of the metal island, toward the stone oven. A fall of flour, glinting weirdly under the lights. She drew closer, the flour—it didn't smell like flour. An image of balloons exploded into her brain.

This was the worst possible time for her mind to take a joyride. A moment later, she realized why her brain had tried so hard to distract her.

There, in the flour. Something brown . . . no. Red. Alchermes, it had to be that red drizzling liquid so popular on Carnevale treats. Stella tried to convince herself that her eyes spied nothing more dire than spilled alchermes, intended for whatever pastry Antonio had been making.

She'd almost convinced herself when a realization thundered into her ribcage. Alchermes did not smell like swing sets, it smelled like spices.

Her heartbeat quickened, and she dropped the box of *strufoli* without noticing.

Her eyes trained on the drops, Stella barely noticed her feet moving, pulling her forward around the island. A splatter of red drops. There seemed to be more of them toward the edge of the island. Perhaps a bottle of something else red fell out of a distracted hand?

But Stella knew the truth. Even before she rounded the corner of the island and saw the body on the floor.

For perhaps the first time in Stella's life, she swore under her breath.

With Antonio on her mind, Stella immediately assumed the white-clad body at her feet must be him. But no, the blue apron, the smooth face that hardly looked like it could grow a mustache . . . the lack of crow's feet around the staring eyes, still like brown stones . . . this was not the baker.

This was Jacopo.

Her heart sagged. When she'd stumbled across her murdered guest a few months back, it was horrible, and not just because he'd been wrapped like a sausage spilling out of its casing. His still body had represented life and all the possibilities of better tomorrows, snuffed . . . gone.

This, though. This was not that. This death, *this* one, spelled grief. For the butcher, for the baker. For Aramezzo.

She blinked. It did nothing to correct her vision, which careened this way and that. Jumbled, kaleidoscope style, like a restaurant's going out-of-business fire sale.

The police, she'd have to call…oh no, how did she wind up finding *two* dead bodies within a few months? What would they say? Well, it didn't matter what they said, someone had to come. Now. After all…

Stella remembered last time, when she neglected to check for a pulse. She took out her cell phone and dialed, even as she tiptoed around Jacopo's arm, outstretched at a weird angle. She almost pressed her knee against a cell phone smashed on the floor, but kneeled an inch over. Tentatively pressing her fingers against Jacopo's wrist, she inhaled the scent of cigarettes mixed with a floral, almost soapy smell. Stella gasped in amazement at the feel of Jacopo's skin under her fingers, warm and alive. For a moment, she thought she felt a flutter, but then realized it was the sound of the phone ringing in her ear that her brain, keening to deny truth, imagined came from Jacopo's wrist. A wrist that didn't beat with any pulse at all.

The switchboard picked up and Stella pressed the phone against her ear as she launched into English, "A man…dead… at the bakery." The words sounded flat, wrong, surrounded by the pink medieval stones. Realizing, she switched to Italian. "I'm at Forno Antico in Aramezzo. A man is dead." The words still sounded foreign. But at least the person at the other end understood. Stella tried to focus on the distant voice coming through her phone. *Stay put.* Police officers were on their way.

Stella hung up, letting her hand, still clutching the phone, fall to her side. She breathed slowly, trying to steady her heartbeat.

Dead.

She tried to make sense of the words.

Jacopo was dead.

But…*how*? The question landed like a goblin's footfall. The liquid she'd thought could be alchermes—she knew now how deluded that was, a sign of her brain protesting reality, much like that odd image of balloons.

The red, it must be blood. From…where?

Only then did she notice. And once she did, she realized her mind must have refused to let her see. A slash across the neck, a purple seam in what seemed a crimson scarf of fine silk. She recognized the knife work. The line hooked down at the left side, the characteristic mark of a bread lame, run across dough.

She frowned, wondering if another kind of knife could make that mark. It seemed suddenly of grave importance that she understood what weapon had been used to kill Jacopo.

A truth dawned on Stella. If she understood what killed Jacopo, it would lead to the obvious . . . *someone* killed Jacopo. *How* the killer murdered the baker's apprentice could well give information about that killer's identity.

So could it be a lame?

Lames were extraordinarily sharp by design—they had to be to swiftly slash through a dough's exterior, allowing an exit for steam. In fact, that's why most bakers used a lame that fit disposable razor blades. As soon as the blade lost its edge, it got tossed.

Suddenly, Stella remembered the other benefit of a lame . . . the curved shape lifted the top layer of the dough enough to create a nice, crusty "ear." Stella leaned back down to examine the cut once more. She didn't want to get too close, and she certainly didn't want to touch it, but it looked to her that the cut had a bit of lift.

She spun away from the body. How could she have been staring so dispassionately at a dead person? She supposed cops lost their squeamishness (if they ever had any) over time, but she never would have guessed that one dead body and a lifetime of reading murder mysteries would have made her able to control her retching reflex in the face of death. Well, it was hitting her now, with gusto.

Her stomach heaved, and she leaned over the counter, away from the body. Could she splash cold water on herself? Would that interfere with the crime scene?

Because one thing was certain, this was most definitely a crime scene. Not like last time when she had to convince the police to investigate when they wanted to believe it accidental.

But who would want Jacopo dead?

Or maybe...was it possible Jacopo was not the intended target? After all, Jacopo seemed an easy-going enough fellow. Not the kind to instigate enough rage to lead to...*this.*

She heard footsteps hurrying closer and wondered at the lack of sirens. Then she remembered. The ring roads. An ambulance or police car couldn't make its way up the tunnels. Sure enough, the police stormed into the room with what looked like a collapsible stretcher.

Stella groaned inwardly at the sight of Officer Luca. Why must he be present for all her lowest moments? He must have had the same thought as his eyes widened at the sight of her and then he stopped, tense. His head swiveled as if assessing danger in the darkened corridor and the dripping sink.

"No one is here," Stella said.

Luca set his stubbled jaw and gestured for his fellow officer to enter the bakery floor with him. Salvo. Of course. Looks like every time she found a dead body, the cops who turned up would be Luca, who even made a cop's uniform appear stylish, and Salvo, with his outdated walrus mustache.

Luca knelt and put his fingers on Jacopo's wrist. Salvo waited, watching, as the faraway look on Luca's face faded into one of grim determination. "No pulse." Stella readied herself for the remarks about her habit of finding dead bodies, but then realized that this was, of course, not about her. With a fellow villager at their feet, Salvo took careful notes of her story, asking what time she arrived, how she found the body, while Luca took out his phone to make a series of brief calls. He then used his phone to snap photos of the scene.

As Stella finished answering Salvo's questions, he paused and ran the top of the pen over his lip. Finally, he said, "But Stella . . . why are you here?"

She nodded. "Chance, really. Dario said I could probably find Antonio here this morning. We were going to talk bread."

Salvo tapped the pen top against his lip. "Antonio asked you to come?"

Stella shook her head. "No. Dario said Antonio should be working today, though the schedule keeps changing. But I had the *strufoli* made, and I knew Antonio would like them, so I took my chances."

Cocking his head to the side, Salvo asked, "*Strufoli?*"

Stella gestured to the box lying on its side, the balls of dough now smashed.

"Stella, you'd best head on home," Luca said as he slid his phone into his pocket. He turned to Salvo and said, "Get gloves. And grab an evidence bag for this phone. It's cracked, but the last text is there, from 4:43 this morning. There's no name, but let me read you the number."

Stella started to step away, but slowly, so she could listen.

Salvo wrote the number before handing Luca disposable gloves. Once they had both snapped them on, Luca picked up the cracked phone and slid it into the waiting bag.

Salvo looked up. "What's the message?"

Luca said, "*We need to talk. He knows.*"

Stella mulled the words. Who needed to talk? Jacopo and the murderer? Or had someone tried to warn Jacopo?

Luca added grimly. "I've called both the coroner and the Captain."

Stella's heart lurched. Without thinking, and without knowing why, she said, "I'm sorry."

Salvo and Luca looked up. Salvo asked, "What are you still doing here?" as Luca said, "Bad luck, Stella, that's all. Bad, rotten luck."

She touched the pendant on her chest. "Maybe it's run out of charm."

Luca tried to smile, but with his eyes fixed on the body, it didn't quite make it. "I've known him all my life. We played on the same soccer team."

Salvo nodded. "Me too. An excellent forward."

"That's why he played with us, even though he was young." Luca shook his head. "Who would do this?"

Stella ran her hands over her arms.

Luca caught the motion. "Are you cold? Why don't you have a jacket?"

"Not cold." She shook her head. "It's tragic. This kid, he had his whole life in front of him."

Luca understood. "Not like Severini."

"Not like Severini."

They stood in a semicircle around Jacopo, lost in thought. Stella's heartbeat raced as her gaze dragged over Jacopo's lifeless form. A flour scoop next to his hip. He had probably been adding flour when...

Her vision darted to the flour, streaked with red. She shook her head to clear the tears forming in her eyes, creating glints and prisms in the flour.

She looked up to find Luca's eyes on her. "Go. I mean it, Stella."

"But—"

He shook his head.

She tried again, "But last time, I helped. I cracked the whole thing—"

Salvo grumbled as Luca shook his head again. "Yes, but Stella, you have to understand. You're a civilian. Part of the public we're supposed to protect."

"How does being here put me in danger?"

Luca and Salvo exchanged glances before Luca said, "For one thing, we have no idea where the killer is. For another," Luca stared at his feet and muttered, "You're making it harder for us to focus."

Salvo glanced up at Luca before looking away.

Stella nodded slowly. She didn't want to go, but also understood. She wasn't a police officer. Anyway, who was she to think she could help? It wasn't like she had any training. All she had was a keen palate and a penchant for mysteries. She turned to go and heard Salvo say to Luca, "A robbery, do you think?"

Luca started to answer when something occurred to Stella and she spun around. "Okay, I know it's not my business—"

Salvo groaned.

She went on, "But the murder weapon . . . "

Luca nodded. "A knife, clearly. Thanks for your help. We've got it from here."

"But not any knife," Stella insisted. "It looks like the mark of a bread lame."

"A what?"

She pointed at the arc of the wound. "You make bread enough, you can spot it. Bread lames are sharp, the cut ends up being clean, with a curve because of the bend in the razor. But see that notch at the far end?"

Luca shook his head. "Stella."

"I'm serious!" She twitched back her shoulders as if trying to appear more authoritative. "Must be a right-handed person, first of all, with the notch on that side. The . . . killer . . . must have grabbed him from behind, taken him unawares. But I still don't get—"

"Stella!" The sharpness of Luca's voice pulled her short.

"What? I can be right about this, you know. It has been known to happen."

Salvo muttered, "Even a stopped clock is right twice a day."

Irritably, Stella asked, "Do you see a different murder weapon lying around?"

Both men shifted their weight and casually glanced around, no doubt hoping for the appearance of a giant cleaver. Seeing nothing of note, Luca shrugged. "Look, I'm not saying you're wrong. Necessarily. I'm saying you're making a lot of assumptions. And you know we can't take assumptions to the Captain."

She blinked. "He still hasn't retired?"

"He has not," Luca said. "And as complimentary as he was about you to the press, you have to know he was none too pleased by your role in catching Severini's killer."

Salvo nodded in affirmation. "He was in a towering temper for weeks."

Luca went on, "There was talk of him retiring early. But then he said that nothing else could go wrong, so he might as well coast to full pension."

Stella scowled. "Looks like I'm not the only one making assumptions."

The muscle in Luca's jaw twitched. His voice low, he said, "He is the Captain. For another few months. I don't want you tangling with him."

Salvo nodded. "If the Captain sees you skulking around here..." He let his words trail off.

Luca added, "And what I said before stands. This isn't the place for you. Okay?"

Stella bit her lip before saying in a soft voice, "But you get it now, right? That his refusal to see what's in front of him blinds him...blinds you all?"

"Look, Stella," Luca sighed. "He's our leader. And he has a lot to teach us, still."

"About misogyny maybe," Stella muttered under her breath, in English.

"It may be old-fashioned, but it's not misogyny. Civilians, men or women, can't do what we do."

Stella looked up in surprise. Was Matteo right? Was Luca getting some English training with all his American TV viewing?

She stared at him until he flushed and turned his gaze away. Finally, he said, "Lie low and give the Captain, give us, a chance to start the investigation."

Stella quieted her thundering heart and tried to remember what she'd decided just a few minutes ago. She'd gotten carried away. She was a cook and a reader. Nothing more. "Okay, I get it. I'll let you do your thing."

Luca sighed in relief. "I appreciate that."

She nodded and walked to the threshold. Where she stopped and stared at the ground. Her eyes widened. Looking up, she said, "Luca—"

"Please," Luca frowned. "Leave this to us."

"You're right. Absolutely. You're the experts. So I'm assuming you took note of this?" She pointed at the street in front of the open double doors.

Luca and Salvo straightened, on alert. Luca said, his voice throaty, "Note of what?"

She pointed outside the bakery door. "This footprint."

The officers rushed toward her. Quietly, they stared at marks left by a sneaker. It was large, perhaps indicating a man of tall stature? Or at least a person with large feet. Stella examined the tread, peering closer to discover that the white marks pointed toward the bakery looked to be made by flour pressed into the damp cobblestones.

Luca groaned. "This. The phone. What else?"

"Well, the lame you won't listen to me about." Luca turned away, and Stella, afraid of being dismissed again, added, "And you'll have noticed that, of course." She gestured to the metal island where the butter-filled pastry sat for a folding that would never come. The men looked at it, exchanged glances, then turned back to Stella. Salvo said, "So?"

"So. That's a laminated pastry dough. Used for making flaky pastry with loads of layers—*cornetti*, *nidi* with the cream inside, *trecce*."

Salvo said to himself, "*Trecce*. I love those. With the walnuts."

She nodded. "Doesn't that strike you as strange?"

Salvo furrowed his brow as Luca's face registered dawning awareness. Stella prompted, "Why would Jacopo make laminated pastry dough? They don't sell pastries here."

Luca said, "Maybe Aldo makes them in Assisi? So Jacopo is boning up?"

Shrugging, Stella muttered. "Could be." She looked up. "His cigarettes."

Luca said to Salvo, "My turn. What about them?"

Stella looked around. "He smokes. I've seen him and anyway, I can tell he's had one not that long ago. But where are they?"

Luca frowned. "Could someone have taken them? Maybe they had a fingerprint on them?"

"Maybe," Stella said. "But no keys, either? And that baker's uniform doesn't have pockets. There must be someplace where the bakers store their things."

Luca nodded. "Maybe the killer took it all. His wallet too. A robbery gone bad?"

Stella nodded along with him. "Right. Unless it's all somewhere else in the bakery? Where do the bakers keep their stuff while they're working?"

Luca and Salvo seemed to have forgotten their determination to make Stella leave as they all began pacing the internal perimeter of the bakery, examining the shelves. Stella scanned the walls for any hidey-holes. But all she could see were shelves of flours and grains, and a whiteboard covered in what looked like scribble. From the back corner, on the opposite wall from the oven, Salvo called, "Here! I found it!"

Stella and Luca joined Salvo in the back of the bakery, where they found a line of baskets with names on them above a hamper of dirty aprons. Luca pulled one bin after the other. They were all empty save for Jacopo's. Luca didn't touch the objects, but brought the bin down to investigate the contents. Stella spied a slim wallet with bills poking out of it, a pack of cigarettes, and two sets of keys. One ring had three keys, one of which must be for Jacopo's car, on a keychain with a red leather tag stamped with a "J". The other had a single new key with no embellishments. As Luca tilted the bin, Stella caught sight of a purple pack of candy.

"Violet," Stella said under her breath.

Eyes alight, Salvo said, "Does that mean something?"

She shook her head. "Not about this. It resolves a private mystery. I smelled something floral around Jacopo, like soap." She frowned. "It reminds me of something else, but I can't think of what."

Luca's gaze fixed on the keys, he said, "Why two sets of keys?"

Salvo shrugged. "Maybe one is for the bakery?"

Luca murmured, "Sure, that's probably on the ring with the keychain.

But look at this key, on its own ring?'

Salvo frowned. "A shed? A neighbor's key? Maybe he was cat-sitting."

Luca's eyes drifted to the hamper at their feet. "The hamper. Maybe there's a clue . . ."

Stella shook her head. "I doubt it. The bakers toss their dirty aprons in there at the end of each day, and a service washes them on Sunday, their closed day. The service brings each baker a stack of clean aprons so they can come to work each day with a fresh one. Jacopo would have brought that apron he's wearing. And no way the murderer would be dumb enough to put anything compromising in there."

Salvo's eyes widened. "How do you know all that?"

"I skulk." Stella shrugged before gesturing with her chin. "But you know what? Makes sense to check the hamper. You never know, right? Maybe we're working with a dumb murderer."

Luca reached for the lid, right as a voice boomed from the open doorway. "What do you think you're doing in my bakery?"

The thin morning light framed Antonio's shoulders as he stood on the threshold. Stella moved toward Antonio, her heart in her throat, but Luca pulled her back more gently than she would have expected. Antonio looked from one to the other. He frowned. "Was I robbed? Was it Aldo? What did they do?"

"I . . . " Stella couldn't remember the last time she struggled to find words. Usually phrases leapt like sinewy fish into her mind, whether she wanted them to or not. But now . . . nothing. She glanced at Luca. The hardness in his face reminded her, these were not her words to tell. She noticed Salvo slip out the shop door and move behind Antonio, taking photographs of the footprint in the street. With a pang, she realized he was also trying to capture Antonio's feet in the frame.

She had tried not to think about it, but how could Antonio not be a suspect? She tried to decide if the shoes Antonio wore were the same as the print on the cobblestones, but she couldn't tell without seeing the bottom.

Luca stepped a fraction of an inch closer to Stella, who felt grateful for the warmth of his presence. She heard Luca's voice rumbling through his torso before it left his body. "Antonio. Weren't you supposed to be working this morning?"

Antonio shook his head. "Jacopo asked me to switch last minute."

Salvo hesitated, eyes flitting toward Stella. "But didn't you agree to meet with Stella this morning?"

At his confused expression, Stella clarified, her voice coming out creakier than she expected, "Dario, he said..."

"Ah." Antonio's face sagged. "He mentioned doing that. I didn't realize we'd fixed on a day."

Stella nodded. "Dario said I'd likely be able to catch you this morning."

"Jacopo asked me to switch last minute," Antonio said dully. The words sounded strange and Stella realized the baker had repeated himself, as if stuck in one gear.

Luca said, "Then Antonio, why are you here?"

Antonio rocked up on the balls of his feet to peer over Luca's shoulder. "I couldn't sleep. Thought I'd get a head start on the day. With Jacopo leaving, we all have to pitch in a bit more until I get more hands on deck."

She felt Luca shift his weight beside her. "The Captain is on his way. But I need to ask you... where were you early this morning?"

"Where was I?" Antonio frowned, though his long-standing habit of smiling must have fought with his more recent tendency to scowl. His lips arched into a kind of sneer. "Asleep, of course. In my bed. Why? What are you..." Antonio's eyes cast back to the bakery floor but snagged on Luca's broad shoulders. He sagged. "*Madonna mia.* What are you saying? Is someone in there? Tell me!"

Stella heard heavy footsteps echoing toward them, and Captain Palmiro appeared at Antonio's side, his police hat under his arm. Without the cap, his jaw looked wide. "Luca. I've got it from here." He took Antonio by the elbow and led him away, but not without jeering at Stella. "Why haven't you gone home?"

Luca began explaining about the clues she'd found, but the Captain had already turned to walk Antonio away a few steps. She heard Palmiro's low voice, but couldn't make out any words other than Jacopo's name.

She turned to regard Luca, eyebrows aloft. "Oh yes, he radiates respect for women."

Luca shook his head. "Time and place, Stella."

She flushed pink. As much as she hated to admit it, this was not the venue to air her grievances about Luca's captain. Not with Jacopo...she could hardly say the word in her head...*murdered.* Luca seemed to read Stella's thoughts. He lowered his gaze to search her eyes with his own. "You okay, Stella? This has been a lot."

She nodded, unable to say anything. From outside the bakery, she heard Antonio moan, "Jacopo? Are you sure? He's...*Jacopo?*" His voice hitched as he stammered, "But who...*why?* You can't be right... you *can't* be."

Luca gestured for Stella to accompany him outside, and she followed meekly, her gaze darting to the side to see Palmiro's pen moving swiftly across a pad of paper as he muttered questions in low tones. Suddenly, Antonio's voice rose. "Why do you need my shoes? You can't think I killed Jacopo because I didn't want to be short-staffed! That makes no sense!"

Palmiro's voice rose to meet Antonio's. "Since when is murder ever logical? And I didn't say we suspect you, but we need all the information we can get."

Just then, Stella saw Dario come running down the street on her left. He stopped short at the sight of Stella and Luca in the bakery's doorway, and Captain Palmiro talking to Antonio, now white as fine-milled flour. Dario's eyes moved from one police officer to another as he said, "Veronica saw the commotion outside the bakery and called me when she couldn't reach my father. What's going on? Why is Captain Palmiro talking to Papà?"

Luca shot his captain a look, and Palmiro cocked his head toward Dario as he turned back to his conversation with Antonio. Luca took a breath. "I hate to be the one to tell you, but Jacopo is dead."

Dario blinked. "Dead? What do you mean, dead? *Dead*, dead?"

"I'm afraid so." Luca paused before adding, "And it looks like murder."

A wash of pink swept over Dario's face and his eyes bugged toward Captain Palmiro, gesticulating with his pen as he spoke in rougher tones to Antonio. "And you think Papà did it? No way. I know he's been at odds with Jacopo lately, but *no way*. He wasn't even around last night. The two of us went hunting, we slept in the woods. He left me to come to work a little bit ago."

Luca and Stella made eye contact. Luca turned to Dario, his face stiff. "Hunting?"

"Yes!" Dario said, his eyes flicking to his father.

Stella blurted, "He wasn't at home, asleep?"

"No!" Dario said and then paused. "I mean, unless..." He blinked. "Did he *say* he was asleep?"

At a warning glance from Luca, Stella kept her lips firmly closed.

Dario flushed deeper and then stretched a grin across his teeth. "Oh! Ha, I forgot. We'd planned on going hunting, but you know...the rain. We went out for a bit, but then came back home and went to sleep. That's what I meant."

Stella watched the thoughts race across Luca's eyes. She decided that if he wanted to pursue a career in law enforcement, he'd have to learn to adopt a poker face. She could see his full house, clear as consommé. Perhaps Dario could see it too because he said, "Can I talk to Papà? Real quick?"

The baker, now sagging against the stone walls, briefly lifted his hand to acknowledge the Captain turning away from him to approach Luca. Quickly, Dario shuffled to his father. As Captain Palmiro and Luca conferenced in hushed tones, Stella noticed Antonio pale even further.

She couldn't make out Dario's words, only his pleading tones and his hands clasped together.

The next ten minutes blurred like a movie running through a deranged projector. Captain Palmiro, in clipped but courteous tones, asked Stella all the same questions that Salvo had but also grilled her on everything she saw from the moment she left her house to the moment she stepped into the bakery. Luca and Salvo and Antonio and Dario seemed to move in an orchestrated dance . . . police tape strung along the entrance to the bakery floor, Dario seemed absent for a bit, then reappeared. Salvo took more photographs, and Luca slipped Antonio's shoes into a clear plastic bag. Salvo collected keys from either Antonio or Dario, Stella could hardly tell with Captain Palmiro's eyes boring into her as he asked for the third time how she knew the time she entered the bakery.

The bakery. Where Jacopo spent his last moments—in fear? In surprise? Her attention drifted.

"Stella? Stella!" Captain Palmiro snapped his fingers in front of her face.

"I'm sorry, what was that?" She tried to focus.

"I *asked* you if you have any guests at your bed-and-breakfast," Palmiro growled.

Stella's ire rose. Why would he suspect one of her guests? As if anyone in her care could—

She stopped herself, remembering last November. "No. I don't have any guests until next week. Australian," she added irrelevantly.

As she continued to answer the captain's questions about if she'd seen anyone suspicious in Aramezzo, Stella heard Dario telling Luca in sorry tones that he had gone hunting last night, but the rain forced him home early this morning, around three o'clock. He knew the time because his climbing into bed had awoken his girlfriend, and they'd spent the morning . . . Stella couldn't hear the rest of the sentence, but given the flush creeping across Dario's cheeks, she could guess what had preoccupied the young man in the early morning hours. Captain Palmiro's eyes moved to his notepad, offering her a reprieve from her stint on the witness stand. This allowed her a moment to realize—Dario's camping explained the faint smell of smoke that hung around him. She'd assumed it was cigarette smoke. But no, the smoke smelled like wood, not cigarettes. Not for the first time, Stella wished she wouldn't notice every dang scent.

Captain Palmiro barked at Luca to take Stella's fingerprints. Her eyes widened, "But . . . why . . . "

The Captain ignored her, but Luca ducked his head beside her own as he withdrew a fingerprint kit from his satchel. "Don't worry, Stella," he murmured. "It's in case you touched anything. That way, we can isolate the killer's fingerprints."

She nodded and held out her hand. Luca took each of her fingers in turn, rolling them in the ink and then on a card. His touch was warm and firm, sending confusing tingles up Stella's arms. The card filled, Luca drew out a moist towelette and wordlessly cleaned each of Stella's fingers. Stella watched him, mute, hoping he didn't notice how clammy her palms suddenly became. She never would have expected him to be so gentle. Even when Captain Palmiro made an impatient sound, Luca would not be hurried until no ink marred Stella's hands.

Captain Palmiro tapped his pen on his notepad, his eyes fixed thoughtfully on Stella, as Luca waved the card to dry it. Just then, Antonio's wife came barreling down the street, her robe flapping open to reveal her baby blue nightgown. She stopped in front of Captain Palmiro and panted, "Dario told me."

Luca's eyes cut to Dario. "I told you to stay put."

Sheepishly, Dario said, "I know, I'm sorry. I came right back. But I had to go. You know what this town is like. I couldn't stand her hearing it from anyone else. It would kill her." He winced at his choice of words, his eyes sliding quickly to the bakery.

Antonio's wife clamped onto Captain Palmiro's shirt, like a drowning woman clinging to a life raft. "He was home with me! I swear! I'll swear on anything! I was...I went to the bathroom! Yes! About an hour ago or whenever the murder happened. And he was sleeping soundly right where he was supposed to be!"

Captain Palmiro attempted to pry her fingers off his shirtfront. "Celeste, get a hold of yourself." To Stella, he grumbled, "Stella, that's enough for now, but don't leave Aramezzo. We may have more questions."

Celeste caught sight of her husband and burst into tears.

Antonio wrapped his arms around his wife, his head nodding into her hair, mussed from sleep, as tears leaked from his eyes. "He's gone, Celeste. He's gone."

At this portrait of grief painted in layers, the rest of the assembled crowd hung back, quiet.

Finally, Antonio drew in a shaky breath and staggered into the shop-front connected to the bakery floor. Stella caught Luca's eyes. After a beat, Luca mouthed, "Go."

Stella nodded. As she turned to leave, Antonio shuffled into the street with a piece of paper that he taped to the door. Stella read, "*Oggi chiuso.*"

Closed today.

Well, that about summed it up.

Stella walked home, confused about when the sky had lightened. The shell-blush color seemed in defiance of the brutality she left behind. She opened her door, tense, as if waiting for another surprise, but the only movement was Barbanera, trotting toward her to bump his head against her knee. She patted his head. "Oh, cat. Why couldn't you have been around to protect Jacopo the way you protected me?"

She knew it was ridiculous, everyone told her that Barbanera's heroism on her behalf was simply a cat being a cat. And yet, did she imagine Barbanera's smug expression as he sat down and tilted his head up, his eyes fixed on hers? Anyway, she'd learned from Cosimo about how some of the local cats were byproducts of wild cats, breeding with house cats at the behest of a saint's miracle. Who could say what talents Barbanera might possess?

As if on autopilot, Stella opened a drawer and pulled out measuring cups. Barbanera, sensing a cooking project, leapt onto the back of the armchair to supervise. Stella stood, immobile, staring stupidly at the measuring cups as if trying to remember what they were for.

A metallic jingle shattered her daze, and she drew the phone from her pocket. At the sight of Matteo's photo that popped up when he called, she answered the FaceTime. Immediately, Matteo's face filled the screen. "Stella? What in the world? I'm on my rounds and passed the bakery. Are you okay? I'm coming over."

"No," she sighed. "Don't. I'm baking."

"Of course, you're baking. How am I not surprised?" She knew normally he would grin at her predictable behavior, but his face looked as empty of grins as hers felt. "I won't get in the way. But you need company."

"I told you, no." Stella didn't know why she refused him, other than the thought of having another human around right now made her feel like overstretched pizza dough.

"Why not? It's stupid to be on FaceTime when you are down the road." Matteo's face leaned into the screen, his eyes wide.

"I told you," she said, irritably pulling out measuring spoons and flipping through them as if looking for a key to open answers. Her mind cast back to Jacopo's keys. What about that buttery dough? And who besides a baker would know how to use a lame? "I don't want company. I need to focus."

"Stella, not to get all American psychobabble here, but you are in denial. You found a dead body. Now is not the time to be alone."

She didn't bother answering him as she nudged the flour canister closer with her knuckle and opened the top, peering into the darkness within.

He sighed. "Okay, All right. I know. You think best when you're baking."

"I'll talk to you later, I promise. It's . . . I need a minute. I mean . . . *Jacopo*. It's a lot to process." She spooned flour into a mixing bowl.

At a beeping sound, Matteo's eyes flicked to the top of the screen. Dully, Stella said, "Who's calling?"

"Doesn't matter. Nobody."

"I gotcha. Romance on line two." Stella tried to lilt her voice, but with the accumulated strain, it came out flat.

He sighed. "If you must know, my mother is telling me my laundry is ready. Promise to call me later?"

Stella narrowed her eyes, the spoon forgotten in her hand. "Your mom does your laundry?"

"Not now, Stella."

"Matteo. You are a grown man."

He rolled his eyes, which seemed answer enough. But he offered her a tentative smile before signing off and saying he would check in later, whether she wanted him to or not. So much she still didn't understand about that man, even after all these months. Her initial assessment that he played his *scopa* cards close to his chest proved accurate, but so did her determination that she didn't need to know about the details of his life to appreciate him as a person. Matteo, as a rule, was upbeat, thoughtful, and he didn't take himself too seriously. All qualities she looked for in a friend. Plus, he had an uncanny knack for remembering everybody's birthdays. There was hardly a week when she didn't spy him walking through the streets of Aramezzo with flowers or a beribboned box. A guy like that, how could she not cherish his friendship?

She tried to concentrate on Matteo—his kindness, his quick wit—to keep the crawling feeling from snaking back into her chest. But it came all the same. Shaking her head, she focused on the bowl of flour in front of her. She rapped the bowl over and over on the counter as if trying to minimize air bubbles in finished batter, until Barbanera jumped off the armchair and stalked off, his tail lashing in annoyance.

For a moment, Stella watched him leave before shouting, "It's not my fault!"

Her words rang hollow. Scowling, she cut butter into the flour, rubbing the two together with her fingers before adding a pour of cold milk, soured with a splash of vinegar. Biscuits, she finally realized. Southern biscuits. The kind her old friend from one of the Carolinas used to make from her Mawmaw's recipe. Kneading the dough once or twice on the floured board, Stella sliced the dough into rounds with a drinking glass, shivering as the edge cut through the pastry.

The invasive thoughts wound up her ribcage, and her attempts to shove them away only seemed to invite them to take up more space, until she couldn't turn off the movie in her mind. Over and over, the flickering, mottled film ran, replaying finding the body . . . *over* and *over.*

Weirdly, while the images running across the screen of her mind were as fresh as newly turned earth, the score, soaring and dipping and creaking along, felt old, worn, pulling at her with a kind of resonance only a long-forgotten piece of music can.

She slammed the oven door with a sound that couldn't rise above the blood pounding in her ears. She couldn't escape the cold, like an undertow. It hardly made sense. Yes, she was an empathic person and felt for the butcher and everyone who loved his son, and even so, the waves seemed too big. Pulling her under, leaving her breathless.

Stella set the timer, her heart skidding through her torso. Running hot water over the bowl and cups, she decided she needed another project. A more consuming one. Baking biscuits only slightly quieted her popping brain. She needed to turn off that familiar pull before her extremities froze.

Stella's gaze caught on the fireplace surround, blistered and warped. All winter she'd wanted to replace it, but couldn't bear to leave the fireplace unusable during the cold months. With spring beckoning, now was the time. Tearing off the already cracked wood, that would quell the rising tide in her chest. Now, where had she put the crowbar?

Snapping her fingers, she bustled out to the terrace, where she'd left the crowbar after jimmying the lock on a trunk she'd found in the shed, hoping for family memorabilia. All she'd found were empty picture frames.

Now, she wedged the crowbar's edge into the space between the surround and the wall and leaned hard. Her heartbeat eased as sweat stood on her forehead. Yes, exactly what she needed. Physical exertion. Maybe she should take up running again if she was going to keep finding dead bodies here, there, and everywhere. The Umbrian countryside seemed littered with them.

Stella felt a choking around her neck and dropped the crowbar to pull at her necklace. She untangled the chain, realizing that the pendant had caught on the end of the crowbar as she swung, twisting against her throat. She touched the pendant in thought. When Cosimo gave it to her back in the fall, she figured she'd grow used to the silver intersecting coils. That she'd eventually like them. But instead, the pendant only seemed stranger. She took it off. Given today's events, it had outlived its usefulness. If it ever had any.

Tossing the chain and pendant onto the coffee table, she returned to the crowbar, pushing and pulling it to wedge deeper, to pull harder, until—

The surround splintered with a satisfying snap. Suddenly, Stella realized she really should have waited for Ilaria, who helped her with all things maintenance. This clean-up alone . . . but no, it gave her something to do, and anyway, she couldn't afford help for tasks she could do on her own. After all, she could no longer justify the expenditures by telling herself that Ilaria's husband was out of work and they needed the money. Nowadays, Ilaria and her husband earned enough that they were squirreling away money in case of another on-the-job injury. Which demonstrated more long-term thinking than Stella had ever exhibited.

Stella shoved the crowbar lower in the seam and pulled and pushed again, driving away the creeping thoughts. The red scarf...the lifeless hands...Luca's narrowed eyes. The images faded as she shoved and pulled. Another crack and the entire side of the fireplace surround came away.

Stella reached to pull away the wood before noticing all the fine hairs of woodgrain, lying in wait. She needed gloves. As she turned to find them, a flash of white among the scraps of wood caught her eye.

She leaned forward and realized...a photograph! All thoughts of Jacopo's death pushed against the corners of her brain as she gingerly plucked the photo out of the debris and shook it, freeing it from shards of paint and wood.

Not one photograph, she realized, but three. How had three photographs gotten behind the wood of the surround in the first place? Ah, Stella realized. Some long ago relative must have placed the photographs on the mantle and they'd slipped behind.

She gently pried the most lightly adhered photograph from the others. Two little girls, dressed identically in white dresses with flounces on the sleeves and skirt. Their halos of curls and enormous gray eyes made them at first resemble twins, even though one looked to be around four and the other two. But as Stella studied the photograph, she recognized in the older child her mother's round chin and the left eyebrow that twisted up as if in perpetual questioning. This must be her mother, also named Stella, and her younger sister, Stella's aunt.

Stella felt the breath leave her body.

She'd only brought one photograph with her, the only one she could find in her mother's things. Now she had two of her family. Maybe more, right here in her hand! The realization landed into her heart like a windfall. She carefully peeled the two last photographs apart.

A wedding photo. A bride and groom sat in the middle of a group of people, all in formal wear.

Why would someone put a photograph like this on the mantle, without a frame? The other one, too, now that she thought of it. She scanned the photograph, realizing that the bride in the wedding photograph had her eyes half closed. Maybe this was an outtake? The original framed somewhere while this one sat on the mantle until one day it fell behind the surround?

Stella flipped back to the first photo, noticing a fly on her aunt's chubby leg. Huh.

She turned to the last photograph, which unfortunately had been distorted by the photo stuck above it. But luckily the ruined areas were mostly in the corners, the center remained clear. A candid photograph. She didn't know they even had those back then. Then again, she did remember admiring photographs at her favorite bialy spot on the Lower East Side, all of turn-of-the-century tenement kids—running through a gushing fire hydrant, hanging from fire escapes, playing street games. Maybe a passing journalist took this photograph, or a villager bent on archiving rural life. In the photo, women and men stood under olive trees, the same ones in Stella's yard, if the angle of the terrace and the road below were any indication. Children hung from the boughs, laughing. Stella brought the photograph closer, her eyes moving from face to face.

The timer rent through the quiet of the house, and Stella jumped. Placing the photographs carefully on the wood-chip whiskered couch, which she realized in her foolery she'd neglected to cover, she ran to the kitchen. She yanked the tray of biscuits out of the oven. Usually, habit forced her to check a few minutes before the timer went off, but she'd been too distracted. Luckily, the biscuits appeared perfectly, evenly golden.

She removed the biscuits to a rack to cool, her mind on the photographs. She'd bring them to Domenica and tell her about the murder. No doubt Domenica already knew, but she'd want to hear about it from Stella. In fact, she was likely to read Stella the riot act for delaying the visit. Impulsively, Stella loaded the biscuits into a basket, hoping their tenderness would be enough to soften Domenica's ire. It had worked before, though, with a dead villager in the cards, all bets were off.

At the sound of the bookshop bell jingling, Domenica looked up from pouring her coffee and narrowed her eyes at Stella before hustling to a pile of books that Stella was pretty sure had been sitting on the desk for at least a month. Probably two. Domenica said nothing as she shoved a book of poetry, another about Catholic saints, and a gardening manual onto the already crammed romance shelf.

"Domenica..."

Domenica sucked her teeth and kept her gaze trained on the bookshelf before whirling around with such force, her overlarge glasses slipped down her nose and one scarf fluttered from her shoulders. "I can't believe you didn't tell me. I had to hear it from *Mimmo*. Of all people!"

"Mimmo knows? Already?"

"Of course, Mimmo knows!"

"I'm just saying," Stella shrugged, trying for a look of nonchalance. "He hates everybody, who would tell him?"

"For reasons passing understanding, he seems to not hate you. And might I add, he wasted not one moment before dropping in here. As if he'd ever picked up a book past elementary school! If then! No, he showed up to lord it over me that he knew all about it. Loved adding that the police haven't found the murder weapon. But *you* have all sorts of ideas."

"They still haven't found it?" Stella blurted, but at Domenica's glare, Stella hung her head and nudged the basket of biscuits across Domenica's desk. "I'm sorry. But I couldn't have known—"

"*Jacopo*, Stella." The sudden softness in Domenica's voice caught Stella off guard. "I've known him since he saved his euros for old comic books. This isn't some stranger nobody noticed except to despise. Jacopo *belongs* to us."

Realizing the inaccuracy of the verb tense, Domenica's eyes welled with tears and she turned away.

Chastened, Stella tried again. "I am sorry, Domenica. Finding the body...I couldn't think."

Domenica gestured toward the basket. "You could bake."

Stella shrugged.

Nodding, Domenica sighed. "Yes, of course. To release the tension."

Stella bit her lip. "Plus the confusion, the panic, the whole 'how can this be happening again' crazy-making surety that I'm almost certainly cursed."

Domenica's eyes softened and her voice lost its edge when she said, "You called Matteo."

Stella flopped into the chair, looking for a cat to use as a furry shield. "He called *me*. Besides, it's not like I could have reached you. You know you keep your phone off when you're above stairs."

"Anybody who wants to talk to me can do so during my working hours."

"Exactly. By the time you were open, I was already knee-deep in baking."

Begrudgingly, Domenica pulled the basket closer and lifted the napkin. "What is it?"

"Biscuits, Southern style," Stella said.

Domenica harrumphed before falling back in her chair to nibble a peace offering. "How your baking improves in the aftermath of tragedy is beyond me."

"Not sure I'll be adding that to my resume," Stella grumbled. She reached into the basket to take one herself as Domenica stopped chewing to shoot Stella a look of resentment. Stella ignored her. "What's the word on how Bruno's family is? And the folks at the bakery?"

Domenica put down the biscuit and wiped her hands against each other. "About as you'd expect. Devastated."

"I would not have wanted to be Luca having to tell them, not for all the flour and sugar in the world."

"Hmmm," Domenica said, straightening her headband on her iron-gray hair.

"What?"

"Nothing," Domenica said before changing the subject. "At least you and the police aren't at cross-purposes this time around, right?"

"I guess."

Domenica went on, "I'm not trying to Pollyana this, don't get me wrong."

Stella looked up. "Pollyana is kind of an obscure reference. Even for an American and especially for an Italian."

Domenica shrugged. "You get around, you pick stuff up, what can I say? Anyway, my point is that not having conflict as part of this loss . . . maybe we can be grateful for that."

Stella felt an upswell of the emotion she'd kept at bay since she'd ripped out her fireplace surround. She waved her hand irritably. "Sure, at least we can agree it's murder. But I told them that the murder weapon is a bread lame, and they ignored me. Like I was a waiter trying to tell the sous how to cook!"

"*Cara*, remember that they grew up with Jacopo. The *how* is less important in this moment than the grief."

Stella stood up and paced, not noticing Domenica's eyes trained on her. "Can't they *see*? Somebody *did* this to Jacopo. Somebody . . . took him away."

Domenica said nothing as she watched Stella continue to pace.

"Gone. Forever." Stella snapped her fingers. "Like she never existed."

Domenica waited a moment before venturing, "She?"

Stella spun around to face Domenica with wide eyes before collapsing back into the wingback chair. "*He*. I meant . . . he. A slip of the tongue."

Softly, Domenica said, "Finding the killer is important. But it won't bring Jacopo back. And it won't erase anyone's grief. About this death or any other."

Stella wiped her eyes irritably and said nothing.

Domenica murmured, "Stella. Imagining the family's anguish is going to bring back memories of your own. That's understandable."

"My father and my sister, they vanished in an instant. Like they never existed."

"I know."

"They never found the driver who hit their car. Drunk probably. The guy is still out there, without a care in the world, while I . . . I . . ." The words caught in her throat like a fishbone.

"I know, *cara*. I know."

Stella stared at her knees for a moment before wiping at her eyes angrily. "You have too much dust in here, Domenica."

Domenica looked around to find Ravioli asleep on a pile of magazines. She plucked the cat, who meowed briefly in protest, and dropped her in Stella's lap. Ravioli glared at Domenica before curling into a ball and purring lightly. Stella scratched Ravioli behind the ears. "Well, Domenica. You're right, as usual."

Domenica smiled. "I didn't say anything."

Stella smiled tremulously back. "You didn't have to."

Domenica waited a beat, considering before saying, "You weren't allowed to grieve, *cara*. Your mother didn't leave space for your sadness in the face of her own."

"But that's understandable, right? I mean, she lost the only daughter who mattered to her."

"Stella, that cannot be true."

"You think I would misquote something like that?"

"Wait. Pause." Domenica's eyes widened. "Your mother *said* that? Those words?"

Stella shrugged.

"But . . . that's awful!"

Stella shook her head. "You didn't know Grazie. She softened hearts everywhere she went. Even my mother's. And I would have presumed hers permanently frozen."

"Still. Your mother loved you." Though now Domenica sounded unsure.

"Debatable," Stella said, like she might ask for the bill in a restaurant, a foregone conclusion of little interest or import. "Anyway, pasta water through a sieve. But this reminds me of what I wanted to show you. Look what I found when I pulled out the fireplace surround." Stella pulled the photographs out from between the linen napkin and the basket. She handed them to Domenica.

Domenica flipped through them. "Your family, I'm assuming? You come from beautiful stock."

"It must be my family. I'm sure that's my mother there. And those are our olive trees."

"Plus all the gray eyes."

"What do you mean?"

"I read an article in Science magazine on this years ago. Gray eyes are recessive, like blue or green. If two parents have light eyes, the children will have them too. I always figured that explained why so many people in Aramezzo have gray eyes. Though when I tried to talk to locals about it, they didn't seem interested. Eyes are just eyes to them." She peered at Stella over the rims of her glasses. "Your father must have had light eyes?"

"Scottish blue-green, yes. I got freckles from his side, too, though he didn't have any himself." Stella gestured toward her nose, at the dusting her father had called fallen stars.

Domenica waved her hand noncommittally. "You could have gotten the freckles from your Italian side. You'll see plenty of people in Aramezzo with freckles. Part of the link with some interbred Minoan society from Crete who formed an exclave here a zillion years ago. Or so Cosimo would have you believe."

"Really?"

"Yes, Cosimo insists you can find evidence of Minoan matriarchal society in the archaeology of Aramezzo. For some reason, he believes Minoans carried the genetic marker for freckles. Then again, he also credits those Minoans with magical abilities that are passed down in deeply rooted families, like your own."

"No, I mean, I hadn't noticed anyone with freckles in Aramezzo."

"You will in the summer." Domenica returned her attention to the photographs. "Did you find more?"

"No. It's so strange, I've found so many mementos in the house, old receipts, ledgers, even a sketchbook. But no photographs."

Domenica leaned back, staring at the ceiling.

"What is it?" Stella asked.

"Hold on a second. I'm remembering something."

Stella stroked Ravioli under her chin, and the calico lifted her face to allow Stella to scratch more fully.

Finally, Domenica said, "You should ask someone who knew your family back then, but when there was a spate of robberies some time ago, I'm pretty sure someone mentioned how your grandparents were robbed when they took your mother to the airport to fly to the States to marry your father. It stuck in my head because someone said that when your family got robbed, the only thing stolen were photographs. And maybe some letters? I might be misremembering."

"These weren't stolen because they had fallen behind the surround, years ago." Stella looked at the fronts and back of the photographs.

"Nothing else taken?"

"Not that I remember. You could ask Roberto and Romina. Or Cosimo. Or even Mimmo, actually."

Stella's eyes widened. "Unless ... maybe ... do you think Mimmo might have *taken* the photographs?"

Domenica cocked her head, staring at the ceiling momentarily. "He's hardly sentimental. I can't see him caring about photographs."

"Who knows what that man gets up to." Stella pulled the photos towards herself to examine them again. "But why would anyone steal somebody else's pictures?"

Domenica smiled, "At the risk of sounding like a broken record, and also at the risk of dating myself since you probably don't know what a broken record is ... therein lies the mystery."

Stella smiled. "Oh ... this reminds me. I didn't tell you what we found at the bakery, when ... you know."

Domenica nodded and pushed her glasses higher on her nose, pivoting in her chair until she faced Stella and gave her full attention. "Do tell."

"A phone, with a cracked screen. I didn't get to look at it before the cops arrived, but Luca said it read, 'We need to talk. He knows.'"

"That sounds serious."

"Right?"

Domenica frowned in thought, her forehead creasing. "I don't suppose you saw the phone number?"

"I didn't," Stella grinned. "But Luca read it off, and I remembered it."

"What! How can you remember it after hearing it once?"

Stella shrugged. "My memory palace."

Domenica nodded sagely. "Ah, yes."

"Oh, Domenica, you can't know what a memory palace is. I learned about it from watching Sherlock. You don't even own a TV."

"Stella," Domenica clucked as she rose to remove a pile of shawls from the ancient computer. "A memory palace, or whatever you want to call it, is a modern name for the method of loci, invented by an ancient Greek poet. Simonides, I believe."

"Oh."

"Don't worry, *cara*," Domenica said over her shoulder as she sat down and began typing, "I'm sure you'll discomfit me with your pop culture knowledge any day now."

"I doubt it," muttered Stella.

"So," Domenica sat down again with an expulsion of air. "Digits, please?"

Stella recited them.

Domenica turned to her. "Wait, did you try calling the number?"

Stella nodded. "What do you take me for? I called on the way over. No answer, no outgoing message."

"Not terribly uncommon in Italy." Domenica turned back to the screen. "Any guesses before I hit on the winner?"

"Honestly, I'm just hoping it's not Antonio. Or anyone who knows Antonio, since then Antonio could be the 'he'."

"Well, then, ding ding ding."

"Well? Don't leave me in suspense."

Domenica spun to face Stella. "It's Forno Fontana. In Assisi."

Stella inhaled. "Aldo's bakery?"

Domenica shrugged and peered toward the screen. "If memory serves." Her fingers flew across the keyboard. "Yes, here it is. Forno Fontana. The owner is Aldo." She spun around to face Stella with even more force, knocking her glasses down her nose. Pushing them up she asked, "Do you think this implicates Aldo?"

Frowning, Stella said, "I don't know. I mean, he was getting what he wanted with Jacopo coming. Why would he kill the goose he thought would lay him a golden egg?"

"Hmmm. That's true." Domenica stared up at the ceiling. "What else did you find?"

"Keys, candies, cigarettes. Nothing really of note." Stella thought. "Except the keys were on two different key rings. One that had keys for probably his home and car and the *forno*, on a ring with a keychain on it, and another key that was just key on a ring."

"One for Aldo's bakery?"

"Maybe." Stella sighed. "Oh! And here's something weird. Jacopo had been kneading a laminated dough."

"Huh. But Antonio doesn't sell *cornetti* or anything with those layers."

"You got there much faster than the cops did." Stella grinned.

Nodding slowly, Domenica said, "Maybe part of his job at Forno Fontana is baking *cornetti* or sweets?"

"But that's odd, right? I mean, Aldo is going through the trouble of poaching Jacopo for his bread and *torta al testo* experience. Why put him on pastry detail?"

"That *is* odd."

"I think I should go to Assisi. Ask some questions."

"Stella."

"What?"

"Give it a minute. Aldo probably doesn't even know yet. Let it unfold."

"Wait, is what you're saying."

"Yes." Domenica nodded with a smile. "Wait."

Stella grumbled. "I hate waiting."

Stella trudged around the ring road, not in the mood to return home to Barbanera's baleful staring at the wood splinters littering his favorite couch. Then again, his favorite couch tended to be whichever one he was currently deprived of.

She ran through the contents of her pantry, wondering if she needed to pick up groceries. She sighed. Maybe a chocolate bar to tide her over.

As she approached the *alimentari*, she spotted Mimmo exiting the shop, empty-handed. No doubt he'd sauntered in to sneer at the patrons who lacked the stomach, or ability, or more likely both, to procure their food from the forests all around them. One look at his smug face, his bumpy nose gleaming like a kerosene lamp, and Stella knew she was right. A throb of anger jolted through her.

He probably *had* taken her family's photographs. She and Domenica had minimized the possibility because there didn't seem a viable reason for him to want them, but she'd forgotten about Mimmo's joy in the take.

"Mimmo!" Stella called out to Mimmo's back.

He turned with a scowl at being recalled like a paunchy dog on a leash. His face briefly brightened at seeing Stella, before his heavy eyebrows knit together. "Stella. What are you—"

"Can it, Mimmo."

"Can what?" His eyes widened.

"What?" Stella had no idea what he meant. They stared at each other for a moment before Stella shook her head and tried again. "I know about the robbery. At Casale Mazzoli."

He startled. "Robbery? But . . . how? when?"

"You know when. When my grandparents sent my mother off to America. They came home and all the photographs were stolen."

Mimmo squinted at Stella as if trying to put together the pieces of a child's jigsaw puzzle. "You know, some olive oil on your forehead and around your mouth would help those lines. You frown too much."

Anger throbbed through Stella. "How could you, Mimmo? They *trusted* you!"

Mimmo frowned in concentration. Then his face cleared. "You think I did that?"

"Who else!"

He scoffed, "Why would I take photos of a bunch of people I didn't care about?"

Stella started. She'd always heard that Mimmo and her grandparents were fairly close. For Mimmo. Then again, she remembered how derisive Mimmo sounded when he spoke of Marta and Ascanio, and yet he always showed up for them. "You did care about my grandparents, my aunt."

"Did not!" Mimmo's yell rent the quiet of the street.

"Did too!" Stella clapped her hand over her mouth, suddenly realizing how she sounded.

"Listen, missy," Mimmo growled. Great, she was back to being unnamed by Mimmo. "I worked for those people. If I was going to steal something, it would have been the jewelry."

This stopped Stella cold. "Jewelry? What jewelry?"

"You haven't found the jewelry?" A shadow passed over Mimmo's face. Guilt? Did he take it? Then why would he bring it up? Then again, his logic did not resemble human logic.

She shook her head.

He frowned. "I know your aunt said she put it somewhere safe. You better not have let someone steal it, with all those people you have coming and going."

"Those are guests, Mimmo. Paying guests."

He shrugged. "Plus all of Ilaria's family. Who knows what they get up to?"

This comment on the men Stella hired to do the heavy renovations sounded vaguely racist to Stella. Though Ilaria's family came from Albania, by way of Puglia. Surely no one could be so xenophobic that they feared people who looked much like them but hailed from a country a ferry ride away? She realized she'd lost the thread of whatever they were supposed to be talking about. "Mimmo, did you or did you not take my family's photographs?"

Mimmo rolled his eyes and shoved his hands into the pockets of his stained pants. Cocking his head as if mildly interested, he said, "Didn't the accordion-playing baker show up to work dead? Are you sure this is what you want to talk about?" He turned and walked away.

"Mimmo!"

Mimmo winced but kept walking.

"What do you want with Mimmo?" At the words, Stella whirled around to find Matteo. He tried to smile, but his wan face only approximated the gesture.

"Matteo."

He opened his arms, and she stepped into his embrace. "Oh, Stella. How can he be gone?"

She closed her eyes and said nothing. Finally, she pulled back, wiping her eyes.

Matteo gestured down the street, where Mimmo had rounded the corner and disappeared. "What was all that about?"

She blinked. "Honestly? Probably misplaced anger."

He frowned, looking into her eyes. "His or yours?"

Biting her lip, Stella pointed to herself.

"Aw, Stella."

She shook her head. "That wasn't fair to him."

He nodded and said, "Mimmo can take it. In fact, I expect he'll forget by lunch. People are always sniping at him for something or another."

"But he usually deserves it."

"Even so. He's a porcupine. Always bristling at somebody and fundamentally unaware when someone is bristling at him."

Stella nodded, her eyes fixed on the ground.

Softly, Matteo said, "How are you?"

She shrugged and said nothing.

Matteo nodded and said nothing.

Stella felt gratitude for how the best of friends didn't need to talk. She pointed at his sanitation worker uniform. "I didn't know you were still working."

"Oh, right, that's what I wanted to tell you. We're all working overtime.

All the trash in public canisters needs to be hauled to the police station. I guess they want to make sure some clue wasn't tossed in one of them."

"Like the murder weapon."

He nodded. "Like the murder weapon."

"So they still haven't found it."

He shook his head. "We're also supposed to be keeping an eye out for anything suspicious."

Stella asked, "Have you found anything?"

"The footprint, which you know about." Stella nodded, and Matteo went on, "The police are figuring out the brand and size. Everyone is in an uproar."

"I imagine so."

"Anyway, I'll fill you in if anything comes up. I figured you'll want to know?"

She nodded.

"Then I'll keep my ear to the ground."

"Thanks, Matteo." She nodded at the *alimentari*. "I'm gonna buy a chocolate bar."

He grinned. "Good call. In fact, I'll get it for you. And one for me, too."

Her eyes pricked at the simple gesture. "Thanks, Matteo."

"What are friends for?"

The murder weapon.

As the sweet chocolate faded from her palate, the thought returned with redoubled energy. It had to be a lame. It *had* to be. Something about the lame bristled in her mind. Why?

All the way home, Stella ruminated. She flopped into a chair next to Barbanera who stretched and pressed his silver-spotted side against her, leaning his head back to look deep into her eyes. She grinned and accepted his invitation, scratching him under the chin. His purr rumbled, sputtering at first like an old motorcycle, but then it caught hold and rose and fell with his breathing. She smiled at the cat she never asked for or even wanted during her first months of living in Aramezzo, and now couldn't imagine life without. Her breathing synced with his, and a kind of contentment unspooled over her shoulders. Cats, man. Who knew?

Barbanera opened one eye as if hearing her thought and chiding her for the insult implied in the question.

She grinned. Whether or not Barbanera was descended from magically summoned wildcats, he sure seemed a miracle.

Miracles... Stella thought about Easter approaching. She had never been a religious person, though nowadays she did go to Sunday mass from time to time, reveling in the comfort of sitting with her neighbors. Sometimes she wondered if it was okay that her devotion was not the same as theirs. They worshiped their Catholic saints and rituals, where she worshipped the quiet. If there was one thing the events of November had taught her, it was the value of quiet. A good quiet, full of souls leaning back, nestled in the moment. She enjoyed her Sundays of Don Arrigo's voice rolling over her, his goodness an echo of the love she felt standing in front of the Madonna in the church's prized niche.

She'd probably attend Easter services. Why not?

Easter... even in her non-religious household (and non-American— no Easter bunnies or purple wicker baskets or jellybeans, unless her father sneaked her a few when her mother wasn't looking), Easter meant something special. Mostly because, though you could evidently take the Italian woman out of Italy, you couldn't entirely erase Italy from the Italian woman. Hence, the weeks leading up to Easter, the period celebrated as Carnevale in Italy, were a time of decadent sweets.

Her mother didn't fuss with the fried Carnevale treats so popular in Italy, but she never failed to provide a *colomba*. Making the sweet, enriched cake involved a complicated procedure, shaping the *colomba*'s paper collar to hold the rising dough into the dove shape that symbolized Easter's peace. Her mother made one herself only a handful of times and, Stella realized, never again after the accident that halved their family. Even so, a *colomba* unfailingly appeared in the Buchanan household, sometime between Ash Wednesday and Easter. Even if left without comment on the cluttered dining room table, like one more bill or a half-eaten sandwich.

Easter and the sweet, risen cake twined together in Stella's heart. When Stella staged at restaurants in Italy throughout her training, her stay would sometimes overlap with the Easter holidays, and she always sought out *colomba*. Its sweet springy dough juxtaposed against the crackling sugar top strewn with almonds tasted like heaven itself.

She'd practiced making *colomba*'s Christmas cousin, *pannetone*, this past December. It had suited the days of healing and bonding she and Barbanera had needed. She remembered those stretched-out days of sunlight seeping through the omnipresent fog, the long rises of dough that scented the air with yeast and sugar. And at the end of all that, by the time Christmas rolled around, she had *pannetone* to hand out to her neighbors, lighting one face after another. Even Mimmo—who, at the sight of Stella at his door with a festively wrapped *panettone* had turned away so quickly that if Stella hadn't known better, she would have thought he'd needed to rearrange his face to his usual scowl.

Strange to admit it, but making *panettone* and giving each away had made her little quiet Christmas one of her very favorites. All the free-flowing, bubbly Prosecco at each of her deliveries certainly didn't hurt.

So, *colomba*...perhaps the perfect project to throw herself into. Maybe in the flow, she'd figure out why the bread lame stuck in her thoughts.

Barbarnera gave a short meow of protest as Stella got up to practice shaping leftover decorative baking paper into a dove. Taking out her scale and measuring cups, flour and sugar and eggs and yeast, her thoughts flicked back and forth to the lame. The way she figured it, only someone with intimate use of the lame would consider it a viable murder weapon. First of all, they were usually kept sheathed in leather to avoid slicing careless fingers, so it was hardly the tool someone without familiarity would go looking for.

Furthermore, she realized with a start as she added cool water to the flour, even if Jacopo had been about to slash the bread, and so had the lame out and unsheathed, a stranger to baking would never see a lame and think, "Aha! There's my murder weapon!" It looked surprisingly innocuous for such a sharp instrument, just a razor blade affixed to a handle.

Which meant whoever killed Jacopo had to both recognize the slashing power of a lame and know where to find one, since Jacopo wouldn't have had one out while making laminated dough.

Stella tipped yeast into the flour in a practiced motion, her lips moving as if she was counting each tiny grain, but in reality she was, quite without her awareness, counting the seconds of pouring, stopping at three. She suspected *colomba* required a bit more, perhaps closer to the four or five seconds of *panettone*, but she'd begin here.

As she waited for the inevitable bubbles that showed the yeast to be active, she settled the matter. The lame was definitely the murder weapon. Therefore, it must have been handled by someone who not only knew the tool's power but knew where to find one.

She picked up a wooden spoon and then put it down. Unless the wound was self-inflicted? She couldn't reconcile her image of Jacopo, laughing as he snapped a towel at a fellow baker, with someone who wanted to end his life.

She picked the spoon back up and then put it back down. No way that could have been self-inflicted. No one could draw the knife straight across their own neck that quickly. It would have dragged down at the end or showed evidence of a sputtering line. Unless he focused on keeping his elbow straight out, and why would he have bothered?

No, she thought, as she separated four eggs. Someone murdered Jacopo and that someone knew how to manage a bread lame and where to find one. Stella added egg yolks to the dough and then stopped again. Someone who knew how to manage a bread lame...

No murder weapon had been found at the scene. Sure, someone could have thrown it in a river or buried it. But...maybe they hadn't. If they were very used to using a bread lame, then he (or she, Stella amended to herself), perhaps after using it to kill Jacopo, cleaned it and put it away by habit.

Which meant...could it possibly still be in the bakery?

She couldn't picture a murderer carting a lame to the bakery as a prospective weapon, even if they had one. Far more likely they either planned on using one of the bakery's lames, or they grabbed it in a moment of rage. Either way, was it possible that it was still there, innocently sitting in its sheath?

If she could only get in there and search.

She shook her head. No way anyone would allow her into a crime scene. The bakery doors remained shuttered, though Stella knew even if the police gave the okay, Antonio would keep the bakery closed. The murder shook up the employees too much to return to work.

The butcher, of course, was closed, too. Stella couldn't imagine their heartbreak. From what she understood, the butcher's wife, whom Stella had never met as she seemed to keep to her room, wasn't particularly well. Stella couldn't imagine how she'd ever rally again.

Stella's thoughts flitted to her own mother's grief. Yes, her mother had two daughters, but her heart only had room for Grazie, so the loss had been akin to losing one's only child. Like the butcher and his wife.

Stella kneaded the dough until it was silky. Leaving it in a buttered bowl to rise, she washed her hands and cleaned all the bowls and utensils. Well, she might as well go to the bakery. She could at least examine the street for clues the police might have missed. Plus, maybe she'd overhear news on the investigation.

Stella stalled. Hadn't she resolved to mind her own business? A resolution that had served her well for months? Shaking her head, Stella decided that resolutions were hardly iron-clad, and if anything was worthy of breaking her intention, it was this.

A final peek at the dough, full of promise in its buttered bowl, and Stella gave Barbanera a pat before heading out.

A thread of ice wound through the early spring air, stinging her cheeks. Maybe she should have worn a scarf. Never mind. Once she got moving, the air would be perfect for sharpening her senses.

She slowed as she approached the *forno*. Luca stood outside, his hands plunged in the pockets of his uniform as he stared, unblinking, at the bakery. Stella's heart twisted as she noted his expression, like a little boy standing alone on the playground, suddenly aware that the world could be a chaotic, lonely place.

He didn't notice when Stella appeared at his elbow until she softly said, "Hey. You okay?"

He startled and then tried to hide it with a shrug. "I came for bread before I remembered."

"You got all the way here before—"

"No. I remembered when I pulled out my scarf. But I seem to be on autopilot." His eyes flicked to Stella. "Aren't you cold?"

"My father used to say I have hot blood."

"*Sangue bollente,* we say here." He smiled, though his eyes remained dull.

The words sounded familiar. She thought her mother might have used boiling blood to describe Stella's temper. "Still no murder weapon?"

"No, though the medical examiner will tell us about the characteristics of the knife. Which will help the search."

"I really think—"

"The bread lame, yes I know. You've said it already."

Stella felt herself bristle, but at the softness in his eyes gazing steadily into her own, her defensiveness shattered. She turned her attention back to the bakery door, contemplating her next move. She felt his eyes still on her, as if trying to decide something.

Finally, he said, "Stella, I've been wanting to ask you."

Her eyes fixed on the *forno*, she wondered if the police had gone through the bakery's trash yet. Did Luca ever search the hamper? Something had interrupted him. Right, Antonio. Poor Antonio. Unless... no. She couldn't believe it of him.

"I...I mean..." Luca coughed. Then he cleared his throat and coughed again.

Stella looked up at Luca, eyebrows lifted in surprise. He never seemed unsure. At her sudden eye contact, Luca said all in one exhaled breath, "This whole thing, it's got me thinking. Time...we don't always get as much as we deserve. So, I guess I'm asking...when this murder investigation is over...maybe you want to have dinner together sometime?"

Her heart lurched. Maybe Luca was putting her on. Some sort of game with the officers? A bet about humiliating the new girl?

But she knew in her bones that couldn't be right. The last few months ran through her mind, all the simple and easy interactions she'd had with Luca. She had to admit, she'd grown to enjoy running into him on the street. He'd take off his police hat, tucking it under his arm as he inquired after what she was reading, how Barbanera was healing, what she was cooking. He often added an interesting aside about a restaurant with a hyperlocal specialty, like *strigoli*, a green found only on Monte Subasio that tasted like lemony arugula. All the while keeping his eyes trained on her, listening carefully to her every word.

Somewhere along the way she'd been forced to acknowledge that though she'd initially written him off—after all, men who resembled cologne models tended to ride on their looks and therefore lacked emotional maturity—Luca had surprised her, time and again, with his curiosity, his interest, and his humor.

Her thoughts stormed ahead and behind... shouting at her to remember her checkered past with men. Every relationship she'd had flamed out. Not with a whimper, but with a bang, a blaze of un-glory. She had so few people here, she couldn't stand to lose any. And frankly, though she trusted herself in most ways, she did not trust her gut when it came to men. If she felt a pull to Luca, it probably meant she should stay far, far away.

Luca stepped closer to her, a hesitant smile making his dimple appear and reappear. "I guess you aren't afraid of leaving me in suspense. Can I... should I assume your silence means you've thought about it too?"

A sliver of annoyance rippled through Stella. She tried to ignore it. She needed to control herself, let him down easy. It was the only way to protect the friendship.

"Stella?"

Pushed to answer too quickly, she blurted, "I'm sorry, Luca. But we wouldn't be good together. It would end badly."

Luca's eyes widened. He clearly hadn't expected a refusal. Stella felt herself bristle again at the presumption. Into the awkward silence, Luca said softly, "Because you're American? I can be okay with that."

Stella recoiled as if slapped. She reminded herself that he'd just put his heart on the line. Or did he? Maybe he was only interested in a physical relationship, if he could barely tolerate her background. "Don't do me any favors."

Luca took a step backward. "Favors? I'm trying to say—"

She struggled against her trademark impatience as she said, "I know what you're trying to say. What I'm saying is it's not possible."

"Wh-why?" Pink crept up his strong jaw as he stammered and looked away. "What's not possible? You need to back up. You don't have many allies here. I thought you could use a friend."

She frowned, suddenly unsure. She had known Luca for months now and had never seen him blush like this, his olive-toned skin turning apricot under the stubble. She tried again, softer this time. "Luca, I'm flattered, of course I am," she babbled, but let her words drift as his eyes narrowed.

He ducked his gaze away from her. "I *said* it wasn't a date, I was trying to be neighborly. So much for that."

Stella opened her mouth, but at the hardness of his eyes, she closed it again.

"What are you doing here, anyway?" he bit off.

She tried to look innocent, but her glance at the bakery must have revealed her true motive.

He rolled his eyes. "Don't tell me, I know. Here to nose around, gather evidence for another one of your wild theories?"

This stung. She lashed out, "Maybe if you listened to me the last time, you would have caught the killer before my cat's ear got blown off."

He laughed mirthlessly. "Oh, I get it. It's all my fault. Sure."

"Whatever." She straightened her shoulders and tucked her curls back into her bandana. "If you can't look outside the box, that's certainly not my fault."

"That's rich, coming from you."

"What's that supposed to mean?" Stella fought the urge to stamp her foot.

His jaw tightened. "Let's speed this up. What do you want?"

The answer flew from her chest, a thrown dart. "I want to see if there's a bread lame in there with any evidence of foul play."

"We checked. You must know that."

"Did you now? So tell me, did you find a bread lame? What did it look like? Straight or curved?"

He scowled.

"You don't know what you're looking for. Even if you found the lame, you don't know how it's used, so how could you examine it?"

"Ah. And you do, I suppose?"

"More than you!"

"All right, hotshot. Let's see." He took a key from his pocket and opened the door to the bakery floor. "Show me what you've got."

She stalled. "You have a key?"

"Of course, I have a key. I'm the lead officer."

"I thought . . ." She swallowed and then lifted her chin. "Fine. Let's do this."

She stormed in and started throwing open drawers, looking for the characteristic wooden handle and the curved blade. On the edges of her awareness, she heard Luca muttering, "This is a bad idea. What was I thinking?"

Ignoring him, she continued pulling open drawers, her eyes scanning for a wooden handle. But this drawer and the next held only spoons and whisks. Her breath caught at the sight of a handle of the right size, but she realized it was a fold-up electric thermometer.

When she found it, she doubted her eyes, as if she'd manufactured it by picturing it so vividly. But there it was, the handle worn down; the blade sheathed in brown leather.

Luca's voice bit out sharply, "Stella! Wait, stop!"

She reached for the lame and unsheathed it, right as Luca grabbed for her arm. She torqued to avoid his grasp.

At Luca's wide eyes, Stella debated telling him about the sharpness of the curved blade, how it created a flap perfect for creating an ear of sourdough, or, perhaps, for creating a corpse. But he didn't deserve the explanation after his behavior. And his efforts to thwart her now out of spite or whatever were beyond aggravating. Jane Austen had it right—the most incomprehensible thing in the world to a man was a woman who wasn't in love with him.

She turned her body further away from Luca's shouts to stop and examined the blade. At first, she thought it had rusted and she wondered, who would wash but neglect to dry their blade? Then she remembered. Razor blades were stainless steel, they *never* oxidized. The brownish-red color wasn't rust.

It was blood.

A glance at Luca and she realized he'd seen it, too. His eyes widened, and he ran his hand through his hair, staring at the lame.

Stella flipped the blade over to pass it to Luca, handle side toward him. She gave him a wry smile. "Feel free to tell your captain you found this all by yourself."

WEDNESDAY

*S*tella hardly remembered storming out of the bakery. She flew home and flung herself on her bed. Though she'd only planned to wait for her heartbeat to slow, the next thing she knew it was morning. An odd smell, like ripening gym socks, greeted her and she groaned, remembering the dough she'd left out to rise and then forgot about. She comforted herself by remembering that a proper *colomba* likely required a *biga*, an overnight starter, anyway. She'd try again later.

She inhaled a yogurt, which wound up being poor sustenance for her debate with Domenica.

"Domenica, I'm telling you. It was Antonio's lame, it had to be." Beams of light flickered across the floor of the bookshop as a patchwork of clouds filigreed the sunlight.

Domenica shook her head. "No way. I've known Antonio for years, it's impossible."

"I agree, it's hard to accept. But it was his lame and there was blood on it."

Domenica dusted a bookshelf farther away from Stella before turning to say, "Maybe it's his own blood! Maybe it slipped—"

"Impossible."

"Hear me out!"

"No, Domenica, I know what you're going to say. But someone doesn't use a lame as often as Antonio does and make such a careless mistake."

"He had a lot on his mind. You know that!"

Stella blinked. "Yes, Domenica, he did. The thing he had on his mind was Jacopo taking his secrets to Assisi. Which means Antonio not only had the means, he also had a motive."

Domenica let her hand with the feather duster fall to her side. "So you think he did it."

Stella ran her hands over Ravioli's ears. "No. I don't."

Domenica exhaled loudly. "Then what was all that for?"

Shrugging, Stella said, "I'm stating the facts and you seem to think you can argue me out of them. Old as that lame is, it's got to be Antonio's, and there was blood on the blade. We have to come to terms with the very real possibility that when the lab report comes back, it'll show that the blood is Jacopo's."

Domenica stalked around her desk and dropped into her chair. "Then why don't you think he did it?"

Stella shrugged again. "A hunch I guess."

Domenica furrowed one eyebrow. "Stella. You are holding out on me."

Stella offered a vague half-smile. "Well for one, he doesn't seem the type. Even when Aldo taunted him, the most he did was make a show of his toughness. Plus, I've seen him when the butcher mutters snide comments at him. Antonio shrugs it off. A guy with that much self-control? I don't see him flying into a murderous rage."

"Exactly," Domenica nodded slowly. "And for two?"

"Even more of a hunch. I wouldn't say this to anyone but you, since I know you won't roll your eyes like some people I know."

"Like who?" Domenica pushed her glasses higher onto her nose.

"It's not important." Stella waved her hand. "As I was saying, since I work in the culinary arts—"

Domenica pretended to fling a feather boa around her neck. "Well, aren't you Miss Fancy. The 'culinary arts' now."

Stella lifted her eyes to heaven as if praying for patience.

"Really, Domenica?"

"Sorry. Can't resist a Steinbeck reference."

"In English no less. I'm wondering if you are more fluent than you let on."

Domenica adopted an air of deep mystery before saying, "Go on."

Stella sighed. "Antonio and I, we have cooking in common. Not as a job or even a passion. Food is our life. Which means we treat the tools of our trade with extreme care. Devotion even."

"Where are you going with this?"

"I can't see Antonio taking a tool he uses for creation and using it for destruction. It would be . . . unseemly." To Domenica's blank expression, Stella added, "Anyway, even if he did, he'd have cleaned the blade."

Domenica thought for a moment. "I'm not following. I mean, I'm all on board for not pinning Jacopo's death on Antonio, but just because he regularly uses baking tools doesn't mean he wouldn't use them for murder."

"Think of it this way," Stella went on. She looked around the room. "How likely would you be to thwack somebody over the head with a copy of your favorite book?"

"Not *Leaving Tabasco*!" Domenica paled.

Stella grinned. "You see my point."

"I suppose I do." Domenica sat in thought. "But how can you convince the police of that?"

"I can't. My guess is that as soon as the lab report comes back on the blood, they'll arrest Antonio."

"But he was asleep!"

Stella shrugged. "It doesn't help that his son came barreling in, insisting that Antonio was out hunting with him."

"Poor Dario. He's going to beat himself up if the alibi he tried to give his father winds up being a nail in his coffin."

Stella shivered at the phrasing. She lifted Ravioli off her lap and stood, brushing off the white, caramel, and brown hairs. "Well, I suppose I better go see Cosimo."

"Cosimo, why?"

"I need a new fireplace surround."

"You mean you tore off the old one without first securing a replacement?" Domenica said with a lift of her eyebrows.

"Was that wrong?" Stella asked, innocently.

"Not at all, *cara*. I would expect nothing less of you. Nothing more either, when it comes to that."

Stella grinned. "I'm hoping he has one lying around with zero historical interest. I can't afford much. Fingers crossed these old photographs butter him up. You know how he is about this stuff."

"Do I ever," Domenica nodded. "Oh! Ask him about the robbery. He'll remember the details."

"I'm sure he will," Stella grinned. "Good idea."

Stella patted Ravioli goodbye and stepped out into the warming air. With a start, she realized the grapevines, the ones in derelict-looking yards as well as the cultivated ones threaded through the arbor above her head, were budding. Her olive trees couldn't be far behind.

It made her realize—this stay in Aramezzo, it had been her longest sojourn in Italy. Her previous visits lasted only a couple of months at a time, so she'd rarely witnessed one season transitioning into another. Here, she'd seen fall turn to winter and now winter to spring. Plus, she reflected, she'd only ever lived in cities, without the seasonal cues from vines and trees.

She'd never been a country girl. In fact, she'd always assumed she'd live her whole life in big, tumbling cities, given how much she loved the roar of street life and the cavalcade of human activity. Stella assumed she'd always crave the stimulation of people in the act of inventing, connecting, aspiring. Back in the fall, she remembered wondering how long a place like Aramezzo could hold her attention.

BREAD AND MURDER IN ARAMEZZO

She stopped in the street, considering. How strange, she wasn't bored at all. Even without the murders—which she could frankly do without—she found that in the days of unfurling quiet, she noticed more details. She smiled to see a pair of old women walking toward the town gate with their sticks and bags, clearly out to hunt asparagus.

No doubt on a normal day, without the specter of grief hanging over the town, she would hear about the women's foraging adventure later in Bar Cappellina—the snakes they scared away with their sticks, the heaving bundle of wild asparagus they'd found, the frittatas and pastas they planned to make (how did Umbrians know that the sulfur in eggs highlighted and elevated the depth and greenness of asparagus? Years of experience, she supposed). The women's appearance underscored her realization. In days without the racket and overboil of city life, she noticed the smaller moments and appreciated them in unexpected ways.

Stella pushed open the door of Cosimo's shop. He looked up from his work behind the counter, a magnifying loupe still held against his eye. "Stella! How lovely to see you."

"What are you magnifying?"

"Magnifying?"

She gestured to the loupe still held against his eye.

He chuckled. "Ha, I've grown so used to holding it, I'd forgotten all about it."

She nodded. "Sometimes I find myself in the bathroom still holding a whisk."

His chuckle warmed before he grew serious. "How are you, my dear? What a trying time."

She nodded, wondering if she should mention finding the lame. Probably best not to until it was common knowledge. She shouldn't have mentioned it to Domenica.

"It appears you are getting yourself quite the reputation, my child." Cosimo nodded sagely.

"I am?" Stella adjusted her bandana nervously before rubbing at a spot of chocolate on her sleeve.

"Indeed." He nodded. "So...given Jacopo's imminent defection to Assisi...it seems the baker did it?"

"I can't believe it of him," she answered slowly.

"The man has a cheerful exterior," he intoned, nodding.

She echoed his nodding until she realized his meaning. "Exterior? You don't think he's actually as sunny as he seems?"

He paused. "Well, I don't like to tell tales, child, but I have reason to believe that his mask is just that. Haven't you yourself referred to him as...what was that...a kind of children's puppet?"

"A Muppet, yes." Her eyes narrowed, trying to follow his line of reasoning.

"Well, I should have thought it would be obvious," he said, his mouth in an O. "I assumed you were picking up something quite astute. Puppets are controlled. They are not authentic."

She shook her head. "You're giving me credit for far more thought than I put into that caricature."

He shrugged. "Whether you meant to or not, you seem to have hit the nail on the proverbial head. The baker...he holds himself apart. The only thing people know about him is his near brush with fame and his disconcerting cheerfulness."

She frowned. "I never found his cheerfulness disconcerting."

"Too right, too right," Cosimo nodded. "My opinion likely comes from years of trying to really know the man and only learning of his ambition."

"Ambition?" This visit to Cosimo was proving far more interesting than she'd expected.

"Surely you've heard. Antonio himself mentioned it to me last month...he is angling to expand his baking empire."

"Isn't that good?"

He blinked slowly. "I confess, I don't believe everyone is interested in that kind of exposure."

"The mayor certainly is," Stella smiled.

"Indeed," Cosimo chuckled. "I suspect the mayor would leap at the opportunity to put Aramezzo on any map."

"I know he's invested in Antonio's success."

Nodding, Cosimo said, "I imagine so. And that success did seem around the corner. Dario came in a few weeks ago, chatting about how his father was in talks with investors from Rome." He inclined his head, remembering.

"Once this blows over, I'm sure he'll be able to pick up that thread."

"Perhaps."

She waited a beat to see if he'd illuminate further. "You don't think this will blow over?"

"Maybe Antonio will be too sidelined with grief, losing such a valuable apprentice." He shrugged. "Or maybe he did it."

She thought about it, debating once again if she should tell him about the lame. But it would only prejudice Cosimo further. "No, I don't see it."

"Perhaps you are right. If nothing else, I applaud your optimism." He studied her with a smile. As his gaze moved away, he did a double take at her throat. "Where is your pendant?"

Oh, no. She'd forgotten to prepare an excuse. The truth was, she felt so much lighter without the pendant. She tried to laugh, unsure if it would be better to tell him she didn't buy into his evil eye nonsense or she didn't believe it was working. A dead body was pretty much the epitome of bad luck. She decided on neither of these. "Oh! I forgot to put it on this morning."

He paled. "Has something happened to it, Stella? If so, please tell me and we'll find you another."

"No," she objected, "like I said—"

"Because you really should be wearing it at all times." He examined her face closely, as if looking for signs the black cloud of evil had already taken up shop in her soul.

She found his concern touching, but she still didn't like the pendant. Something about the shape felt . . . she didn't know how to describe it . . . *dark*. Dark and cloudy and oily, like smoke from burnt sausage. But she'd wear it to appease Cosimo. "It's on my nightstand, I promise." A small white lie. But she was sure it was somewhere in the kitchen. Or the living room. Hopefully not in the pile of debris she'd left all around her fireplace. "I'll make sure I wear it all the time from here on out."

He paused, as if weighing the veracity of her words. Something he saw must have satisfied him because he nodded. "Good girl." He patted her hand affectionately.

Stella smiled in return before pulling the photographs out of her pocket. "I brought photographs I thought you'd be interested in. I was ripping out the fireplace surround—"

He frowned. "Why would you do such a thing? A vintage fireplace surround can bring a room, a home, together."

"It was crumbling as it was. Anyway, it wasn't original or anything. According to Mimmo, though . . . you know. Take that with a grain of salt."

"Noted," Cosimo smiled.

"Which is the other reason I'm here. I am down one fireplace surround."

"Oh, joy! I have quite a selection!" He jumped down from his stool and began rummaging at the other end of the store.

"Any that would fit the budget of an out-of-work chef?" she called out.

"I'm sure that can be arranged." She could hear him chuckling to himself. He straightened. "Here's a simple one."

Cosimo ran his hands over the surround. "It's from a farmhouse in the valley, I believe. Carved of walnut, from the early 1900s, so even with its simplicity, it might be a bit out of your reach." He showed her the price tag. She blanched, and he added. "But I think I could manage a 50% discount. If you promise to wear the pendant . . ."

"I promise!" She clapped her hands to have this problem so easily remedied. It really was a lovely surround, with simple lines running up and down along the side pieces and a carved rose in the center.

"Excellent." Cosimo grinned and leaned the surround back against the others before returning to the counter. "And you mentioned photographs?"

"Right, goodness, I almost forgot. My brain is a sieve lately."

He tapped his temple and said, "Well, you have quite the cacophony in there, I expect."

"Ain't that the truth," Stella muttered in English. "Anyway, behind the surround, I found these."

"Photographs!" Cosimo clapped his hands together like a child in front of a candle-filled cake before returning to his side of the counter and settling on a stool. "Wonderful! Let's see them!"

As she handed the photos to him, she said, "I heard a rumor that my family's house was robbed the day my grandparents and aunt took my mother to the airport when she moved to America. Do you know about that?"

Cosimo settled his glasses on his nose and let his gaze drift over each photograph in turn. She thought maybe he hadn't heard her, but then he looked up, "Oh, the robbery! Yes, such a shame. And so strange, only photographs taken."

"That's what Domenica said, but I couldn't believe it. Are you sure? No jewelry, no cash?"

Cosimo blinked in thought. "Not that I'm aware of. Only photographs. Your grandparents were relieved, certainly, to discover that nothing of financial value had been taken, but at the same time, they had just sent their daughter to the United States. They longed for a memento, a way to remember her, to hold her close."

She pressed her lips together, thinking. "They never caught the robber?"

"No, not unless he was captured in another town."

She considered. "Were they the only ones whose house was ransacked?"

"Oh, my dear, I think ransacked is too strong a word. But yes." Cosimo paused. "Now that I think of it, there have been other break-ins, though those homeowners reported other items missing as well. So perhaps those are unrelated. Or perhaps the homeowners hoped to cash in on insurance by reporting valuable items stolen."

"In those cases, the robber definitely stole photographs, though?"

"That's my understanding." His gaze slipped back to the photos in his hands. "It's lucky you found these. Behind the fireplace surround you said?"

"Yes. They must have slipped behind the mantle."

"I suppose," he said softly. "I remember your family when they looked like this. Look at those children's clothes! I wonder if they are still somewhere in your house."

She shook her head. "There are trunks of adult clothes—maybe from my grandparents or my aunt—but nothing for children."

"And nothing of your mother's? Not clothes, or any other keepsakes?"

She shrugged. "Not that I can tell."

He nodded. "Perhaps they donated them. Or she took them with her."

"Maybe. Though I didn't find much beyond one photo in my mother's things." She hesitated before adding, "My mother . . . she wasn't exactly fond of Aramezzo."

He looked up, sharply. "What do you mean?"

"Just that," Stella shrugged. "She never mentioned the town. If she did, like when teachers at my school noted her accent and asked where she was from, she, well . . . she talked about her home in a pretty negative way."

Stella tensed, waiting for Cosimo to bristle. He took incredible pride in his village. She feared he might ask what her mother had said, and how could Stella tell him her mother described Aramezzo as a bland oatmeal kind of backwater town full of people with more superstition than brains, and not a drop of imagination among them.

But Cosimo didn't bristle. In fact, he didn't even respond. Instead, his eyes slid back to the photographs, lost in thought.

"Cosimo?"

"Hmmm?" He looked up and his eyes cleared. "Ah! Yes, your mother. Well now, we often resent the soil that feeds us."

She wasn't too sure about this. She loved her hometown of Cedar Grove and considered it the jewel of New Jersey. But it wasn't worth arguing about. She gestured to the photographs. "Did you notice all the gray eyes?"

He nodded. "Impossible to miss. Then again, I'm always drawn to eye color since that's how I found my way here."

Stella's eyebrows furrowed. Did she misunderstand him?

At her expression, he chuckled. "I'm sure you've noticed my child, but I have one green eye and one blue. It's an anomaly. I wondered about it for years, annoying my parents with questions about who else in the family had eyes of two colors, if it meant anything. Finally, they admitted they had adopted me as a baby."

"You were adopted?"

"Indeed. It took quite a bit of digging, but I finally found my birth certificate at a Roman abbey that houses women in need. I discovered that though my mother was a vagrant living in Rome, her last name connects her to ancestors hailing from Aramezzo."

"Did she have eyes of two different colors, too?"

"That I do not know. I unfortunately don't have any photographs of her."

Stella thought about mentioning what she learned from Domenica about the heritability of eye color, but she didn't want to break the spell of Cosimo's words with anything as pedestrian as science. "Wow. Are you related to people living here now?"

He shook his head. "Possible. But only vaguely. My ancestors left Aramezzo generations ago, and before that records weren't that well kept."

She thought about this and noticed that he stared at her, as if wondering whether or not to go on.

She tilted her head. "Is there more?"

He didn't answer right away. "It's not something I tell many people, Stella. I know most find me unusual to the point of fatigue. But I feel like I can trust you."

She held her breath and waited.

He nodded, as if to himself. "You've seen the Madonna in the church."

"Sure," she said, confused. "The first time was when I met you."

"Did you notice the Madonna's eyes?"

"Well, yes. Because they looked like my mothers'."

He paused. "Yes, at first blush. But if you look at the Madonna in a certain light, you'll see the artist did something quite masterful. View the Madonna from one angle and she has gray eyes. Look at her from another angle and her eyes change. One blue and one green."

"You're kidding."

He smiled. "No. I've looked through more local art than I can say, much of it right here," he waved to indicate his shop. "And I can tell you that, while we don't have much in the written record, you'll notice a higher proportion of art featuring people with two different colored eyes than you'd expect in a town this size."

"Fascinating." Stella ruminated on Cosimo's backstory, his quest to find his roots. She wondered if this explained his interest in artifacts. He certainly valued historical attachment more than anyone she knew. Without knowing she did so, she finished the thought aloud. "And this is why you lean so strongly into the town's history."

He nodded, pleased. "My roots, they are intertwined with that of the town."

Stella wondered what that would feel like, to feel like yourself, your past and present and future, were part of a landscape.

He seemed to read her mind as he said, "As are yours, my dear."

At the light dimming in the shop, Stella arranged for Cosimo to deliver the surround later in the week. He waved off her attempt to pay and said they could settle up later. And hinted that maybe he'd knock another few dollars off if she offered him *strufoli* at the time of delivery.

She grinned and asked for the photographs back.

"Photographs?" he said, his eyes cloudy.

Stella pointed at where he'd moved them without realizing, next to the register.

He laughed. "Oh my goodness, Stella. These events have befuddled us all, haven't they? I'm afraid I couldn't find my way out of a paper bag today."

Stella waved goodbye and made her way to the tunnel that led back to the bottom ring of Aramezzo. She shivered walking through the shadowy passageway and breathed a sigh of relief to come out into the fresh, if cold, early evening air. For a moment she stood, wondering at the empty tables where the men of Aramezzo usually played cards into the evening hours.

Just then, she spotted the mayor stepping out of his office, cell phone pressed against his ear. Stella pulled back into the shadows of the tunnel and breathed a sigh of relief as Marcello passed. His words trailed behind him, "I'm telling you, *cara*. There's no need... That's what I'm saying, the problem is behind us. No. No, that's not what I mean...mmm-hmm...why would he... Exactly! Who would believe him?"

Without making a decision, Stella found herself following the mayor, as close as she dared. She stopped quickly when Marcello paused in front of the obituary board, yanking on a flapping poster. Stella squinted but couldn't tell who the poster was for. Maybe it didn't matter and Marcello didn't like it fluttering about without his express permission.

Marcello paused and Stella ducked into a doorway right as he spun around. She pressed against the shadows, heart beating so wildly, she was sure he could hear it. She tried to quiet her breath, to listen for Marcello's footsteps, drawing closer or moving away. Finally, she heard him mutter,

"I'm still here. I thought I heard someone. Must have been one of those blasted cats."

Stella, who a few months ago would have counted this last comment as a sign that maybe she underestimated Marcello's competence, now had to stop herself from yelling, "Hey!"

She tentatively stepped out of the doorway, but then recoiled back at the sight of a villager approaching the mayor. She heard Marcello mutter into the phone, "Speak of the devil. Home soon."

Then she heard the mayor call out, "Bruno! The pride of Aramezzo."

She couldn't hear Bruno's answer, but it didn't sound like he felt the full force of the compliment.

Stella peered out from the doorway in time to see Marcello clamp Bruno on the shoulder, "Ah, Bruno. Our hearts are with you. Such a loss for us all. The pride of Aramezzo."

Did Marcello call everyone the pride of Aramezzo? The mayor seemed oblivious to his repetition. Before Stella could ponder this further, she heard Bruno's voice slice the air like a cleaver. "How could you?"

Stella could imagine the expression of deep confusion wreathing the mayor's face. Certainly his voice rang with exaggerated innocence as he said, "Bruno. What can you mean? I'm afraid your grief—"

"You forget, Marcello. I've known you since you were the scrawny kid tied to an olive tree on field trips. You will always be that kid, friendless and small. Always."

Quiet. Then Stella heard Marcello growl, "Thanks for the walk down memory lane, Bruno. What's your point?"

Bruno's voice seethed with rage. "Did you really think threatening to make my life difficult if Jacopo left would make him stay? Did you think he wouldn't tell me?"

Stiffly, Marcello said, "I don't know what the boy told you, Bruno, but it's not my fault he was high-strung."

"High-strung?" Bruno's voice escalated. Stella wondered how many people were currently leaning out of their windows to hear this drama unfolding. Bruno must have thought the same because he dropped his voice until Stella, a few meters down the road, had trouble catching the words. "You thought threatening me would make him abandon his dream? You thought so little of him? Of me?"

"Sounds like he didn't tell you the whole story—"

"He didn't have to," Bruno cut the mayor off. "You ruined the peace of his final night on this earth and I will never, not ever, forget that. I'm going to take you down if it's the last thing I do."

THURSDAY

*T*hursday morning, Stella struggled to open her eyes.

The night before, she had drifted home and scarfed down a can of tuna while searching for the pendant. She had finally found it under the couch where it must have fallen when she tossed it, or maybe Barbanera had used it as a toy. She'd fastened it back around her neck and then climbed into bed to stare at her book, not processing a word, even as she turned pages. Finally, she had resigned herself to being useless and turned off the light, Barbanera standing guard at her feet.

Exhaustion had enfolded her like a straightjacket, and yet she'd rested only fitfully, her dreams populated by whales and birds and bears floating in a funnel shape, as if suspended in the still air, above vivid blue-green water, framed by red rocks. She had awoken with a start, panicked, though she couldn't say by what. Her memory of her dream included nothing jumping or threatening, only those eerie animals hanging in the air, blinking.

Bleary and listless, Stella could decide on only one thing—she needed coffee. Okay, two things—she needed somebody to make it for her.

So nothing suited her more than stepping into Bar Cappellina to Roberto and Romina's worried faces, the cup of warm *cappuccino* placed into her hands, the pastry she hadn't known to ask for left wordlessly at her elbow.

Within ten minutes, Stella felt more herself and though she refused to enter conversations about the murder (nobody could believe Antonio could have done it, but some voiced the opinion that stranger things had happened), and tried to shut her ears to the words of their collective grief at losing Jacopo, she happily engaged into the conversation Romina seemed to know she needed as much as the pastry, about how the predicted spring storms would boost the area's truffle production.

Stella's shoulders had loosened by the time Marta entered the bar, Ascanio astride her hip. "He tells me he cannot walk another step without a sip of juice."

Romina plucked two oranges from the enormous bowl on the counter and juggled them to Ascanio's gasp of pleasure. He bucked to get down and ran to the bar. "Do it again, Romina, do it again!"

Laughing, Romina said, "You got it, *tesoro*, but don't ask me to toss more than two. That's my limit."

At Ascanio's giddy clapping, Stella smiled and said, "I wish my morning doldrums could be so easily solved."

"I can't believe he's gone." Marta patted Stella's arm warmly. "And what a trial for you. How horrible."

Stella nodded. "Mostly, I'm sad for Bruno and his wife. Losing their son, so young. What a tragedy."

A flash crossed Marta's face.

Stella leaned toward her friend. "Marta? What is it?"

"What you said . . . about tragedy. *You* know." At Stella's silence, Marta cast a quick glance at Ascanio and lowered her voice. "You mean you don't know? About . . . " Her voice trailed off.

Stella shook her head. What could Marta be referring to?

Marta hesitated and Roberto caught the gesture and walked around the bar to pick Ascanio up. "Why don't you help make the juice, Ascanio?"

Ascanio turned to Marta like a sunflower toward light. His face beaming, he said, "Did you hear that, Mamma? I get to *make the juice!*"

Marta bit her lip. "I heard, my love."

Roberto lifted Ascanio and murmured to him about oranges and their juice while Marta ducked her head to speak quickly and quietly to Stella. "I would have told you, Stella. Only I assumed you knew."

Stella waited, leaning closer to Marta.

"Where to start?" Marta closed her eyes briefly. "Ascanio's father . . . goodness, I haven't had to tell this story in so long."

Stella's eyes darted toward Roberto with his hands over Ascanio's guiding the lever down to press the halves of the juicer together. Stella hoped Marta would figure out how to tell the story before Ascanio finished and ran back.

Marta inhaled and tried again. "Okay. The beginning, I suppose. Cesare and I fell in love at the organic farmer's market in Perugia. We had stands beside each other. We dated for only a few months before I got pregnant. His family . . . well, they didn't approve. Accused me of trying to entrap their son to get his property. I was pretty sick at the beginning of the pregnancy, and dealing with their resentment . . . it was too much, to tell you the truth."

Though this happened years ago, Stella couldn't help the leaping feeling of rage in her chest. How could anyone not love Marta, who always carried the tender scent of her farm's lavender? She focused on Marta's words.

"Cesare had always been close with his parents and couldn't stand disappointing them. I felt for him, to feel so divided. But then he started to blame me, too. Blame the pregnancy for everything that had soured between us."

"As if you got pregnant alone," Stella grumbled.

"I broke it off with him," Marta said, nodding at the memory.

Stella's eyes widened.

Marta sighed. "Maybe because of that, or maybe all the pressure together, but . . . he partied one night with his friends and then decided to hang glide off Monte Subasio. He loved hang-gliding, even at night, though when we were together I convinced him to give up the nighttime flights. Anyway, his friends tried to stop him—night time is so dangerous even with that full moon, and how could he make split decisions when he was, well, high—but he laughed them off and said it would be fine."

Stella's brain raced ahead.

"Maybe the wind was wrong. I doubt he checked carefully. Or maybe he got into a stall and couldn't recover. His friends believe clouds got in the way of the full moon he assumed would provide plenty of light." Marta stared at her hands and whispered, "He didn't survive the accident."

Stella breathed, "Oh, man."

"After that, his parents, well . . . they tried to mend fences. Begged me to come to Aramezzo so they could be on hand to help raise my child."

Stella nodded. "They lost their son and wanted to bond with yours to patch their wound."

Marta nodded. "That's what I figured. They offered me the house they'd intended for Cesare, and they built a smaller house that requires less work outside of town. My parents split up long ago, and anyway they're pretty unstable, if I'm honest. I leapt at the offer of a free place to live and help with Ascanio so I could earn enough to support us."

Stella sipped her coffee which had grown cold. "And are they still involved with you and Ascanio?"

"They adore Ascanio," Marta said, casting her son a fond look. "Me, they could do without."

Stella winced. "You're kidding. You are a dream daughter-in-law."

Marta shrugged and turned her gaze to Ascanio, carefully placing a lemon in the juicer.

In a small voice, Stella ventured, "And now . . . you're dating Leonardo."

Marta laughed so hard a few curls broke free of the braids she'd wound around her head. "You don't know about my son's father, but *that* you've heard?"

Stella shrugged. "I only heard you went for a drive. I admit I was testing the waters there."

Marta laughed again, freeing yet another curl until the wisps framed her face. "Nicely done. We've only been out a few times. I'm not sure that counts as dating. He's very sweet. Not at all what people imagine him to be."

Stella cocked her head. "And what do you imagine people imagine him to be?"

"You know. A tough guy." Marta shrugged easily. "And . . . well, this feels weird to say. But Jacopo made it very clear he didn't approve."

"Jacopo!" All heads turned to Stella, and she concentrated on the bubbles drying on the sides of her cup. As the conversation around the bar picked back up, Stella lowered her voice to say, "Did he . . . were you . . . "

Marta's eyes widened. "Stella. He's like my kid brother. Besides, I'm pretty sure he was seeing someone."

"Who?" This was new information to Stella. If Jacopo was in a relationship, it added twists to this story.

Frowning in thought, Marta said, "He never said her name. Now that I think of it, he didn't even tell me he was dating. He just blushed when I asked about it and made more references to love lately. It seemed unlike him."

Stella nodded. "So why didn't he like Leo? And I can't believe I have to use the past tense."

"I know. This whole thing." Marta bit her lip in thought before remembering Stella's question. "I don't know why Jacopo was so down on Leo. It seemed to go back years, some grudge, maybe? All I know is he said I could do better."

Stella sort of agreed, but made no comment. She looked up with a start. "*That's* why Leonardo wasn't at the shearing."

"I didn't want any tension, and Jacopo comes every year. Leo didn't mind, he had to do some repairs on the *porchetta* van, anyway." Marta sighed. "Honestly, though, I can't imagine it'll go anywhere with Leo.

He's not exactly commitment material. But it's nice to date again, to have someone think I'm pretty."

Stella recoiled as if slapped. "You are gorgeous."

Marta patted Stella's hand. "Ascanio thinks so, and that's enough for me most of the time. But if there's one thing I've learned, it's that life is short and we're only young once."

Stella had no idea how a woman as ethereally beautiful as Marta failed to see herself clearly. She frowned, and then wondered at the oddity of Marta losing her son's father in an extreme sport, and now she was dating a race car driver. Or a former race car driver. She supposed Marta saw him mostly as a guy in a *porchetta* van.

Life is short.

Stella heard the truth in those words and remembered Luca saying something similar. She lowered her voice. "Jacopo . . . who do you think killed him?"

Marta's eyes widened. "You don't think it's Antonio? I thought the police almost have enough evidence to arrest him."

"You can't think it's him."

Marta paused, watching Ascanio now walking in slow motion, holding his full glass of vivid orange juice with both hands and staring at the surface as if terrified of spilling a drop. "I guess it is hard to imagine. But he was awfully angry at Jacopo. You heard about their huge fight?"

"I heard the fight. When I walked home from the sheep shearing."

Marta nodded. "People down the road heard the pans crashing."

"That part doesn't look good." Stella paused. "But I still don't see Antonio doing it."

"I hate to think it could have been him. But if it wasn't . . . then who?"

Stella picked up her cup and took a last sip before shaking her head. "I wish I knew."

Marta frowned. "I don't know how this figures into anything, but yesterday I heard Orietta telling Cristiana that Jacopo had stopped into the pharmacy to ask what vitamins helped with headaches. He didn't want to say more, she said he looked nervous enough talking about it, but he said something about not being able to take the tension."

"That fits with what I heard about the bad feeling between his father and Antonio. "

Marta went on, "Especially since Mimmo said Bruno had upped the pressure on Jacopo, ordering him to leave the bakery."

"Mimmo told you this?"

Marta grinned. "Bear in mind, he's not a huge Bruno fan. He doesn't trust anyone who sells farmed meat. For him, it's hunted wild or not at all." Stella laughed and Marta's eyes danced before her face grew serious. "Honestly, the thing that bothers me is that I've seen Aldo with Jacopo and it was obvious Jacopo couldn't stand him. I can't imagine why he'd want to work with someone like that."

A realization struck Stella so forcefully she didn't know how she missed it earlier. "Wait. This can't be the first time Antonio has lost a worker. Don't his apprentices usually wind up at other bakeries? Why is Antonio so worried about his secrets getting out now?"

Marta shrugged. "Jacopo is . . . was . . . the first of Antonio's apprentices to love baking. The previous apprentices did it for a few years, then went off to do other things. From something Jacopo told me, I think Antonio shared more with him. I wonder if he was grooming Jacopo to take over. At least until Dario joined the crew."

"And maybe with Dario on board, Jacopo had to rethink his future." Stella mused aloud.

"My guess? Jacopo never meant to betray Antonio, he needed to get out and tend his own path, " Marta said softly, smoothing Ascanio's wild curls and letting them spring back up. "And now, in a way, he's left Aramezzo. But he's also here forever."

Something bothered Stella, like the lingering scent of garlic on her fingers. "But there must be more to it. Especially given what you said about Jacopo not liking Aldo. I mean, why not go to a different bakery?"

"Money?" Marta guessed. "Maybe Aldo offered more."

"Maybe," Stella said. "But that doesn't sound like Jacopo's main priority. I think I need to talk to Aldo. Maybe as part of leaving Forno Antico, Jacopo mentioned something to him."

The door flew open, and the mayor strode in, flinging his arms wide. "Oh, friends! Can you believe how tragedy has befallen our fair city?"

Ascanio put down his empty juice glass and gazed up at Marta. "Mamma? Did something happen?"

Marta tried to smile. "Nothing at all, sweetheart. Let's get home." She dipped her head to say to Stella. "I haven't told him yet. I will, of course. I'll have to. But I have to figure out a way to explain."

Stella nodded and quickly said, "Go. I've got this. Who knows what Marcello will say next."

Marta quickly hugged Stella in thanks before picking up Ascanio and dashing out.

Marcello turned in time to watch her go. He rapped on the counter. "I remember when Jacopo was Ascanio's age. So innocent! And now, Jacopo, the pride of Aramezzo . . . killed!" The mayor swept his hand to the right, knocking the hat off a farmer who had bustled to the bar for an espresso. The mayor didn't seem to notice. "Killed! With a . . . a . . . baking razor, of all things."

Stella's eyebrows went up. How did he know about the lame? She wondered if this meant the lab confirmed the lame to be the murder weapon. The blood test results couldn't have come back already.

The mayor dropped his head into his hands with a loud gasp of a sob and then raised his head to tell Romina to make him a cappuccino, skim milk, not too hot.

Stella's brows furrowed, remembering what she heard the night before. Which led her to remember seeing Jacopo leaving the mayor's office. Marcello had held Bruno's business over Jacopo's head. Was this threat the solution Veronica had alluded to? Moreover, during that meeting, might Jacopo, in his youthful tenderness, have confided something to the mayor? She could easily imagine sweet Jacopo, crumbling in Marcello's authoritarian grip.

She arranged her face into one of innocent curiosity. Sidling up to the mayor, she said, "And Jacopo met with you the night before he died. Did he—"

"To think!" Were the tears welling in Marcello's eyes for real? She couldn't tell. "I may have been the last person to see him alive." He added in a rush, "Aside from the murderer, of course."

"Of course, but did he—"

Marcello flung his head back. "Thank the Madonna! My last conversation with him was so positive. At least he died with his mind on civic responsibility. A proper and decent reflection in his last moments."

"Civic responsibility? You mean about how you told Jacopo how difficult things would be on Bruno's butcher shop if he left?" Stella winced as the words left her mouth. Blast her impetuousness. She tensed, waiting for him to ask how she knew about a private phone call even as she ran possible excuses for her knowledge.

He patted Stella's hand as if she'd offered a condolence. "It's what we all want, isn't it? To go with good, clean thoughts in our hearts."

He and his wife certainly deserved each other. "But what you told Jacopo about Bruno—"

"Yes, that too. I reminded him of how hard his father would take his leaving, how in missing Jacopo, Bruno's work would likely suffer."

"No, but—"

"A son's duty! Yes. A son's *duty*." Marcello shook his head with a small smile, as if contemplating his own wisdom. "Ah, how we'll miss the boy. Taken too soon."

The villagers around the bar muttered, "Too soon . . . too soon."

Stella stifled her huff of impatience. The self-aggrandizing of this man. He seemed to consider Jacopo's murder an opportunity to grand-stand. It's like he didn't care at all.

All these people around, falling in the mayor's line. What power did he have over them? Suddenly, Stella felt suffocated. She needed to get out.

Her mind darted to Jacopo's cracked phone, Aldo's phone number . . . "He knows" . . .

Stella tossed down her napkin and stepped to the register to pay for her coffee and Ascanio's juice. She didn't care what Domenica said. It was time to go to Assisi.

"Domenica, I need your car!" Stella blew into the bookshop.

Domenica looked up from the book propped in her lap. "Well, hello there, Stella. I'm doing all right, all things considered. How kind of you to ask."

"Sorry, but I'm going to Assisi. Don't try to stop me this time," Stella said firmly.

Domenica closed the book. "I won't."

Stella, ready with her list of justifications, practically stumbled forward from the lost momentum. "Really? I thought for sure you'd preach patience."

Chuckling, Domenica said, "I'm surprised you waited this long."

"It's only been two days!" Stella blanched. Had it only been two days since the murder? It felt like a lifetime.

"Two whole days." Domenica smiled fondly at Stella. "I rather expected you to hitchhike there back when we talked about it on Tuesday." At Stella's scowl, Domenica added, "You needed to catch a breath, *cara*."

Stella flopped into the wingback chair. "Honestly, I'm not sure I have enough breath to catch."

"Of course," Domenica nodded. "But you are no longer fueled by panic. Now you can make a good go of it." She opened her mouth to add more, but then closed it, pressing her lips together in thought.

Stella stayed silent, letting her gaze drift to the cobweb that had been in the window's corner for as long as she had known Domenica.

Domenica stammered, "There is something . . . well, probably nothing . . . just speculation, I'm sure . . . "

Stella's gaze returned to Domenica. "What?"

Domenica sucked in her lower lip, thinking, and then said, "Nothing, never mind. You know. Rumors and gossip."

Stella grinned. "Sometimes value in that."

Slowly, Domenica nodded. "Sometimes."

Stella sighed and then she said, "Two things I need to know."

"Who killed Jacopo, and why?"

"Besides that," Stella said. "I need to know what Aldo knew about Jacopo and what the mayor said to Jacopo the night before the murder."

In a flash, Stella realized Domenica hadn't heard the latest. She filled Domenica in on both the argument between Marcello and Bruno, as well as her recent run-in with the mayor at Bar Cappellina. "By the way, the mayor referenced the lame as the murder weapon."

Domenica's eyes widened. "Results are back already?"

"Apparently."

Domenica frowned. "I'm surprised the police are making this common knowledge. Don't they usually keep this stuff under wraps? So they can hold all the cards?"

Shrugging, Stella said, "Somehow, Marcello found out. I guess the mayor gets special dispensation."

"I'm not sure they'll take kindly to him spreading that around."

Stella shrugged again. "Not my problem. I only wonder if they're investigating Aldo."

"They have to be, right? With that text? It was easy enough for us to track it. I'm sure they must have done the same."

"But Aldo as a suspect doesn't make any sense. Aldo lost something with Jacopo's death, didn't he? Now he'll never get what he needs to elevate his bakery. I can't see what he'd gain by murder."

"I guess," Domenica conceded. "But I don't like him."

"Join the club," Stella chuckled. "It sure would be easier to have the killer be Aldo. It's so hard to believe it's anyone here."

Domenica picked up her purse and rummaged around for a few moments before pulling out her keys. "Pick me up some cat food while you're at it. Not all of us will make gourmet meals for our pets."

"Sure," Stella grinned. "From the pet store on the ring road, by the parking lot?"

"The same."

Stella stood. "All right, I'll be back soon. Hopefully."

Domenica nodded. "Come straight back though, okay? To check in?"

"You're that worried about my driving?"

Domenica pressed her lips together as if deciding whether or not to say something. "I . . . don't laugh at an old woman. But I have a bad feeling. I've overheard pieces of conversation. Something is brewing."

Stella whipped around. "You think they'll arrest Antonio today?"

"Maybe," Domenica said. "I mean, it makes sense if they've confirmed the blood on the lame was Jacopo's. But . . . I don't know. I feel like I've been hearing . . . Never mind, *cara*, it's probably nothing."

Stella leaned over and kissed the top of Domenica's iron-gray head. "I'll be careful. I promise."

Domenica clasped Stella's hand between her own. "Promise promise?"

"Promise promise," Stella agreed.

Stella had to stop herself from sprinting down the road and then through the tunnel to the road that encircled Aramezzo, which brought her to the parking lot.

An engine roared and Stella jumped back, just as a red sports car careened into the parking lot. Through the cloud of dust raised by the car's thrust of speed, Stella saw Leonardo leap out of the car, locking it with a sleek beep of his key fob. Stella coughed as she watched several police officers, one of them Salvo, rush toward Leonardo.

She shook her head. Looked like Leonardo would not get away with reckless speed today. But by the time Stella reached Domenica's car, she realized the police officers assembled around Leo's car were nodding in admiration. Stella heard at least one impressed cooing sound as Leo walked around the vehicle, stroking it like a wild animal as he recounted features of its handling.

Stella turned the ignition, struggling to imagine Leonardo and Marta together. *Allora*, she didn't need to understand it. She only hoped Marta came out of it okay.

It had been a while since she'd driven a car. As she drove, she remembered the last time she drove, to the polenta festival in Perugia last month when Domenica and Matteo got food poisoning. Stella had skipped the Ascolana olives, even though she adored the fried, meat-filled olives ubiquitous at festivals in central Italy. Her sensitive nose had curled at what she assumed must be spoiled meat and she'd tried to warn her friends, but they'd mocked her for being overly precious and fussy, refusing commoners' food. She'd reminded them about her love of boxed brownie mix and how she'd fed them both her homemade mac-and-cheese, but Domenica and Matteo continued making theatrical "yummy" noises right up until they found themselves tossing the olives back up into the bushes. Later, they curled into themselves in the backseat, green and chastened, the whole way home to Aramezzo, quietly vomiting into trash bags.

At the memory, Stella felt her stomach lurch. She'd never been able to abide being around people vomiting, but then again, she assumed only insane people would be okay with it. Taking a breath, she felt glad that she had the car to herself this time. She opened the windows and blasted Radio Subasio, singing along with Cher. It never failed to amuse her how much 90's American pop played on Italian radio stations.

After barely three songs, she turned into the parking lot. First things first. She swung by the pet store to pick up Domenica's cat food. Looping the handles of her tote bag over her shoulder alongside her purse, Stella continued to the bakery, following her phone's directions into the center of Assisi. She stopped outside the door, stepping back to take in the bread in the window and the scent outside the shop. Forno Fontana lacked the sunlit, almost almond scent of Antonio's *forno* in Aramezzo, but, surprisingly, it didn't smell of whatever restrained, almost tame, scent she'd noted on Aldo back in Aramezzo.

Opening the door, Stella inhaled. There it was—the tame yeast. Wait. She sniffed again. Actually, it smelled midway between Antonio's bread and what she initially smelled on Aldo. Aldo must have made some changes that approximated Antonio's bread.

She approached the counter, and the baker greeted her blandly, his tired eyes slipping past her. For some reason, she was glad the outfit at Forno Fontana wasn't the same as Aramezzo's bakers' get-up. Aldo wore white slacks and a white shirt, unbuttoned to reveal the white v-neck below it, along with a smattering of chest hairs.

"*Ciao*," Stella said, swallowing her revulsion. "Do you remember me?"

His gaze flicked over her face and lingered at her chest before moving back up. She would not have considered jeans, a work shirt, and scuffed Doc Martens remotely seductive, but apparently that hardly mattered. Stella sighed inwardly as Aldo's once-over seemed to click something in place for the baker. He licked his lips, reminding Stella of a lizard. "Ah, yes. From Forno Antico?"

"I'm Stella," she said.

"Stella." He ran a hand over his round, moon-like face. "Nice."

Stella did not know what was nice about that and didn't care to find out. "And you are Aldo, I remember."

"You remember well." Aldo smiled, his gaze drifting back to her chest. His high voice grew husky as he said, "I hope you're not here only for bread."

Stella was saved the trouble of answering by a woman dressed in white pushing through the swinging doors. She stopped when she noticed Stella, but then turned to the baker. "Giorgio is here with the flour."

The baker kept his eyes trained on Stella. "I'll be there in a minute."

Stella herself said nothing. Something about the woman felt familiar, and Stella gazed so long at her dark bob and brooding eyes, she likely violated all kinds of social niceties. Nobody seemed to notice, as the woman had her gaze trained on Aldo, and Aldo had his gaze trained on Stella's torso. How did she know this woman? The only image Stella could summon was a field of purple. Maybe the woman resembled someone in a movie? Stella shook her head, frustrated.

The woman shifted her weight impatiently as she snapped at Aldo, "Giorgio said he's leaving if you don't sign for it right away. You know how pissed he was that you weren't here last time. Tuesdays and Thursdays. It's not hard to remember."

The baker growled, words escaping between his clenched teeth. "I told you, I saw a car broken down on the way to work and I stopped to help."

"So you say," the woman grumbled, "We're running out of flour here, Aldo."

Stella realized how strange it was to have an employee talking this way to her boss, especially in front of her. Italians' ideas about customer service varied quite a bit from Americans'. But still, Stella had never seen a drama play out like the one in front of her now. Except perhaps at her first Aldo sighting.

The woman practically stamped her foot, and Stella noticed her eyes were bloodshot and rimmed with red. Had she been crying? Or, with the blossoms bursting forth all over the countryside, it could be allergies. Stella had never suffered from allergies, but had worked with enough chefs over the years who spent weeks of every spring looking like wrung washcloths. Sadness or allergies, the woman had plenty of stamina. "Aldo! *Helloooo*? How do you expect to bake bread with no flour?"

At Aldo's non-response, the woman muttered, "*Madonna mia,*" and stormed out. The air around her shifted as she pushed through the doors, which swung back and forth in her wake. In a flash, Stella realized—the woman didn't look familiar, she *smelled* familiar. Like violets.

Violets!

The violet candies! Stella felt like thwacking her forehead. Violets. That was the floral scent she caught on Aldo the first time she met him. That's what she couldn't remember when she saw the candies at the crime scene.

She needed to ask Aldo about why his employee smelled so strongly of violets and could this reason have anything to do with Jacopo's candies, but she didn't know how to begin without sounding deranged.

Stella adjusted her bandana, thinking, and decided to open with innocence. "Sounds like you have your hands full?"

"On the contrary, my wife leaves me with empty hands." His lips stretched across his teeth.

Wife? She had to be like half his age, and he looked at least fifty, maybe pushing sixty. Stella frowned. "That's your wife?" This changed everything. A motive shimmered into place. Stella just needed to clarify the stock.

He shrugged.

Stella cleared her throat. "Oh. I see. A lovely woman, certainly. And do I detect a hint of violet perfume? My, erm, my aunt loves violets, and I'm looking for a perfume for her birthday so—"

Aldo put his hand out to stop her words. "No perfume. This is a bakery, are you nuts? You can't wear perfume in food service."

"Oh, yes. Of course. Though your wife carried an unmistakable—"

"She's always sucking these violet candies. It's revolting, if I'm honest. Her family is from Toulouse. That's in France."

"Yes, I know where Toulouse is."

"Well, her grandparents grow violets for perfume and lotion and candy or whatever."

Stella blinked at this simple act of family connection. Aldo's wife's family grew violets, and she kept them close through a preference for violet flavored candies. Right then, though, two things snapped together. One, Jacopo's candies. Violets may be popular in Toulouse or even France, but it was not a common scent here. In fact, Marta, who made jellies and was even breaking into soaps from flowers and herbs, used French tarragon, but never violet. The scent connected Aldo's wife and Jacopo . . . how? And two, the wife had said Aldo was late to work on Tuesday. The morning of Jacopo's murder. Could this be a coincidence?

Only one way to find out. Stella widened her eyes and made a show of examining the bins of bread behind the display case. She adopted a breathy voice and said, "I remember the day we met in Aramezzo. You said you wanted to make bread as good as Antonio's. I have to say, though . . . your bread looks out of this world."

Aldo's lip curled as he grinned, and she couldn't help thinking of one of Mimmo's dogs spotting a darting mouse. He scratched his round chin with his gaze fixed on her and said, "Yeah, I had a plan, and it didn't turn out how I wanted, but before the . . . deal went sour, I got enough information to change my formula."

"Jacopo, you mean. Yes, I heard he was going to come work here."

Aldo scowled at the name. "Then he got himself killed. After all his whining about how hard he had it, being pushed by his father to leave Antonio's and pushed by Antonio to stay. Idiot."

Stella winced. But then played on, "So he told you some baking secret before he . . . died? Something you could use?"

"No, but he told my wife about the wild fermentation a while back, and the other day I found shelves full of their 'experiments.' I didn't think something that simple could make a difference, but . . ." he shrugged before suddenly narrowing his eyes. "Why do you care?"

She stretched her mouth in what she hoped resembled a friendly smile. So Jacopo and Aldo's wife had worked closely together. Perhaps closely enough for her to pass onto him an affection for violet. She wondered...the wife was older than Jacopo, but not by a lot...maybe their connection had another level? She thought quickly, "Oh, none of that really matters. Only, with Aramezzo's bakery closed, I need a new bread source. For, er...for my bed and breakfast." *Very smooth*, she chided herself. "If you have gotten hold of Antonio's secrets, then at least I know I can come here. For *quality* products."

His eyes widened. "Oh, yes. We have plenty of that here. *Quality.*"

She pressed her lower lip down into a pout. "But is it consistent?"

"What do you mean?"

"Without Jacopo...to guide you..."

"Oh, don't worry. My wife got everything he had to offer." Stella didn't miss the sarcastic edge to his voice.

"Say, was he going to be making sweets here? *Cornetti*, things like that?" Her eyes raked over the display case of breakfast pastries.

Aldo rubbed his lower lip. "No. Why would I hire him for that? My wife bakes those, and anyway, why bring him here to make sweets when his specialty is bread? That makes no sense."

"No, I suppose it doesn't," Stella muttered to herself. Shoot, she was hoping to make sense of the laminated dough Jacopo had been working on.

Aldo picked at the knot of his apron until it came untied. "Listen, if we're going to keep dancing around this, let's go out for a glass of wine."

Dancing? What dancing? How was she going to turn the conversation to his tardiness on Tuesday? "It's ten in the morning."

His leer widened. "And?"

"And you're married."

"You don't have to worry about that," he leered as he took off his apron. "She sure doesn't."

"What does that mean?" Stella thought she knew exactly what he meant, but didn't want to let on.

"Evidently, I'm too much man for her. She likes her chickens young and stupid." He shrugged, the storm clouds in his eyes at odds with the casual gesture. "Let's get out of here." His presumption left her tongue-tied. Not for the first time, Stella wished she could bottle the assuredness of a middling man and pass it out to the astonishing women she knew who somehow felt they needed to hide their luster. Meanwhile, this guy swanned around confusing libido for personality.

She took a breath. "One question first." If she couldn't work it into conversation, she'd shoehorn it in. "You were late to work on Tuesday?"

"She's overreacting, as usual. I was fine, a few minutes behind. The bread all got out in time and we have a backlog of flour." His eyes narrowed. After a moment of intense concentration, his lips smashed against his teeth in irritation. "Why are you here?"

"I told you. For bread."

"Then what's with all the questions?"

She licked her lips. "I'm curious?"

"I'm not buying it." He shook his head. "Who sent you? Antonio? Dario?"

She lifted her chin. "No one sent me. I can have an original thought, you know."

Tying his apron back on, he sighed. "Get lost."

"Fine by me!" Stella turned so quickly, the cat food knocked against her hip, throwing off her trajectory so that her exit lacked the flair she'd intended. To add insult to injury she crashed into a man standing outside the bakery.

Stella began a litany of apologies as she straightened her bandana. She looked up at the man's face and groaned. "Oh. *Ciao,* Luca."

His eyes narrowed. "Stella. What are you doing here?"

"Can't a woman buy bread anymore without it amounting to a

capital offense?"

He looked pointedly at her single bag of cat food.

She adjusted her bandana again and tried for a vague air of boredom. "He didn't have what I needed."

"I told you, Stella. If you mess with the investigation..."

She waited for him to continue. When he didn't, she prompted, "Then..."

"Then?"

"You're telling me to stay away, and it seemed like there was an 'or else' hanging out there. Might as well serve the butter alongside the rolls, as they say."

"Stella, I'm pretty sure nobody has said that in the entire course of human history." A flicker of a smile made Luca's dimple appear on his stubbled cheek, but he pressed his lips together and it faded as if it had never been. "Listen...be careful, okay? Remember what happened last time you insisted on interfering."

She shook her head but decided not to remind him that without her, they might never have caught the killer. Partly because she remembered that without him, she likely would be dead herself. Maybe they were even. Instead, she said, "Just a tip? Aldo's not a big talker unless you flash some cleavage."

"What's that?"

She shrugged. "Never mind. I'll let you figure it out."

"Stella, wait." Luca ran his lips together. "I don't know what's going on with the investigation, the captain is burying me under pointless paper-work. But I can tell something is brewing. Something big. I know you like to hang out in the center of the action, but please...consider retiring to the margins? For a few days?"

She hesitated. Was this genuine concern or a ploy to avoid her intrusion? Finally, she said, "I told you. I came for bread."

"Whatever," he muttered, and turning into the bakery, she heard him add, "I tried."

Walking away, Stella rolled her eyes. When would he let this childish reaction to her rejection go? Maybe he didn't have a bunch of experience getting rejected, but it was time to man up. She didn't like him that way, and it was as simple as that. After all, he wasn't *that* good looking. Even if he was, he could be so aggravating! She remembered the condescension dripping from his voice during the last investigation. How could he think she'd forget that!

Stella paused in the street, hiking the cat food higher as she thought about how one of Luca's front teeth overlapped the other, and the way his eyes flashed light and shadow like an approaching storm.

Okay, maybe he was a *little* good looking.

And he wasn't actually condescending. Not anymore. Not for a while. In fact, he genuinely seemed interested in her opinion.

Still ... there was no denying how irritating he could be.

Anyway, one thing Stella learned from her checkered romantic history was that she was terrible at picking men. One after another, her relationships ended in flames. Why ruin a good thing with all that drama? She was done with drama.

As soon as she figured out the killer.

She paused, her mind running over the last twenty minutes.

Perhaps she just did.

As Stella wove the switchbacks home to Aramezzo, she thought about Aldo. She hadn't considered him a suspect before because he gained nothing from Jacopo's death. But his wife's association with Jacopo changed everything.

Perhaps, at bottom, this murder had nothing to do with Jacopo's baking talents or the threat of his taking Aramezzo's secrets to Assisi.

Perhaps, instead, it was a crime of passion?

Stella ran back over the clues—the wife's red-rimmed eyes (was she mourning her lover?), the violet candies they shared (perhaps a way to keep each other in their hearts when apart), those sessions together in the bakery (nothing sexier than messing around with strains of wild yeast).

The text message! With the number linked to the bakery, she'd assumed it had come from Aldo, but now she realized it came from Aldo's wife—the phone plan must be under the business account so they could claim it as an expense.

Perhaps Monday night, the very night of the day Stella met him, Aldo stumbled across his wife's experiments. Obviously, he would demand to know what his wife had been up to. Though she no doubt tried to explain away the fertile yeast playgrounds, citing the business advantage, Aldo would have noticed the faint flush creeping up his wife's cheeks, still smooth with youth. In her embarrassed confusion, his wife might have let something slip, something that even Aldo, dim as he was, recognized.

Then she must have texted Jacopo. Too late to warn him. With the text still showing on the screen, he'd either not seen it, or perhaps he'd ignored it, too caught up with his baking. Stella could empathize—one couldn't let the butter soften while working with laminated dough. Or perhaps it arrived when the phone smashed to the ground.

Stella frowned as she turned into Aramezzo's parking lot. Aldo didn't seem to care enough about his wife to fly into a murderous rage over an affair. Though Stella often observed that jealousy was often less about love and more about territory. Aldo's anger might be rooted more in being made a fool—a cuckold, to use the antiquated British word—than in fearing the loss of his wife.

Killing the engine, Stella realized the irony. Just as Aldo had poached a baker without compunction, that baker had poached Aldo's wife.

She shook her head at the folly of humans in this crazy world.

Stella leaned back and closed her eyes in thought. She wondered if

Aldo, once he realized he could strong-arm his wife for Antonio's secrets, didn't feel like he needed to turn the other cheek. He could get rid of Jacopo, thus freeing him of two problems—revenge for trespassing and saving a salary for a baker Aldo no longer needed.

Antonio's lame was the piece that felt out of whack.

Other than that, the pieces certainly fit. She felt excited by her revelations, emboldened enough to think that if she worked on it a little more, she'd be able to deduce how Aldo would have gotten Antonio's lame.

As she got out of the car, Stella decided maybe today was the day to tackle *colomba* again. Last time, she hadn't even used candied orange peels. This time, she'd do it right—get the starter going overnight, candy the orange peel . . .

Maybe it wasn't even Antonio's lame! Maybe it was Aldo's!

She grinned as she locked the door. Simply thinking about cooking seemed to hone her thinking.

Stella dropped in on Domenica but found the shop dark. She backed up and looked for a sign or explanation for the locked door; this was far earlier than Domenica usually closed. She kept walking and as she passed the butcher shop, she noticed the light on. Bruno, back at work already? She thought about the guilt he must carry. As far as she could see, guilt was always a part of grief, whether or not there was anything to feel guilty about. She imagined Bruno rehashing his last conversations with his son, wishing he had conveyed how much he loved him. How wrong that Marcello inserted himself into that conversation. Stella's heart twisted.

The twist decided it. She'd go home and make a meal for Bruno and his wife. She felt the need to do something for them, and cooking would allow her to think more logically. A kind of two pastas, one sauce sort of situation. Ooh. She'd make a pasta sauce! Perfect. She still had Bruno's sausages and some other meats in the freezer.

However, an hour later, despite the sauce burbling on the stove, Stella's thoughts remained a jumble. She kept getting stuck on how Aldo would have known to find Jacopo at the bakery. The best she could figure, as she stirred the simmering pot of tomatoes, beef ribs, pork sausage, and pancetta, was that she needed to talk to Antonio. She knew he didn't leave the house, scared as he was of people's suspicions. Would food open that door?

Stella startled at a knock. A kind of booming, impatient knock that prompted her to fling down her kitchen towel and race forward, still in her chef's coat. Throwing open the door, she found Matteo, his normally animated face oddly still. Drying her hands on her chef's coat, she said, "Matteo? Is everything okay?" She peered up and down the street as if expecting to see marauders chasing her friend. But only an orange tabby sauntered along the cobblestones. Stella exhaled with a smile. "How am I not surprised that you show up when the sauce is almost done?"

Matteo shifted his weight. "Stella. I'm not here for dinner."

She held open the door and gestured for him to come inside. "What's up?"

He shook his head and took a step backward, down the stair. "I only have a minute."

The smile vanished from Stella's face. "Matteo? What's going on? I've never known you to refuse food."

He tried to smile as he touched his belly lightly. "My stomach is in knots. Please stop being charming."

Her mouth turned down. "Wasn't aware that I was being anything."

"Sorry." Matteo shook his head. "This is hard. Harder than I expected."

Her stomach dropped. Oh, no. First Luca and now . . . Matteo? But they'd been friends for months and she'd never picked up on even a hint of interest. She assumed he felt as she did, like the best of buddies.

He opened his mouth to speak and then closed it at the sound of a door opening. Luisella from down the street stepped outside, dropped a minuscule bag of compost on the step (did the woman eat?), and spun back around into her house with a decided click of the closing door.

Matteo rubbed his hand across his forehead, as if trying to reduce the pressure in his brain. "Stella...I can't believe I'm saying this—"

"Then don't." She held out her hand.

"What?" He looked up, confused.

"Look, Matteo. It's taken me some time, but due to...circumstances...I've had to consider this. I'm not in a place to date."

Matteo blinked. "Congratulations?"

Meaningfully, Stella added, "Anyone. I can't date anyone."

"Check. I'll bat away the hordes for you."

"Matteo."

"What?"

Beat.

Stella sighed. "I'm trying to be gentle here, but it's hard with your oblivious act. I can't date you. Not that I'm not flattered—"

Matteo snorted. "You think I'm in love with you?"

She tipped her head to the side. "Well, aren't you?"

Matteo shook his head sadly. "Honey, I wish I had half your confidence."

She frowned, images from the last few months spiraling through her memory. "But the hugs, the meals, the hanging out late at night, the sharing a bottle of wine. It seems like you like me."

"I do." Matteo ran his hand down his long face.

She smiled, gratified they finally arrived to the same destination.

"Only not like that."

Her smile disappeared.

Matteo chewed his lip before choosing his words carefully. "Listen, I don't have a lot of friends."

She waved her hand dismissively. "That's ridiculous. Then who are you delivering presents and flowers to all the time?"

"I mean good friends. That I can be myself with. You're easy to talk to. And delightfully weird."

She scowled. "I am not weird."

"It's not an insult," Matteo said without a smile. "I am fond of you. Though maybe a little less fond of this version."

Stella pressed her lips together. How could two men in such quick succession both declare their feelings for her and then backtrack so hard to save face? Unlike with Luca, though, Stella *needed* Matteo to save face. So . . . fine, if he wanted to pretend what happened didn't happen, she'd go along with it. She waited, and when he didn't say more, just looked down the street as if waiting for an answer to pop out of the sewer, she ventured, "So we're agreed. We're both weird and we're both friends. What did you want to tell me, then?"

She girded herself for some nonsense reason that she'd have to pretend was his intention all along . . . would he tell her that Domenica got a new book in or let her know Bruno had opened his *macelleria*?

"The police are asking questions. About you. I heard them talking when I was emptying the station trash."

Stella stumbled from her high horse.

He raised his eyebrows.

"What do you mean? What questions?"

He sighed and replaced his scornful expression with one of softness. "Stella. They found your fingerprints on the murder weapon."

Stella started to laugh, to explain, to tell Matteo that she'd been with Luca, he would untangle everything. Then she remembered Luca wasn't exactly in her corner.

She went white.

Back in the house, Stella stirred the pasta sauce without seeing it or smelling it.

How could the police suspect her? They couldn't.

Could they? Matteo must be wrong, or at least wrong about the severity of the situation. Maybe he overheard idle speculation and made too much of it.

She lifted a spoonful of the sauce to her lips to taste and then froze, remembering.

She found the body. *She* did.

She found the body, and her fingerprints were on the murder weapon.

Motive, she remembered, as the muscles behind her knees loosened and she felt herself crumpling in relief. She had no motive! Why would she want Jacopo, a man she barely knew, dead?

Then again, who else had a motive? Everyone loved Jacopo. Looking back, she realized that the jocular, ebullient energy that rolled off the bakery floor came from him. Antonio was cheerful, sure, as cheerful as Jacopo, but he felt his years.

Jacopo brought life to the bakery, as he brought life to the sheep shearing, as he brought life wherever he went. Is it any wonder Aldo's wife, no doubt jaded and calloused after years of living with her oaf of a husband, became entranced with Jacopo's shiny openness?

Which reminded her . . . suspects.

Antonio. It was presumably his lame. But she didn't buy the apparent motive. Sure, he was angry with Jacopo, but that wasn't a motive, was it? Antonio would have to be in a blind panic about releasing his secrets for him to fly into that kind of fury. She remembered Dario saying Antonio would be happy to walk Stella through his process. That didn't sound like the behavior of someone paranoid about his hold on a recipe. Then again, perhaps he trusted Stella.

Then there was Aldo. He had probably the most classic murder motive of all—revenge. Maybe his attempts to hit on Stella came from some sort of mutinous rage to get back at his wife? The same kind of mutinous rage that would lead him to kill Jacopo? He *was* late to work. She frowned. How would he know to find Jacopo at the bakery, alone? And again, how did he get his hands on the lame so swiftly? There were no signs of a struggle . . . if he'd entered the bakery and started throwing drawers open to find the lame, it would have given Jacopo plenty of time to ready himself for an attack.

Stella shook her head. She had to figure it out, and she had to figure it out soon, before the police came rapping at her door. For a moment, she thought she heard a knock, but realized the sound came from Barbanera running down the stairs. He bolted to the back door and sat, staring at the space between the door and the jamb.

Touching the side of the pot, Stella realized she had at least an hour before it was cool enough to bring to Bruno's. "All right, you little beast, I can take a hint."

A flick of Barbanera's remaining ear was the only sign that he'd heard her. His gaze remained unmoving. She opened the door, and the cat pranced out, tail as upright as a mast. He jogged down the stairs and stopped cold. He glanced over his shoulder at Stella, his ear flattened like an airplane wing.

Even with so much on her mind, she couldn't help worrying about Barbanera. Would he ever get back his swagger, his confidence? She hadn't been his biggest fan when they first met, to be sure, but even then she'd admired how little he cared about anyone's opinions. He'd leave, and sleep, and eat, as he wanted, when he wanted.

Now, he appeared to tremble at the movement of the olive trees in the wind. Stella walked down the steps and sat beside him. He leaned against her and closed his eyes.

The two of them sat like that for a few minutes. Quiet, still. Comfortable in this kind of liminal space, between action and inaction. Stella felt her heartbeat slow, and her pulse soften.

The sight of Captain Palmiro walking the ring road with Salvo shattered the fragile tranquility. Catching sight of Stella on the steps, he hailed her, indicating that she wait there while he walked through the olive trees toward her. Stella bolted to standing, sending Barbanera whisking back into the house. She sighed briefly before crossing her arms in front of her chest. Wait, that probably made her look defensive, guilty even. She dropped her arms. That didn't feel right, either. In a panic, Stella tried to remember what one did with one's hands. She tried one hand on her hip with the other hanging loose, but realized she had all the gravitas of an underwear model. She tried clasping her hands in front of her but that felt wrong too, like she was about to break out singing, "How Do You Solve a Problem Like Maria?"

Before her arms could find a natural landing spot, Captain Palmiro arrived in front of her. He skipped the pleasantries of saying hello or asking after her health. Not that she expected those sorts of niceties from Captain Palmiro, but nonetheless the suddenness of his question took her by surprise. "Where were you Tuesday morning?"

Even with Matteo's warning, the Captain's words punched her in the gut. She gasped, "You can't think I did it." Her eyes cut to Salvo.

He snarled, "Again. Where were you Tuesday, March 4?"

"In bed. Asleep. Salvo, tell him—"

"From what time to what time, Signorina?" Captain Palmiro barreled on.

"I went to bed around ten and woke up around four thirty."

"When you went to the *forno*."

"That's right," she nodded. Why were her arms suddenly crossed over her chest again? "I told you all this."

"Can anyone testify to your timing?"

She shrugged. "Not unless my cat counts."

Palmiro's lip curled. "This is where living with a man like a proper lady comes in handy."

Stella, thrown by the remark, said nothing. She looked at Salvo. Did he think she had something to do with the murder? Did he think she *did* it? "Salvo?" she murmured.

Salvo glanced at the captain and then opened his mouth, but closed it when Captain Palmiro shot out his hand to silence him. Salvo's gaze dropped to the ground.

Captain Palmiro went on. "We found your fingerprints on Antonio's lame."

"So it was Antonio's? Is the blood Jacopo's?"

"Did you hear me? *We found your fingerprints on the lame.*"

"But I—"

"Save it."

"No, but Luca was there, he can tell you—"

Shaking his head, the Captain said, "He already told me. Unfortunately, he is so compromised, he missed the very obvious conclusion that you wormed your way back into the bakery so that you could cover up your old fingerprints with new ones."

"What! That's not what happened—" Stella could hardly catch her breath. "Please, let me explain."

Palmiro's words rolled over her like a military tank. "We also know that Jacopo was planning to open a pastry shop. A shop that would put you out of business."

Stella's mouth fell open. Bewildered, she murmured, as if to herself, "But I don't own a pastry shop."

"Calm down, Signorina."

Had she been un-calm? Wait, un-calm wasn't a word. What was wrong with her? Her heartbeat lurched, skittering around her ribcage. This couldn't be happening.

Palmiro went on, "Everyone knows you've been giving away free samples to gain customers for your pastry business."

This felt impossible. She tried a different tack. "Have you interviewed Aldo? From Forno Fontana? Don't you think—"

At Captain Palmiro's braying laugh, Stella's words stalled in her throat. Catching his breath, he turned to Salvo. "I told everyone her catching the killer in November was luck. Remember, Salvo, how many people joked, saying a little American nobody waltzed in here and solved the crime that stumped the police. Remember that?"

Salvo tried to laugh along with his Captain, but instead, he winced as if his stomach hurt.

Captain Palmiro stopped laughing. "Keep telling everyone this theory about Aldo, Signorina. I'd love to correct the record on what a natural crime-fighter you are."

Perhaps trying to be helpful, Salvo ventured, "Aldo has no motive, Stella. No reason to want Jacopo dead. In fact, it's the opposite—"

"Stand down, Salvo," muttered Captain Palmiro. "Let her be the laughingstock for a while. See how she likes it."

Captain Palmiro glared at Salvo until Salvo stared back at his shoes. Meanwhile, Stella rearranged her arms, stopping to tuck an errant curl back into her bandana. Then her arms fell naturally to her side. Right. This was how arms hung. Loose. Taking a breath to keep her tone even, Stella said, "But if Jacopo was opening a pastry shop like you said, it sounds like he decided not to work for Aldo. Leaving Aldo in the lurch after he'd been telling everyone he was on the cusp of big changes. Which means Aldo has a motive."

Stella noticed a small smile flick across Salvo's face, but the captain stared at her, his eyes like weathered stone. She went on, "I mean, you're probably right, it was probably luck the first time around, and I know you smart and savvy policemen no doubt have it all figured out . . . but . . . it's kind of a plot hole, isn't it? Are you sure about his starting a pastry shop?"

An image of the single key on the ring leapt into her mind. Could it be true that Jacopo was going to open a pastry shop? If so, it upped the possibility of Aldo being the murderer and decreased the possibility of it being Antonio.

The men still had said nothing. Stella widened her stance. "While you're mulling that, you might be interested to know that Jacopo was having an affair with Aldo's wife."

"How do you know that?" Captain Palmiro asked, iron in his voice.

"More of that little lady American luck, I guess." Stella shrugged, hoping her hunch was correct about the affair. "Also, you may be interested to know that Aldo was late to work the morning of Jacopo's murder."

Captain Palmiro stared at her, his lantern jaw working.

"So, are you going to arrest me or what?" Stella lifted her chin.

"Don't leave, Aramezzo, Signorina. You're a person of interest in an active crime investigation."

"Where would I go?" Stella spun on her heel and as she climbed the stairs, she called over her shoulder, "If you'll excuse me, I have a pot on the stove. But next time, Captain Palmiro, I expect you'll do me the courtesy of a hello. And please come to the front door. That's where I receive guests."

She slammed the door behind her and counted to ten, as slowly as she could manage, before peeking out through the curtains. Seeing the backs of Palmiro and Salvo striding away, Stella sagged against the wall. She was safe. For the moment. But she had to figure out who killed Jacopo before they came back with some other "evidence" that pointed at her. What it would be, she couldn't imagine. She never would have guessed they'd arrive at a motive. Could it be true? About the pastry shop? How could she find out?

Stella felt the pot. Still too hot to carry.

Anyway, did she want to sashay through town right now? The villagers could have heard about the police suspecting her. What if someone yelled at her in the street, accusing her of killing Jacopo?

Stella shook her head. She couldn't let that fear keep her from Bruno's. Her anxiety was nothing to his grief, and if she could make him feel even a little bit supported in this time, well, he deserved that. She paused. Unless he had heard about her being a suspect? What if he flew into a rage at the very sight of her? Well, that was a risk she had to take. Besides, who would be crass enough to mention theories of the crime to him? And if they hadn't, maybe the sauce would soften his hard edges, get him talking. Maybe he'd even mention who he thought did it—leads Stella could follow to clear her name.

She wrapped the pot in a towel, dropped it on a tray, and hefted it into her arms, staggering under the weight. She made her way to the butcher shop and found the light still on. Bruno glanced up with a scowl when the door opened, and Stella paused, her heart beating fast. *He'd heard.* But then his face lightened. She breathed a sigh of relief.

"No sausages, Stella. I haven't been able to—"

She shook her head to cut him off as she heaved the pot onto the counter and lifted the lid to set it on the pot sideways, allowing the steam to escape. "I'm surprised you're open."

He sighed and cast his gaze over the display of meat. "We really can't afford to be closed. There's all this meat. It will go bad if I can't move it."

She nodded. "Bruno, I want to say ... I mean ... I brought you dinner. I don't know how to say anything ... " She stopped talking at the painful sight of him closing his eyes as if guarding against a blow.

When he opened them, he said, "Please, Stella. Don't. I thank you, but don't."

She nodded. "I understand. My mother was the same when my sister ... passed."

"You lost your sister?" Bruno's eyebrows lifted.

"When we were children."

The door to the back creaked open, and a small woman appeared. Stella realized the inanity of calling anyone small when she herself barely cleared five feet, but this woman, her clothes hung off her as if from a hanger. Enormous, smudged glasses broke the jagged planes of the woman's face.

Carefully, Bruno said, "This is Stella. She brought us dinner."

The woman flung a glance at Stella before she pointed at the pot, her voice lifted querulously, "Is that what I'm smelling?"

Stella smiled. "If what you smell is good, then yes. If it's not, then I can't take credit."

The woman looked at her husband, as if asking him to translate. "Bruno?"

"Come, Benedetta." The butcher placed his arm around his wife, as if she might break, and led her to the pot. "What do you smell?" he asked Benedetta with a tender smile.

Benedetta breathed in with her eyes closed, the steam further fogging her glasses. Her face shifted, looking younger and briefly fuller. "Oregano. Mint. Clove?"

Bruno cast a questioning glance at Stella, who grinned. "That's right!"

Bruno smiled at his wife, gently stroking a lock of graying hair off her forehead before turning to Stella. "An old game of ours."

Stella felt a pang deep in her ribcage. She searched for something to say and babbled, "I'm sorry I don't have bread. I went to Aldo's in Assisi, but—" She felt like kicking herself. As much as she had imagined she could impose on these decent people by asking them questions or prompting memories, she realized in their company there was no way she could intrude on their grief in this macabre way. She wished she could take the words about the bakery back and leave them unsaid.

Bruno winced a little, but his wife didn't seem to notice. Stella wondered how much she'd known about her son's plans to leave his job in Aramezzo. As his wife looked for a spoon, Bruno whispered to Stella, "You went to Aldo's?"

She nodded. "But I got . . . distracted. I didn't bring anything home."

A thoughtful look passed over Bruno's face. "If only Jacopo had gone to work for him years ago."

Stella didn't know what to say, so she bit her tongue to say nothing.

Bruno seemed to have forgotten Stella's presence as he shook his head, muttering, "I was an idiot for trusting him with anything of mine again."

Stella doubted he meant Aldo.

As Bruno led his wife back through the door to the apartment above the shop, Stella slipped away. They had the sauce. It was enough.

Suddenly, Stella felt awash with exhaustion. It had been a very, very long day. Talking to Marta at Bar Cappellina seemed an age ago.

Coffee.

Just the thought of it perked up her brain.

She walked up the stairs to Aramezzo's middle ring road, unzipping her hoodie as the sun unfurled a final glow.

Only when she arrived at Bar Cappellina did she realize it was far too late in the day for coffee. She could get a glass of wine. That's what she usually got in Italian bars in the afternoon, at least before summer heat made her think longingly of Aperol spritzes—those chilled glasses of sunset-hued Aperol, bubbly with Prosecco and redolent with bitter orange and herbs.

But no, this was not the time for alcohol. She needed all her faculties. She also needed normalcy. Warm milk, maybe? She'd done that before.

As she stood outside the bar, watching the villagers within talk and laugh, she realized. Her hesitation was not about what to order—it was not knowing what would happen if she walked in this bar that had started to feel so familiar. Would the room go stone quiet? Could she bear it? She could overcome her fear of the villagers' animosity to bring someone food, but not with empty hands.

Her shoulders sagged, and she turned away. She noticed Antonio's son, standing outside the florist shop, gazing at the window without seeing. This must be hard for him . . . his friend murdered, his father a suspect. She stepped beside him and touched his arm. "Dario?"

He startled, but when he saw her, he attempted a smile. "Stella. Sorry, I didn't see you."

Stella gestured to the flowers. "They're pretty."

He shrugged. "I guess."

"Listen, I'm really sorry—"

"Please," he cut her off. "I appreciate it, I do. But I need a minute to not think about it."

Stella thought of how much she needed to cook when overwhelmed. "When are you opening the *forno*?"

He shook his head. "I wish I knew. That's up to Papà, and right now he's in no condition. I told him, people need bread, we need income. Standing idle won't bring Jacopo back, but he won't do it."

Stella faltered, unsure how to mention it. "Maybe he doesn't want to face it? The questions I mean."

Dario nodded. "That's probably true. But he won't let me do it either. I think he considers it disrespectful. But Bruno opened up his shop, and Jacopo was his son." He paused. "The police suspect him, you know."

"Bruno? That's ridiculous."

He stared at her for a moment as if checking to see if she was joking. "No. My father. They're gathering evidence. I know they are. Even now. Trying to prove that Papà was so angry at Jacopo for leaving the bakery that they fought and it got out of control."

Stella bit her lip and touched his arm lightly, noticing that his hand gripped a scratch-off lottery ticket. "For what it's worth, I can't believe it was him. He couldn't have."

"I know that." He sighed.

Stella thought for a moment. "When you said he'd been hunting with you that morning—"

Dario ran his hand over his forehead. "That was so stupid. I saw what the police were thinking, it was so obvious. I mean, Papà and Jacopo had been fighting the night before, then Jacopo winds up dead on the bakery floor, sliced across the neck like a loaf of bread. Plus those angry marks on our scheduling whiteboard."

"Angry marks?"

He regarded her for a moment. "You didn't see them? Crossing out Jacopo's name on the schedule?"

She shook her head. "I saw the whiteboard, and now that I'm thinking of it, I did see scribbles, but I didn't think much of it."

"Well, you can bet the police thought something of it. It looked unhinged." He shook his head, muttering, "He keeps digging his own grave."

Stella adjusted her bandana. "So you wanted to give your father an alibi."

He hung his head. "Stupid, I know. I mean, you were right there. You could tell them he was supposed to meet you at the bakery that morning."

"So you and your father didn't go hunting?"

He shook his head. "I went alone. He was supposed to join me, but he never showed up. I wound up going home around three."

"Did you catch anything?"

Dario ducked his head, grinning. "No. We never do. I know it drives Mimmo up a wall. We go out to the woods, cook sausages over a fire, and come home empty-handed. More than once, we've forgotten bullets."

Stella nodded. "And you tried to give him an alibi."

"I had to. Asleep at home? That's hardly ironclad."

Stella flushed. That was her alibi. She ran her toe over the ground. "So, where do you think he was that night?"

"In bed, of course." He regarded her with widened eyes. "Didn't you hear Mamma telling the police? Then again, she hardly looked reliable, she was so flustered. If only one of us had kept our wits about us. "

Stella nodded.

"Anyway, hopefully, the police will figure it out soon and we can all go back to normal." He thought for a moment. "You're helping them, right?"

"Me?" The laugh took Stella by such surprise it triggered a coughing jag. Finally, she caught her breath. "No way they allow me around."

"But you have to help anyway," he pleaded. "You found Severini's killer when they couldn't."

"Severini's killer showed up on my doorstep."

"Because you figured it out! You have to help the police. Whether or not they want you to."

Stella said nothing.

The pleading in his eyes pulled her back to face him before he said, "Please."

"Dario. I'm a suspect."

"You?" His head snapped back in surprise. "Why would you kill Jacopo? I mean, I guess you'd know how to use a lame. But still, that makes no sense."

"My fingerprints were on the lame."

"*What?*"

She frowned. "It's my fault. I found the murder weapon. I shouldn't have touched it."

"You *touched* it? Without *gloves*?" He shook his head, muttering incoherently. Catching his breath, he sighed. "It doesn't matter. You're way too small to take down Jacopo."

Shrugging, she said, "I guess they figure I had the element of surprise on my side?"

He pressed his lips together. "No way. They can't suspect you for long. I'm sure they'll figure out who the real killer is."

She hesitated. "You knew Jacopo. Do you have any guesses?"

"The police asked me the same thing. I'll tell you what I told Luca and Salvo—no. Everyone liked Jacopo. We were like a family on the bakery floor."

Stella ventured, "I'm wondering about Aldo, the baker in Assisi—"

"Yeah, me too. I don't know where he could have gone."

Stella paused. "Gone?"

"You didn't hear? Aldo, he took off."

"But . . . why? Where?"

Dario shrugged, his gaze once again fixed on the branches of yellow blossoms in the window. Listlessly, he said, "I've always liked the smell of Spanish broom."

"Dario...does anyone know where Aldo went?"

He shook his head and for a moment Stella didn't think he would answer. But then he said, "All I know is Luca went to Aldo's bakery yesterday. In Assisi. He says Aldo was agitated throughout the questioning. When Luca went back later with Salvo, Aldo was gone. His wife said within an hour of Luca dropping by to ask questions, Aldo flung up the closed sign and sprinted home. She followed him, but he'd disappeared. The bakery is still closed. Can you imagine, Stella? No one is making bread."

"Dario," she ventured. "There are many bakeries around here. And plenty of home bakers as well."

He shook his head. "None of them use the old way."

She realized what his comment implied—Aldo's discovery. "So you know...that Aldo replicated the yeast?"

"Oh, sure. He couldn't resist calling me and telling me all about it. I guess he didn't consider it polite to wait a minute. Out of respect." Here, Dario hiccuped.

Stella wondered aloud, "And no one knows where he went? His wife must know something."

"She says she doesn't." Dario shrugged. "Also, she told the police that Aldo was late to work the morning of the murder, which piqued their interest, but she went on to tell them that Aldo couldn't have killed Jacopo. Apparently she cried all through their questioning, but she did say that she and Aldo left for work at the same time that Tuesday, but took separate cars. He arrived a half hour after she did and at the time she figured he'd stopped somewhere, which annoyed her since they were expecting a delivery. Anyway, according to her, that's only a half hour of time not accounted for. Not enough to get to Aramezzo, park, walk to the bakery, pull a lame on Jacopo, and then reverse course."

"I'm surprised she's giving him an alibi. When I saw them, she seemed to have nothing but contempt for her husband."

Dario shrugged again. "Who knows? Maybe she's worried about their livelihood. Or maybe she's loyal. Or maybe what she says is true. We won't know until the police find him."

Stella asked, "Do they have any leads at all? About where he could be?"

"I think I heard they were looking for him in places where his relatives live. But that's all I know." Dario sighed and shook his head. "What a mess."

Stella wished she could get Luca to talk to her. Her mind raced. "But this is good, right? I mean, it makes him look pretty suspicious. Which should take pressure off your dad."

Dario considered for a moment and then shook his head. "I don't know, Stella. It was my father's lame. How would Aldo even know where to find it?"

"But—"

"Anyway, I can't envision Aldo driving to Aramezzo, creeping all the way to the bakery and then out again, without anyone seeing him. This isn't a big city where you can have a getaway car with blacked-out windows waiting outside a crime scene."

It did seem strange that no one had seen him—or anyone, actually—in the streets. Sure, nobody but bakers got up at that hour, but somebody must have had insomnia or got up for an early flight for even a drink of water, and peered out the window and seen...*someone*.

She realized she had tuned out in thought, then focused on Dario's words. "I appreciate your optimism, I do. My girlfriend's parents, as soon as they heard, forced her back to Perugia, even though she keeps telling them my father didn't do it."

Stella nodded. She guessed she could understand why parents wouldn't want their daughter fraternizing with the son of a murder suspect. "I'm sorry. I bet you could use that support."

Holding up his lottery tickets, he said, "Plus, she keeps me from buying too many of these." He gave a rueful smile. "Anyway, it's nice to hear when people believe in him. I know my worry can make me look on the dark side."

"You can't think your father did it."

"He loved Jacopo. " Dario sighed. "He might have been angry with him. He might have felt betrayed by him. But I can't picture him hurting one hair on his head. At the same, time...well... I guess I don't know what I believe anymore. "

This Stella could understand.

He frowned for a moment and then shook his head. "I hate all these unknowns. It's making me jumpy. Please. I don't know you well, but Papà speaks highly of you. Stay on this until you figure it out? For him."

She patted his arm. "If the police don't arrest me first, sure."

He pressed his lips together. "They won't. Even they aren't that foolish."

She gestured to his lottery card. "Any luck?"

He tried to smile but failed. "I wish. It's always the same. Even so, I can't help hoping."

Stella's mind whirled as she walked away from Dario. She needed to go home and bake, but she also needed to talk to Domenica and return her keys. She hoped the shop was open now.

As she strode toward the bookstore, she did a mental inventory of the items in her pantry. She was pretty sure she had everything she needed to make the overnight starter and candy the orange peel for *colomba*.

When she arrived at Domenica's, she exhaled with such force, she realized part of her had been holding her breath, wondering why Domenica would close the shop. She pushed open the door and Domenica looked up from a pile of books on her desk. At the sight of Stella, she immediately said, "Where have you been? You wouldn't believe the rumors flying around! I've been so worried!"

"Where have *you* been?" Stella said, dropping into the chair beside Domenica and tossing the keys onto her desk. "I came by and the shop was closed."

"Delivering books to Romina's grandson, so he has something to read while he's recovering from his accident." Domenica patted Stella's knee. "I'm glad to see you. I heard the most ridiculous gossip."

"About me being a suspect?"

Domenica inhaled sharply. "Who told you?"

"The police."

"What! It's *true*? They think you did it? Why in the world would anyone suspect you?" Domenica's rage puffed her up so much, she looked like she might sail right out of her chair to tell the cops a thing or two.

Stella touched her tongue to her top lip. "Well. The thing is, I handed the lame to Luca. So my fingerprints are on it."

"You *what*?" An unfamiliar tabby, the color of pencil lead, vaulted from the printer and dashed to the back of the store, tail lashing.

"I know, Domenica. It was stupid."

"Stupid is one word for it. I can think of a few others." Domenica closed her eyes as if praying for patience and then, not finding it, shook her head in aggravation.

"I said I *know*. You don't have to flambé me for it. Believe me, I feel the full force of my error." Stella rose and began pacing.

Domenica shook her head. "You are simply going to have to learn to control yourself."

Stella spun to face Domenica and considered storming out.

Domenica's sigh recalled her. "I apologize, Stella. Give me a moment. This... threw me. I couldn't stand it if anything happened to you."

Stella turned back, surprised. She'd never known Domenica to talk like this.

"I love that reckless part of you, Stella, I do. Your impetuousness makes you creative and spontaneous, and I enjoy your refreshing lack of a filter."

Stella's mouth dropped open. Nobody had ever, ever articulated a positive side of her impulsiveness.

Domenica went on. "I guess this is the rent for your adorable gift."

Stella thought for a moment. She hadn't heard the notion of rent used this way before. "Kind of steep rent."

"Indeed," Domenica smiled. "Anyway, we'll have to hope the police come up with a better suspect. *Madonna mia*, you must have been shocked when the police told you."

"I had warning. Matteo heard when he was emptying trash at the police station."

"Ah."

"But I didn't believe him at first. Thought he was trying to deflect from me rejecting him."

"You rejected Matteo? But why? You two are such good friends." Domenica frowned.

"Domenica. That's why I had to reject him. It's kinder. I don't like him in that way, and he's better off knowing that."

Domenica's eyes widened, drawing her mouth open until she let out a huge belly laugh.

"I don't think it's all that funny, to be honest," Stella grumbled.

Domenica kept laughing until she had to double over. Her glasses slipped onto the floor and she reached around, trying to find them.

Stella knelt to snatch them up, cleaning the grime off the lenses with her shirt before putting them back on Domenica's nose, muttering, "How you see out of those things, I'll never know."

"Oh, Stella." Domenica tried to catch her breath.

"What, is he like, married or something?"

"Or something." Domenica launched into fresh peals of laughter.

"Are you quite through? I have work to do. A reputation to preserve.

Et cetera, et cetera."

"Oh, my dear. Matteo is gay. Did you not know that?"

The frown vanished from Stella's face. "Gay?"

"Quite."

"Why didn't he tell me?"

"I suppose he figured you knew. Don't you have heaps of gay friends in New York?"

Stella nodded. "Of course. But they're . . . I don't know . . . *out*."

"Oh, *cara*, Matteo *is* out."

"No, I mean, *out* out. My New York friends talk about their relationships, they embrace their lifestyle."

"Not much of either of those in Aramezzo for Matteo to embrace."

Stella thought for a moment. "So everyone knows this?"

Domenica removed her glasses to wipe her eyes. "Sure. Of course."

"It's not a secret? It's strange this is the first time it's come up."

Domenica shook her head. "This is small town Umbria, my dear. People don't carry soapboxes. They accept and move on."

"Does Matteo date?"

"I expect so."

"You don't know?" Stella asked.

Domenica shrugged. "How would I know?"

Stella considered for a moment, then said, "Who does Luca date?"

"He'd like to date you."

Casting her gaze heavenward, Stella wondered how Domenica knew. "Fine. How about before that?"

"Oh, how to count? There was the tourist, but that obviously couldn't last. He dated his high school sweetheart for years, but she went to a different university and it fizzled. Four or five other women over the years, I'd say. He's a romantic, that Luca."

Stella ignored Domenica's eyebrows, their height full of unspoken suggestion. "How about Leonardo? Who has he dated?"

"Why do you ask? Are you interested?"

"Humor me."

Domenica sighed. "You'll know about Marta, of course."

Stella nodded.

Musing aloud, Domenica said, "I don't give that one long. Leonardo is a bit of a player. And Marta . . . well, she might find Leo exciting, but ultimately a single mother needs a constant."

Emphasizing each word, Stella said, "So you know about the love lives of people in this town you hardly talk to, but you know nothing about Matteo's."

Domenica shrugged. "Matteo doesn't talk much about his personal life."

"I get why," Stella muttered.

"Who are we to say? Maybe he's private."

Stella sighed. "Well, that's why I didn't know. That he's gay, I mean."

Domenica shook her head and went back to shuffling her books. "Well, I still say it's pretty heteronormative of you to assume he was straight."

Stella cocked her head to the side. There was something to that.

But where did Domenica pick up lingo like "heteronormative"?

Stella walked home through the cobblestone streets without even relishing the part where the street dipped into a tunnel whose ceiling was the floor of the house above. The nodding heads of the burgeoning grapes on the vine, the irreverent red of a poppy forcing its way through mortar to bloom where nothing should—all of it went unnoticed. Her thoughts swirled, from the murder to the puzzle of Matteo to the murder again.

Once home, Stella took out fresh bowls and made the starter from flour, yeast, and cool water. Putting it aside, she plucked the oranges from the drawer in the refrigerator. She scored the peel into quarters and then pulled them off the orange. She cut each piece into strips and boiled them.

As she worked, she tried to organize her thoughts—about the murder suspects, about Matteo. She realized that she had plenty of friends who identified as queer. So many that in New York, she never bothered to assume that someone walked on one side of the street or the other. Her friends were in and out of relationships with men and women so fluidly, she didn't trouble herself to define them as gay or straight. So why did she assume Matteo was heterosexual?

She fished the orange peel strips out of the pot, then dumped the water and poured in fresh with sugar, heating it until the sugar melted. Then she added back the orange peels.

It hit her. In Aramezzo, she had never seen two women or two men walking hand-in-hand in a romantic way (though there was plenty of affection, including hand-holding, of the platonic type, even with men). Not tourists and definitely not villagers. No pride flags flapped below windows. No flamboyant hairdressers chatted with passersby outside their shops (the woman on the edge of town who cut Stella's hair that one time looked as if she colored her own hair in between clients and spent the entire time chiding Stella for not conditioning as much as her curly hair demanded). No organic farmers with eyebrow piercings and tattoos that looked like the-artist-formerly-known-as-Prince's symbol.

In this small Italian town, there were no options for an alternative life—the only stream was main. So what did people do who didn't quite fit? Those whose gender or sexuality were more fluid, those who trended to spiky dog collars and black lipstick, or even those who prayed to Allah or lit Beltane fires? She guessed they either withstood the spotlight, they moved, or they washed out their bright colors until they blended with the landscape.

Suddenly Stella's stomach twisted. Sad for Matteo, who, yes, was comfortable with who he was enough to be out, but not comfortable standing out enough to chat about his dates or (and she was speculating here) chat about a film's portrayal of a gay relationship. Then she felt angry. Angry at Aramezzo, angry at the world—people should get to be who they were, wherever they lived, not only if they had a New York zip code! And angry with herself for unwittingly contributing to the relentless push toward some imagined normalcy.

Stella tested an orange peel, but it was still opaque.

Could this be what Stella's mother hated about Aramezzo? No, homogeneity couldn't be what Stella's mother despised. After all, Stella's mother had nothing to compare it to, how could she understand the provinciality of the village? Plus, Stella realized a deeper truth. Though town regulations demanded everyone paint their houses in the same color palette, at the level of people, Stella, herself, even as an outsider, had never felt so accepted. She felt sure if she dyed her hair blue tomorrow, it would certainly be fodder for conversation, which could be enough to deter some from outrageous behavior, but she would still be loved.

Stella remembered a phrase from her college psychology course, one of the few she enjoyed before dropping out to go to culinary school. Unconditional positive regard. She had that in Aramezzo.

In fact...

She stopped removing the shiny strips of candied orange peel to a rack as the thought struck her. Stella had found an acceptance from her mother's people that she'd never gotten from her mother—the one person in the world who should have loved her unconditionally. To her mother, Stella never measured up. Except the day she packed her knives for her first job in a Manhattan restaurant.

Sprinkling the orange strips with sugar, Stella wondered how the people of Aramezzo could be so aware of her limitations and yet accept her, when her own mother couldn't even pretend to see her. In fact, Stella's mother could more easily summon warm feelings for the vagrants who showed up at the back of her shop and left with an aluminum tray of baked pasta.

Then again . . . what would happen to Aramezzo's unconditional positive regard toward her if the villagers thought she'd taken one of their own? She had to prove her innocence. But how?

Stella washed up and climbed into bed, shoving aside Barbanera who had curled on her pillow. She felt the cat watching her for a few minutes before curling against her hip. She smiled despite herself and fell into a dreamless sleep, not noticing she'd left the lights on.

FRIDAY

*S*tella woke up on Friday morning, remembering that Domenica mentioned Jacopo's funeral would be held on Monday. If she was a suspect, could she even go to the service? It seemed disrespectful, to say the least.

She thought about Bruno and his wife at the funeral, burying their son without knowing who killed him and why. Her heart ached. They needed resolution.

At the thought, her stomach roiled. She knew she needed to eat, but she was too pent up. Her mind turned to the starter. She itched to get out of the house, but she couldn't bear to come home to another batch of wasted flour.

Stella removed the towel over the bubbling starter, adding more flour and a sprinkle of salt and more yeast, plus a yogurt canister of sugar, and half a stick of butter, as well as two whole eggs and one egg yolk. She debated the flavorings in her cupboard. On impulse, she grated the peel of her last orange along with the lemon. Then she added her last jot of honey and a splash of vanilla. She was about to wrap up when she went to the liquor cabinet to pull out a dusty bottle of rum, adding a tablespoon to the dough.

She kneaded the dough together and noticed her shoulders relaxing. Really, people should make bread instead of doing downward dog. Then again, most people probably didn't have thoughts zipping around in their brains in this kind of unbridled fashion. Stella knew plenty of people who did yoga without even once constructing a grocery list. As for her, she only found that kind of peace while cooking.

The dough formed a smooth ball, and Stella added in the candied orange peel from the night before. She covered the bowl with a clean kitchen towel.

Ideally, she'd be back in a few hours to shape the dough. But then yesterday had gotten completely away from her. Today she needed to connect with Matteo, broker peace with Luca, and track down Antonio. He and Jacopo had been close, and if he didn't kill the boy, he must have some information about who might have wished Jacopo ill.

Stella put the dough in the refrigerator to give herself more time to get home. She liked a slower rise anyway, more flavor in the finished product. That done, she put a plate of food out for Barbanera on an antique tea saucer rimmed with fading gold and stepped outside, breathing in air that seemed rinsed and pure.

Spring in Aramezzo felt like a bit of a miracle.

Shrugging on her hoodie, she decided to take a walk around Aramezzo before beginning the onslaught of her day. She needed the refreshment of cool and soothing waves of silvery olive trees undulating into the distance. The vast distance, the mountains towering as a backdrop, all of it called to her.

Approaching the park where she knew Don Arrigo played *bocce* with the village elders, Stella's ruminations vanished. On the bench, facing the rolling hills . . . could that be Antonio? She hardly recognized him out of his white uniform and sneakers. His reddish hair seemed tousled, as if he'd been in bed for days.

Tentatively, Stella approached him. She inadvertently stepped on a twig and, at the cracking sound, Antonio's head swung around, his eyes landing on her. He recoiled as if burned and shot up, glancing once more at her before bolting away. His feet slid out from under him on the muddy edge of the park, but he regained his balance and fairly ran down Aramezzo's ring road.

Stella remained in position, watching after the baker as he rounded the corner and disappeared. She shook her head and gazed around, noticing Matteo for the first time, at the other edge of the park, trash spear held motionless in his hand. Stella bit her lip and then walked toward him. He dropped his arm with the trash spear and watched her approach, his eyes unblinking.

She'd hoped she would figure out what to say by the time she reached him. But of all times to have a head free of thoughts, she came up empty. All she could do was search his eyes with her own. Initially, his eyes held nothing but coldness, but they softened until both of them stood with tears welling, though not falling. Finally, Stella reached up and embraced Matteo. For a moment, she wondered if he would stand there, motionless, but eventually his arms wrapped around her, one hand still clasped around the trash spear. She squeezed him, breathing in his familiar Matteo scent, like a breeze through a forest. As she drew back, she said, "I'm sorry."

His lip twitched. "For what?"

She thought for a moment. "I'm not totally sure. I know I did something wrong, but I can't articulate what."

He shook his head, smiling. "Stella."

She thought for a moment. "I made assumptions. I guess I'm sorry for not seeing you."

He inclined his head in acknowledgment. "I'm not sure I was showing you what to see."

"Still," Stella said.

He ran his hand over his face. "I'm not good about opening up."

She nodded and gestured toward Aramezzo. "Maybe for obvious reasons."

"Maybe," he shrugged. "But sometimes I wish I could be braver.

Like you."

She laughed mirthlessly. "Oh, Matteo. I am not brave."

"Sure you are. You are your own person, no matter what Aramezzo thinks of you."

She thought about this. "Matteo, that's because I'm already an outsider here. It's easier. You should have seen me in kitchens. I promise, there were plenty of times I hid my true feelings, my true self." Then again, there were other times when her reckless need to say her truth landed her in boiling water. Like when she revealed to a *New York Times* journalist that one of Manhattan's favorite chefs had a history of offensive behavior to up-and-coming women in his kitchens. Sometimes it took nothing but a cold cocktail, a hot meal, and warm conversation to lull her into a sense of security that prompted her to drop her guard. She sighed, remembering the backlash that forced her to flee New York's restaurant scene.

Matteo's eyes stared into hers, joining her wince of pain at the memory.

She sighed. "Anyway, I guess we all do that, right? Keep a part of ourselves hidden?"

"I wish we didn't have to."

"And maybe we don't." She considered. "I can tell you this much, Matteo. I'm here for it. Whenever you're ready to bring out the hidden stuff."

He smiled. "I know."

"Unless you are the murderer, in which case, honestly? I'd rather not know."

His face fell. "I've been asking around. Stella, there's no way they can believe it's you. I think Captain Palmiro is on some sort of power trip."

She adjusted her bandana. "We had what probably passed for a conversation in his book, and he let it slip that he was none too pleased with the attention I got for finding Severini's killer."

He sighed. "Palmiro needs to retire. He is way too old for this."

"Or too tired."

"Or too tired. Or too something." He grinned. "Yes, I can say quite definitively he is too something for this."

She grinned back, but then her face fell. "But my fingerprints..."

"Psh!" Matteo said, waving his hand. "Come on. You are half Jacopo's size."

"Hey!"

Matteo put his hand on her shoulder and looked into her eyes. "Stella, I adore you. But you have to know you're tiny."

Her chest swelled. "I prefer the term 'pocket-sized'."

"Ha! Well, the point is the same. How could someone of your...diminutive stature—"

"Better. Points for creativity."

"—reach up with a knife at the level of Jacopo's neck?"

She thought for a moment and then sighed. "I guess they aren't trying to figure out how I couldn't have done it. They're having too good a time figuring out how I could. If pressed, they'd probably come up with some notion like I dropped something on the ground and when Jacopo went to pick it up, I did the deed. Or maybe in their heads, there's a chair involved. Who's to know?"

Matteo frowned and gazed off. "You really thought I was hitting on you? You got that vibe from me?"

She startled at the about turn. "I *never* got that vibe from you, Matteo. That's what threw me. I think because Luca had asked me out about two minutes earlier—"

"What!" But he looked more bemused than surprised.

"You knew, didn't you?"

A smile inched across his face. "It was pretty obvious, the way he kept asking questions about you. And the way he always happened to turn up."

Stella gave him a withering stare. "I'm sure you have a good reason for not warning me."

He grinned. "I thought I had."

"Anyway," Stella went on. "He clearly is not used to anyone spurning his advances. He got all cold and defensive, and well, with one thing and another, I made the colossal mistake of handing him the lame."

"That'll show him." He smiled.

"Right?" She smiled back. "My point is this . . . when you began telling me I was a suspect yesterday, you sounded a lot like Luca. Sheepish or whatever. Hence the taste of foot in my mouth."

He chuckled. "Anyway, back to the main point. Even if the police are enjoying this little dance—and say what you want about Luca, I doubt he's in on the entertainment value of viewing you as a suspect—"

"Salvo didn't look too keen, either."

Matteo's eyes flashed. "Yes, your prints are on the lame. And now that I'm thinking about it, you were the one who found the body, which puts you at the bakery around the time of death. But still . . . no way! It's physically near impossible. And furthermore! What motive could you possibly have for wanting Jacopo dead?"

She sighed. "According to them, Jacopo was planning on starting a pastry shop and I feared he'd put me out of business."

Eyebrows constricted, Matteo said, "That makes no sense. You don't sell pastries. You give them to guests. And to the rest of Aramezzo. At the bargain price of free, I might add."

Shrugging, Stella said, "They didn't seem to want to notice that part."

"Besides!" Matteo rolled on. "That's ridiculous! Where would Jacopo get the money to open a bakery? It's not like Bruno has extra euros lying around. The man had to open up the week between the murder and Jacopo's funeral! And I happen to know that apprentice bakers don't even make as much as civil service employees like myself."

"These are all good points, but like I said—"

"Plus! Where would this bakery be? In Aramezzo?"

"I'm guessing, otherwise it doesn't work as a plausible motive for me."

"This town isn't rolling in real estate. There aren't that many empty shops. We'd hear about it if someone was taking over a lease to open a pastry shop," Matteo said.

"Especially Jacopo. I mean, a pastry shop would have solved everyone's stress. His father would have him out from Antonio. Antonio would still be the only bread baker using traditional methods."

"Exactly! This would be every third conversation at Bar Cappellina."

"Unless." Stella cocked her head in thought.

"Unless?"

"Unless," she thought aloud. "Unless this fell into his lap right before he died. Like maybe he and his girlfriend—"

"Girlfriend? What girlfriend?" Matteo frowned. "He wasn't dating anyone."

She lifted her eyebrows. "Or he was keeping it under wraps. I think he was dating Aldo's wife."

"What!"

She nodded. "I know it sounds crazy—"

"Aldo is like, what, sixty? His wife must be the age of Jacopo's grandparents!"

She shook her head. "No, I met her. Or at least saw her. She is older than Jacopo, but not by a lot. Maybe five years, ten at the outside."

"Whoa, Aldo must have robbed the cradle there."

"I know. But I'm fairly certain she and Jacopo were . . . involved. I also know she makes pastry." She wondered aloud, "Maybe the two of them were going to open a shop?"

"I guess that's possible."

Matteo and Stella looked up as the mayor passed, whistling. Stella's gaze followed Marcello as he sauntered through the tunnel that led to Aramezzo. "He's caught up in this somehow."

"How do you figure?"

She shrugged. "I don't know. He seems to know things. And

something he said after Jacopo died . . . it didn't sit well. Like a bad clam."

Matteo chuckled. "You are too much."

She returned her gaze to Matteo. "About the trash. Have you found anything suspicious?"

He shook his head. "No. But I do know they are trying to find the shoes that match that footprint."

"Right, the footprint. I almost forgot."

He nodded. "So far, nothing. The shoes Antonio wore to the bakery the morning of the murder didn't match the print. And the police have taken shoes from him and the rest of the apprentices. Nothing. Which is strange right? You think there'd at least be blood on something."

She shrugged. "Lots of ways to get rid of blood on clothes—bury it, burn it, send it downriver."

"I guess." He looked around. "Well, I'd better get back to work."

She patted his arm. "I'm glad I ran into you."

His smile flowed easily, lighting his face. "Same." As she walked away, he pointed at her muddy footprints in the street. "You know, we're in a good place. Don't make me nag at you about my freshly cleaned streets."

She laughed, but her laughter cut off quickly, air escaping a balloon.

"Stella," Matteo said. "I'm joking. I don't clean the streets around the park. I'm collecting trash. See?" He held up his spear.

"No, it's not that. It's . . ." She looked back at her footprint and then the spot where the baker had slipped. "It occurred to me. Antonio, he was just here. Did you see him?"

"Sure. I saw him when he arrived and tried to give him his distance. I can tell he didn't want company. He did the same thing yesterday. Poor guy must have a hard time catching a clean breath."

"Did you note his shoes?"

"His shoes? No. Why?"

She looked down at her Doc Martens and the tread they left on the ground. "He slipped when he sprinted away. And now I'm realizing . . . his shoes. His shoes were *dress* shoes. The kind with no tread."

"Okay. And?"

"Well, have you ever seen him in anything other than those white sneakers?"

"No, but I hardly ever see him not baking."

"The footprint outside the bakery, that had a tread."

"Yes, I know. I saw it before the rain washed it out."

"And now the baker is sporting dress shoes. Even though it's not a dress occasion. In other words, he's wearing shoes without tread. Why?"

"Well," Matteo thought. "Why not?"

Stella shrugged and turned away, saying, "Maybe it's because we were just talking about shoes, but something about this seems strange to me." She started walking away, lost in her thoughts.

"Okay, well, I'll catch you later, Stella," he called to Stella's receding back. She gave a distracted wave and moved as if on autopilot to Bar Cappellina.

It felt risky to enter the bar. After all, her reluctance to bear the brunt of everyone's accusations hadn't faded. But she needed to do this. Something in her knew she needed to confront the fear.

Stella paused as she opened the door. The conversation hit her like a wave and didn't slow with her presence. She felt her heartbeat slow. People either must not know, or they wrote off her being a person of interest as easily as Matteo and Dario had. She could hardly squeeze through the villagers to reach the bar and flag down Roberto for an espresso.

She stood quietly, rotating on the spot to eavesdrop on the conversational pockets all around her. All of which seemed to be centered on not being able to get bread. She heard snippets:

"Why can't the police figure this out already so we can get back to normal?"

"How could it ever be normal, with Jacopo gone?"

"I mean, it's sad, sure, but come on. We need to eat."

"So eat! Nobody is stopping you."

A new voice: "I went to Assisi for bread."

"Not Aldo's!"

"No, though I would have. It's stupid to not go there because Antonio has a beef with him."

"Some loyalty you have!"

"You can't eat loyalty. Anyway. His shop is shuttered up tight. Nobody knows where he is! So I went to another one, can't remember the name."

"And? How was it?"

"Eh. About what you'd expect."

"I heard about a bakery in Spello that bakes their bread the old way."

"What! Why haven't I heard about it? Spello isn't that far away."

Stella could practically hear the shrug. "I asked Dario about it, and he says that's a rumor. Though he thought I meant the bakery on Spello's outskirts, and I found out later the good one is in the center."

"Why can't Dario open the bakery? He's worked there for years. He must know how."

"You know how it goes. Antonio won't let him."

As Stella accepted the cup of warm and nutty espresso from Romina, she leaned forward to ask, "Has it been like this all morning?"

"All morning."

"Can't they give it a rest?" Though she was mostly grateful that word of her "guilt" hadn't trickled to the bar yet. If it had, there was no way all eyes wouldn't be on her. She sighed. It was only a matter of time.

Romina stared at Stella for a moment before saying, "In the midst of all this sadness, you'd deprive them of some excitement?"

Stella sighed. "Excitement is overrated. I'll stick to boring. Bland. Give me an Umbrian bread sort of life."

Romina stiffened. Her husband Robert must have noticed because he looked up, concerned, and moved towards her. Finally, Romina said, "What do you mean?"

Stella shrugged, stirring her coffee. "It's simple. The bread here is unsalted. So it's a great vehicle, it makes the best bruschetta once you slather it with local olive oil and sprinkle it with sea salt. And I love how it works in a *panzanella*. Best bread salad I've made. But on its own? It's uninspiring."

The room went silent. Even Luisella, in her corner, went chillier than usual.

Cristiana, who Stella hadn't noticed down the bar, spoke slowly, stretching out her words in case Stella was slow to understand. "Stella, is this your American sense of humor?"

Stella shook her head and opened her mouth to further articulate her issues with Umbrian bread, but at the steely stares all around her, she paused. "Um, well. I mean. Yeah? Yes, I'm kidding around. Don't know what came over me, there."

Roberto carefully dried his already dry hands. "Do you know why Umbrian bread is unsalted?"

She aimed for a casual shrug that she feared came off as a twitch. "I think so. Isn't it that in the middle ages, the pope tried to levy a huge tax on salt?"

Cristiana's bandy-legged father piped up, "But Umbrians didn't want to put any more money in Pope Paul III's pockets! So we stopped using salt!"

Orietta, the pharmacist, added with a note of pride, "It's that kind of stubbornness that helped us weather all the skirmishes between popes and the Holy Roman Empire."

Cristiana's father went on, "Our ancestors had to decide what to do with the limited salt—put it in bread or use it to cure prosciutto. They made the only sensible decision. After all, we can live with unsalted bread—we can even make it great!—but we cannot preserve pork without salt. Which is why our prosciutto is saltier than other regions. We put all we had into curing."

Cristiana narrowed her eyes at Stella. "Do you have a problem with our prosciutto, too?"

Stella raised her hands. "No! I love it! It's better than the prosciutto from Parma!"

Muttering broke around the bar, and Stella could hear voices debating why Umbrian prosciutto was so much better. Some argued for Umbrian pig diets, some for how Umbrians processed those pork legs. Cristiana looked slightly mollified, but still suspicious.

Unfortunately, Stella then blurted, "But there were lots of things Umbrians did in the middle ages they wouldn't dream of now. Why not salt the bread?"

At the prickly silence, Stella muttered the rest of her thought under her breath, in English. "People ate dormice in medieval Italy, but I don't see them on menus today."

Silence continued, so Stella tried to explain. "All I'm saying is, progress isn't all bad. Why not add some salt to the bread? It's not like Pope Paul III will cackle in his grave, smug that he always knew we'd cave. And everyone would enjoy it much more."

Romina shook her head. "But Stella, our cuisine has grown up around that unsalted bread. If we salted it now, everything would be out of balance."

Stella ran her lips together, thinking. "Okay, you may have something there."

A collective sigh washed over the bar. Romina reached around the bar to pat Stella's hand. "You'll get used to it. I bet within a year or two, you'll gladly reach for Umbrian bread over any other kind."

Stella tried to smile. But there was no chance. No chance she'd ever prefer Umbrian bread, and no chance she'd still be in this bread wasteland in a few years. Then she remembered . . . the *torta al testo*. That could very well absolve Umbrian bread's sin of saltlessness. But it couldn't be reason to stay.

With the weight of all those eyes boring into her, she had never been so happy to have Veronica, the mayor's wife, step into a room. The woman commanded all attention, leaving Stella to sip her espresso in peace. After a few moments, she tuned into Veronica's conversation with Cristiana, who looked all around the room as if wishing to be somewhere other than here. Stella could relate.

Veronica ordered two glasses of milk and then intoned. "We've simply got to get Antonio to open the bakery. He hasn't been arrested, so why not? I've sent Marcello to reason with him."

Cristiana's father didn't seem particularly impressed with Veronica's assurance. "There's no way. I brought Antonio and his wife groceries last night. He is in no shape to open the bakery."

"Ah," tinkled Veronica. "But you don't understand the power of my Marcello's influence."

Cristiana's father shook his head, muttering.

Veronica nodded, as if everyone had voiced loud agreement. "Right? When Marcello wants something, he gets it. I should be the first to know about that!"

Okay, this grabbed Stella's attention, and more eyes turned to Veronica, who looked around simpering as she added, "I mean, with my theatrical star rising, it's not like I had aspirations to become the wife of a small-town mayor. But Marcello convinced me, and here I stand!"

Stella couldn't help herself. "You were an actress?"

Veronica's wide smile seemed at odds with the coldness glittering in her eyes. "You know that! I'm sure you Googled me when we met. One article called me the darling of Italy's Hollywood on the Tiber. Remember, Luisella? It was the same article that failed to mention you."

All eyes turned to Luisella, still propped on her stool in the corner with her pink quilted leather purse set neatly on the tall bistro table, its gold link chain glinting. Luisella glared at Veronica and then pointedly looked away.

"Poor Luisella," Veronica clucked. "Always following my shadow."

Stella's eyes widened. She remembered the day she first met Luca, how he'd looked into Bar Cappellina and mentioned that since he saw Veronica at the bar, it meant Luisella wouldn't enter. What was the beef between these two? Veronica always lorded over anyone, that was hardly new. But why this bite of menace towards Luisella? And how did their backstories collide to bring two actresses to Aramezzo? Stella wished Luca were here. She could imagine his slow grin, the flash of a dimple and his one tooth overlapping the other, the way he would lean toward her until she could smell the musky woodsiness that must be his aftershave. How he'd lower his eyes, until his eyelashes, thick as paintbrushes, rested on his cheek as he murmured an aside to clarify the dynamics playing out in front of them.

Now that the bar was silent, all eyes on Veronica, when they weren't darting to Luisella, Veronica lifted one of her dachshunds to the bar to lap at the glass of milk she'd ordered. Drops of milk mixed with drool speckled the gleaming bar. Stella sensed more than heard Romina's sigh. Veronica waved one ring-laden hand as she said, "In any case, Marcello will know how to compel Antonio. He always does."

Veronica placed the dog gently on the floor and picked up its twin to lap up the second glass of milk. "Rest assured, the bakery will be open by Sunday. Monday at the latest."

"Sunday is the bakery's closed day. And Monday is the funeral." Cristiana looked like she regretted the words as soon as they flew from her mouth. Stella smiled, glad to see she and Cristiana shared a certain heedlessness.

Veronica turned to arch one perfectly shaped eyebrow at Cristiana.

The bar door opened and Matteo popped his head in. "Stella? I need you. Something's come up."

Matteo's voice seemed to break a spell, and the bar resumed its chatter. Stella threaded through the villagers in the center of the bar to work her way to the register. She counted out ninety cents and waved a goodbye to Romina, who, she was happy to see, seemed to have let go of Stella's bread insult. Perhaps she'd forgotten? No, based on Stella's recent revelations, she figured it more likely that Romina, and the rest of the bar, chalked up Stella's bread ignorance to her eccentricity, hopefully without altering their conclusion that she was a worthy member of their community.

Stella slipped outside and said, "Thanks for rescuing me."

He peeked back into the bar and his gaze landed on Veronica, still holding court as Cristiana inched away. He grinned, "Veronica in rare form?"

She hooked her arm through his, glad of their ease again. They began walking, Matteo leading the way as Stella responded, "She was going on and on about some history between her and Luisella—"

"My mother mentioned that a few times, but I don't know the details—"

"And she kept hitting this point about how Marcello would get Antonio to open the bakery."

He thought for a moment. "How? We both saw how skittish Antonio is. I doubt he'd even open his front door for Marcello, let alone open the bakery."

"I was thinking the same, but then I remembered . . . The night before he died, Jacopo had a meeting with the mayor."

"I heard about that." Matteo nodded.

"I'm sure everyone did. But I saw Jacopo after, and he looked, if anything, more stressed than he had earlier. I tried asking Marcello about that conversation, but he was pretty cagey. Do you think the mayor could have threatened Jacopo?"

"I wouldn't put it past him. Or, more likely, he pushed Jacopo where he knew he'd crack."

"Like threatening Bruno, or his butcher shop." Stella sucked in her bottom lip, thinking. "I know he tried that angle, too."

"That's why I'm here."

"Did something happen to Bruno?" Stella's voice escalated.

"No, that's not what I mean. I'm thinking about the situation in general. Remember back at the park?"

"You mean like a half hour ago?"

"Yes, that." Matteo smiled.

"You have to give me credit for a better short-term memory than that."

"Can I finish? Or shall we spend the day bantering?"

"Sorry." Stella grinned. "I guess I'm enjoying things being normal between us again. I've missed you."

"We were at odds for like three minutes."

"Four," Stella countered.

Matteo nudged her shoulder with his own, then pulled her through the town exit. "So we were talking about the clothes, about how someone might have gotten rid of them."

"Bury, burn, or send downriver."

"*Esatto*. Well, it reminded me. About once a year, Mimmo complains about people throwing garbage off this cliff."

"Why should he care about illegal dumping? He's hardly a paragon of societal virtue."

"True, but—"

"Hunting," they said together.

Matteo nodded and went on. "So I thought . . . it's not burying, burning, or sending downriver, but . . . if someone was in a pinch, maybe that would be a quick option?"

"So you want to talk to Mimmo?"

He shook his head. "I think I can spare us that particular

unpleasantness. Whenever he complains, I bring the truck to haul off the illegal trash. So I know the spot."

Stella nodded, understanding where Matteo led them. "It's always the same place?"

Matteo shrugged. "As long as I've been working here, yes."

"But . . . why? Why would people always dump in the same place? Unless it's the same people?"

He shook his head and gestured toward his trash truck, waiting at the town exit. "I doubt it, based on the assortment of bags. Some paper, some black plastic, some white plastic. Sometimes an old toaster or a broken shovel. I suspect it's all flung off the same spot because it's a short walk from Aramezzo, and you can drop things off a precipice, which means they fall far below, out of sight."

Stella climbed in the tiny cab, and they rolled away. As they drove, Matteo pointed out the spot above where people could stand while tossing trash and then aimed the truck down the hill.

Stella said, "It's not a road. Can the truck make it?"

Matteo nodded. "It's never been a problem. Farmers use this space between the trees to get to their fields, so there's an informal track, even though there's not a road."

The trash truck jerked and bumped over the uneven terrain. Stella was on the verge of asking if she could get out and walk when Matteo pulled to a stop.

The hush of the forest made talking feel vulgar and crass, but it did nothing to quiet the thoughts ping-ponging in her head. She followed Matteo, pushing branches away from her face. Strands of blurring gossamer tickled her cheeks, and she jumped, realizing she'd walked right into a spider web.

Matteo stopped and pointed to the ground between the trees ahead of them. Three bags, two black and a white, lay in a heap at the foot of the cliff, along with what looked like the remains of a rabbit pen.

"Not much here," Stella breathed a sigh of relief. She'd imagined a pile of bags and didn't relish the idea of rooting through heaps of someone's refuse.

"I cleared it out not that long ago," Matteo said. "Should we start?"

"No time like the present," Stella agreed. But neither of them moved. They caught each other's eye and broke into chuckles. Stella added, "You'd think you at least would be used to this."

He shook his head. "This may be hard to believe, but I never pick up a bag of trash wanting to investigate the insides. And also? I faint at the sight of blood. Not looking forward to losing any masculine status I've acquired by collapsing here in the woods."

"You have to know I'd run straight to Mimmo to tell him all about it."

"You wouldn't dare."

She gave him a mysterious smile. "Better not faint on me, then."

He nudged her. "Then you better go first."

She nodded with a sigh. "All right." She picked up one of the black bags. "Should I open it right here? It'll get trash everywhere."

"Good point," Matteo agreed. "Let's cart all three bags to the truck. I have to take them in, anyway. This gives me longer until Mimmo's next complaint."

"And the rabbit pen?"

"Leave it," Matteo grunted, picking up the two black trash bags.

Stella picked up the last one, pleased with its lightness until the odor seeped out and she dropped it. "Aw, man! This one smells like stinky diapers!"

Matteo turned, drops of sweat standing on his forehead. "Did you want to switch?"

"No," Stella muttered, kicking at the bag. Its give suggested she'd accurately guessed the contents. She heaved it up and tried not to breathe through her nose as she jogged to the truck.

Once they loaded all three bags, they paused, staring. The bags looked so innocent. What might they hold?

Stella poked at a black bag. "Should we open them here? Or . . . somewhere else?"

She realized she had no idea how landfills or garbage dumps or whatever worked in Italy. This seemed the kind of moment where Matteo could opine on local trash systems, deriding her lack of informed opinions on the matter. Luckily, he only dragged his hand over his face, squeezing his chin before saying. "I dunno."

"Matteo. You need to have an opinion."

"I don't know! It's not like I've ever been in search of bloody clothes before."

She waited.

Finally, he exhaled in such a controlled way she wondered if he'd discovered some mindfulness app. He nodded to himself and said, "Let's take it to the dumpster outside Aramezzo. That way we can trash them as soon as we're done. And if we find something, we can cart it directly to the police."

Stella didn't like the idea of the police knowing about her "meddling," as they'd call it, and Matteo must have picked up on her hesitation because he added, "If we find anything, I'll take it in. I mean, that looks pretty plausible, right? A trash man bringing in some suspicious trash?"

She nodded. "You were depositing trash from the vicinity of the bakery to the police. Easy enough to say you figured they'd want this. You don't even have to say you looked inside it."

Matteo ran his hands over his face. "Plus, there's probably nothing in it. No bloody clothes at all."

"No bloody clothes. Super unlikely."

They nodded at each other and hopped back into the truck, Stella trying vainly to not imagine what they might find in the bags. Even if they didn't find bloody clothes, she hardly relished the idea of sorting through the trash someone felt deserved a pitch off a cliff rather than the sensible option of putting it out for Matteo to cart away.

At a slapping, grinding sound, Stella's ruminations on the bags' contents shoved themselves into the corner of her brain. She asked Matteo, "What's going on?"

Matteo grimaced, throwing the truck into gear and alternating the clutch and the gas. "The rain the other night. It's made the track muddy. And the engines in our 'pocket-sized'," he paused, grunting, as he barely avoided stalling the motor, "vehicles are finicky at the best of times."

Stella knew what he meant. A neighbor had offered her the use of his three-wheeled Ape when she said she needed to get her olives to the *frantoio* for pressing, and she'd found the mechanism so baffling she'd abandoned the attempt and carted her olives by foot. Luckily, there had only been the one bucket.

The truck seized and then slipped. Stella braced herself against the dashboard as the truck rolled downhill. She wondered if she should get out and walk, but she could hardly leave Matteo in the truck, his face white and grim as he alternated the pedals with some wizardry on the steering unit. At the very least, she needed to not distract him.

They slipped another few feet and Stella tensed, waiting for the inevitable slide down the hill. Would they crash against the trees, be thrown clear of the truck to land in a heap with the garbage, which she was now convinced contained bloody clothes because of course they would.

The engine caught. The wheels spun for a heart-stopping moment before they found purchase, and the truck chugged slowly up the hill. Stella swallowed her cheer, not wanting to annoy Matteo, whose eyes stared fixedly at the road as he continued fluttering his feet against the pedals.

Finally, they cleared the top of the hill and Stella inhaled deeply. They made it. Now she cheered and Matteo tossed her a look of tired triumph as he chugged along the road. He assumed his casual air—pointing out the communal ovens, the baker's house, Matteo's best friend from high school's house who had gone on to play professional soccer, and the water fountain that villagers still used despite the ubiquitous running water, because they believed it sacred.

"Sacred? Why sacred?" Stella asked.

Matteo shrugged, pulling alongside the industrial dumpster. "I can't keep all the folklore straight. You'll have to ask Cosimo."

Stella touched the pendant hanging around her neck and nodded. She hoped Cosimo was writing all this stuff down. If the current generation was like Matteo, soon those stories would be as extinct as those dormice on menus.

Matteo threw the truck into park and climbed out. Stella followed, and they stood staring at the back of the truck. Matteo said softly, "I guess we should feel grateful that we didn't lose any of these bags?"

"Hardly feels like a treat worth savoring, but yes. I guess." Stella nodded.

"Let's flip a coin for who starts and we'll alternate."

"Okay," Stella said, relieved to have a plan. "But . . . there's probably nothing in there, right? Maybe banana peels or something innocent like that."

Matteo turned to look at her. "Why banana peels?"

She shrugged. "Seems the most innocuous thing I could think of."

He kept his eyes on her. "You don't think an enormous bag full of banana peels would be sinister?"

"Matteo," she practically stamped her foot. "You're stalling."

"You're right, you're right, I know you're right." He pulled a coin out of his pocket. "Call it in the air. Heads or tails."

"You do that in Italy, too? Or did you get this from watching American cinema?"

He sighed. "Not everything is borrowed from you Yankees, you know. *Testa o croce*, heads or tails. Ancient Romans did it, too."

Her eyes lit up. "You're kidding!"

"No, in fact . . . " He stopped and glared at Stella. "Now who's stalling?"

"Okay, okay. Not the moment for intercultural comparisons. Heads!" she said, realizing Matteo had tossed the coin.

"Tails." Matteo grinned, holding the coin out to Stella for verification.

Stella sighed. "Just my luck." She twisted the pendant between her fingers.

Matteo made a chivalrous gesture of allowing her into the truck bed, and she chose a black bag. She already knew that the contents of the white bag were foul. Hopefully, she hadn't gagged too much carrying it. She hoped Matteo would choose it next, rather than leaving it for her.

Stella picked at the knot at the top of the bag, until Matteo nudged her with his pocketknife. She nodded her thanks and opened it, pushing the tip against the top of the bag carefully so it didn't rip, spilling the contents all over her. Pulling open the hole until she could peer inside, she moved the contents around from the outside of the bag. She sighed in relief.

From behind her, she heard Matteo say, "Banana peels?"

"Better," she grinned. "It's clothes, but not the kind you wear to a murder. It's all...shoot what's the word?"

"What word?"

"The Italian word for what ladies wear to seduce men. Like skimpy nightgowns. This may say too much about my Italian sex life, but in all those kitchens I worked in, I never learned the word."

She heard Matteo chuckle. "*Biancheria intima*."

"*Biancheria intima*," she said and then straightened. "Well, that's all that's in here."

She hopped down from the truck.

Matteo frowned. "Why would someone dump a bag full of lingerie over a cliff?"

"Beats me," Stella shrugged. "My guess is someone is desperate not to let her husband, partner, or parent know about her...proclivities."

"You know the word proclivities but not lingerie?"

"You'd be surprised how much chefs talk about their inclinations in the kitchen," she shrugged. "And now who's stalling? Again."

He nodded grimly and leapt up into the truck bed, reaching out a hand for his pocketknife.

Stella folded it closed for safety and handed it to him. Matteo pulled it open and reached for the other black bag. *Rats*, Stella thought, the stinky one is mine. He slashed at the top of the bag and stretched the slit into a hole.

He froze at a shout from up the road. "Hey!"

Slowly, they turned to see the mayor striding toward them.

Matteo offered a tentative smile. "What's up, Signor Sindaco?"

The mayor seemed to have misplaced his usual genial pomposity. He glared from Stella to Matteo and back to Stella. "What do you two think you're doing?"

Matteo gestured to the bags. "We found these bags below the cliff over there." Was it Stella's imagination, or did the mayor pale a bit? Matteo didn't seem to notice anything as he continued, "We're putting them where they belong. It is part of my job." Matteo failed to sound as sure of himself as Stella assumed he'd intended.

As Matteo reached again for the bag, the mayor threw up his hands. "Stop! I've decreed all trash as police property. Until this murder is solved."

Stella's eyebrows rose. "You decreed this? I missed a decree. Matteo, did you get a decree?"

But Matteo was standing with his mouth hanging open, like a cartoon character bonked on the head with an anvil. Stella sighed. She loved her friend, but he was no good in a crisis. Turning back to the mayor, she said, "We found this trash. Seems like it's ours until we see fit to hand it over."

Marcello's eyes narrowed. "Signorina Mazzoli—"

"Buchanan."

The mayor ran over her correction. "As I understand it, you are a suspect in this murder."

"That's 'person of interest,' actually." The whole thing suddenly felt ridiculous. Was this man seriously telling her she had no right to poke through trash she found? Through her simmering anger, she pretended to look around. "I don't see anyone arresting me."

"A matter of time, I'm sure." The mayor turned to Matteo. "Matteo, you've always been a good boy. Since you were small, even when your brother ran off the rails, you have been a model citizen. Don't let this bastard corrupt you."

Matteo stared at his feet for a moment and then he jumped down from the truck bed. Marcello smiled and patted Matteo's shoulder. "That's right. Now get along with you. I noticed some bird droppings on the garbage can in the *piazza*."

Nodding, Matteo trudged away. Stella couldn't believe this. She stared from the mayor to Matteo and back to the mayor. This felt like a scene from Dracula. Did the mayor have Matteo in his thrall? Was he really an ancient vampire? Of course not, that made no sense, but neither did Matteo's blind submission to an out-of-bounds mayor.

She shot a look at Marcello, bile rising in her throat. "You can't talk to him like that."

Shrugging, Marcello said, "I can talk to him any way I like. Perk of the job. Now you best get out of here before I call Captain Palmiro."

"But I didn't do anything!"

Marcello lifted his shoulders in an approximation of a shrug. "Frankly, I'm not sure he cares. He seems pretty intent on making your life as difficult as you've made his."

The truth of this was too much for Stella to deny.

The mayor made a flicking gesture. "Go clean up. You need a shower."

Her anger rose again. She watched Matteo, still trudging away. Despite his lanky frame, he looked like a child, grounded by a stern parent. Seeing the inward set of his shoulders, her sense of betrayal shriveled like grapes in the sun. She cast the mayor one more furious look. He'd already turned away, as if he could no longer be bothered with her.

Stella watched as the mayor prodded the hole in the bag open to peer inside. The contents shifted, rotating the opening downward until Stella caught a glimpse of white. Marcello snatched it back closed and glared at Stella before taking out his cell phone. Dialing the police, no doubt.

She sighed. At least it wasn't a flash of red. Of course, the bloody clothes could be buried deeper in the bag. She shook her head and jogged to catch Matteo, now approaching the park on the right, while Aramezzo towered over them to the left. She reached his side and breathlessly said, "What was that?"

He paused and looked at her, as if surprised to no longer be alone. "Oh. Hi, Stella."

"Hi? Why did you take off?" She gestured behind her, where the mayor now seemed deep in conversation.

He shook his head. "You heard him."

"I heard him spouting off like a TSA agent on a bad day."

Matteo ran his hand over his face. "Right."

"That doesn't mean we have to listen to him."

"Doesn't it?" He retied his ponytail, mumbling something Stella couldn't catch.

She stared at Matteo.

He dropped his gaze to a spot on the ground and said, "I'm sorry, Stella. I let you down. I should have stayed and . . . fought for your honor. Or something."

Her eyebrows screwed up. "Wait. What, now?"

"I don't know. He said mean things about you. I shouldn't have let him. I guess."

She shook her head "Matteo, this isn't the middle ages. Neither of us fits the narrative of the damsel needing a knight to rescue her."

His gaze remained on the ground as he said, "I didn't know what to do. I didn't like what he was saying, but he's the mayor."

She nodded. "I bet you always got your homework turned in on time, didn't you?"

Finally, he looked up. "Of course."

"Pencils always sharpened, chores always done before the TV went on."

He nodded. "What does this have to do with—"

"Unlike your brother," Stella added.

After a pause, Matteo said, "You think I'm a rule follower because my brother wasn't."

She shrugged. "Makes sense."

Pressing his lips together, he said, "I don't know if that's the reason. I always figured my mother needed me, since my father died when I was young."

"Oh, right. That too."

"Anyway, I guess I did what I always do. I felt uncomfortable, so I got out of there. But I left you there alone."

Stella threaded her arm through Matteo's. "Like I said, I didn't need you to take care of me. I just didn't like you allowing Marcello to talk to you like that. You deserve respect."

He looked at her, surprised. "From the *mayor*? You think so?"

"I know so." She squeezed his arm. "He's a small time mayor, it's not like he's the president. Anyway, my bet? That lingerie was his."

He grinned. "You're kidding."

"Most certainly not," Stella said. "Why else would he be so intent on getting us out of there?"

He shrugged. "Maybe his wife's?"

She nodded. "Maybe! They could be turning over a new bedroom leaf. From now on, it'll be all nurses' uniforms and maid's aprons."

He smiled, then said, "What was with him calling you a bastard?"

She shrugged. "I figured in Italian that worked like mongrel or mutt. You know, someone so irredeemable it calls their parentage into question."

He frowned. "I guess. I haven't heard it used like that before."

They walked under the town arch. When they got to the ring road, they paused. Matteo said, "So we did all that for nothing."

She shrugged. "It was a good idea. Maybe we should ask Mimmo if there are other dumping spots."

"I'll let you take over that conversation." He gestured to the stairs. "Are you going up?"

She nodded. "Yes, I need to talk to Cosimo about getting my fireplace surround." She caught sight of Luca walking toward them and said, "But I'll do that later."

"Cosimo's shop is closed, I saw when I was sweeping."

She turned to him. "Closed? It's not his closed day."

He shook his head. "It's not like the town is in dire need of antiques. The man can move slowly."

"Still . . ." Her eyes returned to Luca, now peering down an alley.

Matteo said, "Okay, I'm going to grab a coffee and then explain to my boss why I no longer have my truck."

She laughed and waved goodbye.

Luca caught her eye and moved toward her, his face impassive. They stood toe to toe, saying nothing, until finally Luca said, "I'm off the—" just as Stella said, "How could you not warn me?"

They gazed at each other. "What?" They said in unison. Luca said, "You first."

"Palmiro and Salvo questioned me yesterday. Seeing as I'm their number one suspect."

Thunder crossed his face. "That's ridiculous. You found the body. And the lame!"

She paused, watching the emotions cross his face until he said, "Oh. I see."

Shaking her head, Stella said, "I don't believe this innocent routine. How could you not know all this?"

"Stella," he sighed, running his hands through his dark hair until it stood at attention over his moody eyebrows. What a ridiculous thing for her to focus on! Stella reprimanded herself as Luca went on, "That's what I was trying to tell you. Captain Palmiro took me off the case."

"*What?*"

He shrugged. "He says I'm . . . compromised."

The anger washed out of her. "Oh, now that makes sense."

"What does?"

She shook her head. "Something he said."

He waited to see if she'd add more and when she didn't, he said, "When I told him you found the lame . . . I've never seen him that mad. On and on about how my head was in the clouds, and I should never have let you into an active crime scene."

"Well, you shouldn't have," Stella said, the corner of her mouth tugging up.

"Tell me about it. I regretted it as soon as I opened the door, but you were flying around and, well . . . I guess I got caught up in the moment. For the record, I did try to stop you, but . . . " He looked away.

"What?"

Luca said nothing, his eyes narrowing.

"Luca, spill it."

His eyes still fixed at some spot in the middle distance, he said softly, "Stella, you're a phenomenon. Watching you at work, I couldn't have stopped you for the world."

Stella's heart caught.

Luca's gaze slid back to her and he shrugged. "I deserved to be taken off the case. Salvo said I should fight it, but I realized. Stella, when it comes to you, I can't see straight."

Stella fought the urge to peer over Luca's shoulder for cameras filming this prank. Luca couldn't possibly mean it, could he?

He looked into her eyes and moved closer, murmuring, "I guess it's not macho or manly to say these things."

She swallowed. "Was our conversation on Tuesday macho and manly? When I turned you down so you rejected me? Because I got to say, I'm not sure that was working for you."

He ducked his head, smiling. "Ah, *ma dai*. Come on, Stella. Give a guy a break. I knew I was behaving badly the whole time, but it was like I was on a runaway horse and couldn't catch the reins. As soon as you stormed off, I wanted to call you back. To do it all ... differently."

She wanted to do it all differently, too; to say, why the heck not? Let's give it a whirl. Why not see where things went? She opened her mouth, but then Luca went on, "Even if you felt like I do," here Stella again wanted to blurt out a run of words, but stopped herself. Maybe just in time, or maybe a fraction too early, she knew she'd spend some time wondering. "Maybe you were right. Why mess up a good friendship? Especially since you're always talking about leaving. Right? You *are* leaving?"

She nodded, mute.

He reached up as if to tuck a curl behind her ear, but let his hand fall. "It's too bad. I've gotten kinda used to you."

Stella cleared her throat. "Well, I'm sure you won't miss my ability to get caught up in your investigations."

He grinned. "I don't know. I'm kinda used to that, too." His face sobered. "Do you think they're pursuing evidence that you're a suspect? Or is the Captain rattling your chain?"

"If I had to guess," Stella said, "I'd wager a little of both."

Luca shook his head. "Salvo isn't supposed to tell me about the investigation, but from hints he dropped, I figured they were pursuing Aldo."

"Not Antonio?"

"He's also a person of interest. A stronger candidate, really, as much as none of us can believe it. Antonio admits the lame is his, and his whole alibi seems weak."

Stella nodded, "But Aldo was late to work, and I'd imagine the fact that Jacopo was having an affair with Aldo's wife is a classic motive."

Luca's eyes widened. "I hadn't heard that part. Are you sure?"

She tapped her nose. "How many people do you know who smell of violet? Sounds like they cozied up for some time tinkering with wild yeast."

Luca ran his hands through his hair again. "Weird. I didn't pick up on that when I was in the bakery."

She shrugged. "Well, a woman's brain is far more attuned to nonverbal cues."

Furrowing one eyebrow in a gesture of mock disbelief, Luca said, "Sounds self-serving."

"Science doesn't lie."

Luca chuckled. "To tell you the truth, it explains a lot."

She nodded. "It's why kitchens do best with men and women working together. It's like brick and mortar, you need them both to build a strong wall."

Luca put his hands in his pockets and thought. "I can see that for police stations."

"Especially police stations. Talk about an excess of testosterone."

Luca chided warmly, "Hey, now."

Stella went on, oblivious, "And think of interviews! You should have women in there, picking up on everything a suspect isn't saying."

"We *are* trained in that you know."

Stella shrugged. "But women have been reading social cues since we were old enough to diaper dollies."

"Isn't that sexist?"

She shook her head. "Nah, just real talk. Girls are praised for being good friends and supportive peers. That glass ceiling is so heavy, we have to do a lot with the tiny bit of territory we're given."

"Huh," Luca said.

"You don't believe me?"

"I never thought about it." He looked at his watch. "I better get back.

Those reports aren't going to write themselves."

She touched his arm. "I am sorry. That you're off the case. I feel like it's my fault."

He shrugged. "It's okay. I didn't much like looking for evidence that a guy I've always thought of as an uncle could have killed Jacopo. It'll be nice when things return to normal."

Stella had hardly closed the door behind her, her thoughts occupied with if she wanted to take time to feed herself or finish the *colomba* or fall into bed, when she heard a soft rapping on the door.

Stella tensed. The police? If they came for her, would they knock? Or barge in, waving handcuffs? She called out to ask who was there. No answer came. Hesitating for a moment, Stella gathered her courage and threw open the door. She found Benedetta, the butcher's wife, standing on the stairs with Stella's pot, scrubbed clean. Not simply "I'm returning a pot" clean. The woman must have scoured with industrial-grade pads to pry off years of flame marks and stains.

Stella smiled, confused. She'd heard that Benedetta never left the house. Unless that was classic village hyperbole, and she just didn't dine out or socialize much?

It didn't matter, a wan soul stood before her, pot in hand, and Stella knew her role. "Please, Benedetta. Come in."

As Benedetta stepped inside the entryway, Stella closed the door and said, "You didn't have to go through the trouble of bringing the pot. I would have come by."

Benedetta shifted her weight, pushing her wispy hair off her glasses with the flat of her hand. She stared at Stella for a moment before gushing, "It was so good."

Somehow this feedback, lacking though it was in specificity or detail, felt more rewarding than her James Beard Rising Star award. She grinned. "I'm delighted you enjoyed it."

"Enjoyed it! I ate two heaping bowls for dinner." Benedetta paused for a moment and looked around as if expecting *paparazzi* hiding around the corner. She lowered her voice. "I even had pasta this morning for breakfast."

Stella smiled anew. The logical part of her knew good eaters weren't necessarily good people, yet she always thought well of people who enjoyed their food. And for an Italian to eat pasta for breakfast, Benedetta must have considered the meal extraordinary.

Benedetta patted the lid with the palm of her open hand, once, then twice. "I haven't tasted a sauce like this since I was a child."

Stella impulsively stepped back to invite Benedetta further into her home, to offer a seat at her table. The older woman shook her head as if she couldn't, even as she moved into the house. Stella plucked the pot out of Benedetta's arms as she passed. Obviously, the woman had no trouble carrying it across town, but Stella didn't know how she'd managed. Those thick bottom enamel-coated pots were workhorses, the cooking implement version of a Clydesdale.

Depositing the pot in the kitchen, Stella ushered Benedetta past the couch, still furred with splinters, and pulled out a chair for her. Benedetta shook her head again, indicating she couldn't stay long enough to sit, but then sank into the chair. Stella stilled her breath. She couldn't help but imagine that one abrupt gesture and Benedetta would bolt. She needed to control her movements, even her thoughts. Else the waif sitting across from her might float off like dandelion fluff.

In modulated, quiet tones, Stella said, "I'm so sorry. About Jacopo."

Benedetta stared at her clasped hands, pinched like a vise between her knees. But she stayed.

Stella went on, "I didn't know him well, but nobody could miss what he added to a room."

For a moment, Benedetta sagged back into her chair, but then she seemed to lean into a wellspring of hidden strength. She smiled. A shaky smile, but a smile nonetheless. She looked Stella in the eye as she said, "People call him a light. Not much to me, over the years. I . . . I don't often see people anymore. But Bruno, he tells me. A light, they say."

Stella couldn't mistake the pride in Benedetta's voice. "Very fitting."

Her eyes fixed on her clasped hands, Benedetta said, "Honestly, I never thought I'd be lucky enough to have him. We tried for years. When I got pregnant, we called it a miracle. So every day with my Jacopo, I felt like he could be taken away from me. At any moment."

Benedetta gazed up at Stella, as if seeking advice from an oracle. "I didn't deserve him. So how can I be surprised God agreed with me?"

Shaking her head, Stella leaned forward and clasped her hands around Benedetta's. "God didn't take him."

The woman lifted her chin, and with steel in her words said, "He's with God."

Stella nodded, alarmed at her accidental insinuation. As a non-religious person, she often felt awkward treading spiritual waters. "Of course he is. Of *course*. I only meant that God didn't make this happen. A monster did."

Despite the thick glasses, Stella saw tears welling in Benedetta's eyes.

Stella didn't know what to say, so she stayed quiet. Benedetta's hands in hers felt like a cold bundle of sticks.

Benedetta whispered, "I heard people talking. From the window above the *macelleria*. I heard people say you did it."

Stella bit her lip. Word was, apparently, out.

Was bringing the pot back a ruse to attack Stella? Benedetta didn't look like she had enough strength to attack a fruit fly, but Stella had seen her mother keen over the body of her younger daughter. Hell may hath no fury on a woman scorned, but a scorned woman had nothing on a grieving mother.

When Benedetta didn't go on, Stella said, "You probably know this, but I'm the one that found your Jacopo. On Tuesday, I mean. And because I also found the murder weapon, my fingerprints were on it. I foolishly picked it up without wearing gloves."

Benedetta seemed not a the last sentences. "Did he look . . . peaceful? When you found him?"

Stella remembered those eyes, like brown river pebbles removed from the water, staring at the ceiling. No panic in them, only surprise. The scent of violets. The scarf of red, that was no scarf at all. How could she sum this up for his mother? Then she realized, she didn't have to. The right thing here was not perfect honesty. That right thing was perfect kindness. "He did look peaceful. Yes, very much so. He knew how loved he was."

Benedetta looked down at her hands intertwined with Stella's, murmuring, "You didn't do it."

Though Stella wanted to shout, "Of course I didn't!' she kept her tone even, low, modulated. "No. No, I did not."

Benedetta nodded as if to herself. "I know. I can tell." The words seemed to tire Benedetta. She slumped back, her face empty.

Stella turned at the sound floating in from the open window. Music, played by a flute or a pipe. As ever, Stella couldn't tell, as it sounded closer to birdsong than anything else.

Benedetta snapped to standing so quickly, her glasses slid down her nose. She shoved them higher with the back of her hand. "I have to go."

"Now?"

"Oh, yes."

Stella looked around the tidy kitchen. "Can I at least send you home with a plate of—"

"No, no. I must go now. I'm not supposed to be out." Benedetta looked around hurriedly, as if looking for a goblin hiding behind the furniture. She breathed in relief at spotting nothing but Barbanera, snoozing in the chair. "Thank you, Stella. For the sauce. And your kind words about

Jacopo. I'm glad you knew him."

Stella's heart snagged. Her blunders hardly counted as kindness. When would she learn to hold her tongue? "You are welcome."

As they reached the door, Benedetta pulled Stella close and kissed her on each cheek, a flutter like the wing of a butterfly. At such close range, Stella could see past the thick glasses to the tears still standing in Benedetta's gray eyes.

The door closed quietly behind Benedetta as Stella stood, immobile. Gray. Gray eyes.

She thought for a moment and then yelped, grabbed her phone, and darted out the door.

As Stella raced to Domenica's, she spotted Cosimo, walking slowly, his fingers trailing along Aramezzo's stone walls. Her steps slowed as she called, "Cosimo?"

He turned, and she caught sight of his pale face. Though her feet itched to keep moving—she had to get to Domenica's!—she couldn't walk away from Cosimo. His mismatched eyes drew her closer.

His lips tugged up, but he didn't smile. "Good evening, Stella. You're in a hurry, as usual, I surmise."

"Are you okay?"

He looked down at his suit, rumpled but in good shape. "As you see."

She nodded, unsure of whether to pry. Finally, she said, "I heard your shop was closed, and it's not your closed day."

His eyes flicked to her pendant, hanging below her collarbone, the interlocking coils shining in the near dark. "And you worried about me."

She shrugged. It didn't seem polite to observe that he was of an age that his unexpected absence could well suggest a dire situation. After her gaffes with Benedetta, she endeavored to think before speaking. "I did, yes."

Smiling, Cosimo said, "I am quite well, *cara*. Quite well."

"At an antiquarian function?" she asked. She loved his stories of his fellow relic collectors.

"Something like that," he nodded. "I see that you're wearing the pendant. All the time, I hope?"

She nodded, then remembered her mission. "I gotta run, Cosimo. But it's nice to see you. I'm glad you're feeling well."

"Come by soon, my dear. We'll have tea. I've been wanting to ask you . . . oh, it can wait."

Stella spun around. She hated dangling sentences or obscurity of any kind. "Ask me what?"

"No. You're in a hurry." He waved her along.

"I have a second," she hoped.

"I was thinking about our earlier conversation, about the robbery at Casale Mazzoli."

"Thirty-whatever years ago?"

"Less than that. When your family went to Rome to see your mother off for her adventures."

Adventures? Stella blinked. That hardly seemed the word to describe her mother's life with her two children: endless dishes, endless laundry, and the banging hot water heater she complained about to Stella's father everyday until he died and she opted to stop complaining about it rather than getting it fixed. "What about it?"

He smiled, and began, "As we age . . . " He paused as if searching for words. Stella wished he'd hurry. Maybe she should have waited to talk to him later. When she had endless time, she loved listening to the man spin a yarn, but right now . . .

She swallowed her impatience.

He went on, "As we age, our memories don't so much fade, as become buried under the piles of every day nonsense. After we spoke on Wednesday, I thought more about that robbery and I remembered something. Something I hadn't thought about in so long, the memory itself felt dusty."

He chuckled, and Stella camouflaged her irritation with a grin. Cosimo went on, "A medallion of your grandmother's, from her mother, and her mother before her. An item not of traditional worth, perhaps, one would hope overlooked by the common thief, but seen by your maternal line as an object of great power."

"Power?" Stella's frustration vanished at the oddity of the word.

"Yes," Cosimo nodded genially. "Power. You've heard of the gift that runs in your family, I'm sure."

"No," Stella answered. Though, now that he mentioned it, she remembered Domenica talking about Cosimo's belief in her family's—and other ancient Aramezzo lines'—magical abilities. She'd meant to ask him about it, but she'd forgotten. So perhaps she should have more patience with Cosimo's memory. "Actually, it does sound familiar."

He glanced at the sky, narrowing his eyes at the darkness, clotting in navy stretches across the indigo sky. "After thieves plundered Casale Mazzoli, I asked after that medallion, knowing it to be of great sentimental value to your grandmother. She said that in the disarray the thieves left behind, she couldn't find it. But she remained hopeful that it would turn up. Perhaps behind a shelf or fallen in the back of a cupboard. Apparently, she had lent it to your mother, so she had half a mind to wonder if your mother had thrown it in with her own things and took it across the ocean. I avoided asking after it again because she grew sick and I didn't want to trouble her with memories of a lost heirloom. I did always hope, and even pray, that she found it. And now I wonder, perhaps you found it behind the surround? Or . . . might you have found it among your mother's things?"

She shook her head. "The thieves could have taken it, though, right?"

He cocked his head to the side. "Certainly possible, though, as I said, it didn't have any noticeable value."

"But neither did the photographs."

"Ah," he nodded. "This is true."

Stella tipped her head to the side. "I'm glad you mentioned it. There are loose floorboards and sticking drawers all over the house. I'll have myself a scavenger hunt."

He clapped his hands in glee, and Stella realized he wanted in on the action. She grinned at how his old-world speech and white candy floss hair were at odds with his earnest enthusiasm. She said, "I'd be glad of the help. If you want to come by."

"Yes, my dear! Oh, a quest for an ancient relic! What a thing to make an old man's heart go pitter-pat."

She smiled. He was so easy to please.

His face sobered. "When should we begin?"

Stella tipped her phone back around to check the time. If Domenica wasn't closed, she was locking up. "Tell you what, let's get through this murder investigation and we can put our calendars together. We'll find a time when I don't have any guests."

"Excellent, excellent. I can even bring your new fireplace surround." His face grew serious. "By the way, I overheard the rumors. About the police suspecting you. Preposterous! Dario and I agreed that the police must be playing this angle to make the actual murderer complacent. Perhaps then he'll make a mistake."

Stella grimaced and said, "From your lips to the gods' ears."

"That too," Cosimo said. Before Stella could figure out what the old man meant, he added, "But I feel quite certain the police will be locking Antonio away anytime."

"What about Aldo?"

He shrugged. "I never thought he was a real suspect, did you? I mean, Aldo suffered a real loss with Jacopo's death."

So he hadn't heard about the affair.

Perhaps Cosimo noticed Stella's far off look because he patted her arm. "Don't worry. It'll be over soon. I feel sure. Then we can have a hunt!"

She laughed and waved goodbye. As soon as he turned around, she dashed to Domenica's, groaning at finding the lights off. She pushed the door, but it didn't move. Stuck? Or locked? Stella pulled and pushed again, holding back yelps of frustration.

Stella peered in through the glass. She noticed the lamps still on. Maybe Domenica had started to close and then grown distracted by another article about the Venetian influence on the Aeolian islands or something. Was it only a week ago that Stella had sat beside Domenica in this shop, cats on each of their laps, as Domenica told Stella how the foodways in Corfu and the other Aeolian islands varied from the rest of Greece because Venetians had cleared the forests of timber to outfit their celebrated ships during their 400 years of rule? Stella remembered talking about the ancient Venetian language while the coffee burbled in the corner, Domenica's eyes flashing behind her oversized glasses as they wondered how the lack of easily accessible firewood changed the gastronomy of the islands, before the conversation turned to the promise of green lasagna for dinner at Trattoria Cavour. So it must have been a Monday. Adele always made green lasagna with mushroom béchamel on Mondays. Which Stella enjoyed as much as the wild boar tagliatelle Adele made during *cinghiale* season.

Focus! Stella chided herself. She knocked on the door and when that failed to recall Domenica from the netherworlds of the back stacks, Stella began slamming her hand against the glass. "Domenica? Domenica!" Stella yelled.

She heard Domenica's footsteps thundering through the shop. Domenica appeared from behind the bookcase, her hand clutched to her heart, unlocked the door, and threw it open. "What is it? What's wrong?"

"I need you to look something up."

Domenica paused. "That's the big emergency? I thought you were being chased! The murderer hot on your heels!"

"It *is* an emergency! I need you to look something up!" Stella practically clapped her hands between the words for emphasis.

Domenica frowned. "You have a working computer, what do you need me . . . oh."

Stella put her arm around Domenica and guided her to her chair. "Yes. Oh. I need you to do what you do so well."

"Hack, you mean."

"Well, if that's what you kids are calling it these days . . . "

"Cute, Stella. Very cute." Domenica pulled her chair toward the computer and flicked it on.

"What are we looking up? Someone's financial records? Autopsy results?"

"You can do all that?"

Domenica shrugged.

"Okay, yes, you can do all that." Stella collapsed into the armchair. "Do you remember what hotel Antonio and Benedetta stayed in the night they were held hostage in Rome?"

"Can it be called a hostage situation? The station had them stay at the hotel; the mob didn't force it."

Stella waved her hand to bat away Domenica's words. "Not the point."

Domenica pushed back and stared at Stella. "I don't think I ever heard the name of the hotel. Why would it matter?"

"Can you look up news articles from that time, and see if that's mentioned?"

Domenica furrowed her brow. "What are you up to?"

"Just do it. Please?"

Domenica shook her head and began typing. Pages flew across her screen and she pushed her glasses higher as she peered closer, her nose practically smudging the screen. Finally, she said, "The Hilton Roma. Which makes sense, it's across the street from the TV station."

Stella nodded. "Okay, can you do that thing you do where you look up secret stuff and find out if, the night of the Mafia attack on the studio, the station reserved one or two rooms for Antonio and Benedetta?"

A dark look creased Domenica's face. "Stella. You don't think—"

"I don't *think*. I hunch."

Domenica turned back to the screen and somehow accessed a dark box that she began typing furiously into, which made one page after another appear on her screen. "They booked several rooms. Five, to be precise."

Stella sighed. "I guess that makes sense. Antonio and Benedetta couldn't have been the only guests of the studio that day." She pulled Ravioli onto her lap from where she'd been drowsing on the bookshelf. Scratching the cat under her chin, Stella said, "Shoot."

She leaned back, defeated, mindlessly petting Ravioli. Suddenly she bolted up and snapped her finger. "Hold on! I can't believe I didn't think of this, especially after Severini. Hotels and inns have to take identification from every guest, not just the ones paying for the rooms. In fact, when that Australian family stayed at Casale Mazzoli last month, I even had to log their kids' passport information."

"So? That's all hand written. No way I can track down a literal paper trail. I'm good, but not that good."

"*Aspetta*, wait. I jot the identifying information down in a book because I host a few visitors a month. There's no way a big hotel could be that old school—they'd need a whole room just for the logs! They must be storing identification information on the computer."

Domenica cocked her head to the side. "Maybe so. Now. But twenty some odd years ago? Do you think hotels were creating electronic records back then?"

Her eyes wide, Stella said, "Probably not the smaller, more local hotels. But a big chain like the Hilton? They probably joined the information age back when you and I were still figuring out how to program our TiVos."

"Speak for yourself, *cara*."

"Noted." Stella grinned. "Anyway, only one way to find out, right?"

With renewed vigor, Domenica hunched over the computer. Stella leaned into the sound of clacking keys, her heart rising in her throat every time Domenica paused, and then sinking every time she renewed her typing. Finally, Domenica stared at the screen and spun around. "Got it. Room 514. Antonio Grella and Benedetta Zanetti."

Stella released her breath in a loud sigh of relief. She muttered, "I can't believe it. It worked."

"There's more. Room service for lunch and dinner. Two meals each time, both brought to room 514."

"They did stay in one room."

"Looks like it. So, Stella. Spill it."

Stella shook her head slowly. "It started with the eyes. When Benedetta kissed me goodbye, I noticed her eyes behind her glasses. Gray. She was asking me about when I found Jacopo, and I remembered his eyes, they were brown. Which made me think, Bruno has gray eyes. Antonio has brown." A flash of Jacopo's eyes, fixed and rigid in death swam up into her vision and she forced it down. Later she could fall apart. For now, she needed to get to the bottom of this. For everybody's sake.

Domenica nodded. "They're also both tall and thin. Antonio and Jacopo, I mean."

"Yes, but what struck me was the eyes. Bruno and Benedetta, they have gray eyes. According to that article you read, they should only have light-eyed children."

Domenica thought for a moment. "Go on."

"Then I remembered, how strange, when Matteo told me the story, he included that bit about the two rooms."

"It's part of the narrative."

"Exactly. But *why* is it part of the narrative? My thinking is that when

Antonio and Benedetta got home, they hit the 'two room' part of the story hard, to throw any gossipers off the scent. After all, if people knew— one room, certain danger, holed up together . . . it's a recipe for an affair, isn't it?" Stella's brow furrowed as she muttered to herself, "Then again, with so much to jaw about, the whole Mafia drama, maybe nobody would have wondered anyway. Not even when Jacopo came along nine months later. Nobody thought to do the math, since the flashy part of the story was the near-fame thwarted handily by the mob."

Domenica shook her head. "The affair, that's the part that doesn't make sense to me. They both have strong marriages."

"You never know what goes on behind closed doors. Anyway, a night like that, with the specter of death knocking on the door in the form of a near bomb miss. Maybe with a bottle of wine to loosen their inhibitions?"

"Two bottles of wine. It's on the receipt."

"You see? And maybe they talked about their fears, opened up to each other. Nothing is sexier than emotional intimacy."

Domenica nodded. "Okay, I see what you mean."

Stella nodded. "Then . . . when Benedetta and I were talking—"

"When was this conversation with Benedetta?"

Stella waved her hand. "She was returning my pot."

Lifting her hand, Domenica said, "I have questions."

"Let's stay on topic for the moment. The point is, she talked about Jacopo like he was a surprise. It reminded me, my mother used to complain about how I arrived too early in her marriage for her to have a real honeymoon period with my father. I guess I'm saying, both Jacopo and I, we were accidents. Only my mother regretted it as if I cursed her to motherhood, and Benedetta found it a blessing, the gift of motherhood. Benedetta even said something about her not deserving Jacopo. That stuck with me. Why wouldn't she think she deserved him? Maybe because of how she 'got' him? And also . . . she let it slip that she and Bruno had tried for years to get pregnant. So, what could have made this pregnancy flourish when her previous ones hadn't? Maybe a different father. One with brown eyes."

"Wow." Domenica exhaled loudly and stared at the ceiling. Her gaze dropped, and she said, simply, "Stella."

"I know, right?"

"What does this mean?"

Stella shrugged. "First of all, I need to know if Antonio knew Jacopo was his son. If he did, it cements the theory that he can't be the murderer. There are all sorts of inborn moral mandates against that, from an evolutionary perspective alone."

The color vanished from Domenica's face. "Bruno. Do you think he knows?"

"I'd like to know that, too. But there is something more pressing." Stella hesitated. "I don't suppose you're willing to do a little more computer magic?"

Domenica shrugged. "Since I'm here . . . "

"It's Aldo. The police can't find him, but I bet you can."

Domenica grinned. As she typed, she said, "Easy enough, I'll find out what numbers are associated with the bakery. We already know one is his wife's. The other would be his. So I just need to hack the cell provider's records to access the phone's GPS data, and then . . . " She pushed her glasses higher on her nose as she continued muttering and typing, screens appearing and vanishing with strings of numbers Stella couldn't make out.

"Huh," Domenica said, her eyes fixed on the screen.

"What?"

Domenica spun her chair slowly. "He's in Assisi."

"He's back?"

Domenica's gaze flicked back to the screen. "According to his phone's GPS, he never left."

SATURDAY

Stella hardly slept, wondering why Aldo had pretended to flee Assisi when he was hiding out at home. And why wouldn't his wife report his presence? Should Stella tell the police? It would take them so much time to get whatever permissions they needed to track his phone, who knows what he might get up to?

Stella pushed open the door of Bar Cappellina. Immediately, the bustle and conversation cut off, like a curtain falling. The spotlight trained on her.

"So you've heard," she announced, hanging up her zippered sweatshirt on the coat rack in the corner.

"We know you didn't do it," Romina said, all in a rush. "No way. It doesn't make sense." Stella noticed some villagers nodding and moving closer as if to assure her of their belief in her innocence. But Cristiana's father's face grew grim, and he stalked out of the bar. Stella watched him leave, the door closing behind him.

Orietta, the pharmacist, appeared beside her. "Don't pay him any mind, Stella. He's been friends with Palmiro forever, of course he'd believe whatever the Captain says."

Stella stood still, her eyes fixed on Cristiana's father, now hurrying away as if racing from a landfill's stench. "But Cristiana, does she—"

Orietta grabbed her arm. "No, absolutely not. She knows you're innocent. I heard her and her father fighting about it this morning."

Flavia rushed over and added, "I saw Salvo this morning and I gave him a piece of my mind. How dare they waste their energy on you when the real killer is still out there!" Stella blinked. Flavia must be very sure of Stella's innocence if she'd dropped her regular speech pattern of ending every sentence like a question. As if to punctuate her punctuation, Flavia seethed, "The nerve!"

Another villager, one Stella knew by sight but not by name, overheard the conversation and stood, throwing money on the counter. The villager tied her scarf around her neck and pulled so taut Stella wondered why it didn't choke her, saying, "If the police say she's a suspect, she's a suspect. That's good enough for me. And I won't be in the same room with a murderer. She never belonged here. I don't care who her parents were."

Everyone watched her leave. Stella sighed. She couldn't really blame anyone. This was the logical consequence of her stupid impulsivity. "I found the murder weapon. That's *all*," she said aloud to nobody in particular.

Leonardo, who she noticed in the corner with Marta, laughed. "And got your fingerprints all over it."

"Luca was right there when I touched it. Why would I hand him the murder weapon if I did it?" She hoped no one would land where the police apparently did—that she did it to cover up her earlier prints.

Leonardo shrugged before gently teasing a curl out of Marta's braid to pull it down and watch it spring back up. He murmured, "Who knows why murderers do what they do?"

Roberto shot Leonardo a look. "Leo. That's enough."

Raising his arms in a gesture of innocence, Leonardo laughed again. "I'm kidding! Stella has a sense of humor. Right, Stella?"

Stella studied his face, all strong planes and dark lines. She didn't know what to believe.

Softly, Marta chided, "Leo. Be kind."

Instantly, Leonardo adopted an apologetic expression and pressed his palms together. "Honestly, Stella. I'm sorry. Of course you didn't do it. Why would you?" A glimmer of a smile made Stella doubt the sincerity of his apology.

Flavia sighed, "Oh, Stella. How hard this must be for you."

Romina said firmly, "They can't have any real evidence or they would have arrested you already. It'll be okay, Stella. Soon they'll figure it out and this will be all forgotten."

Stella heard a huff from the end of the bar near Flavia, but couldn't tell who made it. She only knew the faces vaguely, other than Luisella, and she'd never heard the woman make any sound at all.

Grabbing the one empty seat, Stella sat and asked for a *cappuccino*. Marta reached over and grabbed Stella's hand. "How are you, really?"

Stella shrugged. "As well as can be expected, I suppose."

Leonardo arched his eyebrows. "Trying to nab the killer again? Snatch some fame from the cops?"

Stella stared at him. "Wouldn't you? If the police suspected you did it, but you were dang certain you didn't? Wouldn't you be a bit desperate to prove your innocence by showing someone else's guilt? "

Chuckling, Leonardo said, "Yeah, I guess."

Marta leaned closer to Stella. "How about Antonio? Any more reason to think he did it?" She looked at Stella hopefully and added, "Or any evidence to suggest he didn't?"

Stella accepted the coffee from Roberto with a smile of thanks and reached for the packets of sugar. "My gut says no, but as we all know, I'm not always the best judge of people."

She shot Leo a meaningful look, beginning to understand why Jacopo loathed him. Once she'd felt the *porchetta* driver's charm, but now she realized that he played his aloofness like a card in poker. He could focus his attention on a person, like Marta now, or, Stella realized, like herself months ago. When she first met him, she felt pulled not only by his pervasive scent of roasting pork but by his attentive gaze. It felt charged. Seductive. But he could withdraw that quickly, leaving a rather mean edge.

Leo missed her glare or didn't deem it important. "My gut tries to tell me all kinds of things, but mostly that it's hungry." He slapped his belly and rubbed it until his shirt lifted. Stella spied his muscular abdomen and turned away, trying not to roll her eyes. She glanced at Marta, who flushed pink and sipped her coffee.

Flavia said, "I don't think it's Antonio, either. He loves all his apprentice bakers, and so many have moved on, he's never gotten angry about it before, has he?"

Stella wondered. She had asked the same question of Marta a few days ago. But now she knew that Jacopo was Antonio's son. Which perhaps made Jacopo's leaving more of a betrayal, but again...would Antonio hurt his own son? If he knew?

Marta nodded. "I hope the police find Aldo, and soon. Take him in for questioning. If you ask me, he's the suspicious one, not Antonio."

Leonardo traced a line from Marta's cheekbone to her chin with his fingertips, murmuring, "But you can't bear to think that anyone close to you can be anything other than good, can you? Thank goodness for that. Selfishly, I mean."

Marta dipped her eyes to the ground and Stella realized what was missing. "Where's Ascanio?"

Marta lifted her hand, pausing briefly before resting it over Leonardo's, now cradling her cheek. She tore her eyes away from Leonardo and turned to Stella. "With his grandparents."

Leonardo grinned. "Overnight."

Flushing again, Marta said, "Leo."

Leonardo chuckled and shrugged, his eyes never leaving Marta's face.

Stella felt a pang. She missed the first flush of a relationship—the newness, when everything sparkled like the day after a snowstorm. Ah well. The crash and burn that inevitably followed never made it worth it.

But, she couldn't help but wonder, would it have been different with Luca?

No, definitely not. Yes, she enjoyed talking to him when he wasn't irritating the stuffing out of her peppers, and she couldn't deny the tingle she felt around him or the upswell of emotion she felt when he stood between her and chaos, but they were too different. He didn't seem to have any goals in his life other than honoring authority figures and playing by the rules. Not her style.

Besides, she did have too full a plate for romance. The bed-and-breakfast for one, but for the moment, getting out from under suspicion of murder. Which reminded her. She took a sip of coffee and asked, "Anyone seen Antonio lately?"

Romina shook her head. "He hasn't come in once."

His eyes fixed on Marta's clavicle, Leonardo muttered, "I saw him after the farmer's market."

"It's Saturday." Stella realized. "I forgot about the market."

Shrugging, Leonardo said, "Seems like most people did. We had as many vendors as customers, so we all broke down early. Anyway, I saw Antonio after that, at the park. Sitting there. Looking at nothing."

Again? She supposed if one needed to get out of the house and didn't want to talk to people, the options in Aramezzo were thin.

She knocked back the last of her coffee, paid, and said goodbye to the assembled villagers. Only one or two pointedly ignored her, but their silence was eclipsed by warm goodbyes and catch-you-laters. Honestly, that might be how it usually was, even when she wasn't accused of murder. A significant proportion of Aramezzo still didn't know what to make of her, and this current state of affairs couldn't help.

As Stella walked to the park, she went over the clues, comparing the ones that implicated her and the ones that implicated Antonio. There weren't that many for either of them. No smoking gun, as it were. Antonio might have a motive, but those were her fingerprints on the murder weapon. Maybe he had fingerprints on the lame as well, but that could hardly be a clue, since it was his lame.

She rounded the corner and spotted Antonio, back on the same park bench. Her gaze focused on his shoes—dress shoes again, at odds with his rumpled sweatpants and ill-fitting sweater.

Stella sat beside him.

Antonio didn't move or even register her presence. After a minute of stillness, Stella wondered if perhaps he'd passed out or had a stroke or something. As she lifted her hand to touch his arm, Antonio's words fell into her lap, weighted and leaden. "You, too?"

She nodded. "Me, too."

Antonio nodded. "If it helps, I'd be more inclined to assume I did it and forgot than you did it at all."

Her eyes smarted.

He said nothing, his eyes on the blackbirds strutting around the *bocce* court.

"Antonio?" Stella began. "I know."

He turned to her, his ginger eyebrows so high they got lost in the hair coming loose over his forehead. "You know who did it?" he breathed.

"No, not that." She closed her eyes. "I know about you. About what happened in Rome. About you and Benedetta. About Jacopo."

She held her breath, waiting for him to lash out at the accusation. He turned away to stare over the hills.

Her voice wavered. "I know he was your son."

Antonio continued staring. Finally, he said, "How did you guess?" He shook his head before she could answer. "It doesn't matter. Of course, you guessed. Everyone else accepted the story as town lore. You came with fresh eyes."

Stella turned to stare out at the horizon with Antonio. When he added nothing more, Stella said, "Did he know? Jacopo?"

Antonio breathed deeply enough for Stella to hear the air entering and leaving his body. "I can't count the number of times I almost told him. But I couldn't do that to Bruno. To Benedetta. He was their boy. As much as I loved him, valued him . . . who was I to claim him? A man who knew his mother that way only one night, and who offered him no more than a place on the bakery floor."

Stella nodded. "You could tell the police, you know. I imagine it less likely that they consider you a suspect if they know he was your son."

"If they consider me capable of murdering any human, I don't see how Jacopo being my son would make a difference." He sighed. "Anyway, even if I knew it would help, I couldn't tell them. My wife . . . the betrayal would kill her."

"Celeste never suspected? About Jacopo?"

"Why would she? She was so focused on raising Dario, on looking after both of us. Which hasn't always been easy. And after that one lapse— and believe me, Stella, I had only one—I've always worked to make sure my wife knows how much I love her. How much I treasure her." His voice cracked. "I don't want Celeste to think our life together has been an illusion. Because it's not. That was one moment of weakness. Never before or since have I even thought of another woman that way. It's Celeste. It's always been Celeste."

Stella took his hand, and he squeezed it.

He went on, "So no. I can't do that to her. I can't cheapen our marriage that way."

"Even if it means setting yourself free?"

"Even so." He checked his watch. "I better go. It's almost lunchtime and nowadays, Celeste worries if I'm not home on time."

"Worries?"

He nodded, standing. "You have to understand, Celeste sees all of this differently. In her mind, a baker at our bakery got killed. When I was originally planning on working."

Slowly, Stella said, "So she thinks you're next."

Shrugging, Antonio said, "I suppose. And how can I argue? Arguing would only aggravate her."

Stella fell in step with Antonio as he walked home. "It's not an unreasonable theory. Are the police looking into it?"

He shook his head. "They aren't exactly keeping me apprised, but I doubt they would find a random serial killer intent on bakers to be all that plausible."

"But Antonio," she stopped, her hand on his arm to stop him, too. "What if someone was after you and got Jacopo by mistake?"

"Why would someone want me dead?"

"Why would someone want Jacopo dead?" She sighed. "None of it makes any sense."

"Tell me about it," he smiled. She wished his face would light the way she'd grown accustomed to after all these months here. Though it seemed an unreasonable wish. On top of losing an employee, on top of being accused of murder, she now understood that he'd lost a son.

He rubbed his arms. "Well, I better get home."

She stood. "I'll walk you."

He turned to regard her. "You can't be concerned for my safety."

She shrugged, not wanting to admit that Celeste's uneasiness had settled like chili in oil. "Better safe than sorry."

Smiling a little, Antonio said, "Stella, no offense, but you don't offer much protection."

"I know. I'm hardly threatening. But something about Jacopo's murder, it seems the work of a coward, doesn't it? Using the knife from behind, nobody around."

Antonio's face paled, and he said nothing.

Stella went on, "Frankly, I think the presence of a warm body is enough to keep you safe." She hoped.

Antonio seemed lost in thought, but he didn't protest Stella accompanying him home. One less argument, that was worth something, she supposed. They walked in companionable silence until they passed the town entrance. Stella's ears perked at a sound, a kind of shouting.

She stopped walking. Antonio didn't seem to have heard anything, but he stopped when Stella did and, seeing her expression, he tipped his head to listen. Some kind of hubbub, but Stella couldn't tell what. "Come on," she said to Antonio, a gnawing feeling growing in her gut.

He resisted, saying, "Ah, no Stella. You go on. I need to head home."

But Stella was already at the tunnel. She listened and then spun around, running backward as she said. "I hear people shouting something. Something about the bakery."

His face tensed, and he nodded once before rushing up beside Stella. As they hurried forward, he said, "But let's hang back, okay? It's probably nothing, and I don't want anyone to see me."

Stella didn't answer because that gnawing feeling had grown and she felt certain that this nothing was actually something. She tensed at each spike of volume, the villagers' high-pitched calls.

Their footsteps slowed as they approached the crowd milling about in front of the bakery. Stella noted police tape blocking off the street on either side of the bakery doors.

Stella's stomach dropped. The thought that perhaps Jacopo hadn't been the intended victim had barely crossed her mind until twenty minutes ago, and now it looked like something bad had gone down on the bakery floor. Again. But Antonio stood here beside her. Could it be Dario? Or one of the other assistants?

"I'll see what's going on," she told Antonio, who stood ashen on the edge of the crowd. He looked like he was trying to fold his large form against the wall, to stay invisible as long as he could. She nudged her way forward, listening to chatter, but gleaning nothing. Finally, she spotted Matteo and wedged further into the fray to pull his sleeve. "What's going on?"

He looked down at her and said grimly, "Looks like you're off the hook."

"What do you mean?"

He gestured toward the bakery. "The police got an anonymous tip."

She heard Captain Palmiro yelling at Salvo, "I told you to check every inch! How could you have missed the hamper?"

Luca appeared beyond the police tape strung on the far side of the bakery doors. He heard the last comment and stepped forward. "We did. Right, Salvo?"

Salvo winced and said nothing as Captain Palmiro growled at Luca. "This is why I took you off the case. What are you doing here?"

Luca said, "You called for all available officers."

Stella whispered to Matteo, "Did somebody... did they find another...?" She couldn't get the words out but Matteo knew what she meant.

He shook his head. "No, nothing like that. But they found *something*. Cristiana saw the police entering the bakery and told everyone at Bar Cappellina and when we rushed here, officers were stringing the tape to block access. Palmiro got here a minute ago."

Stella watched as Luca approached Palmiro, his words obscured by the tense exchanges of the crowd. She asked Matteo, "Do we know what it is?"

He shook his head. "Something in the hamper. That's all I know."

She tried to remember the morning of the murder. She remembered they'd talked about the likelihood of having clues within, but then Antonio showed up at the door and everything happened so fast.

Salvo's voice rose, whining, "It was *Luca's* job."

Luca straightened, and his voice likewise carried over the crowd. "I know! That's what I *just said*! But I'm telling you, the morning of the murder, there was nothing suspicious in the hamper. Nothing but dirty linens!"

Palmiro's eyes looked like they were about to pop out of his head. "How can you be sure, Luca? After all, I remember a certain American hanging off you that morning. Distracting you from your duties."

Stella didn't know if Palmiro was playing for the crowd, but he certainly looked pleased as the assembled villagers gasped and laughed. Stella's cheeks flushed. She was no monkey and she hung off nobody. Matteo put his arm around Stella and squeezed.

"I am writing you up for this, Luca. You'll need to decide what's important, your job or," Captain Palmiro paused meaningfully, "fraternizing with witnesses."

"That's right." Luca raised his chin, ignoring the hoots of laughter. "Witnesses. This evidence proves Stella is not a suspect, she's a *witness*."

A man yelled, "Tell us what you found!"

A woman's voice rose to join his. "Come on, we need to know! Who killed Jacopo?"

Stella turned to dart her gaze towards Antonio, still standing in the back. Thankfully, unnoticed. Police officers arrived and stepped under the tape to stand along the line of villagers, as if anticipating them to push forward in a mob.

Meanwhile, Palmiro pointed toward the bakery, and Salvo hesitated only briefly before stepping inside. After a few moments, he returned to stand in the open doors with something wrapped under his arm. The way he carried the parcel reminded Stella of something. Then Salvo stepped into the street, and Stella's height prevented her from keeping her gaze on him.

"Matteo! What's *happening*? I can't see!"

"Should I lift you onto my shoulders?" Matteo asked with a grin. She scowled. Matteo leaned down and narrated. "Salvo must have been ordered to get something from inside the bakery."

"I saw that part!"

"Keep your shirt on! Anyway, that's Salvo's grandmother in black at the front of the crowd, against the police tape. She's been lighting candles for him every day. Having him on another murder investigation is too much for her nerves. He's probably reassuring her. He's been doing that pretty much full time since the murder. Yes, he's talking to her. But...weird. She doesn't look relieved. She looks like...like my grandfather's old peacock preening its feathers."

Matteo watched the action silently until Stella yanked on his arm. "Matteo!"

"Sorry, sorry... Salvo's *nonna* is telling her friend something. Judging the way they are both watching Salvo, I think it's about what he's carrying."

Stella held her breath. If the game of telephone she'd seen play out at Bar Cappellina was any indication, she wouldn't have to wait long.

The woman in front of Matteo turned and said, "It's the apron!"

Matteo nodded, his gaze fixed on Salvo, now approaching Palmiro. They consulted quietly for a moment, and Matteo muttered to Stella. "Can you see?"

Palmiro stood with Luca and Salvo, back where they began, far enough in front of Stella that she could make them out ahead of the crowd. She nodded, her eyes fixed on the item in Salvo's arms.

Apron? It couldn't be Jacopo's, he'd been wearing his. The only reason an apron would be worthy of all this attention was if... Matteo grabbed Stella's upper arm. "Can you see it?"

She got on her tiptoes and peered as much over the crowd as she could. "I see them talking. Is that it?"

Matteo shook his head and stayed silent for a moment before saying, "Salvo is showing it to Palmiro. It's Antonio's apron."

At this Stella jumped up and down, trying for an unimpeded view. "How do they know it's Antonio's?" She answered her own question. "It's white, right." Stella remembered Antonio walking to work all those mornings with his clean, white apron tucked under his arm. "Only apprentices wear blue."

Matteo nodded. The villagers standing in front of Stella shifted until she had a direct view of the white apron in Salvo's hands. Or parts of it were white. The parts that weren't streaked with dough. And the parts that weren't covered with blood.

Stella's stomach lurched. The sight of the apron seemed to shake the villagers. The jockeying for position, treating the scenario like a game, it all faded like a radio program too far from the station. Suddenly, everyone seemed to realize. That blood, it belonged to Jacopo. And the killer was still among them.

Stella pulled Matteo's arm. "How did they find it? You said an anonymous tip?"

He nodded. "That's what I heard."

Suddenly, she remembered. Antonio. She spun around to find him, still at the back of the milling crowd, his face now streaked with tears. A shout from behind her, "Get him!" Captain Palmiro must have noticed Antonio right as Stella did.

She turned to Matteo and clutched his arm. "He didn't do it, Matteo, I know it."

He shook his head. "I don't want to believe it either, Stella, but—"

"No! This isn't—" her words cut off as Palmiro and Salvo pushed past them. She followed them with her eyes as she pleaded, "The apron. Something about it isn't right!"

"Stop!" Palmiro called, now practically climbing over the villagers who couldn't get out of his way fast enough. His eyes remained fixed on Antonio as the baker slipped through the dispersing crowd and disappeared.

"Matteo, I need to find Antonio!"

"Stella . . . if he did it . . . it's not safe."

She shook her head angrily. "But he didn't do it, Matteo, I know it!"

"How do you know it?"

She scowled and said nothing.

Matteo sighed. "Stella, I love your belief that good people can't do bad things. But let's get real."

"I've never believed that." She stormed away toward Domenica's. Matteo ran to catch up. "Stella . . . there's more."

Stella whirled around. "More? What do you mean?"

He pulled her arm and forced her to sit on a stoop. A cat napping in the window box beside them opened one eye and then yawned before nestling back to sleep.

Matteo took a breath. "The trash bag. I found out what was in it." Stella's head turned to stare at Matteo. He went on, "This morning when I walked to Bar Cappellina, my supervisor called me. He said the police just finished searching my truck and I could get it."

"So the mayor did call the police."

"Sounds like it. But it took them a day to get to it, they've been so busy pursuing Aldo. I asked my supervisor if the police found anything in the trash, and he said they found a bag of shoes."

"Shoes?" She thought back—the stinky bag she assumed to have diapers, the bag of lingerie, and the third bag, the one the mayor had stopped them from opening. The flash of white . . . her heart sank. "Shoes. The baker's shoes?"

He nodded, quiet. "I'd hoped to find you at Bar Cappellina. Right when I got there, Cristiana ran in, shouting the police blocked off the bakery."

"How can they be sure the shoes are Antonio's?"

He shrugged. "I guess nobody else would have that many pairs of white shoes. And . . . well."

"Just say it." She covered her face with her hands. "Only, I don't think I want to know."

"One of the pairs of shoes matches the footprint. The one outside the bakery the morning of the murder."

"Oh, no." She shook her head in her hands for a moment before looking at Matteo with wide eyes. "This is why he's been wearing dress shoes. He tossed all his baking sneakers."

"I guess so." Matteo shook his head. "I didn't think it was him. I really didn't."

"But Matteo," Stella said, "was there blood? On any of the shoes?"

He shrugged. "I don't know."

"Also, why would he get rid of all his shoes? Why not just the ones that left the print? It doesn't make sense."

"Stella, remember, it may be hard for you to think like a murderer. How can you know the lengths people will go to erase their tracks? Maybe all his shoes are the same brand and style, he gets new ones each year. And so he had to get rid of all of them."

"Maybe," she said. "But if there was blood on the shoe, we would have heard of it. I still don't buy it."

"Stella—"

"I can't, Matteo! Something about this isn't right."

"Whether or not you believe it, you need to keep yourself safe, okay? No more cozy conversations with Antonio."

She paused. "I guess this rules out Aldo?"

Matteo shrugged. "It'll be interesting to see if he comes out of hiding."

Her thoughts spooled to Assisi, imagining Aldo in some closet. She shook her head and thought about Antonio, now similarly evading police capture. "Where do you think he went? Antonio, I mean?"

Matteo cocked his head in thought. "I'd guess home."

Stella stood up. "Which means they'll be taking him to the station. I can't bear to be on the street when that happens. I'm going home."

Matteo nodded. "Okay, I'll walk you."

"Matteo."

"What?" He smiled guilelessly.

"I can walk home on my own."

"Stella. First of all, there is a killer on the loose."

"My money is still on Aldo. Way too many suspicious things about that guy."

He ignored her interruption. "Second of all, I'm sorry, but I don't trust you. You're likely to go skipping off to find Antonio and probably bake him a cake or something."

She made no comment when he fell in step beside her. For a moment, she thought about pointing out that the last time they were in a scuffle he hadn't been much use in the protection department. But luckily before she opened her mouth, she remembered Matteo's shame when the mayor told him to leave, and he fled with his tail between his legs. No use bringing that up. But it reminded her. "What about the other trash bags?"

"What about them?"

"Did your supervisor say anything about them?"

Matteo shook his head. "He didn't mention them, only the bag of shoes."

"Hmmm."

Matteo waited to see if Stella would state her thoughts aloud and when she didn't, he prodded, "What?"

She shrugged. "I don't know. That whole thing with the mayor was bizarre, wasn't it? How do we know he didn't plant the bag of shoes as soon as we walked away?"

"Stella. Why would he do that?"

"I don't know. But shouldn't someone be asking? It's pretty suspicious."

"Do you also think he put the bloody apron in the hamper?"

"See, there's something weird about that, too." She adjusted her bandana. "The whole anonymous tip thing. Could *that* have been the mayor?"

"Why would the mayor call in an anonymous tip?"

"I don't know! The whole thing doesn't fit together." They arrived at Stella's house and she paused at the door. "Do you think they arrested Antonio by now?"

Stella's phone rang before Matteo could answer. She drew it out and said, "It's Domenica."

Matteo waved his hand for her to take the call while he slumped onto the stoop.

"Domenica. What's up?"

"Stella!" Domenica yelled. Despite her acumen with technology, Domenica yelled into the phone, even if she was calling to borrow a cup of sugar. She also signed her texts, "Love, Domenica," but that was beside the current point.

"I'm right here, Domenica. You don't need to yell."

"I'm not yelling," Domenica yelled. "Cosimo told me! About Antonio! I want to make sure you are locked *inside your house.*"

Stella sighed. "Geez, Domenica. Relax. Why would I be in danger?"

"Orietta just came in," Domenica shouted. Stella held the phone away from her ear. Better to save her eardrum. Matteo caught the motion and grinned. "She said Antonio booked it! He's on the *loose.*"

"And you think he's going to come after me?"

"No one is safe," Domenica boomed. "Especially bakers. I've called all my cats in. We're going upstairs. Let him see if he can get past all these locked doors. I'm so glad I had them reinforced."

Stella covered the mouthpiece and muttered to Matteo, "She's as paranoid as you are."

He shook his head and said nothing, his eyes searching hers.

SUNDAY

*S*tella tossed and turned all night. She couldn't summon panic about Antonio on the loose, but she did feel uneasy. Two bakers on the run. It sounded like the name of an off-brand buddy comedy. She must have finally fallen into a deep sleep sometime in the early morning because she woke up with a start close to noon.

Bleary, she shoved her feet into slippers before padding into the kitchen. Barbanera ran ahead of her, so eager for his late breakfast that he got tangled in her feet. Stella portioned out his stewed lamb and carrots onto a saucer, this one trimmed in navy blue with a garland of pink roses. As Barbanera tucked into his breakfast, Stella poked her *colomba* dough. It would have to wait a little longer.

She filled the moka with coffee grounds and water. Waiting for the water to heat, her mind replayed the events of the last few days. Once the coffee bubbled into the moka's upper chamber, she poured a cup and took it out to the terrace. The warming spring sun burned through the fog. It looked to be a lovely day.

She sighed. Barbanera, bits of carrot still clinging to his whiskers, paused at the threshold before venturing cautiously onto the stone terrazza. He jogged to her chair and balanced on his hind legs to rest a questioning paw on her thigh. For a moment she thought he might launch into her lap, but though he gave her legs a proprietary once over, he jumped onto a nearby empty chair.

As she sipped her coffee, she turned over the evidence in her mind. It stubbornly refused to unjumble.

She sighed again. She seemed to be developing a sighing problem.

Barbanera tossed a gaze at her and opened his mouth as if to meow, but no sound came out. She wondered if sighing was contagious.

She remembered the dough, waiting in her refrigerator. Stella rose. Even if she had to leave it unfinished, she needed to start. Barbanera's eyes followed her as she picked up her coffee cup and walked toward the back door. He looked around as if checking for any forthcoming worthy company before leaping from the chair to follow her heels into the house.

Stella removed the dough from the refrigerator, admiring its puff-iness. She divided the dough into two pieces, one slightly larger than the other, and she rolled them into logs as she thought about Domenica and Matteo. If their reaction was any indication, she expected much of the population of Aramezzo to stay indoors until the police caught up with Antonio.

Placing the longer log lengthwise on a greased baking sheet, she used her hand to crease the center. She looked up. Maybe the police had caught Antonio. Or maybe Aldo! She shook her head, wouldn't someone have called to let her know? She wondered if she was on any Aramezzo phone chains.

Stella lay the shorter log across the longer one, along the crease she'd made. As she shaped the shorter log into dove wings, she decided she couldn't sit on her hands and wait. She regarded her vaguely dove-type shape and realized it would need to rise again for another couple of hours. She shook her head and put the sheet in the refrigerator to give her extra time in case anything came up.

The rising time seemed a directive to go, to gather more information. Plus, she realized she didn't have enough almonds to grind for the top.

She nodded to herself and brushed off her pajama pants, ignoring the half-finished cup of coffee in her haste to buy one at Bar Cappellina.

A few minutes later, Barbanera securely indoors stalking a skink across the living room floor, Stella closed the door behind her and stared at it. Though she never locked up anymore, she supposed it only prudent to start now.

Stella breathed in as she walked to Bar Cappellina. Luisella must be making coffee, the scent drifted out of her window. She wondered if everyone had slept in.

Down the street, she noted the scent of scorching. Someone must have let milk boil over. As Stella walked around Aramezzo's lowest road, she wondered why she could still smell the scorched milk. Then she realized, that burned smell wasn't milk that bubbled over onto a hot oven surface. It was burned bread.

Was someone making bread? Had villagers grown tired of having their one bakery closed and baked their own loaves, much as their ancestors had? But this odor, it smelled like bread crust burned by flame, not over cooking. Were villagers even using their wood-burning ovens to make their bread? That seemed a little ambitious, but she imagined there must be some old women that remembered their mothers making bread in the outdoor ovens.

Almost without meaning to, Stella followed the burned smell and surprised herself by arriving at Forno Antico. She blinked, wondering if she was dreaming. Her sleep had been so fitful, it would be like her to include open bakery doors among the other jarring wisps of dreams.

No, the bakery doors were thrown open. This was the source of the burning smell. Stella wondered if maybe the oven was cooking off old crumbs or something. But the loaves she spotted behind Celeste at the counter sported the injury of hot flames. They appeared mottled. Unappetizing.

Celeste herself looked mottled, a pale rendition of herself.

Stella stepped in, "*Buongiorno*, Celeste."

Celeste looked up, her expression flat. "No *torta al testo* today. Only loaves of bread." It sounded like she'd repeated this multiple times already this morning.

Stella hesitated and then said, "I didn't know you were opening."

Dario poked his head into the shop from the bakery floor. "Stella! I thought I heard your voice. How are you?"

"I'm fine, I guess." Stella gestured to the bread. "Looks like you've been busy."

Dario wiped the sweat off his brow with his forearm. "About time the bakery opened, right?"

Stella paused. "Your father ... is he ..." She didn't know how to finish the sentence.

Dario's smile fell. "I wish he hadn't run. Now he looks guilty." He shook his head and tried to smile. "Anyway, Mamma and I agreed that with my father gone, we needed to open the bakery. That way, when he returns, we haven't lost all our best customers. We've already lost our employees, but Mamma and I can make it work, right Mamma?"

Celeste smiled stiffly. She certainly didn't seem to be an enthusiastic proponent of this plan, but then again, her husband was on the lam. She'd probably look enthusiastic about nothing short of a time machine.

At the flush on Celeste's cheeks, Stella realized what the older woman probably dreaded was knowing looks and probing questions. Stella could relate to that. She offered Celeste a wide smile of reassurance, but Celeste didn't seem to notice as she asked, "Did you want a loaf?"

No, actually, Stella did not. The loaves looked dried out where they weren't burned. But it was worth the euro to be supportive of her neighbor. It couldn't be easy for Dario to fill his father's shoes, especially on his own. "Yes, one please."

Dario rolled onto the balls of his feet in pleasure.

Stella offered what she hoped was an encouraging smile, asking, "Are you baking alone? It's so much work. And on Sunday! Your closed day!"

"We have ground to make up." Dario nodded. "But I think you'll appreciate what we're doing here."

Stella handed over the euro and on receiving the bread, she pretended enthusiasm she did not feel. She applauded Dario trying, but perhaps he was in over his head. She shook her head at the foolhardiness of youth before remembering she couldn't be more than eight years older than Dario. It wasn't like she was fully baked, either.

As she walked, Stella broke off the end of the loaf and nibbled on the inner crumb. She chewed thoughtfully and then swallowed with difficulty. No, she wasn't a fan of unsalted Umbrian-style bread, but Antonio turned out expertly made loaves. She may not prefer them, but she could taste the experience. This bread could not be called well constructed. First of all, it was flat. Dario probably hadn't kneaded it enough to work the gluten. Worse, the close structure suggested it was under-proofed. She wondered if both these errors came from Dario's haste to provide bread for the masses. As he settled into the role, he'd find the patience needed to bake an excellent loaf.

At least, Stella hoped so. She also hoped she could get this loaf away from her and quickly. Checking to make sure nobody saw her, she chucked the bread in a trash can. A job made more difficult by the fact that the can overflowed with flat, burnt bread. So hers wasn't the only disappointed palate.

Stella continued walking to Bar Cappellina. What a difference this time when she pushed the door open—instead of hushed tension, Stella sank into the burble of warm conversation. She made out individual voices from the rushing words:

"He must be hiding in the house somewhere."

"No way! The police tore the house up."

"Maybe he's at Dario's?"

"Nothing doing. They checked Dario's place, too."

"How about the car, can they see where it's gone?"

"His car is still here!"

Stella wondered aloud, "I wonder if they can track him using his cell phone?"

Romina shook her head. "He didn't take it. He has no money, no phone, no keys."

Someone piped up, "Unless someone is helping him? Dario maybe? Maybe Dario is getting him money. Or food?"

Another villager answered, "He might be. He has been so distraught about his father. But he would have to do it when the police aren't watching him. Which is all the time."

Flavia pushed open the door and hustled in. "Did you hear the news?" she panted. "Dario opened the bakery!" Stella hadn't even thought to mention this, assuming everyone knew.

Romina looked up, her eyebrows furrowed. "What do you mean?"

Flavia pointed in the direction of the *forno*. "He's there now, making bread."

Stella asked, "Did you buy a loaf?"

Flavia stammered, looking at the ground. "Umm. I was going to. But the line. I'll get some later?"

Stella smiled to herself.

Roberto shook his head. "How can Dario run the bakery without Antonio?"

Flavia shrugged dramatically. "Hasn't he been working there for years? How long does it take to learn to make bread?" She seemed to catch herself, no doubt remembering Dario's feeble loaves. "Anyway, he'll learn. He needs a running start on Aldo."

Stella asked, "Isn't Aldo's still closed?"

Romina nodded, murmuring, "I heard the police found him. Outside Genoa."

Stella looked up. This was news. Her brow furrowed . . . how could he be in Genoa and Assisi at the same time?

Flavia said, "All I know is, I'll sleep better when all this is . . . over?

Whenever my neighbor's chickens start clucking, I wonder, is Antonio in there?" She shook her head and turned to Stella. "You must no longer be under suspicion, right?"

"I'll believe that when I hear it from the Captain himself," she said. "And I can't imagine he's in any hurry to remove this dark cloud from my good name."

It wasn't until she got home that Stella remembered she'd meant to buy almonds. She thought about turning back, but grew distracted by the sight of her couch still littered with wood scraps, the table mounded with kitchen towels she'd meant to fold, and the fine layer of dust over it all. Before she could convince herself that living in near squalor wasn't so bad, she grit her teeth. She had guests coming in less than a week. Time to get busy. She threw on an apron and got to work. Almonds could wait.

She blared Italian pop music from her phone as she systematically went through the house, clearing splinters, wiping down surfaces, and scrubbing floors. Only when she drew off her gloves, her eyes surveying the bags of refuse by the door, did she remember she hadn't eaten anything all day.

Noting to herself that no self-respecting Italian ate dinner at six o'clock, she nonetheless boiled a packet of pasta and doused it with olive oil and a sprinkle of grated Pecorino cheese. She ate it standing up, watching the clouds move in across the valley.

Stella blinked. Had the whole day disappeared? She still needed almonds to finish her *colomba*! She washed her dishes and decided the spring cleaning had helped. Her muscles felt looser, her mind felt clearer. Maybe now she was ready to think. Unfortunately, the only thing she could think about, the thing that she realized she'd been thinking about the whole time she deep cleaned her house, was the funeral tomorrow. A funeral, and still no confirmed killer.

So unfair to Jacopo. So unfair to the people who loved him.

As far as she could tell (her own experience being convoluted by youth and her mother's grief), funerals were supposed to be cleansing—a way to say goodbye, to provide closure. How could anyone feel closure with a killer at large?

Stella shook her head to clear her suddenly clouded vision. She tied a scarf around her neck, locked the door, and headed out to the *alimentari* for almonds.

Cristiana's seemed full of grandmothers picking up pasta or tomatoes or a bundle of fresh *agretti* for dinner. She wanted to ask a woman how she prepared the *agretti*—so far Stella had only landed on boiling the succulent-like greens and tossing them in an anchovy dressing—but she wasn't feeling particularly social. She paid for her almonds and escaped back into the alleys of Aramezzo.

When Stella arrived home, she found Luca waiting outside her house. Before she could even greet him, he said, "The police found Aldo."

Stella's breath left her body.

Luca went on, "They're questioning him now. He's insisting, though, that he didn't do it. With Antonio on the run, I wouldn't be surprised if they let him go."

"But Aldo took off—"

Luca shook his head. "He's saying there was a family emergency—his great-aunt had a heart attack outside Genoa. He left when he got the news, he didn't know the police wanted him for questioning."

"How did the police find him?"

Luca said, "It was hard. He fled so fast he didn't bring his phone so they couldn't track it." Well, Stella thought, that explained that. "But his wife had given the police a list of all Aldo's relatives. They'd worked their way through all the father's side, and as soon as they got to the mother's side, they figured it out."

Stella wondered. "But wouldn't his wife know about the family emergency? Why didn't she mention it to the police?"

"Aldo didn't tell his wife. Some marriage they've got there," Luca added. He sank onto the step. "The captain still has it in for me."

"Join the club." Luca said nothing, and Stella sank beside him. "Luca, it'll be okay. Once this case is behind you, you'll be Captain Palmiro's shiny star again."

"That's not it." Luca shook his head. "What I hate is not knowing what's happening in the investigation, in real time. I buy off-duty officers glasses of wine until they forget I'm on the outside and they start spilling, but that's hardly the same thing."

Stella hadn't realized Luca was this invested. As if in answer to her question, Luca said, "I had to know what they have on you. Which, as far as I can tell, is nothing but the prints."

She nodded, relieved. "Thank you."

"Of course," Luca said. "But it's still frustrating. Not knowing. Maybe it sounds weird, but I hate . . . no, I *loathe*, unresolved riddles."

Stella paused. Was he kidding? "Oh, I don't know," she said airily. "It doesn't sound all that weird to me."

He grinned and held her eye contact for a moment before saying, "I guess it wouldn't."

Luca said, "Anyway, from what I gather—and understand this is coming from half-inebriated police officers on the outskirts of this case—Aldo seemed surprised to see the officers. He returned to Umbria willingly. Then he revealed his wife's relationship with Jacopo and suggested *she* may be the killer."

Stella's head picked up. "His *wife*?"

Luca shrugged.

Stella repeated, "His wife. Who protested her husband's innocence when they couldn't locate him. That guy seems to have a loyalty deficit."

"Or she did it. Stranger things have happened."

Stella considered. "Why in the world would she kill her lover?"

Luca shrugged again. "Maybe she wanted them to run off together, Jacopo refused, and they got into an argument. Or maybe she wanted Jacopo to kill her husband, and he refused, and *that* got them into an argument."

Stella frowned. "That sounds familiar."

"It's the plot of a Netflix docuseries." Luca offered up a sheepish smile. "Anyway, I wanted you to know about Aldo. Have you found any more clues?"

Widening her eyes, Stella said, "I thought you didn't care what I think?"

"Ah, Stella," Luca ducked his head. "That is the official position, but it's not mine."

A burst of warmth exploded in her ribcage. "No, I'm still stuck on how Aldo would have gotten Antonio's lame. What about Antonio? Any news?"

Luca shook his head. "That's the other reason I'm here. No, we haven't found him."

Stella wondered if he noticed he'd used "we."

Luca went on, "But we have to assume he's lurking about. Some food from gardens has gone missing, with big footprints in the soil. Someone's bag of groceries disappeared from her step when she went inside to put down another bag. Stella, you need to be careful. I've heard from three people that you've been walking through town on your own."

"You think Antonio is going to grab me in broad daylight and drag me . . . where exactly?"

"You're caught up in this somehow, Stella. You see that, don't you?"

She lifted her chin. "I don't. Not at all. In fact, quite the opposite. I seem to be the only one Antonio is talking to."

"When he's not in hiding," Luca reminded her. "And that's the point. If he feels connected to you, then you're in danger."

"No. That can't be right."

"It doesn't matter if you agree with me. Understand, people who care about you are worried. You won't do anyone any good by making yourself vulnerable."

Ah, this was why she found Luca aggravating. Now she remembered—he assumed he knew everything. For a moment she thought about protesting further, but realized a more expedient route. She nodded. "Okay, then."

"Stella."

"What? I'm agreeing."

"Too easily."

"I know when I'm beaten."

Luca gazed at her levelly. "I had more arguments in my back pocket."

"Keep them." Stella rose and brushed the seat of her pants. "Well, I appreciate your stopping by."

He didn't answer, his eyes trained on her. Finally, he stood up. In a soft voice, he said, "Please, Stella. Don't go looking for Antonio. I'm afraid you'll find him."

She widened her eyes to approximate innocence. "No way. I have a *colomba* to finish, a cat to feed, and *gialli* on my nightstand. Cozy night in for me."

Luca didn't look like he believed her, but also knew he didn't have a card to play. He nodded and walked away, his hands in his pockets. Stella watched his broad back retreat into the darkness.

Slowly, Stella climbed the steps and pushed on the door before remembering she'd locked it.

Evening's darkness pressed against her. Her heart sped up as she considered the locked door. Yes, she'd locked this one, but had she locked the back? She couldn't remember.

Was Aldo still in police custody? Maybe Luca had old information. Maybe Aldo had walked out of Aramezzo's police station, intent on finding the person who informed the police of his wife's affair.

Could Aldo...or Antonio...or anyone...have entered her home while she was gone? Could someone even now be crouched in a dark corner, waiting?

Stella held her breath as she turned the key in the lock and swung the door open with a bang. Her hand reached in and swiped the wall, finally finding the switch. She flicked on the light, already recoiling from the expectation of a man hunched against the shadows, ready to strike.

But the light only revealed Barbanera, sitting in front of her, blinking at the sudden light.

She exhaled.

If there was someone in the house, Barbanera wouldn't have been waiting so placidly. Still, she faltered, moving deeper into the house, flicking on light switches as she went until she illuminated the whole downstairs. Shrugging on her chef's coat, she set to work.

She could still hear her heartbeat thundering, so Stella made as much noise as she could in the kitchen, turning on the oven to preheat, removing the *colomba* from the refrigerator along with an egg and then slamming the door, and rummaging through her cabinet until she found the sparkling sugar she'd last used on Christmas's *panettone*.

As Stella separated the egg white from yolk and ground the almonds to make the *colomba*'s crackling coating, her breathing slowed. Surely, if someone was hiding out in her house, they would have made themselves known by now. She mixed the ground almonds with the sparkling sugar and stirred to combine them. Stella picked up the cup with egg white and started to pour it into the almonds and sugar when her hand snatched back.

She stared at the ground almonds and the sparkling sugar. Something tugged on her brain. This looked familiar. It reminded her of something . . . something she'd neglected at the time, but now felt important. But what?

An image of Forno Antico rose in her mind.

The bakery. Something at the bakery. But what? And when?

A series of images played across her mind—the fallen scoop of flour, the cracked phone, the smell of butter-rich dough . . . Jacopo. Without realizing she was doing it, she flung off her chef's coat.

She cast one regretful look at her dove-shaped pastry before sticking it back in the refrigerator. Sending up a prayer to all kitchen gods that the *colomba* could withstand a bit more waiting, she dashed out the door, stopping briefly in the street before running back up the stairs to lock the door.

Clinging to the walls of the streets to avoid notice, Stella crept as quickly as she dared, around the ring road. Almost there . . . she'd almost made it.

She exhaled.

"*Ciao*, Stella." She recoiled like fish skin in a hot pan.

"Mimmo," she whisper-screamed. "What are you doing here?"

"I live here," he said blandly in his regular voice, which seemed to ring extra loud in the twilight. "Same as you."

His eyes followed hers to the bakery as the lights within switched on. Stella's stomach dropped. Did someone hear her? But what was anyone doing in the bakery? Was Dario prepping for the next day, realizing that his opening hadn't gone as well as he hoped? But no, she heard voices. It reminded her of the night she heard Antonio and Jacopo arguing. Drawing closer, she realized that unlike that night, and the morning she found Jacopo dead on the bakery floor, the doors of the bakery were latched closed. Light showed only around the cracks. She wondered if perhaps the shop door remained unlocked.

She knew she should walk away and leave it, but the image of the ground almonds and sugar—she had to know if there was anything to it.

She held up a finger to show Mimmo he should stay where he was. Then she slunk forward to the bakery door. She heard Dario's voice. "It's not like I've gotten paid, don't you think I deserve something for picking up your slack?"

"You can't be serious. You think you deserve *more*?" With a shock, Stella recognized Antonio's voice. "Look at that stack."

Dario said something unintelligible and Antonio sighed, "You'll never learn."

"From you? No, you're right about that. I'm finished learning from you."

Mimmo appeared at Stella's shoulder. "What's going on?"

"Shhh!" Stella jumped, waving her arms. She heard the action within the bakery still. Quickly, she whispered to Mimmo. "Mimmo! Get the cops! Tell them Antonio is at the bakery."

"Cops?" Mimmo scoffed.

"Yes! They need to know Antonio is in here!"

Mimmo leaned over as if to whisper, but his voice sounded regularly pitched to Stella. "Cops are no good, with all those stupid rules. You can't hunt here, Mimmo, you need to leash your dogs, Mimmo. Psh. Who needs all that? We'll take them down ourselves."

"We. Most. Certainly. Will. Not. Take. Them. Down." Stella could barely get the words out. "One of them might have a gun!"

Mimmo nodded, proud. "I have a gun."

"Please, Mimmo! I'm begging you! Just *go*."

He nodded and hurried away, calling over his shoulder. "Okay. I'll get it and be right back."

Stella's heart collapsed. His gun. He was getting his gun. He lived a fifteen-minute walk outside of town.

Just then, the shop door flung open. Dario stood in the doorway. He frowned and cast a nervous glance over his shoulder. "Stella? What are you doing here?"

Before she could stop and think, Stella stepped to the doorway and sidled past Dario, into the shop. Antonio leaned against the bakery sinks, arms crossed over his chest. Flour and streaks of dried dough marred half the bakery's surfaces, the other half looked scrubbed and sprayed. Dirty paper towels filled the trash can. Stella noticed an enormous pile of pans and tools on the drying rack beside a sink full of water and a few bubbles.

Stella's eyes widened. She'd never seen the bakery in disrepair. On the edge of the island, Stella noticed a stack of scratch-off lottery cards, their silver-gray curls littered all around them.

Dario slipped into the bakery and stood in front of his father, as if blocking him from view would make Stella doubt her eyes. In soft but sure tones, Dario said, "Stella, this is a bad time. A very, very bad time."

Behind Dario, Stella saw Antonio, anger thundering across his face.

Stella stuttered, "What-what's going on?"

Dario shook his head, leading her to the door. "It doesn't concern you, Stella. You get home now, okay?" As he put an arm around her shoulder, he muttered. "It's not safe, Stella. Please."

Her breath stalled at his words. Stella nodded and started to leave, when Antonio's voice stopped her, a boulder plunging into a deep, still lake. "It doesn't matter. It's over."

Dario cast his father a nervous look. "Papà, you can't mean it."

Antonio sank onto a stool. "No. You were right, Dario. It's time I turn myself in."

Stella paused. "Antonio . . . *you* did this? You killed Jacopo?"

Antonio looked up, eyes beseeching Dario. "I didn't mean for any of this to happen. You have to know that. None of it."

Dario hurried to his father and patted his shoulder, murmuring, "I know, Papà. I know. The argument got out of control. It was a side of Jacopo that most people didn't see. But we did."

Antonio said nothing, as he dropped his head until his eyes fixed on the ground.

Stella couldn't believe it. All this time, she'd been so sure it hadn't been Antonio. Especially once she understood Jacopo to be Antonio's son. She ventured, "Antonio. Then what was all that yesterday on the park bench?"

Dario's eyes narrowed. "What park bench?"

Antonio cut his gaze to Stella and said firmly. "Nothing. I must have convinced Stella I was innocent."

"Stella is so trusting. She probably didn't need much convincing." Dario nodded as he mindlessly brushed the lead-colored shavings from the lottery tickets off the table, where they landed in the flour.

Antonio nodded slowly. In a quiet voice, Antonio said, "Promise me you'll be good. Okay, Dario?"

"Of course," Dario smiled, gently. "Like father, like son."

Stella's stomach lurched at the words. Her eye caught on the flour, now speckled with the leavings of scratch-offs, blurring the honest smell of flour with something chemical, like latex.

Her heart stopped. Her gaze inched toward the hamper—inner wheels turning, locking, and shifting until the pieces fell into place. She turned back to the bakery floor, taking in the half-cleaned mess, Dario still in his blue apron, and Antonio standing dejected by the sink. The baker's hair needed a wash, and he was disheveled from his time in hiding, but still, his white shirt shone bright white.

Just then, Stella heard footsteps racing toward the bakery. Antonio and Dario both tensed at the sound, Antonio moving to stand behind Stella. Stella's heart pounded.

Dario clocked Antonio's movement. He sighed. "Papà, don't make this harder than it needs to be."

Antonio nodded and looked down at his dress shoes, neatly tied but dusted with flour.

His dress shoes. The final clue fell into place, and Stella's mouth sagged open. Images from the morning she found Jacopo fell like grains of yeast into sugar water, blooming and bubbling until her mind, for the first time in a week, felt clear.

Captain Palmiro and Salvo burst through the shop door. The Captain's eyes quickly scanned the room, assessing the situation. He drew his gun out of its holster and spoke slowly, his voice low and gruff. "Antonio. Get away from Stella. Now."

Antonio didn't move. Stella couldn't move.

Dario, eyes on Captain Palmiro's gun, whispered, "Papà . . . don't make it worse. Please?"

Antonio held up his hands and stepped to the side.

Stella's voice shook as she said, "Captain?"

His eyes fixed on Antonio, Captain Palmiro said, "Not the time, Stella. Salvo, check Antonio for weapons." To Antonio, he said, "Keep your hands up where I can see them."

Antonio's mustache twitched as he nodded.

Stella took a step toward Palmiro. "Captain, please. You have to listen to me."

He shook his head, his eyes still on Antonio. "Mimmo told me. I've never seen him so out of breath. What in the world were you thinking, trying to take Antonio alone?"

Stella's gaze moved around the room as Salvo patted Antonio down, removing a switchblade from his pocket to show Palmiro. Antonio twitched toward the knife, and Palmiro shouted, "Freeze! Antonio, just because we grew up together, don't think I won't shoot you to keep my people safe."

Antonio blinked rapidly and then straightened, raising his hands higher, his eyes straight ahead. Stella watched a muscle twitching in his jaw. She couldn't take it anymore and blurted, "Captain Palmiro. Antonio didn't kill Jacopo."

All eyes turned to her.

Stella inhaled to still her jackhammering heart. "Dario did."

"Don't listen to her, Captain." Antonio barked before turning to Stella and pleading, "Stella. Don't do this."

She shook her head. "You can't protect him any longer."

At the exchange, Palmiro finally looked at her. "Protect who? Dario? Stella, what are you talking about?"

Stella steadied her words. "You remember the footprint, I'm assuming, Captain?"

"Of course I do."

"Then you also remember how it faced *into* the bakery? Strange, isn't it? You'd think a footprint made with flour would be found exiting, not entering, the building. Unless that footprint wasn't made by the killer leaving, but by someone trying to frame a baker."

Captain Palmiro screwed his eyebrows up and Stella knew he was trying to remember which direction the footprint faced. He shook his head and said, "The sneaker that made that print, it was in a bag of the baker's shoes, tossed over a cliff."

Stella nodded. "That tripped me up, too. Then I remembered, the morning of the murder. Dario left the scene to alert Celeste. A perfect opportunity to plant the floury shoe in Antonio's closet." Stella turned to Antonio. "I'm guessing Celeste dumped all the sneakers she could find? Leaving you with only your dress shoes?"

His eyes welled with tears.

Stella went on, "Then there's the apron—"

Dario's voice cut her off. "Stella, now I see why the police can't stand you. Can't you let them do their job and get all of this over with? You must know I have an alibi for the morning of Jacopo's murder."

Salvo agreed. "It's true, Stella, he does."

Stella mused aloud, "You were with your girlfriend."

"Yes," smirked Dario.

Pages from her *gialli* flipped through her mind. "And she confirmed the time." Stella gazed at Dario levelly. "You changed the clocks."

"What?" Captain Palmiro yelped, his eyes darting at Dario, whose smirk slipped off his face.

"He changed the clocks," Stella repeated. "It's a trick straight out of a *giallo*. Dario came home from killing Jacopo, burned his clothes—which explains the scent on him the morning of the murder, which I assumed was campfire—changed the clocks, woke up his girlfriend so she could see the time, and after she went back to sleep, he changed the clocks back."

"Tha-that's ridiculous!" Dario scoffed. "You can't prove that."

Stella shrugged. "Luckily, you frame people with as much attention to detail as you bake bread. I don't have to prove it. All clues lead to you. My only question is, where did you hide the apron?"

"What?" Dario sputtered, laughing. "What nonsense is this? I'm *wearing* my apron. Next, you'll try to convince me I'm not?" Dario continued laughing and turned to the police as if they were in on the joke. But both Palmiro and Salvo looked from Antonio to Dario with steely looks.

Stella continued, "You took your father's Monday apron out of the hamper to kill Jacopo Tuesday. But I can't figure out where you hid it."

Dario gestured to the hamper. "Stella, you must have heard. They found the apron. Right there."

She shook her head. "They found it after you called in the anonymous tip. And that's the part I don't get. You moved the apron to the hamper after I told you the police were searching for Aldo, and that I, too, was a suspect. Why not let one of us take the blame? Why work so hard to convince me you believed in your father's innocence?"

Stella watched as Antonio turned to Dario, his wet eyes narrowing. Dario turned away, his face turning purple.

Stella nodded. "Oh. Oh, now I understand. Of course."

Palmiro grumbled. "Care to fill us in?"

Stella bit her lip and waited for Antonio or Dario to speak. When they didn't, she said, "It wasn't enough to kill Jacopo. He needed his father to go to jail. It was the only way to get the bakery. Or else his father might take a shine to another young baker."

Dario spit out, "Who knows how many illegitimate children that man has?"

Palmiro looked between Antonio and Dario and then aimed the gun at Dario.

Stella tsked her tongue against her teeth. "That was the part I wasn't sure of. You did know. That Antonio fathered Jacopo."

"So what if I did?"

Stella thought for a moment. "All those times Jacopo alluded to being harassed for working here. We all just assumed he meant the tension between your fathers. But I see now . . . he meant you. You made his life so miserable, he had to leave. It was you all along."

Dario growled and lurched toward Stella until he noticed Captain Palmiro's gun trained on him. His words like ice, Captain Palmiro barked, "Don't be impulsive, Dario."

"Impulsive!" Dario shouted. "I planned this for months! Ever since she solved Severini's murder!"

Stella said, "You figured if you laid the right clues, I'd dutifully follow them, leading the police to your father."

Antonio regarded her. "But you never believed it was me. Why?"

Stella thought about how to answer and finally said, "Nobody who cares so much for a loaf of bread could hurt anyone. And even if you did, even if it was an accident, you'd turn yourself in. Because you wouldn't be able to live with yourself."

Dario shook his head and shouted, "You stupid cops can't possibly believe what she's saying! She's insane!"

Stella shook her head and sighed. "Men often think women who don't do what they want are insane. I'm my own person, Dario. I make my own choices. You may have to examine the real possibility that perhaps you're not as smart as you think you are."

Antonio said softly, "Stella."

She whirled to face the baker. "Why are you shielding him? You would let him stroll around Aramezzo while you went to jail for his crime?"

"It's my fault." He closed his eyes. "Though I did try, that I know. I've loved Dario so much, and I could show him, in a way I could never show Jacopo. But at some level, Dario must have known. Because Dario told me, all the time, that I never gave him enough. That I was a terrible father. Don't you see? I made a child out of sin, and somehow, it impacted Dario. That's why he's always taking the easy way out."

Antonio went on, "But I kept trying. I encouraged him to work here, hoping it would finally bring us together. But I failed again. So I owed him. I've always owed him." He opened his eyes, staring at the wall. "I guess I believed that if I turned myself in, gave him this last chance, it would finally be enough. That he'd do … better. By all of us. When you love your child … you never lose hope. You never stop trying."

Silence descended. Dario grumbled and Stella turned to him, saying, "But how did you know about Jacopo?"

He shrugged. "I don't know how anybody missed it. The way Papà fawned all over him."

Antonio held his palms against his eyes. "I failed you, Dario. I'll never forgive myself."

Glowering, Dario muttered, "You couldn't even turn yourself in without blowing it. Such a coward. And Mamma was too stupid to throw you out on your ear. Always mooning all over you for any crumbs of attention. It's sickening."

"Don't listen to him, Antonio," Palmiro intoned. "Nothing has ever been good enough for Dario. Not you, not Celeste, not his teachers. Not anybody. Is it any wonder he's been fired from every job he's ever had?"

Salvo spoke slowly. "I remember, now. Antonio, when you coached our soccer team. You'd always play Dario and then he'd fumble and yell it was everyone's fault. Especially yours. Meanwhile, whatever position you played Jacopo, he'd find a way to get the ball to someone to score. Dario hated him for it."

Stella nodded. "I should have figured out his true feelings when he made that comment about Jacopo's fan club. He couldn't stand his half-brother being so beloved."

Salvo gasped. "The fires. All those fires in middle school, when Jacopo started standing out in soccer, in school. There were rumors it was Dario, but no one caught him."

Stella caught on the word. Fires? Then she remembered, Dario himself had mentioned starting fires. She'd thought it was hyperbole.

Dario leered. "Is it any wonder I couldn't trust the police to solve this crime? Why I needed insurance?"

Stella muttered, "That's me, I suppose. Insurance."

Palmiro tossed handcuffs to Salvo, who snapped them around Dario's wrists. Dario glared at Stella. "I'll get you for this."

She shrugged. "I don't see how."

Dario smiled. "I'm not your only enemy in Aramezzo, Stella. This is the beginning. Actually, Severini was the beginning." He writhed against his handcuffs, even as Salvo pulled him out of the bakery.

Stella watched him go, her mouth hanging open.

"I wouldn't worry about that, Signorina." The Captain said, exhaustion softening his words. "All he has left are empty threats."

Stella tried to nod but wound up staring at the ground.

Antonio's eyes followed his son, his face alternating between grief and flashes of anger. Finally, he said, "But, Stella. How did you know?"

She gestured to the flour sprinkled with scratch-off shavings. "When I found Jacopo, I noticed the flour on the floor reflected light in a funny way. Then when I saw those silver curls from his lottery tickets, I realized Dario must have been scratching off lottery tickets as he waited in the back for Jacopo. When Jacopo turned his back, Dario leapt up to . . . you know … and the shavings must have fallen in the flour." Stella adjusted her bandana as she considered. "Once that snapped into place, I remembered—every morning, you bring a fresh apron to work. At the end of the day, you drop it in the hamper. Sundays, the aprons get washed."

"So?" Captain Palmiro said, even as Antonio nodded.

"So, that apron you all found, that was filthy, not simply bloody. Antonio couldn't have worn that apron on Tuesday morning. No, the killer must have taken a dirty apron from the hamper before killing Jacopo, planning to get blood on it. He must have lodged the apron somewhere, hoping someone would find it, but he doesn't seem able to think like other people, so he must have put it somewhere improbable. Like buried somewhere or in an abandoned house. When he realized no one had found it, and he needed someone to see it to implicate Antonio, he brought it back and called in the tip."

Captain Palmiro said in wonder, "So Luca did check the hamper."

She nodded. "I may not see eye to eye with Luca all the time, but he is honest. I didn't see him check it, but when he said he did, I knew he did. Which means the apron wasn't in the hamper the morning of the murder. It was put in later."

Captain Palmiro nodded before saying, "I still don't get how he got you here that morning?"

Stella flushed self-consciously. "I guess I am easy to manipulate. He led me to believe I'd find Antonio."

The Captain added, "And how did he get you to touch the lame?"

Stella's blush now warmed her cheeks red. "I'm afraid I did that all by myself. He wouldn't have wanted that, it got in the way of framing his father."

"There's one part I still don't get," Antonio said.

"Only one?" Captain Palmiro said.

Antonio went on, "What if you hadn't come Tuesday morning? If you'd slept late or decided to wait?"

She shrugged. "If I didn't find Jacopo, someone would have. Probably you. He stacked the deck, but he probably figured even if I didn't stumble across the body, I'm too much of a busybody to stay away from a mystery."

Palmiro regarded her levelly. He opened his mouth and then closed it and looked away. Finally, he muttered, "And thank goodness."

Stella had no idea how to respond to this. She wanted to joke that she wouldn't get a swollen head, but she almost felt like she should pretend the Captain hadn't said anything at all noteworthy. She turned to Antonio. "What I don't understand is why you are here now."

He sighed. "As soon as I saw the apron, I knew what Dario did. And I knew what I had to do. To protect him. To protect Celeste. But I needed time before turning myself in. And then, Dario made that terrible bread—"

"I should've known then," Stella said. "Everything I needed to know was in that one bite."

"Bread that bad, I knew the kitchen must look like a bomb exploded. I figured, one last clean of the bakery, and I'd say goodbye. Goodbye to all of it."

MONDAY

*T*he rain began, softly at first.

Stella looked out at the heavy sky and sipped her coffee. She supposed a bright day for a funeral would be an insult. Rain suited the mood of the village. Even Barbanera seemed to feel it. He slept in a ball on her faded quilt, opening one eye as she put on a black dress, on loan from Marta. Stella had failed to pack mourning clothes in her move from New York. She never expected she'd grow to care about anyone in Aramezzo enough to grieve them, let alone feel the desire to stand with her neighbors in solidarity with a village's loss.

The night before, she'd finally baked the *colomba*. But it felt so wrong, so strange—an icon of peace on a day that felt shattered. Luckily, she'd remembered that *colomba*, like *panettone*, lasted. She had time to decide if she wanted to make more. Time to decide if she wanted to deliver this to someone.

Then she'd fallen asleep, cataloguing the losses... Jacopo, of course. She couldn't imagine the bakery without his infectious energy. Dario—on his way now to a court that would no doubt find him guilty—didn't count much of a loss, but she felt for his parents. Especially Antonio, who had lost two sons in the space of a week, one whom he could not claim. The hole in his heart, it must be huge, and Stella couldn't help but grieve for him. And then, Bruno and Benedetta. Never mind that Jacopo wasn't Bruno's biological son, which he had to know by now, even if he hadn't already suspected. Stella knew how much Jacopo's parents loved him. She only hoped their son had felt the full force of that love.

She sighed and drew on a black cardigan, on loan from Domenica. Opening the front door, Stella paused, wondering if she should bring an umbrella. She turned into the house but stopped at a voice behind her, "It will lighten. The rain."

Stella jumped. She shook her head at herself. How long until she stopped leaping out of her skin at the most innocuous of noises? She spun around to greet whatever neighbor thought fit to advise her. Then she jumped again at the sight of Luisella, standing below Stella's steps, dressed in a black dress that skimmed over the hollow planes of her body. Stella could hardly believe the words to have come from Luisella except at that moment, Luisella motioned to the sky. "See there? The clouds. They're already thinning."

What response was appropriate when one's neighbor of four months suddenly acknowledges your presence? Stella merely nodded and murmured, "Thank you."

Luisella inclined her head in response and set off down the street.

Jacopo's passing changed things for everybody, Stella realized.

She left the umbrella in the house. Calling a goodbye over her shoulder to Barbanera, she realized he'd finally roused and stood beside her at the door. He leaned against her for a moment, blinking at the increasing light.

Stella patted him and then waited for him to whisk around to reenter the house. But he simply looked up at her as if asking, *are you ready?* Stella drew the door closed with a click and Barbanera trotted down the steps, waiting for her. Hardly daring to believe it, Stella followed him. He stayed at her side better than dogs taught to heel, and Stella trusted that if he grew frightened, he'd find his way home.

She spent the first month of her stay in Aramezzo closing up the holes in her house to prevent his entrance, and yet he always found a route inside. If he needed to return, he could.

Stella and Barbanera joined a clutch of villagers making their way along the ring road to the tunnel. A few raised their eyebrows at the sight of the American *signorina*, curly hair pinned up instead of tamed by its usual bandana, with the enormous silver-spotted tabby jogging at her side. But most kept their eyes straight ahead as they made their way to the graveyard.

Stella knew that most of them had gone to the church for the service, and she felt a pang. Perhaps she should have gone as well. But after the events of last night, she squirmed too much at the thought of being indoors with people. As if summoned, Matteo appeared beside her, wrapping his arm around her shoulder. He nodded to Barbanera. "Does he think he's a dog?"

She shrugged.

He smiled. "You're grateful for the company."

She tried to smile. But her face felt weighed down.

Squeezing her shoulder, he said, "The church was full. Nobody noticed, and if they did, they'd understand."

Thus linked—Matteo with his arm around Stella, and the cat still trotting at her heels—they continued down the road to the graveyard. She looked around. "Don Arrigo isn't here yet?"

Matteo shook his head. "You can imagine all the parishioners who wanted to speak with him after the service."

The crowd mingled around the grave. Stella would have assumed the coffin would journey to the gravesite with the mourners, but no, it waited in the ground. She shook her head. Maybe they did funerals differently in Italy. Or, more likely, each town had variations in custom based on history and terrain.

Anyway, she'd only been to one funeral in her life. She hardly remembered it, it had been such a blur, but since then, she'd always found reason to avoid them. This one, though. Having found the body and uncovered the killer, she felt like she had to be here. No matter how much it brought old pain to the surface.

Stella squeezed her eyes shut, trying to block out the memory of the two coffins, her mother's face red with anger as she turned to a quietly weeping Stella, hissing, *"Don't make a scene! What do you have to cry about?"*

Stella focused on the conversation next to her, trying to blot out the memory that pushed against her heart. The mayor was telling Cristiana, "I can't help but think that if Jacopo had told even one person I'd pulled strings to get him a pastry shop, somehow this all could have been avoided. Silly boy."

The key! Stella blurted, "You tried to help him? *You* gave him that key? Why didn't you say so?"

"I can't have everyone trying to call in favors all the time. But now…" He shrugged expansively.

Matteo and Stella locked eyes. Matteo ducked his head and whispered, "Do you think Jacopo was going to do it? Open the pastry shop?"

Stella considered before shaking her head. "Maybe that's what he was doing the morning he was killed—seeing if he liked pastry enough to take that leap."

Matteo nodded. "Maybe if Dario knew, he wouldn't have killed Jacopo."

She pressed her lips together, thinking. "Honestly, I don't think it was ever about the bakery. What mattered to Dario was getting rid of his competition, when the rest of the world was too stupid, in his eyes, to even know Jacopo was Dario's competition. Feeling smug was better than feeling second best."

Matteo looked at her searchingly and his concern landed in her heart as if he'd spoken the words aloud. "It's okay, Matteo. I came to terms with being second best to my sister long ago."

Matteo didn't look like he believed her. In truth, she wasn't sure she believed it either, but she had never resented Grazie, so Dario's anger felt foreign.

She thought about trying to communicate this to Matteo, but Veronica had cornered him as much as one could corner another person in open space. Her dogs sniffed at Barbanera, who sat and glared at them, his topaz eyes gleaming. Did Stella imagine the long-haired, russet-colored dachshunds trembling a bit before cowering behind Veronica's legs?

The mayor's wife drew a card from her purse. "Of course, we were the first to know about the Americans' ball. Even before they sent out these invitations, they cleared the date with us to make sure we'd be in attendance. And how clever they are! A "*masque-rave*"! You probably don't get it, but it's a play on the words 'masquerade' and 'rave', a blend of old and new party styles."

Matteo nodded politely, but then rolled his eyes at Stella as Veronica still held out the invitation. "I imagine their American high society friends will be in attendance. You, of course, weren't invited to the last such party, several years ago. Such a magical evening! Remember, *tesoro*?"

The mayor turned from his conversation with Cristiana. After a moment of not understanding what he was supposed to be agreeing to, his eyes landed on the card. "Yes. Fine people, the Americans. We're lucky to have their patronage."

Veronica laughed throatily. "But their parties, right Marcello? Simply legendary."

His chest puffed a bit. "The talk of the town. Even people who are not invited gossip about the costumes, the food, for years on end."

Veronica's gaze snagged on Luisella, standing at the edge of the cemetery, not twenty meters from them, her hands still clutching her vintage pink quilted purse. "I don't suppose you got an invitation, Luisella?" As an aside, Veronica muttered to Stella, "Just because she was in those movies all those years ago, she still fancies herself a starlet."

In answer, Luisella unclasped the shell snap atop her purse and silently drew out the invitation, holding it out to Veronica with the first trace of a smile Stella had seen.

Veronica muttered. "Oh, that's right. The Americans do invite her to their soirées. So kind of them to show her attention. I hope she feels grateful for their charity."

Once again, Stella wondered about the history these two shared. She also wondered if it would come to a head at the party. There certainly seemed to be quite a bit of posturing around it already. Ah well, no way Stella would secure an invitation, so that drama would be one she could safely avoid. And thank goodness. She could go a good long time without any drama at all.

Her heart fluttered a touch at the sight of Luca entering the cemetery, flanked by an older couple that must be his parents. Taller than those around him, he scanned the crowd until his eyes landed on Stella. He leaned down to whisper something to his parents and then strode to her.

She tried to grab Matteo's hand but he slunk away with a grin, joining Domenica who walked down the steps with Marta and Ascanio. His eyes fixed on Stella, Luca didn't seem to notice any of this. He put his hands on her shoulders, his gaze searching hers as he said, "*Madonna mia*, Stella. How are you? I could hardly believe it when Salvo told me."

Stella tried to shrug, but Luca's warm hands on her shoulders weighed them down. Instead, she attempted a chipper tone. "I'm great, Luca! Really great. Glad it's over."

His eyes bored into hers for a moment, before he said so softly, only she could hear, "I'm not buying it. You know, you don't have to be strong all the time."

He pulled her into a hug, squeezing her lightly against his chest. She pressed her cheek against the woodsiness of his sweater, closing her eyes to breathe in the feeling of his strong arms around her. He pulled away before she was ready and she looked away, biting her lower lip to keep it from trembling. Luca squeezed her shoulders gently and then let his arms fall to his sides. "So it sounds like Dario was using you? Thought he could lay proverbial breadcrumbs and you'd follow them to his father?"

"I guess."

Luca shook his head, chuckling. "Well, he's not the first man to have underestimated you." She shot him a look, checking for sarcasm. Instead, his smile lit his face. He continued, "He didn't count on your gut, your instinct."

She managed to grin back. "Any chance the rest of your colleagues see it that way?"

His eyebrows instantly furrowed. "What do you mean?"

"Well," she shrugged. "Last time your Captain didn't seem to share your admiration for my, what's the word? Right, meddling."

"Ah," said Luca.

"Yes. Ah."

"To tell you the truth, I think Captain Palmiro being on the scene made him reevaluate his opinion."

"He what now?"

Luca grinned wide enough to show his overlapping front tooth. "Salvo told me that Palmiro said you seemed so small in that bakery."

Stella almost tripped on Barbanera as she started. "Small!"

"Hang on, Stella. It wasn't an insult. He only meant that you looked like you carried the world on your shoulders and he wanted to protect you."

Stella glowered. "I don't need him or anyone to protect me."

Chuckling, Luca said, "That's what Salvo told him. In any case, the Captain seems to consider you one of us now."

Stella couldn't believe his words. "A police officer?"

Luca shook his head, still laughing. "I wouldn't go that far. He has some old school notions about women on the force. I mean, you belong to Aramezzo. So while he may find you annoying at times—"

"Ha!"

"—his primary concern is your safety. In fact," Luca lowered his voice, "He asked me to check on you today." She shot him a look of suspicion. Luca added, "I would have anyway! But he asked me when he called to apologize for taking me off the case. He's reinstating me for full service." Luca hitched his shoulders back.

"How nice for you," Stella muttered.

"Oh, look," Luca gestured with his chin. "Don Arrigo is here. Let's find places."

Stella moved to the back of the group. Don Arrigo paused as he passed her. He put his hand on her cheek and said, "Stella. I couldn't believe when I heard. What are the odds that you wind up in the center of two murder revelations?"

She didn't say anything.

Don Arrigo seemed to guess her feelings. "Come by later today. I have some port to share with you and you can tell me all about . . . all of it."

She nodded and said, "Can we also burn some sage? I'm in serious need of a cleansing."

He looked confused for a moment but then his face cleared. "Ah, I have heard of that. I'm not sure the sage in our church kitchen garden would burn particularly well, but before Easter, I go from house to house, blessing homes. I'll bring twice as much holy water for yours."

"You have a kitchen garden? At the church?"

He smiled. "Planted by the cloistered nuns, a couple of hundred years ago. You haven't heard the story?"

She shook her head.

"We'll add that to our agenda when you stop by this week. I'll see you soon, then?" When she nodded, Don Arrigo patted her shoulder and started to move on when he noticed Barbanera. "He's out!"

She ventured a smile. "Just when I thought he'd never gather the courage."

Don Arrigo stroked Barbanera's head. The cat tolerated the gesture but kept his eyes on Don Arrigo without blinking. Don Arrigo grinned and said, "The one thing we can say—as life changes, we change, whether or not we're ready."

Don Arrigo drifted to put his hands on one parishioner's arm, then moved to condole with another. Until he looked up at a sound.

Stella turned.

The haunting melody drifted down from Aramezzo. The group stilled, listening. Heads bowed, as if this were part of the service, but Stella looked for the source of the music.

From Aramezzo's entrance, she saw a figure in black walking, holding a pipe. A woman in a black dress followed, a half step behind. As they approached, Stella realized—the butcher and his wife. Matteo appeared at her side, whispering, "Have you heard Bruno play?"

Stella nodded and whispered back, "Without knowing it was him."

They watched Bruno and Benedetta approach and then Matteo leaned down to whisper again in Stella's ear. "He learned to play when Jacopo was a baby. Only music soothed the colic. Then, when Benedetta got sick, she'd often disappear. But she always found her way home when Bruno played the pipe."

The trilling lifted into the air, scattering the lingering clouds. As Bruno and Benedetta approached the cemetery, the butcher pulled the pipe away from his mouth, tucking it into the breast pocket of his black suit. He pulled his wife's arm through his elbow and then walked through the quiet to stand at the edge of the grave.

Bruno's eyes locked on something at the edge of the cemetery. Stella followed his gaze to find the apprentice bakers with Antonio and Celeste.

One of the villagers gasped, a sound that rebounded in the stillness.

Bruno unclasped his hand from his wife's and strode up to Antonio. Stella watched, unable to breathe. She heard a whisper behind her, "How could Antonio show his face here?"

The answer, offered even more softly, "It's his son we're putting in the ground. How can he not?"

Nevertheless, Stella could see Antonio writhing in indecision. He put his hands up as Bruno approached. "I'm leaving, Bruno. I'm sorry. This was a mistake." He turned to his wife, pleading. "I told you, this was a mistake. We never should have come."

Bruno stood silent, his hands curled into fists. But before he could say anything, a wavering voice rose. "No. He stays."

Stella stood on tiptoe to see the speaker. Benedetta. She grabbed her husband's arm. "Bruno. You told me. You knew the whole time. You knew he was Antonio's."

"That's not it." Bruno wiped at his eyes. "His son. His son took my son. He couldn't control Dario, he let him get away with everything. Until he took... he took our boy." Bruno's voice turned ragged.

Antonio covered his eyes and tried to pull away. But Celeste held him fast. Though tears rose in her voice, she kept it steady as she said, "Bruno? Please."

Benedetta whispered, but her voice carried. "Bruno. This... now. It's for Jacopo. We need to send him off in peace. With everyone who loved him. That's the least we can do for our darling boy."

Bruno gritted his teeth and then gave one curt nod to Antonio. He spun around and marched back to the edge of the grave. Benedetta curled against him, the two clinging to each other. Villagers on either side of them pressed in, surrounding them with love and shared grief.

Celeste led Antonio to the back of the group, holding his hand. Stella pitched her voice low. "That's it? I figured we'd have another murder on our hands."

Domenica and Matteo exchanged glances. Finally, Domenica spoke. "That's not how we do things. We must live together. So we have to pull together, even when we're angry. Even when we're betrayed."

Stella shook her head. Perhaps Aramezzo had something to teach her about acceptance, about forgiveness. But for now, she didn't understand. She didn't understand at all. She didn't understand anything.

Don Arrigo began, but Stella couldn't make sense of the words. Her knees shook as if constructed from marmalade. Matteo slipped to one side of her and Domenica stood on her other side, pressing against her shoulders as if to hold her up. A soft warmth at her calf let her know that Barbanera, likewise, offered his strength.

Stella nodded, to let her friends know she was all right, that she acknowledged their love, when the trees that lined the cemetery shifted, as if vibrating. Stella's mouth fell open as the tree limbs seemed to explode into the air. It took a moment for her to understand, but when she did, her heart eased.

The spring weather brought the swallows, now diving and soaring across the suddenly azure sky. Their calls seemed a sermon in itself, a promise of a new season and new doors to open.

Stella smiled.

I HOPE YOU ENJOYED YOUR VISIT TO UMBRIA, THE GREEN HEART OF ITALY!

More mystery is already brewing in Aramezzo; look for *Unmasked in Aramezzo*, Book Three in the *Murder in an Italian Village* series coming soon! Don't want to miss a clue? Sign up for my monthly newsletter, the Grapevine, at *michelledamiani.com/grapevine*, and you'll be the first to know when the next book is available.

As a welcome to the Grapevine, you'll receive *Seasons of Secrets,* a free novella set in Santa Lucia—where, you may remember, Stella has a great aunt who is married to the mayor. The books will cross at some point, so now is the time to discover Santa Lucia!

Along with top-secret book news and deals, and your exclusive copy of *Seasons of Secrets* (not available in stores), every month you'll receive expert travel tips, delicious recipes, and books reviews for your next wanderlust read.

Hope to welcome you soon!

Ciao for now,

— Michelle

TRADITIONAL UMBRIAN STRUFOLI

4 eggs

10 tablespoons (125 grams) sugar

8 tablespoons (100 grams) olive oil

Zest of 2 lemons

2 tablespoons (30 grams) anise-flavored liquor, such as Mistra or Anisette

3½ teaspoons (15 grams) baking powder

2 ½ cups (300 grams) of flour

½ cup (120 grams) milk

1 pinch salt

Frying oil

Honey, powdered sugar, or alchermes (all are optional)

1) Whisk eggs in a medium bowl. Add sugar, olive oil, zest, liquor, salt, and baking powder, whisking well after each addition.

2) Switching to a wooden spoon, add in the flour and stir until incorporated. Then add the milk, stirring until combined. Cover with a dishtowel and let rest for an one hour (more or less if you're in the middle of a murder investigation).

4) Heat a few inches of oil in a pot over medium-low heat. You'll want the heat to be lower than usual for frying, as the strufoli need to cook all the way through by the time the outside crisps.

5) Drop tablespoons of batter into the oil (they expand, so go easy). As soon as the outside firms a little, flip them. Continue to turn them so the coloring stays even. If they cook too fast (darken too much on outside and/or raw on inside), turn down the heat. If they absorb oil (rather than crisping), turn the heat up. Bear in mind, they continue cooking a bit after you remove them from the oil.

6) Remove strufoli to a paper towel lined plate to cool. Then drizzle with warmed honey, alchermes if you have it, or toss with powdered sugar. Or leave plain!

NOTE 1: Recipe makes about four dozen, but you'll lose some in trying to get the heat to the right temperature. You can easily halve the recipe.

NOTE 2: Get real Umbrian by altering the ingredients to your taste: bump up the sugar or lemon, reduce the anisette or substitute out for another liquor. Have fun!

Buon appetito!

ALSO BY MICHELLE DAMIANI

*Death in Aramezzo: Book One
in the* Murder in an Italian Village *Series*

Il Bel Centro: A Year in the Beautiful Center

Santa Lucia

The Silent Madonna

The Stillness of Swallows

Into the Groves

*The Road Taken: How to Dream, Plan, and
Live Your Family Adventure Abroad*

Find out more at michelledamiani.com

Made in United States
North Haven, CT
10 June 2023

37592939R00171